3·90

# STOLEN L

THE CHRONICLES OF LOVE AND HONOUR trilogy

*The Engineer*
*Stolen Lives*
*White and Red*

# STOLEN LIVES

## JAN KUŚMIREK

DERWEN PUBLISHING
PEMBROKE · DYFED

First published in Great Britain by Derwen Publishing 2010.

Derwen Publishing,
3 Bengal Villas,
Pembroke, Dyfed,
Wales, SA71 4BH

A CIP catalogue for this book is available
from the British Library.

ISBN 978-1-907084-04-1

Thanks must go to Anne Buhrmann and Julian Robbins for the careful editing
and criticism.

Photograph of author courtesy of Toneborough Photos
www.toneboroughphotos.co.uk

Design and production by David Porteous Editions.
www.davidporteous.com

Printed and bound in the UK.

# DEDICATION

To the memory of Marshal Józef Piłsudski, who recognised the strengths and weaknesses of the Old Polish Commonwealth, and to the varied ethnic and religious groups who made its strength in diversity; and for those Cursed Soldiers whom people chose to abandon and forget.

*Do not leave the graves of soldiers with broken souls. Do not leave them with a sense of defeat and hopelessness, but with an irrefutable belief that in this spirit grow new values; the values are not mine, not yours, but for all of us – the value of belonging to the whole nation. It is necessary to keep the memory of them everlasting and living.*

Marshal Edward Rydz-Smigly

# CONTENTS

# FOREWORD

*Stolen Lives* is an historical novel about war, politics, relationships and espionage in the mid-twentieth century. Teddy Labden continues his chronicle of betrayal and trust in the world described in the novel *The Engineer*.

Set mostly in Eastern Europe many of the events in this fictional work actually happened. Many of its characters existed although some of their words and some of their actions are pure fiction and invention. This is essentially a story of heroism. This is the story of people who were never given the opportunity to speak. I hope they call to you across this novel.

For many Westerners, Eastern Europe still remains a strange, separated world. Poor history education has left the young people of Europe with a lack of understanding of their past and their heritage. Leftist politics have portrayed the lessons of history as narrow nationalism rather than admit the crimes and ineptitude of the Socialist and Communist systems. History is an inconvenient reminder of the duplicity and betrayal of the common people by the political systems of the Left. Put another way, the Germans are constantly portrayed as the bad guys but few know that the worst of crimes were also perpetrated by the Soviets and that both countries were Socialist by name.

Throughout Eastern Europe common people fought against Communism and the Soviet Union long after the Second World War. For Poland World War II began in 1939 and ended in 1989. The armed struggle went on well into the fifties. Few Westerners today fully comprehend this reality. It provokes inconvenient thoughts of responsibility. Yet this is the backdrop to Stolen Lives. Polish 'partisans' had to fight the West too; the Cold War made economic sense. It was cheaper than giving actual support to the people living behind the Iron Curtain.

Teddy Labden now prefers to be known by his real name, Tadeusz or 'Tadek' Labycz. He fights on for the freedom of his country, determined to reveal the duplicity of politicians waging a cold war that is little more than a charade. Proxy wars were being fought worldwide, with colossal loss of lives. In the name of 'freedom' on both sides, from Africa to Vietnam, soldier boys died and their people cried.

A line was drawn across Europe dividing two ideologies. Who created that line? Teddy Labden uncovers plot after counter-plot aimed at destroying the potential of peace. Peace sacrificed to the political vanity and self-interest of power-hungry politicians.

The story unfolds to reveal the complicity of government security services trading information in an international club of self-interest and mutual exchange, which destroyed ordinary people whilst preserving the reputation of politicians at all costs. Tadek and his friend become involved in an assassination plot. As they expose the extent to which American and British Secret Services have been penetrated by the Soviets, they grasp the truth. The failure to deal with these real threats to the West lies with the Security Services' desire to cover up politicians' errors rather than expose national threats.

The system wins, the people lose. As Marie Antoinette said, "If the people have no bread let them eat cake."

*Jan Kuśmirek, July 2010*

# PROLOGUE

The bear sighed long and deep. He watched his black shiny nostrils expand and contract with the effort of exhaling long-lost memories, boredom and the restlessness of defeat. What else was there to do except eat, sleep and watch the humans? His tawny eyes stared fixedly at the round cave entrance, a circle of ever dancing light. Grey light today, with flashes of sunshine. Light that was always cold, casting its depressing hue onto this concrete bunker, this representation of how humans felt a cave should be. Cold, grey and very lonely. A mausoleum.

Iran had always been sunny – well mostly. Yes, it snowed there, but somehow the snow was not wet and cold like here in Edinburgh. Libya had been just as hot, but the sun made you happy in spite of the flies and the hell. Italy was hot in another way, running up and down those rocks, dodging bullets. The bear grunted as he thought of his lost comrades. "Jesus, Mary. Oh, for a fag and a quiet smoke... those damn do-gooders never let me drink beer anymore."

His old joints were stiff now with rheumatism, though he still dreamed of wrestling with the lads of the *Kompania*. At least someone had the sense to provide a bench for him to sit on and watch the human world roll by. Ears twitching, he caught the sound of a child's voice. Wojtek heaved himself on to his paws and padded over the dusty concrete to see this new child. Most of the humans here spoke that guttural, high-speed, cross-border English. He had learned to recognise the more refined accent of Edinburgh from the coarser Glasgow, and knew refined tones meant fewer buns. How he missed the soft sibilance and tonal qualities of his own people, the rise and fall of Polish.

The boy pointed excitedly as the bear appeared. His mother said, "Yes, Janek, there is Wojtek the Soldier bear, just as I told you!"

"No, Mummy, it's not 'Wojtek'. Say 'Voytek'. That's the proper Polish way."

"Ah, a boy of good sense. And he has a proper name," Wojtek thought to himself.

"Why did they lock the soldier bear up here after the war, Mummy?" the boy asked. Holding his mother's hand, he leant as far as he could to get the best view of this famous bear.

"He had nowhere else to go. No home to go back to," she answered.

"We were betrayed!" the bear roared, deep from his throat.

Mother and child jumped back, startled by his ferocity.

A man standing nearby chuckled. "Don't be alarmed. You just touched a nerve with him."

"I know the bear's a war hero," the mother replied, "but please don't tell me he understands English!"

"Polish, actually," the stranger answered. "I don't think his English is that good," and he called to the bear in soft, rapid Polish.

The bear smiled, coming close to the perimeter.

The stranger spoke with a slight North American accent. "Do you by chance have a cigarette?"

She hesitated. Was this a pick-up? He looked all right. Clean-shaven. Middling height, blue eyes with a look of mischief. Long, fawn raincoat, yellow silk scarf, brown trilby. Good brown brogues, well polished. Altogether well-to-do, in fact, quite posh for these parts. She realised she had been looking him up and down, and blushed as his eyes held her gaze. "Yes," she said, "I do."

As he extracted a cigarette she noticed his well-manicured nails. She proffered her chromed lighter which he flicked into flame. He lit the cigarette and inhaled.

He turned to the bear, who was watching him intently, and deftly flicked the cigarette. Wojtek deftly caught it and promptly stuck it into the side of his jaw before shuffling back to his cave.

Mother and child looked aghast then laughed.

The man wasn't laughing. His voice had hardened with a trace of bitterness. "This bear's full story has yet to be told. Wojtek fought in the war with the Polish Army 2nd Corps, from beginning to end. And now look at him, grateful for a handout, just like the rest of them."

The boy added tugged at the man's sleeve to get attention. "My daddy was a Polish soldier. He died in the war."

"At Monte Casino," the woman added quietly.

The stranger looked at her for a moment. She expected the usual, "I'm sorry." Instead he said, "You have beautiful eyes." Kneeling down he took the boy by the shoulders, looking at him eye to eye. "You remember who you are. You are Jan or Janek, never John or Johnny. Both your mummy and daddy were brave in different ways. Remain true to them and where your daddy came from. Don't let Britain own you."

The stranger stood and looked at the woman.

A raucous shout came from an advancing uniformed zoo keeper. "I saw what you did to that animal! That's against the rules. I'll have the law on you!"

The stranger replied in an altered tone. "Oh, do stop blathering, Johnny, and run away, there's a good man."

And Tadek Labycz walked away to his meeting, smiling at the thought of a more contented bear. He turned out of the zoo gates as the cream and maroon double-decker bus was taking on its last few passengers. The conductor turned and pressed the bell and the bus began its journey toward the city centre. Mentally calculating the distance at fifty yards, Tadek clutched his hand to his trilby and began to sprint, gabardine flapping awkwardly against his legs. The conductor saw him. Calculating the distance he pressed the bell again. The bus driver must have seen him in the mirror; the bus slowed slightly but the last ten yards still required that extra spring. Tadek grabbed the chrome rail, jerking himself up onto the platform, the conductor grabbing his arm. "You nearly missed it, laddie!"

"Thanks for waiting!"

"Och, we just like to see you young 'uns run."

Catching his breath, Tadek asked for a ticket to Waverley station. The conductor pulled a green ticket from his wooden rack. Having paid his shilling and nine pence Tadek headed for the upper deck.

Princes Street was crowded as usual, Saturday shoppers enjoying a little less austerity. Rationing had ended just two years ago, almost nine years since the war. Colour was beginning to come back to the country. Tadek looked around him, checking automatically for faces like his own, those wearing a look of bland intent, that look of knowing disguised by normality, which somehow still carried a vibration of the opposite.

He headed straight into Jenners Department store, whose polished grandeur almost denied austerity Britain. Britain was held back not only post-war hardship but by its profligate Labour government. Idly examining the counters Tadek surveyed the ties before carefully selecting something silken, a deep indigo blue with red spots. He trailed it over his left arm, swinging round to let the light fall on it, still discreetly observing the faces around him to see if anyone had followed him into the store. An assistant approached. He agreed the purchase, allowing the girl to carefully wrap "a most distinctive and selective gentlemen's choice".

Taking out his St Martin's Bank cheque book he was conscious of her silent recognition of his gold nib, tortoiseshell Waterman's pen. "Thank you, sir," she purred.

Tadek continued through the store and out a side entrance, heading down St Andrew's Street. He walked to the foot of the street, crossing over the wide tarmac with its soaring Georgian buildings either side. Many of the houses were still privately occupied but increasingly they were being turned into solicitors' and other offices for this brave new world of commerce. Tadek noticed a black Wolseley 4/50, its highly polished chrome glinting in the sunshine. There was a man in the driver's seat, studiously reading a broadsheet. At the far end of the street he could make out another man dressed similarly to himself, smoking a cigarette. Clearly two goons. But whose? No matter, goons and minders were not his business.

Crossing into Queen's Street, Tadek turned left and left again into St David's Street, effectively completing a square. Left again, this time into St. Andrew's Square. Reaching Number 37 he turned up the whitewashed steps to the green-painted door, finished to that glass-like polish only the professional painter can achieve. The brass plate read *McKeowan, Guilders & Graveney, Solicitors*. He pulled on the brass bell knob and heard a distant ring. The door opened immediately revealing an impeccable, white-jacketed doorman who oozed ex-military batman.

"Please come in, sir. You are?"

"Kapitan Tadek Labycz."

"You are very welcome, sir. May I take your coat?"

Another staff member, dressed in dark suit, took his coat while the first attendant continued, "If you would stand against the wall, please, sir? Raise your arms above your head and spread your legs a little; I just need to 'frisk you', I believe the term is."

Tadek stood legs apart, arms raised, whilst the man ran his hands expertly over his clothes. He removed the Radom in its shoulder holster, placing it carefully in a drawer and handing Tadek a small ticket, numbered 15. "Up the stairs if you would, please sir, and straight ahead. Give me the ticket back on your way out and I will return your side-arm. Nice piece, sir, if I may say so."

Following his directions, Tadek climbing the wide staircase, its plush red carpet held back by polished brass rails at every step. The atmosphere was quiet. Not depressing. Not even loaded. Just quiet with time. As he walked along the corridor, past traditional pictures of stags and purple heather, he smiled at the Scottishness of its contents. Hearing a murmur of voices from the other side of the door at the end of the corridor he paused, deciding whether to go in or knock. He could feel his chest tighten slightly. Damned nerves. He decided to knock, simultaneously turning the handle and entering the room.

The room was dominated by a beautiful Regency mahogany table, around which sat a group of men. Sunlight poured in through the high windows, silhouetting them against the light. Cigarette smoke rose through the sunbeams, like genies out of lamps. Tadek found it catching his throat. He coughed slightly behind his hand. A few of the figures rose as he walked into the room.

"Over here, Tadek" a voice called. "We've left a chair for you."

"Late as bloody usual!" came another voice.

Another white-coated uniformed attendant proffered a teacup.

"Darjeeling, sir? Milk or lemon?"

"Lemon," Tadek responded, making out faces.

The group were all men, except for one woman. Ages ranging from mid-twenties to perhaps sixties. Mostly Polish ex-servicemen, from the look of them. Tadek recognised one or two faces and nodded acknowledgment.

Then his eye was caught by the eye of an older man, already seated at the table. Though startled, Tadek controlled his features, even as his stomach lurched. He acknowledged the man with a slight nod of his head. The man was watching him intently. His grizzled, bullet shaped head with its cropped, steel grey hair inclined in return. It was all so long ago yet the old uncertainties, hopes and fears returned. It took real effort to stop the cup and saucer in his hand from betraying the turmoil he felt inside. Here was his *bête noir*, his nemesis, seated at this table of allies.

# CHAPTER 1

# MEETINGS

Kryszka's familiar face swam into view. Relieved, I smiled at my faithful old friend, fellow war survivor and partner in the business of espionage.

"Come, Tadek. Sit opposite me," he said, "where I can keep an eye on you."

The Chairman called the meeting to order. "Ladies and Gentlemen, although we have probably all exchanged cards or names when taking tea, I think it would be in order to go around the table and introduce ourselves. I am General Kruszewski representing the Council of Three or General Anders' group. On my right is General Staszewski, representing the alternative and opposing President Zaleski group."

I stifled a smile at these bravura attempts to prove that we might be down and out but we are not ill-mannered. Most of those present could not afford the train and bus fare, let alone a business card. But the older man had spent most of his war as a POW in Germany, so he was due some respect.

The Polish government in exile with its home in London was now split into two distinct warring camps. Influential people present seemed also to be mostly ex-military with an Intelligence bias. There were a couple of politicians, each representing the old Polish parties, but no Communists. Voices droned around the table as people introduced themselves. Lines were being drawn, positions and places established in the order of things. Extra commentary was added by colleagues and friends, some ribald, some witty, some offensive.

When it came to Kryszka, his position was clear. "I am a member of the Polish underground and therefore still consider myself to be a serving officer in the *Dwojka or* Polish Secret Service."

Then it was my turn. "Kapitan Tadek Labycz, ex-member of the Polish Air Force and RAF, also still serving as an officer in the Polish Underground. I'm closely associated with the British Secret Service, now known as MI6, and the CIA."

"And not to be trusted," someone growled.

"Except by his friends," said Kryszka quietly.

I smiled wryly at the comment. "Gentlemen, I'm a pragmatist but also a member of the patriotic cult. Currently I am involved in the business of learning politics."

This provoked a few smiles and a wholesome "Gee!" from the guy opposite, who now decided to introduce himself. "Alan – Al for short – Bonetti, Liaison Officer with the CIA. On my right are Derek Hartstein of Radio Free Europe, and Robert Pullman of Voice of America, both CIA operatives. As you can guess, gentlemen, they have other affiliations. But, for the point of this meeting, their roles are as stated."

Next was the only woman there. Small, dark, in her early forties. Where everyone else was formally dressed, she wore a simple bottle-green twin set, without jewellery of any kind. I registered my second shock of the meeting.

She gave her name as Susan Herman and said she was an Israeli, a member of Mossad.

*And probably ex-Irgun,* I thought. *She's so calm and collected, as though we saw each other every day. Her reactions seem the same as mine, so I guess it was just as much of a surprise for her to see me. No doubt she's had time to talk to Kryszka. He seems at ease with these surprises.*

She returned my smile with genuine warmth.

"Hello, Hanka. Long time no see!"

"Hello to you too, Tadek. I'm glad we survived."

She then introduced herself to the table. "I'm here to represent the interests of Israel, not Poland or the USA. As so many of us in our service started as Poles we continue to cooperate with our friends here in this room, both in America and Europe. We are not special friends of any country however, except those who aid our survival. The Communists in Egypt and the Muslim Arabs want us destroyed. So we survive with whoever aids us, and we aid them."

General Kruszewski carried on, saying that our American friends were here to discuss how the exiled Polish community and the remnants of the Polish underground could be used in this new, cold war. It was an interesting discussion, to say the least.

Al told a tale of how the American CIA had not encouraged the Hungarians to rise. We all knew this to be a lie. It has been a clear demonstration to Khrushchev of what could happen. Just as it was Khruschev's demonstration to the satellite states of what would happen if anyone else tried it.

Someone spoke. "They are dying in the streets".

Another chimed in. "They are appealing for arms."

"They should have behaved like Poland in Poznan," came a rejoinder.

"The issues were different there," another said. "Irregularities in calculating wages. Unrealistic indicators of production growth and efficiency. Poor working conditions in the plants."

"Still, over seventy people were killed by Soviet troops in Poznan, and it was not just confined to the city. We would never have heard of the trouble if it were not for the International Trade Fair at the time."

General Kruszewski intervened. "Gomułka is not the reforming puppy the West portrays. He could only have been rehabilitated due to Khrushchev's secret speech in February, condemning Stalin's crimes. He plays the fool in the West, uses the same tactics as Stalin, becoming happy little Uncle Nikita rather than the now foul Uncle Joe."

It was too much to stomach. I switched into my own world, the dream-time I had learned to live in as a child. There I could hear everything like a drone in the background, only the important words sounding out like sharp notes on a violin. I listened for the pattern, heard the tones. My eyes chased the table edge, taking in the cigarette packets. I had long since decided I could tell the circumstances of any individual by what they smoked. How the mighty were fallen: there was a General with a packet of green and orange Woodbines. A one-time Major, now a grocer's assistant, was smoking Woodbines too. An ex-pilot with Navy Cut. Another pilot, now a school lab technician, drawing on Gold Flake. A lieutenant with Black Balkan Sobranie. Where the hell did he get those from? Clearly some sort of black market spiv, I thought.

Kryszka had placed his silver cigarette case emblazoned with an enamel white eagle and regimental insignia ostentatiously in front of him, a clear display that he had not changed. He was a die-hard. Next to him an ex-Navy man, who I had heard had was now settled in Plymouth with new wife and baby daughter.

So many Poles exiled from their homeland. Difficult, incomprehensible days for these men, learning a new language, settling into a new culture which distrusted them. I had it easier than most; I had learned my Britishness at Cambridge. But I had taken up my true Polish heritage before the war, working for British intelligence in Warsaw. I was a Pole, and there I was treated as a Pole. The fact that I belonged to Polonia, that world Diaspora of Polish people, the largest contingent of which was in Chicago, I found to be immaterial in the inter-war Second Republic. We Poles had not had a country for three hundred years, since being partitioned by various other empires. Most Poles spoke Polish, but even our language had been banned at times, notably in the Russian sectors. Now some Poles spoke German, some Russian, some Latvian, and some Lithuanian. But they called themselves Polish by heritage. In the Second Republic, at its outset, half the government had been pulled from different parts of the world.

My Polishness and my political persuasion were of the Piłsudski mould. I had never subscribed to the narrow nationalism of Dmowski. To me Polish citizenship was a matter of pride. My upbringing and later experience had taught me respect for all Polish citizens, whatever their attributable origin, from Tartar to Jew, Lithuanian to Ruthenian. Following the war, I had found myself in a Poland that had changed greatly since my first experience in 1938. Poland had become a country of politics. So *many* had died in the war. How could we explain to the world that not only had millions of Jews died, but the same number of other 'types' of Poles? That in the early '40s the then allies, Germany and Soviet Russia, had both started a genocidal policy against the Polish nation.

The first to go had been the officer corps and their families, wives, children, parents. Next the intelligentsia, the police, the fire brigade, anyone who could be construed as belonging to local government, even forestry workers. Teachers, professors, artists, authors, dentists and doctors, they all went into camps and *gulags*, millions and millions of stolen lives. As I remembered the numbers, the word 'millions' seemed so artificial, so incomprehensible and so sterile. *Real people* had lost their lives and their liberty in prisons, concentration camps, labour camps, deportation holding camps, slave camps, death camps. They faced, torture, depravity, firing squads, gas chambers, suicides and dozens of other methods used to steal the lives of peoples whose sole crime was to be a Ukranian, a Jew, a Pole...

Today I was still contemplating how to help people who didn't want to know comprehend the immenseness of its cruelty. What would the English think if the northeast and northwest of England were forcibly depopulated within two or three hours, their homes and belongings given to Danish or Norwegian people and all because a thousand years ago their ancestors had occupied that territory? Was this analogy comprehensible? Or would people better understand if the population of the State of New York were forced to leave their homes within an hour or two, be torn from their material comforts and be shoved into a cattle truck with no food or heating but just a slop bucket? If they were transported up to Alaska over the Bering straits to Kamchatka and dumped there? Such an event on his doorstep would have cut Roosevelt's popularity, I mused. Yet that's exactly what he and his pal Stalin had engineered in Poland, on top of the millions of deaths already caused by Germans and the Soviets in the war.

Through the bitterness and resentment of my meditation I heard a voice coming from the corner of the room. For the first time I observed an angular, chiselled-faced man, his jet black hair combed straight back and brilliantined close to his head. He was dressed as a priest.

He spoke English with an educated Mediterranean accent and his words were for the American, Al. "In answer to your question will Poland help the Americans, I can only say that they will help, provided that the Americans assist in a wider context on behalf of traditional values. Poland can play a central role in Europe. But the conflict, the cold war, is on a wider scale, the battle for hearts and minds. Communism is the anti-Christ and needs to be stopped."

I heard myself speaking. "So the Church speaks for Poland, Father, does it?"

The Monseigneur tented his fingers and looked at me with animosity. "My son, it is the duty of the Church to direct its own. Poland, like Ireland, is the jewel in the crown of Our Lady. Poland has always been in the front of the Christian fight and will continue to be so."

I disliked this type of Catholic, so I could not resist the riposte. "I see you have a poor grasp of Polish history, Monseigneur. We Poles, although nominally Catholic, have beliefs fervently based on our attachment to past, matriarchal, pagan beliefs. We have never indulged in your religious wars against heretic s, except to save your necks from Turks and Tartars. Certainly not in the persecution of alternative believers, which is why we Poles welcomed the Jews. Alas we have not always had good relations with our Jewish countrymen. But as a Canadian Pole, I was exceptionally surprised at the Holy Father's Concordat with Hitler, which allowed for the extermination of the inconvenient Jewry as well as the enslavement of sub-human Slavs, including many good Catholic priests. Did the Holy See's policy not foresee the destruction of our country? I certainly don't see it in a position to speak for our motherland now."

There was an uncomfortable silence around the table. At which point Kryszka managed to sink far enough in his chair to reach me under the table with his boot. He kicked me hard and added for the table's benefit, "I apologise for my friend's caustic remarks. He considers himself something of a historian."

The tension I had created eased. In the laughter which followed the Monseigneur coolly added, "We must remember, my son, the Church has great power and influence..."

"And pots of gold," I interjected. A few of the military men smiled.

The priest continued, ignoring my quip. "My point is that the Vatican has one of the best intelligence services in the world. Between us all here, Catholics, Poles, Jews and Israelis, we should be able to know more and do more than any other group to aid our American and indeed British friends, to fight Communism."

There was a pause, during which General Kruszewski invited Al to explain fully the reason for this meeting. A meeting clearly being observed by British goons, whose masters were just as clearly being excluded from it. Unless someone in the room was a stool pigeon. Or a microphone had been hidden somewhere.

As Al cleared his throat, the last man at the table spoke, introducing himself. He had to be in his late fifties I realised, well-dressed, that grizzled hair even greyer now. As always his cigarette lighter twisted and tumbled between his fingers. I watched in fascination as he turned it over and over, catching the sunlight.

"I am known as Witek." The smoke hovered just above our heads, curling from the cigarettes.

Tap, tap, tap. The cigarette lighter turned and, in my head, it hallowed and echoed, taking me to another table far away, where smoke had drifted as men talked.

My mind reeled, turning through my childhood in Canada, then Cambridge, through Warsaw before the war, seeing myself as a junior RAF officer, before turning on and on, through secondment by the Secret intelligence Services as a diplomat, my time as liaison officer with the Polish Air Force, then betrayal by the British of their first ally to the Russians. I thought of those Reds embedded in high places, of my near arrest, of being framed for murder. I was a Pole and a patriot. By circumstance, not by birth, nor choice. The British had made me what I was; their antagonist.

Tap, tap, tap. The lighter turned. Tap, tap, tap....

I glanced at Hanka, now known as Susan Herman and my mind floated far back to a real place far, far from here, away from games such as these to where that same lighter had turned in those same fingers.

I remembered it all so well. I saw Witek as he was then, turning the lighter over and over in his coarse hands. They were muddy and raw from the cold, contrasting with the polished surface of the lighter as it caught the sunlight from the window. He had tapped it on the table then began flicking it on and off, the wick failing to catch from the sparks. A big man, dressed in an old army greatcoat, bulky from the assortment of clothing beneath it, to keep out the cold. His face had that round, rugged look which would have fitted anywhere from Mongolia to the Baltic. Weather-beaten, creased. Blue-grey eyes that matched the steel of his lighter.

He was thinking and struggling.

Struggling to come to terms with the failure of everything around him.

Struggling to come to terms with the bitterness that disillusionment brings.

# CHAPTER 2

# WITEK

Kryszka and I had come from England, the country which, in Kryszka's opinion, had betrayed him and his kind. He called the West, the whole Anglo-American Empire 'the face of treachery'. We were the 'silent ones', the *ciechamnosci* of the Polish underground. The war was over for most, but not for us. We had lost, but we still fought on. We had been sent by the Polish government in exile, a group of betrayed democratic politicians spurned by once-allied Western governments. Even now we were not sure that a legitimate Polish government existed, except in our own will.

It was the spring of '47. We had travelled by train across France and into Germany. Displaced people were everywhere. Not as bad as '46, but people were still travelling, prisoners of war or survivors desperately seeking relatives or recuperating from work camps or slave factories or concentration camps. Wherever the Russians had taken over, people resisted repatriation. Camps were being increasingly ethnically organised. As many Poles saw it, they had no country to go back to. Southern Slavs, too, were cautious, especially those who were non-communist. Or the Croats, who had been pro-German, unlike the faithful Serbs, loyal to the Allies' cause. When the Russians liberated countries, these people had fled, become refugees. Not because they had all been German sympathisers, no. Because they knew what really happened when Communists take over.

Our journey had been difficult, but not so bad as to be frightening. Our papers as engineers had gone unchallenged. We had slipped over the border into Czechoslovakia, heading first to Česky Krumlov, then north toward Ostrava. Barbed wire coils were being replaced everywhere by fixed fences and watchtowers. You did not have to be Intelligence Service to see that the Czechs and Slovaks were being kept in. This was as much a camp to control inmates as any *gulag*. It was just going to be bigger, that was all.

Kryszka's comment was succinct. "We got in, Tadek, but can we get out?" *That* was the question. As Mr Churchill so eloquently put it, this was an 'Iron Curtain'. Since he and his like had put up the fittings, why complain now the blinds were being drawn?

I shook my head. "The West could have stopped this - could still stop it - but another two years and it will be impossible. They could open the curtains tomorrow if they want. There are masses of people who could throw out the Russians with help now. Now, Kryszka, but that would mean admitting the politicians made a big mistake at Yalta. It would mean accepting their intelligence was wrong or had been infiltrated, that high-up officials on both sides of the Atlantic might have been compromised. The Democrats are not going to allow Roosevelt to be tarnished."

We did not debate the issue further: we were on the same side. I talked more than Kryszka, that was all. Gave voice to his thoughts.

The underground in Czechoslovakia still functioned, although it was being hounded now by NKVD Special Forces. The Soviet police organisation was everywhere. We were assisted to new identities and papers then passed to the Polish border, crossing by bus via Cieszyn where Polish border guards gave our documents only cursory glances. We were now Party members after all, returning from a conference in Prague. You think as you travel. We were now home, at least for Kryszka. For me this was the land of my forefathers. Another adventure in the game of chess had begun.

Thanks to the betrayal by Roosevelt and Churchill at Yalta in 1943 Poland now lay under the heel of the Soviets. Secret deals had been made behind the backs of the Poles. Lies and more lies. Stalin had won, playing the other two like a fish. Now Communist infiltrators had crept into every Western Secret Service, even and into the many beds slept in by politicians. Agents, long kept hidden in the depths of the democratic gardens of free societies, emerged to mate. Sympathisers were found to straddle, to inseminate. Their spawn clogged the Unions; their children swam in the media, even in the Church. They shared their love of the working man, of equality, told of the need for class struggle and of the destruction of society, cast as "Change". Journalists and officials, actors and actresses all, quietly working in the name of world peace for the overthrow of the élite, especially the beastly "Right". Carrying out the work destined for them by the Comintern, its acolytes and its propaganda machine.

Kryszka and I were headed for the Soviet Union, a certain *Gulag*. Call it a work camp if you like; it was unfashionable now to call it a concentration camp. The Left in England and America didn't like that word. Those nice Communists under Comrade Stalin didn't have *concentration* camps. Surely, only the nasty Germans had those, not our affable, smiling Uncle Joe, as the Western Press had called him. Or our darling Bolshevik hero and idol, Lenin. No, these were *gulags*, (Westerners would never bother to look up the definition), corrective labour institutions, health camps. I could tell you that a *gulag* is a slave labour camp, a death camp, yes, a concentration camp. But you would not believe that from a Pole, would you? We Poles were pro-Nazi fascist lackeys after all, who had hounded Jews! We were the ones who had started the war, caused all the trouble. We should just be grateful for our handouts, for the carved up country the British and Russians had allowed us.

So here we were, Kryszka and I, deep in South East Poland, travelling by train and bus, truck and foot. Now we had entered the Soviet zone from occupied Germany. Onward we travelled, 'handled' by the Polish underground still in resistance against Soviet occupation. A set of clothes here, tickets palmed to us from a newspaper kiosk there, here a whisper saying which woman to follow, there money, here the necessary papers, all was provided. At the last we were guided by a boy on a bicycle to our destination. We had come to meet a man. We had arrived at the beginning.

Kryszka twisted the newspaper he had been reading violently between his hands and tossed it into the forest, his pithy comment on the news. Poland now had a 'freely' elected democratic Communist government; the Soviets had their major satellite puppet state, gratis the West. And Stalin had his revenge for the Bolshevik defeat by the Poles in the 1920s.

The Polish election had just taken place. Good time to have a vote, January, the middle of winter when many people could not even get out. Poland had overwhelmingly voted Communist of one kind or another, or so the polls said. Eighty percent of the country wanted Communism and Soviet-style government. Even though anyone could have told you the results weeks ago, because the ballot had already been counted. What a farce. Yet Britain, America and even France were going along with it. I heard myself speak out loud. "As long as everyone's happy."

"Let's just get on with it," Kryszka suggested.

So we did.

It was that time of year when winter is still in the highlands whilst spring has begun in the valleys and lowlands. We walked up the stony track in bright sunshine, slipping on the ice-covered stones. Each of us carried a small suitcase, two city-looking gentlemen, walking in the countryside in the time of melting snow when frosted jewels dissolve into mud. We soon passed a small farm that nestled into the steep hillside, its yellow ochre walls making it seem it belonged amongst the clods of turned, snow-peppered earth.

Wood smoke drifted from the chimney. Kryszka had smelled it earlier and wondered whether we should risk this daylight stroll. A small dog yapped at us from the farm and another St Bernard-like animal wandered from a barn to stare at us mournfully without further attempt to investigate. There was no sign of human life. The curtains didn't twitch. Were the occupants thinking as we were; partisans – but which side? Communists? Home Army? Bandits? Poles or Ukrainians? Small drops of ice fell like rain from the fir trees as the sunshine melted crystals from the needles. The cold air froze them to droplets which stung the face. I was sweating and stooped to pick up a handful of snow to cool my face, instantly regretting it. The snow stung my hand, burning like a chain of fires. Kryszka laughed. "You've been away too long. You've forgotten the cold!"

Indeed. This was the cold I had played in as a child in far away Calgary, where I had experienced the dangers of frostbite. It was true. I had forgotten.

The farmhouse we approached was set back into the hillside, just like the place we had passed, but it was squarer, more squat, as though placed there by man rather than blending into the landscape. It was surrounded on all sides by a post and rail fence. There was a small orchard and, at the lower slope, a pond, now iced and solid. There was the smell of horse, and steam coming from a barn to one side of the building. There was the sound of a goat. The scene was peaceful, the track winding upward into the still, silent forests all around us. The view was breathtaking. Out over to the Tatra Mountains and on, on into the wilderness of the Bieszczady. Here there were lynx, wolf, fox, eagle, falcon, beaver, martins, wild boar. All of nature in its wild beauty. Yet, as we looked, I knew that here was also human fear, hatred and conflict that raged from house to house, village to village. Civil war.

The metallic click of safety catches behind us told us we were expected.

"Hands up, on your head. Turn slowly. Don't make any move."

We did as we were told.

There were three of them. One just a kid, no more than sixteen perhaps, and two in their thirties. Gaunt, hungry, haunted. All of them dressed in a variety of military costume, cobbled from God knew which armies. Two wore forage caps, the third the *rogatywka*, the soft square field cap of the Polish army. Each cap carried the crowned eagle of the Polish Republic. Anti-communist partisans, the remnants of the Home Army, the AK. And they were holding Sten guns, pointed firmly at us.

*Rogatywka* was in charge it seemed. "Papers, please. Slowly, no fast movement. We will shoot if we see arms, or if you move too suddenly."

I kept my hands firmly on my head. Kryszka reached slowly inside his heavy leather jacket and produced our identity papers and a letter, addressed simply to 'Witek'. The officer scrutinised our papers, carefully checking the photographs and stamps, even holding them to the light while the other two watched us unwaveringly. Without appearing satisfied, he folded them together then suddenly, almost embarrassingly, snapped to attention, making the Polish military salute.

"Come with me, gentlemen. I am *Kapral* Karol. You're quite safe here."

We followed him as the other two partisans took up their guard duty in the freezing forest once more. We walked up three steps and into the farmhouse. There stood a burly man in a greatcoat, framed against the light, with his hands behind his back, looking to me like a grander version of Napoleon. He grunted a greeting at us, taking the letter from our officer-guard. Tearing it open, he scanned the contents then took a lighter from his pocket and burned it. Flames curled up to his fingers. He swore vehemently, letting the letter fall to the floor where its final flimsy flames could do no damage. Then he stamped on it for good measure.

The man was a grizzled fifty-something. Not elderly, but solid-looking, stocky. His steel grey hair was peppered silver, cut short in military fashion. The smooth skin of his face was rounded, with laughter lines around the eyes, but his cheeks were hollowed around lips compressed in a hard line, set above short white stubble.

Turning to us he grunted. "I am Witek. Sit. You are here with a proposition. I am listening."

Kryszka began our story. "As you are aware our president, General Sikorski, was killed in a plane crash in Gibraltar..."

"Ah, yes, the riddle continues..." Witek interrupted. "Was it an accident? Or was Sikorski murdered? If the latter, then by whom? The Russians? Most likely. The British, perhaps? Churchill would never have ordered it!"

I disagreed. "Churchill had allegiance to the Empire and not to his allies. He was quite as brutal as any war leader when it was required. Remember he ordered the destruction of the French navy."

Witek beamed. "Ah, a fellow historian. Welcome, my friend". Sitting down heavily on a high backed chair carved with motifs of flowers and leaves, he leaned back, putting his big, grime-engrained hands on the table.

"Who is this?" He directed the question to Kryszka, as though I was some underling.

"He is my brother, my partner."

"Good start," Witek grunted. He leant further back, concentrating his glare on me, penetrating eyes narrowed, brow furrowed.

Undeterred, Kryszka continued. "Labycz is one of us. He fought in the '39 campaign and alongside Home Army partisans on a special mission. The Germans got him but I pulled him out. He is as sound as I am. He came to us as a Canadian Pole from the British side. Now we have lost a few of our operatives who have gone over to the British, mostly MI6. They want to pick up our agents and circles. Unemployment in Britain is high, you see, so we Poles have to take what work we can get."

This was a typical Kryszka joke. From Witek's guffaw it was clear they shared a sense of humour.

"My friend was and is on the books of British Intelligence, but he came over to us when they tried to pin a murder on him in London. Someone somewhere thinks he knows something. We believe at least one of those Poles who went over to be a NKVD plant. The British will operate as though they all are, either recruiting or eliminating. They won't shoot them but in the spirit of comradeship will hand them or their names and addresses to the

NKVD when they have what they want. The NKVD want to break us, so they will cooperate with the British for a while. Neither wants to open up the Sikorski affair, by the way'; 'why' is itself the mystery. This mission of ours is either about Sikorski or it's about who is leaking information to the Russkis. But it's our operation, not yours, Witek."

"Okay, okay," Witek responded. "So you absolve the British of involvement in Sikorski's death?" The question was addressed to me.

"No, I do not. But I have learned how the British work at the highest level. It is simple enough. It comes down to a perennial question: 'Who will rid me of this turbulent priest?' King Henry II's famous question when he wanted rid of his Chancellor. The man was murdered by four knights back in 1170. Of course it was an accident, a misunderstanding. The Pope even canonised the dead priest whilst Henry lamented. But the British have been playing the same trick ever since. The deed is done, the politicians wail and benefit from the publicity surrounding their public mourning – this time of General Sikorski's death in such a tragic, unexpected way. It's the British way. Perfidious Albion, to quote Napoleon."

Witek jerked his chair forward and clapped his hands, his eyes boring into me. "I like you," he said.

I felt as though I was being liked in the way someone relishes a plate of good food about to be devoured. He rose and we clomped noisily after him across the wooden floor, the sound indicating a basement beneath, moving from what I would call the parlour into the warm depths of the kitchen. In one corner stood the massive stove, which a family could sleep above in the coldest winters. Along the top of one wall was an array of colourful plates. Hanging below by their handles was a row of similarly patterned mugs. A wooden chest was set in the corner. Upon it sat an elderly woman, her face wizened and brown like a hazelnut kernel. She seemed to have lost her eyebrows and, from the set of her mouth, possibly her teeth. When we ducked through the doorway she stood up. Pale blue eyes emerged above her cheeks. She said nothing but moved towards a blackened kettle, pouring hot tea into glasses, placing them on the table as we sat.

The sixteen-year old boy I had seen earlier was standing in the corner, Sten slung casually across his chest, brown, soulful eyes watching us. He was holding a bowl of soup close to his chin and stopped, his spoon midway between bowl and mouth, as we entered, turning his gaze away. I noticed he rustled as he moved.

Witek, noticed my curiosity. "Paper, to keep out the cold. We smear lard on our bodies and then insulate them with newspaper. It's good. That way we don't get frostbite. So, gentlemen, I have carried out my orders. I have burned my instructions from this exiled government of yours in London. Now I have two people whom I have to nursemaid and do their bidding.

Good, isn't it? I will do as I am told, my duty. But first, I would like to tell you that when your orders were first issued in London I had nineteen people. We are now seven. We had a small engagement, you see. Three of us were killed, the Soviets have the rest. This means you were lucky to get here and we are lucky to still be here. Because it now seems that everybody is out there searching for you."

He turned to me. "Please do not believe yourself betrayed, my friend. I am sure that the hacksaw used to take off the fingers of our captured men was kept blunt. And I am sure that the Comrade wielding it made sure each finger came off one by one. We do not call this a betrayal. It is *usual* for names to be given after finger number three. So, let us leave in the morning."

He lifted the tea and I took a glass in my hand, looking at my fingers as I sipped the tea. I was glad I had sipped. It was laced with strong vodka for warmth.

The boy left the room without a word. As he passed, I noticed, engraved onto his Amazon shield, the lower part of his eagle cap badge, the Star of David.

Again Witek saw my glance. As the door closed he said, "A Jew, yes. Does that surprise you?"

"Not at all," I said. "I had many Jewish friends in Poland before the war. Since you know something of me, Witek, tell me something of yourself. We have to trust ourselves to you and we've had no identity papers from you." I smiled, to make sure he understood this was a joke.

"It was all so long ago. What is there to say? I was a History teacher in Krosno before the war. Got called up for the '39 campaign. When things fell apart, I shed my uniform and went back to school. I soon realised being a teacher was a dangerous occupation. I was intelligentsia, an educated Pole and a threat to the Germans because I could read and write. So I ran to the woods and joined the Home Army. I was too old for running around the forest so I was detailed to lecture on Polish history at various clandestine schools. Then I helped print books, text books in Polish for the underground schools and a few anti Nazi leaflets. All very unromantic, until we were raided. That night I discovered I was pretty savage. I survived the raid, having killed more Germans than I should, and I headed back to the woods to team up with a group of misfits. Because I was a bit older, they thought I knew everything; I found out they knew more than I did. I simply had the intelligence to work out where to place charges on railway lines.

"Our group of misfits became integrated into the *Armia Krajowa*, the Home Army. My unit was concentrated around Krosno. When the Red Army came to liberate us, we did what our government in London told us to do: cooperate with them, assist them. And so we met our Soviet brothers.

"I was promptly arrested as a Nazi collaborator by the NKVD and sent up to Rembertow, outside Warsaw. Surprise, surprise, there I found an old German prisoner of war camp, now run by the NKVD, full of fellow soldiers from the Home Army, along with the soldiers from the Peasant Battalions. The camp was not so bad, you know, cold kills the germs. During the winter we were held in the open, no shelter, just a compound with barbed wire. Thought we were meant to die somewhere else, not there. Those who died were just 'incidents'."

Witek moved around on his chair, squaring himself for the next part of his story. "The camp was run by a Colonel Alexandrov. It was him who decided who was going to be interrogated, which means tortured. The dead were buried in a park near the camp." Witek shrugged his shoulders. "I don't want to talk about that side of it any more. As I said, it was a holding camp to send all of us to Siberia to a *gulag*. As it turned out, in May 1945 Wichura and his unit from the Home Army attacked the camp. They just dressed up as members of the Polish Communist Army and attacked, taking first the gate and then opening the barracks, cutting the wire.

"There were about one hundred and fifty NKVD guards, but they were caught by surprise. The Soviets lost about sixty soldiers. The attack unit didn't lose a single man, but the bastard NKVD opened a machine gun on us prisoners as we ran away. Quite a number were killed. I would have thought about a thousand of us got out. The Russians claim they lost just a few hundred 'criminals'. Well, they had to say that, didn't they, because we didn't officially exist? They were busy telling the world that they didn't arrest Home Army Officers, just as they told the world that they didn't massacre anyone at Katyń.

"Where do you run to when you're running for your life? Next day there were aircraft overhead, they were everywhere. I teamed up with a German, some Nazi. Strange world, wasn't it? They'd kept some Germans in the same camp. The NKVD had made sure those these poor sods had been on display near the camp edge, so that they could tell the locals the camp was for Germans. See, the NKVD are secretive, very clever, not fools. But the Germans escaped with the rest of us. I'm happy to say Alexandrov got into big trouble. Most of us got away, although anybody caught by the Soviets was executed on the spot. The guy I escaped with, the one I thought was a dedicated Nazi, turned out to be a Sorb from near Bautzen. Just a German with nowhere to go. Last week, he was one of those arrested. From what I hear he never said a word until his fifth finger was cut off.

"What with only five fingers left, I suppose a bullet in the head was kind. I'm sure the NKVD man using the pistol was well trained on how to shoot Polish officers, which is very funny, as our compadre was a German. So you see, Labycz, I am not keen on nationality or ethnicity as a determinant of character. Unlike your Lord – what is his name? Astoria? Odeon?

Lord Cinema? Of course I mean Lord *Curzon*, the man who gave Churchill and Roosevelt the excuses they needed to deliver Poland to Stalin.

"So here I am, having collected another group of misfits. And here we sit, all of us, remnants of the Home Army. Not loved by anyone, hunted by the Polish Communist Army, who are run by the Soviets. Hunted by the Red Army who don't actually trust the Polish Communist Army, many of whom, God bless them, are only conscripts, still on our side. Of course, we do have our own NKVD in Poland, the MBP, the Ministry of Public Security, the great Polish secret police and counter-espionage service. At local level it's known as the UB. Let's hope you never get into their clutches."

Witek smiled wryly. "It was the MBP who won the election this week, did you know? Because the election was run by the MBP and the MBP is run by the Soviets. To ensure we Poles know what we should do, the Public Security Ministry is full of 'advisors' from the NKVD, the GRU, the Red Army military intelligence arm, and SMERSH. That particular acronym means 'death to spies'. These are the guys who literally exterminate anyone they want, under the direct control of Stalin. They are the troops who organise the deportations. The mass murderers, in short. Say what you like about the new Polish government and its independence, but I tell you now, the Polish secret service is run by General Ivan Aleksandrovich Serov and he was a SMERSH man. Any 'Polishness' is just a front.

Witek was warming to his theme. "Now, where we are down here in the South East, of course, there is another little problem; Ukrainian Nationalists. We have a few around here. Naturally they joined the Nazis in fighting the Communists. Stalin thinks these people should be punished. To him they are rebels, counter-revolutionaries. He wants a good excuse to break the Cossacks, conveniently forgetting how many he and Lenin tortured and starved in the Ukraine. Is he surprised so many fought with the Germans?"

The question hung in the air. A dog barked, the sound coming from lower down the hill. Immediately we all came to attention. Witek moved swiftly to the window, watching carefully, standing to one side so as not to be seen. The air held tense for a moment or two before he relaxed.

"Just a mangy fox after some chickens. Be careful of them. Half of them are mad with rabies," he observed then continued his treatise. "As you know, Roosevelt and Churchill connived with Stalin to move the whole population of Eastern Poland into Germany east of the Oder and Neisse rivers and expel the resident Germans west of that line. The new Polish government, a Soviet puppet, wants to move the population around here either into the Ukraine or up into the area around Szczecin, into the so-called New Territories. They then take the local population of Ukraine in the West, move them to Siberia and resettle this area with land-hungry Russian peasants and call them Ukrainians. That means that many of the locals don't like Poles. You follow?

Ethnic 'washing up', you see, a mixture of the best china and the saucepans, all in one bowl.

"As a result we now have a civil war going on here in three parts. Anyone told the Western press that? We have genocide and ethnic cleansing on a criminal scale and the Big Three powers are to blame; Churchill and Roosevelt cannot heap the blame on Stalin alone; they were quite complicit."

Witek breathed a heavy sigh. "Drink," he motioned, holding out his glass for more tea to the old lady. She promptly filled his glass with sweet tea and ignored us, settling back to her place, chewing her lips where they folded back into her face. She looked like a wooden doll. Even though she was inside, she wore a scarf bright with flowers over her hair. The rest of her clothing was nondescript, layers of woolens over a thick grey skirt. Her ankles peeked out from under the skirt. From their shape one could imagine wide, bandy legs. Her boots were clean. She sat, hands clasped in front of her, waiting for the Lord knew what.

Witek rambled on. "So we look at the American dream, Franklin Delano Roosevelt, man of the people, creator of the New Deal. Saviour of the economy. "

It felt like I was back at school, listening to the history teacher, which is what he was. A man's ramblings about his history are no more than personal experience and we all have these. But I could sense he wanted to give our visit, our mission, a perspective, a context. We had to listen or his life, which he was now risking for us, would be meaningless.

"In 1944 the American President badly needed the Polish and Jewish vote. Two things he needed to hide. The first was that he knew about Jewish death camps and could have done something about them. Polish intelligence had given him direct evidence. He had even directly interviewed a Polish underground officer who had gone into and out of Auschwitz. So all this nonsense that no one knew is a clear lie. Second, he needed to hide that he had already agreed to give Stalin half of Poland and agreed to mass genocide and deportations. He'd had secret meetings with Stalin away from Churchill. He lied directly to Mikołajczyk, the Polish Prime Minister, and told him no deal was done with Stalin when it was.

"It was pretty obvious that his Vice-President Henry Wallace was a pro-Communist Stalin fan. The Democrats are riddled with Communists today. Then, for whatever reason, he dumped Wallace and the Party chose Truman. FDR won the election and went straight to the Yalta Conference. Where he confirmed with Stalin and Churchill that Poland should be carved up, along with Germany." Witek's lighter turned agitatedly. "How dare they?" he barked the words, jerking back in his chair. "How bloody dare they? Of course, they cut up China too without asking them, so who are we to complain? So you see, gentlemen, everything here is a mess! And thanks to our allies the real terms of this reorganization are secret and the world press compliant." He held his finger and thumb to his eyes.

There was long pause, but this time I didn't interrupt the man. Witek was not looking at us, but rubbing his hand slowly over his forehead as though in pain or even deep thought. His bitterness, his rage was seeping from him in waves. Some of his anger was clearly directed at us, interlopers coming like gods to this forsaken patch of earth and endangering his men. Finally he held his face in both hands as though washing away his thoughts. Hunching his shoulders he stretched before continuing.

"We are now even getting it in the neck here because the British army forced thirty-two thousand plus Cossacks, including women and children, into cattle rail-cars and trucks and repatriated them to the Red Army. We Poles were allies of the British and therefore the nearest to blame! Can you imagine what happened to those people when they got to Soviet Russia? In Lienz, in Austria, about two thousand officers and soldiers were invited to a large conference. They went only on the assurance of a British officer's word of honour. As one Ukrainian partisan recently said, a man with whom we occasionally fight and occasionally cooperate, 'the NKVD and the Germans would kill us with a bullet or a club. The British did it with their word of honour'. You understand now why I am a man less than happy to see you." Witek whistled through his teeth and toyed with his glass in its holder, fidgeting his great bulk in his chair. We remained silent, knowing it was best to let him talk himself out. The bitterness wells inside you. It creases your stomach and reaches your eyes in tears.

At times like this, conversations become oblique.

"How do the British see us?" Witek shot his question at me.

This was difficult to answer. So, like him, I toyed with my now empty glass. I looked at the wall, measuring the distance in my mind's eye between one crack and another, letting the words come, almost without thinking. I straightened up for my response.

"If you are on the Left it's 'Polish shits go home. We went to war for you so bugger off now, you fascist filth'. Poles who do not go back to Poland are unwelcome, to put it mildly. This attitude is especially true of ex-army boys. The RAF is different. They help the Polish Air Force boys a great deal, and they defend them against the Labour government. The government is a mixed lot and clearly has a lot of communist sympathisers. Many of the British people refuse to accept the situation here as the truth, especially thanks to the newspapers and to biased BBC reports. For them the war is well and truly over.

"The Centrists and Right know that Churchill and Roosevelt made a mess of it and feel that we're in for another war. In fact a new phrase has emerged: the 'Cold War'. This will be fought over economics as much as anything, but it will be played out in proxy countries such as those here in Eastern Europe or in the Far East. Both areas now reaping flawed American policy, as you have said. On the whole, the better educated are supportive of Poland and are not blind to what has happened – though perhaps surprised. There is a residual feeling of 'poor little Poland', that far-away place near the North Pole. In fairness there is a Polish Resettlement Corps, to house and help the Poles to settle down and get jobs, as long as they don't take British jobs. The sympathetic press and radio journalists - and they do exist - sometimes talk of Polish heroism, all the nonsense of cavalry charging tanks and talk like that. Mostly, however, talk is of the Polish Air Force..."

"Of which he is also a member. It's is a long story," interjected Kryszka, pointing at me and almost spoiling my train of thought,

"...which was supposedly shot up on the ground. They're saying that the Polish Army fought a campaign for only two weeks before being overrun by a superior German army."

"What you're saying is the British know nothing except filthy German or Russian lies," said Witek. He began shifting about as though he needed to pee badly whilst wringing his hands. Something I said had touched a very raw nerve.

"Look, Witek, the British like gossip in their papers, not facts. The common man rules now and there is a class war going on. The English are a fair-minded lot on the whole, but the Celtic fringe, the London, Birmingham and Liverpool Irish, the Lowland Scots and the Welsh, are all hard-done-bys. They belong to the 'we-don't-have' brigade, so they fall for Red propaganda every time. *Animal Farm* by George Orwell is beyond them."

Witek was clearly trying to wrest himself back into control. "I know the book, a parody on Stalin and Lenin. We pirated it - there are clandestine copies in Polish, though it will never be published here. 'Squealer' would be too easy to identify as Molotov." We laughed, though the laughter was bitter. Despite Orwell's genuine beliefs and war record with the International Brigades in Spain, he was now seen as a major class enemy – or worse, a subversive, according to the Left.

Silence settled in the room. The old lady broke it, as she began to shuffle about, waving her hands in our direction. "Move, move. I have work to do. You men gossip elsewhere."

We clomped back through the house the way we had come. Dark was coming in fast. The low sun streamed into the house, lighting up the log walls, its red light warming and comforting, despite the chill seeping through the casement windows. The old woman's lace-work pelmets cast patterns on the opposite wall. It was almost restful. I realised how tired I was.

We settled in chairs. Witek lit up a cigarette. Tapping his lighter against the wooden arm of his chair, he inhaled deeply then blew smoke into the sunbeams. He proffered a cigarette from his pack to Kryszka, who accepted and lit up from the lighter Witek held out for him. Witek screwed his bulk around in his chair and shook the pack at me.

"No thanks, I'm not a smoker. Just the occasional pipe or two."

Witek looked at me, holding my gaze till it was uncomfortable. The smoke drifted idly upwards and the sun played with the rising smoke and falling dust. A scene a fairy could dance in. Everything was right, the world was at peace yet here we were at war. They were at war too in Mongolia and China, but that was a long way from this still, quiet room.

Finally Witek smiled. "Roosevelt died from smoking. Smoking kills the brain and so countries!" It was a joke of a kind. Kryszka grimaced.

"So, my friends, here we are. What do we do now?"

Kryszka was first to answer. "Our mission is to find President Sikorski's daughter. Whom we believe to be alive and in a *gulag*."

"You're joking!" Witek said.

"No, we are not," I said. "We have reliable reports and photographs. And we need to bring her out."

"Why would the NKVD have kept her alive?" Witek queried.

"Because that's what they do," Kryszka responded. "They keep people alive till they are no longer useful. Zofia Leśniowska would have remained useful as long as things weren't going their way in Poland. In order to turn the population pro-Soviet, they could have used her to prove that the British killed her father. Affidavits and drugs would have been all that was required. Now, since the election *she* is no longer needed.

"If she is alive, then so are likely others from the plane crash that killed the President. People who would know who authorised what and when. They would be British and they would know who the traitors are, both in the Service and in high office."

Witek interjected, "Sikorski's daughter must be dead by now. Your mission is a waste of time. Or if she's not dead she will have been moved and 'lost'. It is their way. Stalin cannot count."

Kryszka took his stance. "You know as well as I do that the Polish Home army and its allies here are finished. The Polish Underground has no future. It is all politics now, not armed struggle. If we find her, find the daughter of the man we were united around, we have a coup. She becomes the Symbol of our betrayal. We can bring down governments with her, twist arms, keep the truth hidden or reveal it. The Home Army is crushed and betrayed. I took an oath to the Republic, as did you, Witek, and as did Labycz. We will die for that oath. She gives us a reason to keep on fighting."

"Otherwise we are dead meat is what you are saying," Witek responded. "We do this job for honour, loyalty and politics. I know my oath, so I do it.

But now you say we should we give up the struggle as though we have nothing to struggle for, no cause, no politics, no allies. If I lay down arms I shall be shot and the others sent to concentration camp or jail. So what do we do? We fight on. We still have good intelligence and we know the same facts as the British. So when you get back to England you tell them facts!" he shouted.

He had been acting disturbed ever since I had mentioned the September campaign. I could see now that he was clearly on the edge of a madness born of deep emotions. Witek stood up and went over to a carved wooden chest covered with a colourful embroidered cloth, out of sight in a corner the sun didn't reach. He knelt down for a moment. As he rose again there was a certain stiffness. He needed to push himself up. Age and life were catching him up on this old warrior.

When he returned he held a small worn leather-bound notebook. Flicking through its pages he glared at me as though I were the enemy. He fixed his eye on me.

"This...." He waved the book at me, stood up in agitation, then sat down again..."This I have from our friends, *and we do have them*, in the Wehrmacht and in American Intelligence. You want facts? I am an historian. I give you facts!" he spluttered. "I write them all down." He shouted at me. "You, mother fucker, should know these things. Then you can tell them to all the bastards who could not care, who treat us like little children who ran away. I'll give you this fucking book, you use it." He began to refer to his notes, turning pages.

"In '39 the Germans sent against us over 550 Infantry Battalions, against our 370. They had three times our number of field guns, five times our number of anti-tank guns. We had nearly 500 tanks; they had over 2,500. We had 400 aircraft; they had 1,500 with 800 in reserve. We have seen the German intelligence now. We know what happened! The Germans did not walk over us in the so-called September Campaign 1939. That is a propaganda lie."

His face had become red with blood pressure and emotion. Kryszka and I sat silent, but his attention was focused on me. It was as though he was angry at me personally, but I knew he was not. I decided not to tell him that no one in Britain would be interested. Perhaps in fifty years, but not now. Right now no one cared now that the truth in Witek's notebook did not fit the 'facts' in the papers. The facts were what the papers presented. What the BBC said, because we all know it only speaks the gospel. I decided not to say a word. It was not my time.

"The French and the British agreed in the summer of 1939 that they expected the Polish Army to engage the Germans for two weeks. Two bloody, shitty weeks, I tell you. The French and British, with over 70 battle ready divisions, were to cross the Rhine in support and open a front. With indefensible frontiers in the West, the Poles were expected to fall back in the

East. We did what we were asked. We fulfilled our obligation. But the French and the British did not come. Whilst we Poles fought alone, 92 French divisions stood idle behind the Maginot line. Facing them were 35 low-grade German divisions. Their first class troops were over our frontiers.

"In the middle of September we did not know we had been let down. We do now. It was not a walk-over. In the month of the September campaign the Germans lost over 50,000 dead and wounded." Witek's hands trembled as he flicked the pages over to cross-reference his point. He cleared his throat. He was wound up like an emotional spring. Tears seemed not far away, yet I found this emotionality a little disconcerting, almost theatrical.

"In addition they lost a thousand tanks and armoured cars, 30% of what they had. They said four hundred artillery pieces were destroyed, and six hundred 'planes were finished, 25% of the Luftwaffe. So don't tell me we were walked over." He punctuated these last remarks by banging his fists on the table, hammering out, glaring at us from under eyebrows that were still blonde, a leftover from youth. His face was fierce, like an angry owl. Comical in a way, but at the same time tragic. A man spilling his history, his bitterness, about a loss which no one seemed to care about, least of all politicians.

"We lost 66,000 killed, 130,000 wounded. There were 420,000 prisoners taken by the Germans and then, and then..." He pointed his finger at me, which was trembling with emotion, "...the Russians took 190,000. Yes, the Russians. Everyone knows that on September 17th the Soviets crossed the border. No announcement of war, they just invaded. It wasn't over in two weeks.

"Witek, we know all this," Kryszka interrupted, "We lived through it too. We need to talk of what are going to do, not about the past."

Witek swung his venom on Kryszka. "So you, London filth, you come here as though you know everything. You waltz in here and expect help. Well, there's no help. We're finished here, bloody finished and you don't give a fuck what happened. You just want to move on and leave us. As if yesterday was nothing. How can we move on if we don't realise where all this shit is coming from, all the hatred, the bitterness? Do you think this is some kind of romantic novel you are living in? Some gangster movie?"

We tried to answer, tell him we were on his side. He ploughed on despite us, his emotions ever heightening.

"The Germans entered Warsaw on October 1st. On September 28th the Commander-in-Chief himself went to the city, with instructions to form an underground army. The last battle took place around here in south-eastern Poland under General Kleeberg, with the operational group *Polesie*. It took place on September 28th and was against the Soviets, not the bloody Germans. Against tanks, artillery and aircraft. Our troops forced the Soviets to withdraw beyond the demarcation line which Ribbentrop and Molotov had agreed. And then the Germans went to rescue the Russians. Yes, my friends. That's what happened." Witek collapsed into his chair trembling. We kept quiet, breathing in, glad it was over. The man was spent, defeated by his own feelings.

But, like the war itself, he unexpectedly began again, this time speaking more calmly. "Kleeburg and the *Polesie* group fought on for five days against the Germans. Why? Why did they go on? For honour, I tell you! They were not defeated. They simply ran out of equipment and ammunition. Kleeburg called an end to it on October 6th. His last order? I have it written here: 'Poland will not perish as long as we are alive'. I tell you this..," and now he was waving a finger at me, "at the same time the cavalry of the 110th Regiment, commanded by Major Hubal, attacked a German unit at Chodkowo. The partisan war had begun and I am still bloody here, still in it, right fucking now."

This was fact, of course; Kryszka and I were living proof of his ongoing fight. I felt very sorry for Witek at that moment. His was a life waiting to end. I studied him closely, looking past his well worn rag bag of a uniform. A proud man, with no hope. Come the end he would have no place to hide. We were newcomers, interlopers, well fed adventurers who had already cost him dearly. Why was he still helping us, I wondered? But as the words formed in my mind I realised the same question also applied to me. Was I here for duty or honour? Or perhaps even for selfish reasons? Why was I so determined to prove I was right about President Sikorski's death?

More quietly Witek went on. "We did not accept defeat. We are still wearing Polish military uniform. So you tell them back in Britain, we are not poor little Poland who was overrun by the mighty Blitzkrieg. You tell them the facts! The French, British, Dutch and Belgian Resistance lasted thirty-nine days. We struggled thirty-six days *on our own* and, you know what, Labycz? We have proof. The Germans are good at records. They used 400 million rifle bullets, 2 million plus artillery shells and 70,000 aerial bombs to defeat us. Against France, Holland, Britain and Belgium, they had to use less than half those figures to get France to capitulate. And..." He had become animated again and started stuttering, "...we had the Soviets and Russians at our back. What I want to know is, did the British and French *know*? Did they *know* the Russkis would attack? That is a real question."

He stopped dead in his tirade. Standing up suddenly, he walked to the door and said, "I'll get you some weapons. Stay put." The suddenness of his movements caught us by surprise. We jerked out of our thought processes. Pausing in the doorway he grinned at me in the failing light. "The sun has gone down, my friend," he remarked. He opened the door. The still chill crept forward across our knees. "Catch!" he said and his notebook sailed towards me. 'Don't lose it. It is yours to keep and do with it as you damn well wish. As you say, it's all history now."

He slammed the door behind him, rattling the china and wooden plates and ornaments around the room. The sun had nearly gone.

It would never rise on the second Republic.

Kryszka turned to me. "I'm sorry you had to take that from him. I suppose he needs to vent his spleen to someone and you were the nearest target. He seemed to think you're British somehow."

"I'm not British," I said, stubbornly. "I'm not even supposed to be Canadian. God knows what sort of a mongrel I am."

We both laughed. Our cigarettes were cold and stubbed out, their ash dirtying a small plate. The sixteen-year-old Sten toting boy came into the room. *There must be another door*, I thought. He just stood there looking at us. Was he guarding us? If so, in what way? I wasn't sure whether we were free or whether we were prisoners.

There was the smell of cooking. I realised I was hungry. Waiting, I leafed through the pages. It was sad, this war record. It was a small book. I should have asked more closely about his sources of information. As I tucked it away in my shirt all I could think was that it still had many spare empty pages.

Was Witek's war over?

# CHAPTER 3

# CAT, DOG AND MICE

When boredom strikes, the mind sends little impulses around to see what's cooking in its recesses. Relaxed, the grey cells are waiting for the happening, some event, some action. When waiting for plans you can't influence to mature, there is nothing to do except work or play or sleep or think. That list excludes copulation, of course, which might also come under the other headings. When you're waiting, strange ideas can overtake your mind, invade your thoughts, niggle away to be later turned over and looked at.

Bored as it was, my mind was looking around.

I had always favoured novels that moved fast. The kind with heroes jumping through windows to successfully do what was necessary, holding the girl as she swooned in his arms during a daring rescue. My old tutor Mrs. Simpson used to call such stories 'Penny Dreadfuls'. Over the years she had tried to interest me in the great works of literature. For her sake I had ploughed through *Pilgrim's Progress* and *Swiss Family Robinson* and done my duty by many Edwardian boys' books. Though I admired them, I still didn't find them nearly as interesting or gripping as a good thriller. I was happy reading Sir Walter Scott and R.M. Ballantyne, with his Canadian stories, had done me proud. As I got older I migrated to Jack London and Dennis Wheatley. Then at Cambridge I had argued with my tutors that Shakespeare had not used forms of language strange to his audience. He hadn't been intent on educating them in the nuances of English grammar. Shakespeare was the modernist tub-thumper of his day. He was appealing to commoners as much as to his wealthy patrons. That's why I could read *Henry IV* as a novel, wonderful, racy history with all the blood and thunder of a crime writer. I doubted that our William would have enjoyed Trollope or the Brontë sisters any more than I did. I only accepted the superiority of Joyce and Waugh because they dealt in conversation.

But real life is punctuated with events that are mundane or boring. Rarely do you read of a detective changing his underwear. So here I was, a clandestine, a soldier, a desperado sort of guy who had all the makings of a hero from a book, and I was living in my head, not in the action around me. I was cold, hungry, tired. Bored? Yes. Confused? Yes. And there was something else troubling me. Had I give my real name to Witek? No. So did he have it from the letter we'd had from England? That I didn't know. But

Kryszka's eyes had narrowed too when Witek used it.

*So what comes next,* my mind wondered? Witek had made me pensive. England had always been a puzzle to me. Here was a country that had built its traditions over centuries on three invading groups; Anglo-Saxons, Danes and Normans. Later it had given asylum to many foreigners, succour and shelter to Flemings and other refugees. Being good to foreigners was part of British tradition. The British were having difficulty after this war with Poles and their ilk. Much of that was down to the press. Often the 'flash points' were as much about jobs and poverty, both points in the Socialist play-ground, as about nationality. I had seen the effect of the Blitz in London, in Exeter, in Plymouth. But in the destruction in England I had not seen anything that compared to what I had seen travelling through Europe. Nothing had happened in America, of course. America had seen nothing except pictures of graves. There were no bombed-out buildings in America. My journey here had been thought-provoking, as was Witek's little book.

Witek's take on identity had stayed with me. Mrs. Simpson, my tutor, a diehard Scot, was British, not English. She had viewed me as a child of the British Empire. Accepted me as a Polish Canadian, just as in the United States you had Polish Americans. She had sometimes said it should be a Canadian Pole and not the reverse. Of course, I hadn't been born in Canada, but she wasn't aware of this until much later.

In Britain, however, the wording doesn't seem to fit. I sat for a moment running over, 'I am Polish British'. It just doesn't sound right. British Pole works better, but then you would be acknowledging premier Britishness. The same applies if you use English. A Polish Englishman sounds terrible, but we could work with 'an English Pole'. Always the Empire comes out top.

Kryszka still had his head in a paper. My musings continued. French Canadians who are no less Canadian than anyone else. There are communities of *La Polonaise* in France. You could have a Polish Scot or a Scots Pole. But somehow the mentality of the English language, its very Britishness lays claim to you. Not easy for immigrant cultures. North Americans understand this muddle of immigration so much better than the British do, I mused. And there was a difference in attitude. Americans said, 'Come here and work, no handouts'. The British in their kindness or devoutness give charity and aid, even if it's grumbling.

The Polish borders had been changed, millions of people forced to move to a new home. This was ethnic cleansing on the grandest scale. Why, I thought, did the British, themselves so split ethnically, believe that a nation like Poland could not cope with minorities? Why did America, built on diversity think that countries should be unitised behind false borders? Stalin and Russia? Those I understood.

The boy had shifted from his standing position and had slid down the wall. He sat with knees tucked up to his chin, Sten gun between his knees. His dark brown eyes had been staring at me for some time.

I decided to start some conversation. It's the way I am. I could sit for hours when I wanted to, ignoring my surroundings. But when I was uncomfortable my defence was to chatter. Inherent immigrant insecurity.

"Tough time for you?" I asked as an opening gambit.

The voice that came back to me was light, but the tone was unexpected.

"That was a stupid question. Life is difficult, was difficult, and you have made it more difficult."

"I was being just trying to be friendly. No offence meant." If it was true that their group had taken so many casualties because of us what he said was understandable.

"Did I say you had offended me?" The reply was thrown back to me.

Kryszka winked at me from behind his paper, clearing his throat as if to say, 'Nothing to do with me – your problem. 'I decided to exit for safety back to my reverie. Food was coming, the smell making the juices flow.

The lad was the one who continued, "Cat got your tongue now? Given up being friendly?"

"No, I was just trying to make small talk." I had been struck by the lightness of his voice, which had a strange, melodic tone. His ripostes seemed mature for his age, so I pressed on.

"Did you go to one of the underground schools?"

Again, the quick smile. "I attended university in Warsaw but before that, yes, I went to the underground state school. I qualified as a medical doctor. Does that satisfy your curiosity?"

"Not really. What were you, some child prodigy? You don't look old enough to treat me. "

"Well, if you take a bullet or graze your knee then don't ask me for help. If you're nice to me I might kiss it better, though," and he grinned broadly at me.

"We would be arrested for that in England," I shot back, grinning too at his forwardness.

"Why ever is that?" he said. "I think a girl is entitled to kiss whom she wants, don't you?"

The truth came like a flash, not a dawning. How could I have been so stupid? He was a she! Dirty, cold, wrapped up like a bear, it was easy to justify the mistake. But now, out of her greatcoat, I saw her, lithe, slim, those beautiful eyes. I had not observed. A primary mistake, such as could cost my life.

"Why, you are blushing? How sweet! You thought I was a boy, didn't you?" She wagged her finger at me, all the time that mischievous smile playing around her lips. "Here, is that better?" she said, pulling off her forage cap and taking out some pins out of her hair. It fell to chin length as she tossed her head. Dark, with a slight wave. "Better now?"

I blustered. "I was just playing your game."

"Liar!" she said. "You are lying to me. I can see it all over your face."

I decided on the best route out of my embarrassment. "Tell me more about yourself."

"Middle-class Jewish family. One brother and one sister. Me, the youngest, spoiled, adored by everyone. Nice apartment in Warsaw. Father a lawyer. Mother gave piano lessons to poor kids from across the river in Wola."

I asked the obvious question she had avoided. "So how did you get to here?"

"I was a runner in the Home Army, and when the Rising happened in '44, I had just qualified. When Berling's First Polish Army Troops crossed the Vistula against orders from their Soviet masters, they were pinned down and shelled from their own Soviet Russian side too. So I was sent down to the sands to help with first aid. When the landings failed I went back across the river with some of the troops. Although fighting in the City was lost, I simply carried on aiding the wounded. No one asked questions. Quite incredible really.

When the Russians eventually crossed there was no Warsaw left. Nothing to go back to. It was a moonscape. Forget Dresden, London, Berlin. I have seen the pictures. Hitler ordered the city to be razed to the ground and that is what the Germans did." For a moment she was lost in her thoughts. "Does anyone in England or America realise the devastation; the atrocity of it? Emptying an entire city, removing its people and sending them into desolation or slave labour?"

She asked the question in a very matter of fact way, without any of Witek's vehemence. I realised she was genuinely curious.

So I told the truth. "No. Telling people the facts too loudly would have caused problems for the Big Three powers. The battle for Arnhem was going on at the same time as the Rising. Afterwards Warsaw was not brought to the public mind. They might have asked awkward questions, you see, like 'Why didn't the Russians help? They can't remember what they were never told. In fifty years' time the French Resistance will be taught in schools, but the Polish underground? Never. Now the Soviet propaganda paints all the Poles as anti-Semitic, pro-Nazi. It is laughable, but the Western press take it up. They repeat the same old workers' paradise stuff. It helps their conscience, I suppose, having given the country to Russia to try to justify their crime."

"What about the Ghettoes? Is their history known?" She was clearly more animated about this than the '44 rising.

"I don't believe the average European has caught up with any of this

Jewish stuff. You and I both know that Hitler ruled most of Europe by agreement, not by war. Plenty of people were glad to see the back of you Jews for whatever reason. They were collaborative – the French were quite cooperative in removing their Jews, for example. At the moment the general public are horrified to see films of the camps being opened up. But the full horror has not sunk in. The average man and woman cannot really believe what they hear and see. So compared to the camps the Ghettoes are still a side show, not spoken about. The inmates were sent to the camps, the fighters killed and their struggles and politics unknown. We need a few books and films."

"Oh, don't worry about that," she answered. "I'm sure the New York and the Hollywood Jews will be wringing their hands all the way to the box office and then to the bank with all those stories of misery, poverty and settlement. I tell you bluntly, the Jewish propaganda machine will claim all this misery, the camps, the gas chambers as their own. We Poles, Jews proud to be Polish citizens, will be forgotten. The Russian prisoners will be overlooked, the Gypsies, the musicians, the Jehovah's Witnesses, the homosexuals, the disabled, these groups will all vanish beneath the Jewish conquest of fate and publicity. Who will remember the real German patriots who opposed the Nazis? I don't mean the Wehrmacht plotters who still believed in a supreme Germany. They were not the heroes. But the few who helped Jews, who gave intelligence to the Allies. As for us Poles, we lost six million in the camps. Three of which had Jewish origins. That means we are level-pegging in the numbers game. Ethnic Poles are just no bloody good at public relations. The Reds are making sure that in the public mind the Poles are daubed anti-Semitic, Fascist and pro-Nazi.

"What happened to your family?" The question hung in the air.

"My parents ended up in the Warsaw ghetto. I believe they went in a transport to Treblinka and then merciful death, I expect. They were not Zionists, just people building a new society and country on their own doorstep by going to work and polishing the piano and having the family around and helping our neighbours. You know, the things ordinary people do. It's called life and getting on with things. "

"Your brother and sister?" I enquired gently.

"My sister became a resistance fighter in the Ghetto rising in '43. This is the badge she wore." She fingered her Polish Crowned Eagle cap badge proudly. "My sister belonged to the Żydowski Związek Wojskowy or ŻW, the Jewish Military Union. Women fought alongside the men. When she went in she placed me with a family in Warsaw with forged papers, even a birth certificate. Now they say Poles did not help Jews. Many did not, but more did. Those people treated me as their daughter. Jacek, my brother, stayed out. He went to the woods to the AK, and in his unit I don't think they even knew he was Jewish. He certainly called himself a Pole." She laughed. "He helped coordinate, trying to get arms to the resistance. That's all I know. Except one day this grubby boy arrived, I would say about eleven years old, wearing an AK arm-band. I think it was day two of the rising. There were worm-holes that kids used to get in and out for, you know? For anything from food to guns, even jewels."

I knew the ghetto was nothing if not a black market paradise. Ultimately it was about survival and of the fittest. Dog eat dog. Heroism and cowardice, side by side. People are just that; people.

"He told me my sister had been shot by a sniper stationed high outside the walls. This kid had risked his life for this bit of metal, bringing it out to me. All because she'd said, when she was wounded, that she'd have liked me to have her badge."

"It was more than metal to her," I observed. "It was to do with all she had left; self-respect, her honour. Don't you think?"

There was a pause. "That kid went back in, too."

She stopped again and looked at me hard. "Why am I telling you all this? You've already had a lesson from Witek. Why would you want to hear my story?"

"Because you need to tell someone? Because you know you may never tell it like this again?" My inflection was a question or statement. "Because the old world is passing to the writers. The story will be distorted. You just want to say what happened, simply and with respect to your family."

"Yes," she said meekly and then she began again. "My brother was not in the ŻW. Mostly those guys were ex-Polish Army. My brother being already part of the AK, he was sort of liaison. They had dug two tunnels to get arms in and to keep contact. He worked with Pszenny, code name Chwacki. From day one of the battle the Polish underground kept supplies going into the Ghetto and even sent in some fighters to support the uprising. My brother took part in some of the actions outside the Ghetto. You know, attacking supplies and reinforcements. They even tried to blow up the Ghetto wall. He helped get some of the survivors out of the sewers when it ended. " She smiled. "We were in contact from time to time. It was he who told me that mum and dad were gone."

There was a little gap of silence.

"He told me how proud he was that when the work gangs were allowed outside the Ghetto for construction work they would march back singing, 'Hej Strzelcy Wraz'." She began to hum the tune in a quiet voice. "*March Soldiers March, Our luck again we're trying. There facing us stands our detested foe. Our eagle white above us will be flying and God will guide our guns' avenging blow*". She was lost in thought for a moment. I waited till she was ready to resume.

"The longest ŻW defence of a position took place around the stronghold at Muranowski Square. That was their headquarters. It had two flags flying high above it for the people to see, the white and red of Poland and the blue and white banner of the ŻW. Those flags really got under the Germans' skin. Himmler apparently shouted down the phone to the German Commander: 'You must at all costs bring down those two flags!' Of course they were all brought down, in the end."

"And what of the other Jewish fighting group?"

"The ZOB, the Żydowska Organizacja Bojowa. More people my age. Left wing Zionists mainly. They went ahead with the fight in January because they felt the leadership was too slow. So the rising was rushed before the arms and bunkers were in force. But how can you criticize anyone in those circumstances? Have you heard the name Askari?"

"I know that the African troops in the British army are called Askaris,"

"Well, our 'Askaris' were Latvian or Lithuanian or Ukrainian, troops or military police. They were particularly brutal in the Ghetto, worse in a way than the Germans. Volunteers too. Today their story is that they were forced to be inhuman! Just like all the Germans. Funny how there are no Nazis now."

"What happened to your brother?"

"He went through the Rising and was sent to a POW camp in Germany as far as I know. That's the last I heard from him. If he is alive I guess he'll head for the USA. He won't come back here. Not with the Communists in power. Besides, the underground here is finished." She sighed. "So much sacrifice. And we came so close. We had a government in waiting, police, a free press, schools, all the levers of administration. All taken from us by three politicians with no thought for the misery they were causing. Some too, I shall head for Israel as soon as I can get you out of the way. Do my duty and then off."

Touched by her, I gripped her hand in friendship and we waved them back and forward for a moment or two before she withdrew her hand.

"Enough. I am tired. Tired of it all." She shifted and got up like a rustling cat, which made me smile.

It was time for food and warm bread and soup.

Somewhere out there a rabbit squealed its death throes. Night has stolen in. A night of stars and moonlight, of shadows, of shifting shapes. A night where animals, caught between the cold of night and the warmth of day, were driven out to hunt or steal from others.

The war was over, but not in this part of Poland. here armies slept; women were raped; shots were heard; partisans were hung; prisoners died; a drunken guard was garotted by a bandit; an emaciated child finally succumbed to hunger; his sister sold herself.

All in the cruelty of moonlight, here in this borderland.

# Chapter 4

# The Hunt

The morning started sunny. Outside the thaw had begun. Though the ground was still frozen the snow was beginning to turn to slush. Puddles formed in our footprints, white turning grey. We moved out as one column, single file, Witek insisting that we walk behind each other. Not in each other's footsteps, but in a single line, so no one could tell how many we were on the trail.

"Had the group not been decimated in the recent fire-fight I would have sent one group south whilst we headed north. Confuse the opposition," he had reasoned. His last act had been to hug 'Grandmother'. "Courageous old bird, ain't she?" he'd observed to no one in particular. "She's been good to us this winter, a life saver!" As he thanked her, the headscarf, which seemed a permanent feature with its cheerful burgundy and embroidered flowers, caught the light. As we turned away I heard her quiet, "God bless you, children," as she raised her blue pinafore to her face, wiping away surprising tears.

We hoisted our packs containing spare clothing and the few rations granny had provided. Arms were slung. The *Kapral*, Karol, carried the group's radio, whilst Kryszka shouldered our long barrelled Polish version of the tried and tested Mauser rifle. The shorter carbine was assigned to me, a turned-down bolt handle version used by the cavalry. In trained hands it could loose off fifteen rounds a minute.

Witek was busy splashing liquid from a bottle as we walked. "Becherowka," he said, in response to my raised eyebrow. *Why the waste?* I wondered. The potent herb-flavoured vodka was used for every ailment internal and external.

Witek read my mind. "The smell will attract the dogs away from the gate. With a bit of luck, they'll pull the search team on past her gate. The old girl will be interrogated anyway, but she might get away with saying she saw us pass by. Otherwise," he gestured a cut throat with his hand, "old lady kaput. Of course, it will depend whether they are Polish boys or Russkis. I hope the former. Most of those lads are peasant conscripts, far from home in the cold. Everyone has a grandmother, eh? That said, the politicos can't have, can they? Because they'd shoot her out of hand."

As he spoke he produced another bottle. By now we were walking through the ever darkening forest, beneath the conifer canopy. The ground was snow-covered though not deeply. Apart from Witek's observations the world was quiet.

He carried out another episode of Becherowka splashing, then stopped. "Our winter dugouts are close by. If you sniff carefully you can smell the wood smoke."

I responded, sniffing the air and breathing it in. I detected nothing that spoke to me of partisan winter quarters, dugouts or log shelters. "All I can smell is the pine needles and the earth,"

"Let's pray that for Granny's sake they're all like you," he guffawed. "If they come sweeping the forest, they'll find the camp. But if they follow our trail they'll miss it. If they do find it, maybe it will delay them coming after us till they make sure it's empty. Of course then they'll head back to granny. That is logic for you. After all, she can hardly say then she didn't know we were there. I told her, if it comes to it, to say we preyed on her all winter. She should call us scum and bandits, curse us for eating her supplies and threatening to kill her if she didn't part with her potatoes. If she's not lucky she will get Siberia. And later some Party big-wig will take the house for its splendid view. Wonderful opportunity for a *dacha*, you see.

"With luck she'll be believed, and then she'll be a star in the government papers. I can see the headlines: 'Old lady terrorised by partisan AK bandits. Saved by the People's Army.' Either way, Tadek, dogs like Becherowka."

"So now you're deliberately making a trail for them to follow?"

He stopped suddenly. Like an elastic band we all cannoned into each other. Witek regarded me for a moment. "So what would you rather have? Granny shot on the spot? Or you taking a chance, risking she get out alive?" He turned and marched on.

I smarted quietly, feeling rebuked.

Soon we came to a small stream in a clearing. The Becherowka bottles were sent spinning into the ice cold water to bob quickly downhill, banging against stone and rock until out of sight. The stream was wide at this point, about six metres across. It had left its high banks and small rapids to flatten and ripple over a water slide of smooth rock, the water running only a hundred centimetres deep. In midstream it broke into a fast flowing channel, at least four times the depth, from what we could see. In places the slide was an ice sheet. In others it slid silently, ice blue against the rock.

"Quiet everyone," Witek commanded, "Now we separate. Karol, you take everyone except Kryszka, Tadek and Hanka. We cross here, and then we go our different ways. Karol, go downstream for about two kilometres then cross back over and double back toward the old winter camp. Pass on and head over to Ogien's group and join them in Podhale. If we make it I will rejoin you there."

The men murmured quietly amongst themselves. Clearly the order was not welcome.

"Boots and socks off, gentlemen," Witek pointed, "otherwise you will freeze in your wet boots as we go on and tonight you will have to cut off your toes."

"My boots are soaked already," I grumbled quietly.

My words were pounced upon at once, even though I hadn't intended them to be heard. "Believe me, wet boots in this weather are not the same as water-filled boots and wet socks, if you are lucky enough to have any." At his words I realised some of his men did not and immediately felt abashed at my extra pair. "I told you already, grease, goose fat, pig fat, any fat is good insulation, and waterproof." He clapped me on the back, I assumed to make me feel a little easier. His men were already binding their feet with strips of cloth. "Better than your socks," a trooper said. "Keeps your toes from dropping off when it's really cold!"

Icicles sparkled from every fern, every dead leaf and every twig that overhung the stream. By now they were dripping fast in the sun. Foam had frozen to the exposed rocks as though suspended by magic, the bubbles biding their time till they could flow the long journey to the sea. I imagined the cold grey Vistula, an eternity away, its banks frozen silver, ice flows drifting toward the cold Baltic Sea.

The barked order, "Move, move!" broke my reverie. Along with a shove in the back.

"Hardly the river Jordan," my brain sang, and then the freezing water hit me. I yelped as had the others. It was no longer pretty or romantic. First my feet went numb as I shuffled across the smooth rock. By the middle I was up to my knees. As the pebbles pummelled my feet, I almost lost my balance. I didn't think till later to wonder why, when my feet were numb, did the pebbles cause such excruciating pain. Step up, and slide my feet forward again, controlling every centimetre. My calves trembled with the strain but I was glad to be clear of the iced water. Then a last stumble to the bank and onto the snow and mud. I fell back into a snow bank and began to rub my feet, which I couldn't feel except for the fire within them. My hands told me I still had them but my feet couldn't sense my hands. Shivering I put on my socks. I had thought that my feet had dried rapidly, but my socks told me differently as I struggled with them. My toes went in but the heels refused to find their right place without a struggle. Next came my boots, which required heaving on. I stood up as the last of the band came across, stamping things into place. As life came back to them my feet began to feel deliciously warm. I smiled, as did the others.

Karol and his group began their farewells, each of them hugging Witek and exchanging a few words. Then it was Hanka's turn. Some wished

Kryszka and I well, though others held back. We shook hands and gave away some of our cigarettes, to use as currency. Karol turned and led the troop off.

In the distance we could hear dogs barking. The crossing and farewells had taken a lot of time.

"They are close; sound does not carry well in the forest. So this is good news, maybe they did not stop too long with granny. But bad news for us.

"Now, do exactly as I tell you. I will walk to that tree and have a piss. You will put your feet exactly in my steps. Take care. From here you see at the tree the ground has less snow - you see where I mean? - and it's covered with brown needles and black leaf mould. You swing round the tree and hop to that point. Be acrobats! Avoid marking the snow. Your life may depend on it.

"I will walk back, making a clear trail, showing how I went to the tree. They should see the yellow urine; I hope it is a good yellow today. And then I will come back again. We then hop from one patch to another for a few yards. They are in a hurry, so I pray they will not check carefully but head straight downstream, following the obvious tracks Karol is making."

We made it across. It did not look convincing to me, but worst case, as Witek said, our pursuers would be forced to split up. We set off uphill at a fast pace, mostly keeping to the forest and tree cover. When we broke cover it was onto strip fields. We kept to field edge tracks where possible. The snow had either blown into the ruts from ploughing or was carpeted onto small pasture plots.

The sun disappeared. The sky became overcast and then leaden. Flurries of snow, small grains, not flakes, began to float around us. Kryszka, bringing up the rear, began proclaiming that there were four types of snow and what we were walking on was 'crust', ice melted over powder snow.

"Remember that you're talking to a Canadian boy, bred in the shadow of the Rockies, Kryszka. And Eskimos claim over thirty types of snow!"

Witek, the academic, paused. Puffing from the exertion, he corrected us. "There are seven types of snow crystal; plates, stellar, columns, needles and... the others I forget."

"It all ends up as slush, no matter what it's called," Hanka added.

We plodded on. I began to hum a tuneless set of notes, whistling through my teeth. It helped with the rhythm of the pace Witek had set. My breath came and went in regular bursts. I felt out of condition. We skirted houses and small farms, moving ever onward, following the line of the Beskid hills to our right. The light began to fade. I dreamt of a second wind, which seemed to have passed me by. My legs ached, my back ached, and my shoulder ached from the slung rifle.

Witek called a halt as we neared a farm, indicating we should kneel to conceal ourselves. We unslung our weapons. Hanka crept cautiously to the right, covering Witek with her snub-nosed Russian PPSh-41 as he edged forward, crouching as he went. The farm was thatched. With thick, dark logs forming the walls it blended into the earth itself. The roof had a massive overhang so that snow, melt water or rain ran right off, leaving a dry walkway by the walls. The windows at ground level were shuttered, but at the far end light from an oil lamp escaped. This time I could smell wood smoke.

To the side were some outbuildings. A dog woofed, not sharply, neither a growl nor a bark. Some chickens squawked in one of the outhouses. A cart was sheltered under a roof, next to what must be a stable. The light flickered at the shutter. Someone had moved, hearing or sensing our presence. The animals had made enough noise to warn the farmers that something or someone was out there.

Witek back-tracked slowly, still facing the door. He waved us sideways toward the stable.

Inside was warm. The horse grunted. In the last trace of light the whites of its eyes showed as it rolled them back. Agitated it shuffled back in its stall, then decided we were not a threat. The animal relaxed and returned to munching; there was a contented sigh as it watched us.

The door had been left open to the elements. We settled down into straw that covered the floor to one side of the building. It was dark, but after the exertion of the day the stable gave an illusion of comfort, even safety. It was like journey's end. Witek struck a match. By its glow he spotted a lantern hung from a nail on a post, worn to a shine from years of the horse rubbing against it. He lit the lamp. The golden glow of the oil lamp gave a further sense of warmth.

"All we need now is a company of angels and a miraculous baby, Hanka," I joked. We all laughed.

Witek swung the door to, securing it with some rope from our side, but leaving an opening wide enough to watch the house. I looked around. Bridles and other harness hung from pegs. An assortment of wooden rakes and scythes adorned the walls and corners. Old, narrow skis hung in the rafters, together with farm implements used by many generations of toilers . Witek was ahead of Kryszka and me with the obvious question. "Don't worry, they know we're here. It's mutual fear. We leave them alone, they pretend we never came."

We shared the bread and wolfed down the cold potato granny had provided. We had no other provisions. It was a feast.

Witek set up the guard duty. My lot fell to the dog watch between four am and eight o'clock. Hanka took the first and we men snuggled down into the straw and were soon asleep. I woke with a start, Kryszka's hand on my shoulder. It was pitch black inside the barn, there wasn't a sound, even from the horse. I tried to rise but my limbs wouldn't work at first. It was cold, very cold. I tried again to get up and finally accepted a hand from Kryszka. "This must be how it is to be old!" I whispered.

"Everything is quiet, Tadek. But no moon."

I set myself by the door, peering into the dark. Gradually I could make out the outline of the house and the outhouse where I supposed the chickens were kept. The patches of snow seemed to throw up what light there was. My eyes were like lead; I didn't know whether I was awake or asleep. At what point did thought become dream and dream sleep? I jerked awake, convinced I had slept standing up. I glanced at my watch but the hands were not luminous enough to show the time. I played I-spy, to keep my eyes open. I convinced myself I saw a rat, though it was probably a shadow. I watched the edge of the forest. I wriggled my toes. I counted to one hundred again and again.

Suddenly a door opened. Had I imagined it? No, it had opened and I saw a shadow, a figure creeping toward the stable barn. It crossed the yard quickly. What *was* this spectre? Were they small? Or just someone crouching low? It was still too dark to see. The figure was coming forward now, Something was hanging from its right hand. I slipped the bolt on my carbine, raising it to point through the gap in the door. The figure paused. It had heard and recognized the sound of the bolt being drawn.

A young female voice called gently, "No, please, I leave food for you."

I kept the carbine raised as the figure came to the door. I felt, no smelled, human warmth. She dropped the package and ran back swiftly the way she had come.

Kryszka called over my shoulder, "Hike the package in here."

I nearly jumped out of my skin. With my finger still on the trigger I could have discharged the rifle. "Idiot!" I hissed. "I could have shot the woman by accident."

I turned to see the others, all standing weapons at the ready. Every one of them had heard the rifle bolt being slid. We were battle-hardened.

I drew in the package. It was full of warm bread, some *Oscpika* smoked sheep's cheese, potatoes and there was a crock of warm milk, which we drank greedily. Packing these rations we decided to move out in the half light. A cow mooed from the far end of the house. Silently we said our thanks to the good people, whoever they were, and we began our trek eastward.

We spoke little, intent on keeping walking. The weather had not changed, unending monotonous grey with the odd snow flurry. Little wind and no feeling of cold, the temperature hovering around freezing point I guessed.

Around noon we began to hear the 'pop pop' of distant gunfire and an occasional thud which we took to be a mortar.

I looked at Witek. I could see his mind chewing. "Well, it's ahead of us so we may as well head for the guns?" It was a question by inflection.

Kryszka responded for the rest of us. "Could be over by the time we get there. Anyway, who is shooting at whom? Russian special troops? Polish People's Army? Home Army? Polish Internal Security troops? Ukrainian National Liberation Army? Or their Insurgent Army, the comedians of this whole bloody, forgotten civil war?"

"Okay," Witek concurred, "we go on. It may even be just a deportation unit clearing out a Lemko village. One of Stalin's little tricks, to move people from one end of the earth to the other. Uproot them, kill their leaders." He shot the question at me. "Wasn't it your Lord Astoria who had this idea of ethnic cleansing which Stalin turned to genocide?"

"Leave off, Witek! I am as much a Pole as you. Anyway, it was Lord Curzon, not Astoria, as you very well know." Even as I snapped back I realised I was too late seeing the mischievous twinkle in his eye.

"Lord Cinema, I shall call him. A transparently celluloid man, in my opinion." Witek twirled his fingers to emphasize his joke.

Perhaps to ease my blunder I agreed with him. "All politicians are clowns with false faces."

Not to be outdone Hanka put in her tuppence worth: "And red noses from all that brandy and cigars."

Still laughing we headed towards the gunfire.

A sudden throbbing in the air heralded the appearance of a plane, low over the ridge. We hit the ground, hugging the earth. Its engine roared as it banked then came straight toward us, just below the cloud. "Ilyushin Shturmvik, ground attack!" I yelled. "Watch for the rear gunner!"

The plane banked again, almost overhead. I screwed my eyes but could see no faces looking down toward us, just the red star of the Soviets overflying so-called free Poland. The plane circled and headed to the smoke now visible, some two kilometres distant. I could distinguish the snap of rifle fire from the occasional burst of automatic and machine-guns or mortar thuds.

"They were after us for sure," breathed Kryszka.

Witek nodded, beaming. "That means they lost us on foot and have no idea where we are. I think that smoke over there saved us. They were looking east at whatever is going on. It distracted them from watching the ground. Keep your ears peeled for another sweep, in case they come back."

"You some kind of expert on planes then?" Hanka queried, directing the question at me.

Kryszka answered. "Tadek's a pilot and an engineer. Aircraft were his first love. Just like women, he says: good lines, always needing attention and a lot of noise and chatter from the front!"

Two hours later we lay in the snow, surveying the scene as best we could. We were on a slight rise, Witek squinting through his binoculars at the road below. It ran in a wide curve through a prosperous-looking village. The houses were mostly log-built, but at this end we could see a couple of block constructions had been added. These houses lay on the slightest of slopes. Further away the houses and outbuildings trailed into fields. Up on the other side of the valley the hills rounded off into the distance. Along the forest line was another run of houses, mere dots in the distance, but with the traditional strip fields running downhill toward the valley.

As the sun struggled to break through, the scene at this distance was nothing but pretty. The nearest farms were painted yellow ochre, their neat palisades and fences screening kitchen gardens from marauding geese and chickens. Others were painted blue and white. Absurd as it seemed the smoke drifting from smouldering thatch somehow added to the beauty. It was like a mist massaging the rooftops, curling lazily skyward. On another roof, a little dryer perhaps or perhaps doused in kerosene, flames flickered like little fairies dancing around the roof edges. One barn blazed fiercely, its contents burning straw.

Toward the end of the village the onion-less towers of the wooden church stood above the farmhouses. Smoke from an ancient stork nest blazed above a chimney. It obscured my view of the gleaming gold cross atop the church dome, proclaiming this an Orthodox or Uniate village.

Witek rolled toward me. "Lemkos," he whispered. "Like the Huculs and the Bojkos, these people have always been here, living side by side with the locals. Lemkos down here, Polish village up on the ridge. But the new Polish government has orders from Stalin to cleanse the area of 'Ukrainians', whatever that means. Operation Vistula, they call this inhuman tragedy. It's criminal." He spat the last words.

We watched uniformed figures scurry from one building to another, crouching as they ran, firing from the hip. "My guess," hazarded Witek as we crouched around him out of sight from the village, "is that either the village has already been cleared of civilians or some are resisting deportation." He squinted through his binoculars. "Government Security forces are down this end. We are behind them. Partisans, maybe Poles from the old Peasant battalions or Ukrainians of some political persuasion, are holding out at the other end. Below us and to our left in the road is their vehicle park. You can see the covered lorries. Could be empty, could be full, though of what I have no idea. There's a half-track at the front, but I can't make it all out."

"So what do you want to do, gentlemen, my lady? There are only four of us and we know nothing of them. Do we help or sensibly mind our own business and move on? What's it to be, dead heroes or breathing wise men and women? " He winked at Hanka.

"Why not scout the trucks and check their purpose?" she murmured. "If it's only a minor guard we could blow them, cause a distraction? We could upset the balance of the fight, tip any balance against the internal government troops?"

Kryszka added his thoughts. "But what if they are Ukrainian nationalists? They are just as likely to shoot us as the Security men, whether Soviet or Polish?"

There was a pause.

"Let's do it!" said Witek. "Okay, Hanka, go around the side. We will cover just in case. And leave that damn Shpagin gun behind. Here, give it to me."

She slid away sideways as we levelled our rifles toward the trucks parked about one hundred metres away. They stood in two columns side by side, blocking the road. A partly hidden half-track was at the front and I could see one sentry occasionally stamping about at the rear. Further forward, from its stocky-looking back, we could just make out a jeep, probably a Russian GAZ. But the angle of the slight bend made it impossible to see if there were any personnel close by.

We watched Hanka. She seemed to slide over the ground like a lizard. Within seconds she was at the rear of the column.

"Look at her, she's like a cat," Witek cut in. "Like a lioness, ready to pounce."

"I was just thinking of her as a lizard," I offered.

"Why so bloody unromantic, Tadek?" Kryszka was unimpressed. "Lioness to lizard, no comparison."

I recognised the sort of inane conversation men have when nervous, even facing death. "I like lizards," I countered, "Slim, elegant, multi-coloured little sun lovers."

Witek changed tack. "She's a great scout. Me, I am like a bear. I stick out in all the wrong places. I roll. I don't glide about."

I thought about Hanka. She did have natural elegance. Even on the march I had decided she walked with a delicacy, pointing her toe. She did not traipse like me but rather placed her leg forward, even in heavy boots. Perhaps she had once been a dancer. Perhaps she had ballet training. My mind began to wander. What would she look like in civvies? Her figure was boyish, true, but quite refined. Her cheekbones were high. She'd be beautiful without that gaunt look.

"Fine look-out you are!" she hissed at me, sliding over our snow-bank, making me start. "There are about seven in total. One man up front, one at the rear. The rest are smoking and playing cards in the front lorry. Trucks are open, no prisoners. All four-wheel ZIS vehicles, no armaments, just there for troop transport. No sign of anyone on or in the half-track. It's American with Polish military marks, one machine-gun at the front, another at the rear.

"That must be an M2 reconnaissance vehicle then, on lend lease to the

Russkis, whatever the markings," Witek interjected.

Hanka had more information. "Two men are smoking in the GAZ on the bend, possibly political officers, maybe Russian. The guys down there are certainly Polish. They all have the KBW internal security red lozenge arm flash."

"Real Commie bastards then," Witek said succinctly.

A prolonged burst of machine-gun fire came from the village. We heard shouting and screams, cut short by an exploding mortar round that sent a column of smoke into the air about half a mile away.

Immediately Witek was in command. "Okay *ciechamnosci*, let's see what you are made of. You take the guards either end, and on your signal we will come down and take the rest. You two move up to the GAZ and take the other two. We will begin by blowing the vehicles. Kryszka, you take the upper window on the right of the nearest house you see there." He pointed out one of the concrete block houses. "Tadek, you cover the side and back of that house. I will take the half-track and hope the machine-gun is enabled. You, Hanka, take the rear of the building on the left. First time they will come running back into our fire. Kryszka and Tadek hit them from the rear. As they pause I open up. This will force them to try to outflank us a second time and on your side, Hanka. So use that damn gun of yours and try to hit someone.

"It's not my fault the damn thing always shoots skyward." Her gun was notorious for always bucking upward as it fired its seventy-odd bullets. At a rate of nine hundred rounds a minute, it was a vicious gun to handle.

"Short bursts then, Hanka," he came back at her.

"I just hope that the magazine stays put," she countered then shrugged. This fault was well known too.

"Whoever else is fighting here should then seize the moment and come like the cavalry, to save us in the nick of time. Go, go!" Witek commanded, blowing a cheeky kiss toward Hanka.

Remembering how Hanka moved I kept to the contours and ruts as I headed to the back of the column. On my right I could see Kryszka moving as fast as he dared, keeping low to the ground. A few feet from the leading truck he sank to the ground, allowing me time to travel the extra distance to the rear. I could smell the battle, but also diesel, rubber and sweat. The guard was no longer at the rear, but halfway along the truck. I could see his legs and feet from my side of the vehicle, so I knew where he was and where he was facing. Clearly no one was expected to come from this end. My fear was that he could be seen by the others in the truck.

I signalled to Kryszka to wait and slid under the truck to get an angle on the other soldiers further up the line of vehicles. Could they see my guard? From the words I caught coming from the back of the truck I took it that a high-stakes card game was in progress. My guard had his back to me. The game was being played in a truck about thirty metres away. Two men were smoking, peering into the back of the truck watching the game and not my guard. I edged back and indicated to Kryszka to go.

Laying down my rifle I took my knife and ducked under the truck again, watching the guard's legs. Rising cleanly behind him I caught his head, my left hand over his mouth, and twisted viciously as I rammed my blade in above the pelvis. Sawing into the spine in an upward direction I felt the knife grinding on bone and he went limp. Gently I eased him to the ground, pulling him as quietly as I could under cover of the truck.

Rolling back out I signalled to the two on the rise. They immediately broke cover and ran toward the column. I picked up my rifle and ran as quietly as I could toward Kryszka. He waited till I was level then we ran hell for leather toward the GAZ. There was no need for caution now. Just surprise.

As I went I pulled my pistol from my belt and we both ran at the jeep.

Two nonchalant faces turned lazily our way. One trooper had his booted foot over the windscreen. The other began to rise, fumbling for his weapon. Kryszka was a crack shot. He dropped to his knee, leaving me to leap sideways to give him a clear line of fire. *Crack* and the standing officer jerked backward as though overbalanced, before tumbling into the back of the vehicle. The other man literally fell from it and was now on all fours, crawling toward me. No weapon evident.

He saw my boots. Looking up and spotting my cap badge he asked, "Home Army?" His accent was Russian. I noticed he wore glasses. .

I walked around him. He would have seen Kryszka standing in the road looking at him dispassionately. A burst of automatic fire winnowed from the trucks. There were yells and shouts then silence.

Still on his hands and knees the crouching officer trembled pathetically. His arms and legs looked as though they were shivering in the cold. I could see a damp stain between his legs at the crotch. Very slowly I placed my boot on his backside, gently pushing him down. He went with little resistance and I pushed him flat. No words from either of us.

Taking aim I watched the bullet hit his skull in the same way as NKVD special unit bullets had entered the skulls of our Polish officers at Katyń. His skull shattered from the closeness of the carbine. The barrel was blood and brain splattered. I felt no remorse.

Kryszka and I turned and sped to our designated fighting positions. Arriving at the first house Kryszka crashed open the door. I heard his boots clattering to some upper viewpoint. I settled behind a wood pile and began heaving some larger logs onto the ground to give me some extra cover. Being grounded was a safer bet than kneeling or standing and would give my short rifle a more accurate firing platform. I saw Hanka sprinting towards the other side of the road then disappearing to the back of the house, out of sight.

One after another the trucks went up. First an explosion with a fireball, then thick, oily smoke billowing into the already battle-tainted air. The noise would have woken the dead. At least one lorry must have contained reserve ammunition. Rounds whined overhead. Witek must have found a way to ignite the fuel tanks.

His portly figure scurried to the half-track and he swung himself aboard. Taking his station he waved at me and I waved back. So far so good.

Everything had happened exactly as he said it would. The man was certainly a good tactician, calculating and fully aware of the predictability of human reactions.

Peering past some logs, I could see six security troops coming down the street. Three my side, three the other. They looked experienced and wary, advancing in twos and covered by four more behind, also in groups of two. On they came at a crouching run. Pause, look and then on again. One clumped past me and threw himself onto the ground about fifty yards from the GAZ. I heard another panting heavily just around the corner from me. Controlling my own panic I breathed into my stomach, slowly and cautiously, steeling myself for reaction. The forward man ran up and threw himself down at the front wheel of the jeep, from where he cautiously surveyed the road ahead. Due to the curve he could only fully see the half-track from this position, which would be the next target for his advance. He waved forward. 'My' man came into view as he headed for the jeep. I heard the boots of the next guy drumming along as he ran in front of my position. He knelt down, rifle levelled but pointing forward to cover his mates. Watching so intently he didn't give as much as a glance at me lying just two metres behind him, my own carbine levelled at his back.

The forward trooper ran at the half-track and slung himself down. All three of the troops I could see were focussed on what might lie down the road. I had no vision of the other side and prayed Kryszka had them in view.

The trooper was struggling with something in his equipment. I saw him bring his arm back and then lob a grenade. It sailed over the half-track toward the burning trucks. It was meant to disturb any gunmen hidden near the trucks. But we were already behind them, thanks to Witek's strategy.

There was a slight pause before the grenade went off. As it did each trooper rose and dashed forward. There was slight movement from the half-track as Witek opened up with the machine-gun. Bullets and tracer whining to my right across the concealed road, I fired at the man immediately in front. Hit in the back, he pitched headlong. I half noted the grenade thrower fall, so my sights followed the second man now diving back for the shelter of the jeep. A bullet struck home – no two. He jerked back and forward and lay still. Kryszka must have fired simultaneously.

Only a minute or two had passed. My hand trembled. It was never the action but the aftermath or a wait that brought the shakes. I concentrated on my breathing. *What next?* According to the Witek's principle it should be another follow up. That would depend upon whether they had noted my or Kryszka's shots. Perhaps they had assumed they had all come from the burning column. It was very quiet, yet the silence was pregnant. I headed for the back, knowing Kryszka would now switch his attention forward. I heard him fire then a prolonged burst from the machine-gun on the half-track.

Two security men came at high-speed round the far side of the house, directly into my line of fire. One managed to loose his submachine-gun in my direction, but as Hanka had said, it bucked on firing and I lay flat. My bullet took him in the chest and his comrade to the ground as the man in front was thrown back. Crawling backwards the second man let off a couple of pistol shots. I had to rise to get a good shot so decided on firing randomly in the direction of the next barn. The racket seemed to do the trick; I could see nothing.

"Clear!" shouted Kryszka.

"Same here!"

*Now we wait*, I thought. *As Witek said, let's hope the cavalry comes*. My mind wandered into a state of neutrality seeking something to centre on to relieve the stress of suspense and adrenalin-fuelled emptiness. I needed to go home to somewhere there could be peace, find a refuge, stillness. So I caught visions of Calgary, my childhood home. My mind filled with images of people I knew. I wondered how my surrogate aunt and uncle were doing back there. We had made a fortune through this war. Was that right? It was a moral dilemma sufficient to occupy my mind and stop the trembling of my limbs, concentrating the mind in abstraction whilst the self preserving pilot inside, hidden in the subconscious watched and waited for the action. I was jerked from my thoughts by the chatter of machine-guns and the pop-pop of small arms but I could see nothing.

I heard Witek screaming, "On the left, on the left!" Crouching, I ran across the road. Witek was trying to clamber from the half-track. I assumed Kryszka was covering. Hearing Hanka's short bursts coming from her Shpagin, I regretted having sent so many wild carbine shots into the blue. I pulled out my Tokarev pistol, knowing that it only carried eight rounds. Reaching the corner I crouched and peered round. I could see and hear Hanka's shots coming from a window. Two troops were coming along the side of the house, readying themselves to shoot through the opening or throw themselves into the house. Because her fire was directed forward she couldn't see them. Without thinking I stepped forward, aimed and fired at the surprised men. The first fell as I emptied my pistol. The second fell sideways, but he had taken an arm wound. The third ran; I had no idea if my shots had struck home.

The wounded man spun, blood spouting. Cut in half by automatic fire. Witek had arrived.

We three paused as our attackers moved back, shouting and gesturing as they ran. Echoing all around us now were bellowed shouts and a cacophony of firearms. We heard more mortar rounds and watched a line of small figures moving back uphill, joined now by some stragglers. They moved in good order, firing back at their unseen enemy. Then it went quiet. Very quiet.

"I'm coming in!" shouted Kryszka, who grinned as he joined us. "Nothing to see, nothing to report," He nodded toward the now distant line of security troops. "About sixty or seventy, I guess. They'll pull back to the Polish village on the hillside up there. Think they'll call air support?"

We all thought of the Shturmvik we had seen earlier.

"They're more likely to ask their NKVD chums for help," Witek replied, rubbing his hands over his face to wipe away the tiredness. By now I recognised the habit. It gave him time to think and clear his head.

Hanka had been smoking a cigarette. Throwing it to one side she came up to me, stood close and put her arms around me, pulling us together, waist to waist. Still holding her body next to mine her hands ran up and down my collar, pushing and pulling. She looked at me intently, into my eyes, at my lips, all the time gently swaying, pushing and pulling. I held my breath. What was there to say? Finally she pushed me away saying, "I think I owe you my life. I will remember."

"And now we wait," Witek said. "When they come, whoever they are, let me do the talking."

We nodded that we had understood.

Heading into the half-finished concrete house, Witek went to the window to watch the road. We three slumped to the floor and saw to our weapons, reloading and checking magazines.

# CHAPTER 5

# NOT A CIVIL WAR

It was some time before we heard Witek say, "Here we go. Let's pray they see us as the good guys."

He stood away from the window. Even over the crackling sound of fire from thatch and vehicle, we could detect the intermittent sound of boots running, stopping and moving again. Glancing through the window I saw these were not the same Polish Security uniforms I had seen coming down the same street. These troops came low, crouching figures, down both sides of the street. They moved from corner to corner, gateway to fence, garden to midden. Cautiously, moving ever forward, weapons at the ready.

There were a great many of them.

Witek spoke. "Smarten up. Arm-bands clear. Shine up your cap badges a bit. Sling your weapons, look at home, and smoke if you want to. Only come out when I call. If things go wrong for me, aim for the half-track and see if you can make a run for it."

We did as he said, buttoning tunics and setting caps. Our white above red arm-bands straight, Hanka's displaying the PW symbol of Fighting Poland.

Witek unbuttoned his short coat, revealing his khaki tunic below , then scrubbed some waste paper over his boots and adjusted his field cap to a jaunty angle. Like the rest of us, he wore the soft, square *rogatywka* cap of the Polish forces. His Crowned Eagle over Amazon shield shone in the light. White over red arm-band pushed up high, creases adjusted. Like Hanka, he squared the band so that the PW 'Fighting Poland' insignia could be easily seen. Witek stepped into the road, walking to the middle then stood there, hands behind his back, legs slightly apart. The sun had broken through; the whole scene looked for all the world like a Hollywood movie. The oncoming troops paused. From each side two troopers detached themselves and lay in the road, weapons aimed at Witek some fifty or sixty yards ahead.

"Good day," he called. "Did we rescue you or did you rescue us?"

There was a brief bustle of movement some one hundred metres back. A tall, stately man came forward, supported to one side by what I guessed would be a senior NCO. The soldier held a Shpagin in the crook of his arm, pointed down and to the side. The leading officer wore a Cossack style *papachka*, the once white sheepskin greyed now by weather and time, cavalry boots and wide breeches. His greatcoat hung around his shoulders, showing his German style tunic underneath. Walking past the two forward troops he gestured to his NCO to stay put.

"So far so good," breathed Hanka.

"So, Polish pig," the officer called as he stopped short of Witek, by about five metres. "What are you doing here in our playground?"

"Saving your tails, dog's blood," parried Witek.

"So Pole kills Pole now and we should rejoice with you motherfuckers, should we?"

"Look, arsehole, I don't need you to love me. Just accept that we did what your lickspittle toy-town soldiers could not!"

"You look after Ukrainians now, do you, Pole?"

"As you do, Cossack. But these people are Polish Lemkos. Their ancestors lived in this place before the first criminal war bands were called Cossacks. This land was always protected by Poles. We gave our blood against Tartar, Mongol, Russian and German."

"You are a fuckin' liar, Pole. Imperialist, fuckin' fascist bastards. Land grabbing Polish *Pan*." The Cossack snarled the Polish word for 'Lord'.

"Just a humble, destitute member of the old *szlachta* nobility. From a clan who probably fought *with* you as well as against your lot, you mangy excuse for a turd, a turd wearing a German uniform."

"It's going well then?" observed Kryszka. The troopers had relaxed, watching and listening to this verbal duel, enjoying the insults being traded. We were all wondering which way the cat would jump now.

The Cossack officer came forward, reaching under his coat.

"Our turn," said Hanka as she stood away from the window. Making sure she was not outlined by the sun she sighted her gun at the troops nearest us.

"Wait!" snapped Kryszka.

The Cossack officer produced his cigarette case, took a cigarette and extended the case to Witek, Taking a cigarette he reached into his pocket and used his lighter to light the other man's cigarette before his own.

You could feel the tension ease from the house and roll down the road. The troops physically relaxed, at ease, arms slung, firing positions abandoned.

By now I was sweating heavily under my arms. The sweat prickled, making me scratch and wriggle.

"Fleas?" teased Hanka.

"Polish fleas. The worst in Europe."

"Ah, but this is a Lemko village," she said, "Welcome to the Ukraine."

"It's still Poland," I reminded her.

"Well, then it depends on the ethnicity of the flea. We have a choice of pure Pole, Political Pole like you, Jewish Pole like me, or Ukrainian Poles like the Lemkos, Bojkos and Huculs. The choice of flea is entirely yours."

"I do not have fleas," I answered back. "And ethnicity is not the determinant of a country. Ethnicity is the integration of thought, culture and much more. You said '*the*' Ukraine, which translates as 'the borderlands'. Ukraine does not exist as a sovereign state. If anyone from this part of the world says differently then they are a secessionist and my political enemy."

"This is precisely why we have civil war. Why they are our enemies and we theirs. Today we just fought a mutual enemy; we are not friends with them."

"I agree," Kryszka added, "but they seem friendly enough." He nodded toward Witek and the Cossack. They were now walking toward us, evidently in good humour, their conversation animated.

The officer called to his NCO and waved him forward. As he began to trot forward the NCO called back. Another officer appeared and also headed our way.

"Military style," said Kryszka. We snapped to attention, clicking our heels as the two came through the door, the Cossack officer stooping to get his headgear through the door. As he did so I noted a blue cockade with a yellow centre on his *papachka*. The eagle-eyed Kryszka had seen them too: the colours of Ukraine.

His black breeches had a broad red stripe but his tunic was German field grey. No German insignia, but his collar flashes showed the yellow lion of Ukraine.

"Relax, gentlemen" he said, "At ease, please, there is peace here."

"No pigs," quipped Witek.

"And no turds," the officer quipped back.

"May I introduce Janek, Marek, and Agnieszka." Witek gestured to us in turn, using our agreed code names. The officer nodded acknowledgement, adding drily, "And I am the emperor of China."

A sergeant clattered into the room, followed by another much younger officer.

"May I introduce Horse Sergeant *Wachmistrz* Kukura and his Lieutenant *Porucznik* Bajuk." He used Polish military terms, I supposed, out of courtesy. "My name is Teon Kuibida. My rank is *Pulkownik*. I gave up code names long before I made Colonel. They always beat you to death to get your true name, which they probably already know. In my youth I thought I was 'the forge' upon which Stalin would be hammered! Romantic idea, no? And one I grew out of. Now I tell my men if they're caught to give their name and rank like a soldier. That way they'll either die quicker, or they might just be let go for not playing games."

The two men grinned, giving us the once over, lingering over Hanka.

Kuibida spoke to them rapid Ukrainian. We could follow most of it as the two languages are so similar. Witek filled in the gaps.

Kuibida addressed his men. "Today, and until I say so, these men these are our allies. If there are any complaints about siding with Poles, you knock them down, put your fist into their teeth and let them spit them out."

I smiled and he caught me grinning. "Just so you understand, 'Janek'. We are a rough people. Some in our *kurin* are not always as polite to Polish people as I would wish."

I was under no illusion about the 'friendliness 'of this unit. "No sir," I rejoined, "I was thinking of the similarity of your words to those of Prince Volodymyr, who converted the Kievan Rus to Christianity by saying something similar. 'Convert or lose your jaw and teeth.'"

"To be followed by a dip in the Dnieper river. And the poor sods couldn't swim." He roared and struck me forcibly on the back. As his laugh his face straightened. He looked the four of us over and spoke seriously. "I thank you for your assistance. Without your intervention we would have been mauled. Witek, you and I must now discuss our next moves and where to go!

"Find these noble gentlemen, these Polish *Pans* and their lady, some quarters in the village. Place them with a reliable family. "

All five of us walked back up the road to look at the trucks. We discussed the spring and the snowline just a few hundred yards away toward the forest. We talked of mud and boots, horses and shoes. We watched the Ukrainians as they cleared up our mess. The bodies had been laid out. Never pleasant, the sight of your own actions. Features deformed and destroyed. Blood congealing and oxidising, turning from red to brown and black. Body parts. Burnt flesh, the smell of roast meat.

Lieutenant Bajuk seemed almost apologetic. "If the ground was workable we would bury the dead, leave their papers and identity tags somewhere conspicuous. We're not bandits."

Troopers were removing the heavy machine-gun from the half-track. I realised that the white eagle of Poland painted on its side wore no crown. It was a far skinnier bird than the one I was used to seeing. *More like a scrawny chicken.*

I must have said it out loud. Kryszka chuckled. "Yeah, too starved to fly."

Sergeant Kukura butted in. "The old bird might've had his crown knocked off, but he's skinny 'cos he's had a red star stuffed up his backside and he's choking on the hammer and sickle they've stuffed down his throat."

"Perhaps it's a girl bird," Hanka chimed in. "The females are always much fiercer than the males."

We laughed, but it was sad to see this Communist emblem. In a strange way something so emblematic made the reality of change more real than the events happening around us. The eagle had changed many times. In 1927 it had been plumper, with wings upswept. This was the version I remembered from my childhood. It had hung on a beam in the kitchen. White eagle on red shield with a golden crown...or as Mrs Simpson would have said, '*Blazoned as Gules, an Eagle Argent, crowned, beaked and armed Or.*' I could hear the words now in her Scots accent, black jet brooch bobbing gently at her neck. '*Gold beak and talons to you, Master Tadek. The rest of the class, take note: this is probably the oldest state symbol or coat of arms in the world.*' That had made me proud. But it was all a long time ago.

When I first came to Poland in 1939 they used the slimmer style eagle I was now looking at, complete with gold crown. But now that crown too was gone.

"The Soviets called it the Piast eagle to give it some dignity," Kryszka mused, evidently in the same frame of mind as me. "Remember the Piast dukes always put a crown on their eagle? I expect when the Communists rewrite Polish history, they'll try and convince us that the Piasts were socialist as far back as the twelfth century. "

"And that Popiel was really a gentle old man like Stalin, looking after his peasants!" said Hanka.

I remembered my folktales. The legendary Popiel was the last member of his pre-Piast dynasty. A despot, he'd been deposed by his starving people and locked up in a tower where he'd been eaten alive by mice. It seemed to me much more likely his grain store had been eaten and that the old tyrant died of starvation.

My father had told me how the Prussians had looted much of the Polish State regalia in the Third Partition, destroying them, crown and all, except the state sword. When it was bought back from the Austrians in 1925 by the Polish Government it consisted of two crowns, sceptres and orbs all made in the eighteenth century. First the Germans stole them as war trophies and now the Russians had them as spoils of their war. Evidently the USSR could cope with crowns as emblems where the Polish People's Republic could not.

Turning to Kukura I asked a question which had been intriguing me. "Some of troopers wear black and red arm-bands, some none. Still others wear the Ukrainian colours, blue and yellow with trident? Why is that?"

Kukura gave a sidelong glance at Bajuk, who gestured it was okay to answer. Still the sergeant shifted uneasily.

"It's our father *ataman* who binds us together." I recognised the Cossack word for commander. "The old man is no fool," Bajuk continued. "He's an experienced officer from way back. Our original *kurin* was decimated as a regiment in the last twelve-month. Of all the original squadrons we're now down to just two *sotnias*. He insists that we are all Ukrainians, no matter what our political persuasion. Each *chot* must carry no allegiance but to the

Ukraine. Right down to every *riy* of ten men he enforces that we serve as equals and only for each other." Kukura looked defiant now. "Some of us, like me, fought with the Germans. Privately I think of the guys with the red and black arm-bands as terrorists. They are Bandera's people, bandits to a man. That's my opinion, but the ataman says first we need to win the war against the Reds and then we can fight each other. So this is how we operate in this unit. It works. Kuibida runs it along Cossack lines; we are free men, but we have discipline. And men like me administer it." Kukura grinned and waved his fist.

Bojuk now added his experience. "Most of the disciplined men came from the alliance many of us forged with Germany."

We set off back up the road, all five of us, attracting some stares. We passed peasants hurrying back home, some carrying large bundles. Some stopped and stared at us. One woman started to shout abuse but the nearest trooper told her to shut up. "It's a twisted road we follow," Bajuk commented.

Kukura unslung his PPS submachine-gun and kept close to Kryszka. Soon the two of them were gossiping and laughing like old mates. Kukura was greeting his men as he went, drawing Kryszka into badinage with the troopers or flirting with girls. There was a cacophony of excited dogs, who had rediscovered their courage now the fighting had stopped. Chickens were running around and a loose cow roamed the street. Up ahead I could see a young girl being tended by a couple of the *kurin*'s medical orderlies. The horse which had reared and trampled her was being calmed by a young trooper. The girl's mother was at her side, wailing.

We had just passed them when a trooper with a black and red arm-band started to walk backwards in front of us, bowing low to the ground and doffing his cap with a sweeping gesture. "Welcome to the Polish *Pans*. Welcome, Lords, to your country. "He grabbed my hand as though kissing it but touched his own thumb with his lips. As he backed away, still holding my hand, he feigned gratitude. "Thank you, Lords, for saving me, a mere peasant."

Kukura ran forward and aimed a boot at his side. "Bugger off, Slavko, you filthy dog!" The trooper turned away, laughing at his own antics.

Kukura looked put out by the episode. "Some of the guys are weak in the head. That oaf's a peasant from Galicia. They're all inbred in his village, half-wits. Unbalanced." *Dangerous killers, in other words.* Kukura turned back toward the man's group and spat on the dirt in front of him. His spittle was yellowed by his chewing tobacco. They watched him silently.

"Friendly crowd," breathed Hanka.

They settled us in a small manor house. The man who owned it was Polish, not Lemko. He showed us around. The *dworek* had a large central hallway running end to end with doors either side. At the far end of the hall passage was a square covered veranda, built out from the house into the garden. The sun poured in through the small glass panes. Outside we could see Witek and Kuibida sitting in wicker chairs smoking, as though they were on holiday.

Every room led to another. I was intrigued when what I thought was wallpaper turned out to be plaster, intricately painted by hand. The most beautiful had a shell-pink background with dark blue feathered motifs. A majolica tiled stove filled one corner from floor to ceiling, its gaudy browns, pinks, yellows and greens a poor match for the décor. One side of the house was pretty much shattered; it had clearly been occupied by one side as a fighting position. Bullet holes peppered the plaster. The furniture was overturned or destroyed. Paintings and photographs hung wildly from their wall hooks. Two had been slashed. A glass chandelier crunched underfoot on a threadbare Persian carpet.

Troopers were clearing up what was clearly intended to become their headquarters.

The old man was watching me quietly as I looked around the room I'd been allocated. "My father and I painted these rooms," he ventured. "We wanted the house to look proper."

Something in his expression moved me. "Your family been here long?"

"When the old Count died he had no children. So he left this house to my family, along with some land. My father was his bailiff. We were never popular but got along with the other *gospodarze* who farmed locally. "But look at it now! First the Ukrainians, then the Russians, both White and Red, then our Poles, and then the Germans..." He shrugged his shoulders. "And now you are here, *Armja Krajowa*, our own Polish Home Army. You are fighting with Bandera men and other Ukrainian nationalists against Polish Security troops who are officered by Russian NKVD men. I have lived to see it all." He spread his hands.

I could understand the old man's mystification. "What happened here today?"

"The Polish Internal Security men came in from both sides of the village. They called all the villagers together, down by the church. Told us we had one hour to collect our things and be ready to move out. No animals, they said, just clothing and some food for the journey. We would be taken to a train by trucks then sent by rail to our new homes."

There were rumours, of course, but hearing the old man's story was a very different experience.

"All Lemkos were to be deported. Poles could stay. Can you imagine your reaction? To be told your home was no longer yours, your life here was finished? We were all stunned! There are about seven Polish families here in this village, plus half a dozen mixed families. I was the first Pole to speak up. As soon as I started protesting that the action was illegal other voices joined in. There was pandemonium. The troopers had to fire over our heads to shut us up.

"Their officer was very clear. The Polish People's Republic had replaced your old, fascist, pre-war government,' he said. He told us that and that the London Government was no more. Polish citizens of Lemko origin were to be given land in the New Territories, land allocated by Comrade Stalin. We had no choice. We were wasting their time. We were to get ready to move out and leave everything orderly. Anybody found destroying property would be shot. Those were his very words."

I could see the old man was mentally reliving the moment.

"There were a few more protests and shouts. The officer identified some culprits. His troops went into the crowd and pulled out some men, along with Mrs. Fedoruk, the wife of our village headman. She was still shouting, 'Our boys will get you!' and calling them Polish land grabbers. 'What about the Poles up the hill?' she shouted. 'Are they coming with us too?'

"'If you mean that hotbed of counter-revolutionaries, those enemies of the state," the officer answered her, "we know they formed Peasant Battalions and we know they fought the People's Militia. Oh, we know where their loyalties lie, the fascist bastards. Don't you worry about the Poles on the hill, old woman. Their time will come. Now out you get out! I want to talk with you.'

"The troops used their rifle butts and boots and stood the ones they'd pulled out of the crowd in front of us. The Colonel strode up and down, hands behind his back, for all the world like Napoleon. Up and down he walked in front of the detainees. Each one had a soldier him, so from where we stood we could not see their faces. Realising this, the Colonel made them turn round and come out in front of us.

"'This is the government of the people, all you rich landowners and Jews. You want to see what happens when you disobey the new government?'"

The old man interrupted his account. "My Lemko neighbours did not consider themselves rich landowners. Of the seventy or so homes in the village, only about twenty could be called *kulaks*. The rest were very small plots, labouring farm hands. Apart from the blacksmith. Pan Babicz." Wiping his face with a kerchief, the old man continued his recollection of events.

"The officer walked up and down the line. Finally he pulled Mrs. Fedoruk forward and demanded her name. 'And where is Mr. Fedoruk?' he wanted to know. 'Over here,' Fedoruk called. And within seconds the Fedoruks were standing together, arms tied. The Colonel roared in their face. 'Where are your 'boys' now, eh?'

"Mrs. Fedoruk whimpered. We could see she was wetting herself. I was so ashamed for her. Such a beautiful woman, so respectable.

"He must have signalled. Without warning his Master Corporal hit her hard in the groin. She collapsed onto the dirt. Fedoruk flung himself forward but the guards held him back. He was shouting to leave her alone. The Colonel pulled out his pistol and shot him on the spot. The Master Corporal kept kicking Mrs. Fedoruk until she lay silent. All you could hear then were their two children. Such good children, a boy of eleven and a girl of nine. What will happen to them now, I wonder?

" 'Anyone else want to stay put or play partisans?' And then he turned on me. 'You, Pole!' he shouted. 'Are you staying here or going out to found the New Poland in the West?'

"'I will go with my Lemko neighbours,' I responded. Someone patted my back. I felt pathetically grateful.

'What about your family?'

"I knew then I was in trouble. 'My wife is dead,' I told him.' Shot by the Germans. My daughter was taken by them too. I don't know where she is nor what became of her. My oldest son is with the Royal Air Force in England. My youngest went to the Home Army. I have not heard from him.'

"'So, so... a whole family of fascists.' The Colonel turned to his Master Corporal and said,' Keep him under house arrest. I want to interrogate him.'

"I moved forward. There was no point in running. No point protesting. I could see Mrs. Fedoruk on the ground. She was still alive but covered in blood. She was on her knees, keening over her husband. They marched me back here and told me to wait.

"Just then, the firing started. Mrs. Fedoruk was not the only one who knew this *kurin* was in the woods. Some lads had run off and told that Polish Security troops were in the village. The rest you know."

I heard Kryszka calling me and then the sound of a Chopin étude floating through the house.

"Ah, your friend has found the piano," the old man said. "I am so glad."

He turned and shuffled into the new world order.

# CHAPTER 6

# THE WHITE COSSACK

My father used to tell me years ago that these people were White Croats, an ancient people who had migrated here and farmed this land since time immemorial. He used to sit me on his lap before bedtime and tell me stories of the steppes, of the marshes and mountains of his beloved Eastern Poland. About the people who lived there. So I knew a great deal about Cossacks and Crimean Tartars, Ruthenians and Russians and all the other nationalities that made up 'the Borderland', the Ukraine.

This journey was taking me to places and situations I had long forgotten. Reaching into the hidden depths of my soul where I stored my sadness, where old fears had been laid to rest, far away from my life, far outside my mind. That wise old spirit who lived in my head and looked through my eyes was beginning to speak again. To tell me 'I told you so'.

I had loved my mother dearly, but now, thinking back to those stories, I realised that somewhere deep inside me I missed my father. In many ways he had been a stranger to me. I remembered the smell of his sweat, strangely, how it gave me comfort and strength. I could recall the shape of his finger nails. I remembered very clearly his anger, the flash in his eyes. He died when I still had so much more to learn from him. Before I could show him my love.

What would my father have made of this situation? The villagers were still debating what to do. These were Lemkos, Rusyn people with no particular allegiance to the Ukrainian Nationalists. People who had tilled this soil from ancient times. Ordinary people, going about their daily lives. From time to time there had been conflict between Lemkos and Poles, much as there had been between the Scots and the English. These people lived in Poland as they always had. They were Polish citizens. This was their village, their place. Any arguments here with their Polish neighbours were about land or boy meets girl or a disagreement over livestock. Now both communities, Lemkos and Poles, were being expelled from their homes, forced out by a Communist regime determined to control and subjugate by fear. These Lemkos, living happily alongside Pole and Jew were not inherently drawn to Ukrainian Nationalism.

Was the intervention of these Nationalist troops welcome to them here in this village? Certainly some of the younger men would be drawn to the idea of a Ukrainian State. But most of the villagers were just as content with Poland. The biggest or real divide in their life was not about the everyday affairs of village life, but about religion. Poles were Catholic, Lemkos Greek Orthodox. This religious divide was where extremists applied pressure.

In every civil war allegiances shift quickly. The villagers had gathered by the Church at the lower part of the village. It seemed their deliberations would go on into the night. They had a lot to discuss; we four had helped create another mess for them because we had fought against KBW Internal Special Security troops. Killed them because they would have hunted us. We had not fought to defend the village, but rather because anyone who fought the Polish and Russian security forces were our friends.

The Ukrainian *kurin*, having come out of the woods both literally and metaphorically, also faced a dilemma. What to do next? The KBW would be back, no doubt with regular Polish Army men and in some force.

Whilst the village debated, the army cooks were busy. Chickens and goats were butchered and flour and vegetables 'requisitioned'. Some troops were billeted in houses, others in outhouses and barns. As evening fell the atmosphere was relaxed. The evening chill stole through the village. Stoves were lit and open fires burned brightly in the streets.

We three, although assigned to the old man's *dworek* for the night, caught up with Witek and the Cossack in a large barn close by the food lines. The smell of sour cabbage, beans and meat were tempting, the aroma tantalising in the cold sharp air. We settled down with our plates to watch Witek and the Cossack playing chess. A group of about seven or eight troopers had also gathered around and were sitting on bales or boxes. I watched as one young soldier drag over an ammunition box for Hanka. She seemed pleased by the gesture, if her moony smile was anything to go by. I found it surprisingly irritating.

"Bit inconsiderate," I offered, "considering how close we are to the fire. Perhaps he wants to blow us all up?"

She smiled at me too, saying, "Tut, tut, Tadek, I didn't know you cared. Perhaps he meant it as a compliment? Maybe he thought an ammunition box suited a fire-cracker like me? I think he's charming." She smiled at the trooper again, waving a kiss in his direction. He blushed scarlet. Clearly the two lads with him were giving him a hard time about his flirting. One of them picked up a bandura, the little string instrument so loved by the Zaporozhian Cossacks, and began to pick out a traditional love song. All the time he was playing he was making eyes at Hanka, who responded by smiling coquettishly.

Kryszka turned to me. "I've a feeling about this young Ukranian musician's repertoire. First he'll fill our ears full of weeping birch trees. Then we'll all become despondent lovers for a while. Then after a few mournful marches he'll have us all miserably happy with his singing."

To avoid my strange feelings about Hanka's behaviour, which I found so unexpected, I concentrated on the game. Witek played white. He seemed to be losing, but it was a long game between first-rate tacticians. A number of pawns were already gone. Of the major pieces Witek was down by two knights, a bishop plus one castle. The Cossack was similarly down, both bishops and one knight, but had managed to retain his castles. Now it looked as though Witek might lose his Queen, but as a sacrifice of a black castle. The audience waited. The Queen went and Witek moved his castle to support his bishop.

"Check!"

The white king retreated.

The Cossack advanced a pawn. Witek took it with his knight, but too quickly. His hand had hovered.

"Check and mate!" said the Cossack. A sigh went around the group of spectators. Even Hanka came back to her senses long enough to peer at the table.

Alcohol had been forbidden, but from what I could hear, further up the road, that order was being ignored. More and more people drifted in to the warmth of fire and smell of humanity. Cigarettes were exchanged and sweet tea was drunk.

Witek puzzled the board, learning his mistake. He congratulated the Cossack and stretched out his legs contentedly. Kuibida abandoned his cigarette in favour of a pipe. The group waited to see if another game was on offer, content to sit or lie around the table, and listen to a song about birch trees , just as Kryszka had predicted. Before long some of them joined in with the chorus. Others oiled and polished weapons. Some cleaned their boots. Others read or dozed quietly.

Kryszka nudged me. "I feel it coming. Next there'll be tears and 'goodbye ladies' as the soldier boys march off. Yes, here it comes." And the soldier's sweet voice broke into the old tune 'A lonely birch stood in a meadow'.

I smiled at Kryszka's uncanny intuition. But somehow the melancholy song really suited the moment, this setting. I liked it.

Kukura entered the barn, bringing with him the feeling and sharp tang of the cold night air. He walked across to the Cossack, who was gently puffing at his pipe. Cupping his hand the sergeant whispered into his chief's ear before settling himself cross-legged at his side.

Kuibida placed his pipe to one side and then stood. "Gentlemen! My brothers, my children." He was addressing us all and no one in particular. "Tonight our noble Lemkos, for whom we shed blood, have made a decision. They will be moving out tomorrow morning, having accepted deportation to the New Territories. They will be given whatever land they can grab in North

West Poland. When they get out of their first class cattle trucks they will find the Promised Land very cold, flowing with water, no honey. The German farmers and householders have taken what they could before they were forced out. And although this new land is Polish by decree, the Russians are looting everything from factories and machinery to household pots and pans as war reparations, just because it used to be Germany. Our Lemkos will not be made welcome in their new life." He spat.

"We have, however, bought them twenty-four hours. They had been given one hour to get out with one suitcase only and now they have negotiated a truce for 24 hours. This means they can take some more miserable goods with them and a few small animals. So we have achieved a stay of execution. We have won a victory!"

This announcement was made in flamboyant theatrical terms. Kuibida threw his voice as well as any actor. He was pretending to be a little drunk, although I knew he was not. Waving his arms he carried on: "We have won the day, brothers. We have taught the Bolshevik that they do not rule here without a fight. But brothers, all people vote with their feet. The Lemkos go one way, we another. Tomorrow we move out at six o'clock. Pass the word. Full column, skirmishers on flanks. Kukura, you take your men as scouts. We go south."

Some of the men sounded surprised. Shouts of "Why?" were heard.

With his hands he stilled the crowd, which had grown as word had been passed round. He held his arms wide, slowly waving them up and down, occasionally holding a finger to his lips. Quiet descended on the men as they stood n the warm, steady glow of the oil lamps.

"Brothers. Children," he began when they were silent again. "It is time to face the end."

Some of the men called," Never!" One voice bawled "Ukraine for Ukrainians!" but the majority of the men were silent. Kuibida waved his arms again.

"There are no traitors here. We are an army. But we face defeat. I am your commander; I choose to fight my way out. In the morning the column will move south across the mountains, through the Czechs and into Germany, where we shall seek sanctuary with the Allies."

Murmurs rose. Someone called out, "But they sent the Cossacks back home to their death!"

"Times have changed, men. There is a new style of war. Some of us fought with the Wehrmacht, even the Waffen SS. The Russians are becoming the bad guys. Most of you have Polish nationality, so take advantage of it. Claim your Polishness and the Allies will give you refugee status. You will be taken in, now the war is over. Just don't mention what we have been up to!"

At this there were some guffaws from the men. To me it was absurd that a gang of what I considered terrorists would be given asylum by claiming a nationality they despised, so they could no doubt plot further revolutionary deeds. Such, however, was the West.

"I give you leave, if you have families, to stay. Not desert, just stay. Go home, see your wife, see your mother and father, kiss your babies, pray in your church. Go if you want. Lieutenant Bajuk will give you your discharge papers. Go with my blessing."

Kuibida's tone of voice changed. "Some of you want to go north. Mostly our Banderestvi comrades. Do so. Take your weapons. Leave when we leave. But I warn you now, you will die." He became vehement, balefully fixing his eye on the crowd. "You Bandera swine have done for us. You have done for the Ukraine with your terror, your rape, and your needless atrocities. It is you that has caused the whirlwind, the destruction of ancient peoples. You who could not talk to your neighbour with dignity as an equal, you who have murdered your neighbour Pole and Ukrainian." The man's was now so animated spittle was flying from his lips. His face was red with blood pressure and he ran his finger around his neckband for relief. "You have stirred up Stalin against us, him and with his butcher Khrushchev. You revile every Pole as an enemy and every Ukrainian with decency as a traitor. So I say to you now, go. You go north. Go join your brothers on the border and in Wołyn, Volhynia. Go die for banditry. Carve up a few more people on the way but the Poles and Russian security forces will nail you, and with you our Ukrainian hopes."

Men shifted to Kuibida's side and faced the crowd like bodyguards. It appeared no one in this regular nationalist Troop had respect for the Banderestvi faction.

"Your time has passed, Old Man," someone called out from crowd. A group with red and black arm-bands had shouldered themselves to the front. These were the colours of Bandera. A burly man in a battered sheepskin jacket shook his fist at Kuibida while his companions muttered or growled encouragement from around him. "Your time has gone Old Man," he repeated. "I spit on Poles and Jews." Adding emphasis he sent a stream of tobacco coloured spit to the floor. He wiped the back of his hand across his face. "You Poles" he pointed at us, "you watch your backs. You are not wanted in this country!" With that he turned and with his group around him shouldered his way through the crowd who were by no means friendly. The pack resisted the movement with pushes and shoves of their own, jostling the pro Bandera troopers. But mercifully there was no more violence than this. Kuibida shouted to Kukura. "Double the guard, especially on the Polish houses and for anyone in the village who led the decision to accede to deportation. Those murderers could even try a last minute bit of terror."

The commander's audience began to break up. The singing started again. A few village men and women had turned up and now they began drowning their sorrows and adding their aggrieved opinions.

Witek commented quietly, "You did the right thing, old brother. I too have foreseen the end. It is our age. We have seen too much."

The Cossack sank back to his chair and looked at us. "My men and I will have to fight our way through Poles, Czechoslovaks, Russians, regular and security forces. But we will reach Germany alive". His pipe came out, but his fingers were trembling.

Witek dropped into quiet conversation with the Cossack. Kryszka seemed ready now to doze in the warmth. Hanka began reading from a small book she carried, a Polish Hebrew dictionary. "For when I get to Israel," she had said. In answer to my asking why, when she loved Poland and its countryside so dearly, she had come back with, "Let me have my dreams." This was only reasonable, so I did that now, letting her study. So as Hanka dreamed of a land flowing with milk and honey I dreamed of Hanka and what lay beneath her uniform. I smiled to myself, imagining indelible newsprint-like tattoos. I was tempted to ask her but decided against it. She couldn't see her own back after all. ,

Kukura returned and sat himself on the floor. We chatted sporadically, then he asked me how old I was. Kryszka stirred just long enough to comment that we were in our early thirties. This was good enough for a stranger.

"So you keep yourselves secret. I had guessed you were *ciechamnosci*, silent ones."

As this required neither a statement nor an answer we just smiled like angels.

The Cossack commander rose from his seat. "Now I will tell you a story. I, Teon Kuibida, will tell you how life turns out."

Kukura called out, "Oh God, boys, version ten of the war's greatest hero coming up!"

"It's not yet time for sleep, Father Kuibida," one wag called. "No bedtime stories yet." Others sidled over. Kukura joked that these were youngsters who had not heard the stories. Neither had we four. Like a group of Moors we sat and listened.

"I am descended from the Czarnomorski, Black Sea Cossacks." Kuibida began his tale. "Any one of us is equal to three miserable devils from the Don Host and ten of the rest. No one, not Orenburg, Churguevski, Ural, Kuban or Bug Cossacks can equal the panache and dash of us, the best and the bravest of all the Cossacks." Kuibida placed his boot now on a stool, puffing his pipe and blowing smoke contentedly.

"We, the Zaporozhe Cossacks, were loyal to the old Polish Lithuanian Commonwealth. We were the bastion of Christendom against the Muslims!"

He thumped his chest. "Whether Orthodox or Catholic, together we fought like tigers to stop Mongol, Tartar, Turk or whomever the Islamic world sent against us with fire and sword. To them the Commonwealth was the infidel to be destroyed in jihad, the holy war. The Muslim aim is world conquest by any means, of that make no mistake. But we stopped them, boys, Poles and loyal Cossacks that we were.

"Where were your Ukrainian ancestors then, boys?" He waved vaguely at his growing audience. "Ask yourselves: did they fight with us or did they stay at home in the village? And when the Muslim hordes raided, did your ancestors run to their Polish castles to keep themselves? Did they man the battlements with their Slav brothers? Did they run with the Tartars, in the name of freedom, to pillage and rape, to loot and burn?

"True, there is no denying that my great, great, great granda, da, da, da umpteenth grand-daddy was an robber of ill repute who was banished from somewhere between Gdańsk and Kiev for stealing. The story's not clear at this point – was it from a woman Or maybe even the crown jewels?"

"More likely some Polish nobleman's Rusyn house servant from the back end of Drohobycz on the run for getting the squire's daughter up the spout!" shouted Kukura. We roared as the Cossack clipped Kukura round the ear.

The Cossack rose to his feet, casting a baleful eye around the now ring of eager listeners. "As I was saying…"

I felt the closeness of Hanka's lips as she whispered into my ear. "He should have been on the stage." There was a stirring below as I sensing the softness under her jacket against my arm. Had she allowed that pressure deliberately? Was that the softness of her breasts behind that jacket? These were the thoughts which distracted me as I tried to listen to Kuibida's story once more.

"As I was saying… my ancestors were registered Polish Cossacks. We did not believe in Chmielnicki's dream of a liberated Ukraine. We had no time for his common man stuff, revolution and a changed master in Russia. All we wanted was lands and titles." Kuibida beamed at his audience. "That's all Chmielnicki wanted too, at least until he fell out with the other noblemen. We wanted to be equal to the Poles, not fight them. We were with Piotr Konaszewicz-Sahadaczny at Chocim in 1621 We were back at Chocim just fifty-odd years later with the Poles for the largest battle ever set in Europe, when the Ottoman Turks were stopped in their tracks. We were there at Warka against the Swedes. I am the descendant of these Polish Cossack nobles!" And he thumped his chest with his hands like a gorilla.

"That's the real Ukraine for you, boys: a stew-pot. Not this Fascist ethnic nonsense of today. We built the Ukraine together; Cossacks, Poles, Lithuanians, Ruthenians, even Tartars, Armenians, Turks, Jews, so fuck all the bastards. And I mean 'fuck'!" he roared. "Pillage, loot and rape, inter-marriage and slavery. The Ukraine is built on loot, grain, coal, oil and sex! On procreation. And no wonder. Ain't we got the best looking women in the world?"

"Hurrah!" we thundered, clapping or stamping our feet. Despite orders, beer had appeared from somewhere. Foaming wooden tankards were being passed around. Kuibida himself was passed a pot. Soon his drooping mous-tache frothed like spume on seashore seaweed.

His behaviour had drawn the crowd together; many were laughing not only at his words but at his accompanying antics and gestures. 'Sex' had sent his arm pumping up and down. Now 'Women' was accompanied by his own appeals to one of the prettier Lemko girls. She hid her face behind her apron, though you could tell she was enjoying the wolf whistles from some of the boys.

Kuibida took a might draught of beer. "Good of the villagers to share their supplies with us rather than leave them for the Polish newcomers." There was grievance and a bite of melancholy in his tone. Immediately there was bitterness in the air. Not despair but the bitterness of defeat and loss. The mood continued in his story. A story of defeat and acceptance. I knew the feeling well, but right now there was a woman's breath close by my cheek and the smell of the honey mead. Lips sweeter than honey.

"So the Tsar kicked us out of home, boys, away from Zaporozhe for being disloyal. We were loyal to freedom. We Czernomorski kept to Polish names, and even when we got back in favour with the Russians we still had Polish-style uniforms when we had any. Like the Polish nobleman, we always preferred our own clothes anyway. But for the officers always red boots, red shiny boots." He sighed and took another drink. "And if we couldn't get red then Yellow would do!" he shouted, to much clapping and foot stamping from the crowd.

"Quiet, please, your old Ataman speaks. And now to modern times. My father was a *prikazni*, just like that other little Austrian corporal with the moustache. Daddy was a Cossack of the Imperial Russian Guard. A Cossack who remained loyal to his leader Wrangel in Crimea, right up to the end." Kuibida sighed. "The fall of Empires left a void. The nationalists wanted what the Poles wanted. Only trouble was, I wasn't a nationalist, just a boy looking for a cause. We wanted a nation. Only problem was we had never had one before and didn't know who we were.

"Being a Cossack, above all I wanted freedom. Freedom from tyranny, certainly. Well, the Tsar was gone. And so freedom from whom?

"I was told the Poles and Jews had all the money and the land, so they were our class enemies. I was quickly becoming a pink if not a red. If we wanted a nation then we had to get rid of the foreigners, even if they had been there before us, or had put us where we were. Being pink, however, I also believed in the brotherhood of man – except, of course, for Poles and Jews, reactionaries and capitalists that they were. Problem was, half the Socialist leadership I read about were Poles and Jews. No wonder I was confused. " There was much laughter at this.

Hanka called out, "We Jews invented Socialism. All power to the people, as long as they do what the law book says. Then the party interprets the law." The Cossack laughed, and quite a few others caught the ironic nature of her joke.

"I didn't think women were allowed to comment on the Talmud," Kuibida shouted to Hanka.

"Did I say I was a Jew?" she responded. "I thought I was Polish. And in Poland I am my own woman."

This time Kuibida spoke to the crowd once more. "Oh, how I would love to play chess with that girl."

Seeing how the alcohol had reddened her cheeks as well as loosening her tongue I was thinking of more than playing chess with her. Particularly as her uniform buttons had opened.

"I was young, I wanted a fight."Kuibida continued. "So I joined the *Sokolska Brygada*, the Hawk Brigade of the Galician Army. We fought against the Poles. It was a fair fight and we lost, but I got more than a taste of battle. They trained me to be a real soldier. In those days the units were mostly ex-regular Austro-Hungarian, ex-empire troops. We fought with honour, proper engagements. And we didn't murder civilians." He glared around the audience. "And I hope you heard that, your old commander was there!

Someone had found a wind-up gramophone and some records, and a melancholy tango started. Within moments a few dancers had gone into clinches with some local women. The ever popular Russian exile songs stirred their heart-strings, touching melancholia around the crowd. Cigarette smoke, beer, mead and sweat all mingled to a cocktail of longing. *Golubya glaza* wrapped itself around the room, and the song *Dark Eyes* left one young man sobbing. I found in common with many others the chorus rising from my soul to my lips. The tune had been ever-present around my father. He had whistled it gently every time he thought about a machine part or how to solve a problem. I choked on the lump in my throat. Knowing somehow, Kryszka laid a gentle hand on my shoulder.

The night seemed to blur into a sequence of ballads and dances and the aftermath euphoria of the day's action. A sense of 'live for the moment' seemed to fill the air like a demon spirit. Yet practical reality was not far away, for at some point Kukura called for lights out, issuing orders for the move the next day. The unit had to ready itself for battle formation. Guns cleaned, rations issued and equipment stowed and inspected. Kukura issued a string of orders and the night's relaxation ended abruptly as men stood to, following Kukura's orders.

Soon men settled down to sleep around us. Many quickly fell to heavy breathing and sores. In the darkened barn fire flame still flickered and smoke rose from the glowing embers throwing our faces into relief in shadows and orange hues. There was a heavy yet comforting smell of warmth, animals and wood smoke.

Witek spoke quietly, voicing all our thoughts I supposed. "So how did it all end? You are here so the story remains to be told."

Kuibida shifted his position and began again. "When we retreated, we bumped into the Reds who told the remnants of our brigade we had to fight for the Bolsheviks. The Reds started to arrest our officers, so one night I cleared off home to our farm east of Kiev. And what did I find there but the same devils, the Red Bolsheviks! They promised us land reform, and oh yes, we were getting it, Trotsky style. Land to the people all right, my land, my uncles' fucking land. Our village was being collectivised. The people were the State."

Kuibida paused, taking an angry mouthful from his tankard. He rubbed the back of his hand across his whiskers. By now his face was glowing red. He spat before continuing. "Back at home I also discovered the Red Terror. A tiny disagreement with any local decision made by some Comrade Black Sea sailor or some Comrade Moscow Street Sweeper who was now the Party Boss, and you were called a counter-revolutionary, an enemy of the people.

"They tried to run the farms like a factory, with targets and norms. If a crop wasn't big enough they acted like medieval priests on a witch hunt. It couldn't be the fault of the seed or the weather. It had to be some counter-revolutionary plot. Anyone who could read and write was especially suspect but *kulaks* only needed a tin roof on their barn or two cows to be treated as enemies of the state. Anyone with connections to Ukrainian nationalists, anyone who had fought for the Whites or even had relatives who had joined them were deported to a *gulag* or simply exterminated as vermin.

"They would come in the night. Next day Ivan or Timofei, whoever he was, just disappeared. No one asked where. Their goods and implements were collectivised and distributed. Any valuables or cash went 'to the Party'.

"Then the Reds set a quota to feed the workers in mother Russia. They needed our Ukraine grain but didn't need the people. So they starved the Ukraine to death. Every peasant barn was raided. Potato clamps dug out. Anyone caught with a secret store of food was shot or deported and all their property confiscated by the State. And so the 'poor' became rich on State loot and old scores were settled." Kuibida eased himself, rocking on his feet, his mind elsewhere, as if he were thinking through of his next move, calculating the effect carefully, weighing his words. "The Red Army, the NKVD, eliminated us."

He looked at us for a moment as though we should take especial note. "Millions starved, or were sent to Siberia as slaves or were tortured. Seven million died like leaves on a forest of trees."

He turned to Hanka. "Was yours the only people to suffer? That was how the Reds dealt with Ukrainian Nationalism. Starve the buggers. It was Stalin's idea. He needed the grain, not the people. You Jews whine about your ghettos and your gas chambers. Who worried about us?"

The atmosphere was tense, electric.

My head was clouded by honey mead but what I saw before me now a man on the edge. I recognised the madness of Ukraine, a people caught on the edge of insanity, the edge of reason. I thought of Mrs. Simpson's advice to me as a child. 'Observe,' she'd said, 'stay calm. Observe. Look but see, see and look.' Which way was Kuibida headed, I wondered? My father had been a good judge of character. He'd always said, "Don't trust a Russian with a gun when he laughs." It should have been: 'Never trust Slavs on the edge." Despite the situation I chuckled. The honey mead had spoken. But I was coiled for trouble.

Boldly, without hesitation, Hanka answered Kuibida's question, even though it was rhetorical. In her usual wily way she flattered and informed him at the same time: "No, Grandfather, we all suffered together. We travel the same road. We all of us all end in the pit or the flames. It is just a question of when and how. All of us came from the same black earth, drank the same water, and ate the same bread. We all of us welcomed kith and kin, and strangers too, with honey and salt." Her gentle words washed across us like a soft mist. I relaxed back, sensed the beasts inside us easing too.

The Cossack smiled at her. "I wish I were a Grandfather. My wife, Oksana, died in the *Holodomor*. You Jews will have American publicists in New York working to make the world aware of your suffering. Even now some are calling it a Holocaust; a burnt offering to your God. Soon everyone will know of the Holocaust of the Jews. But who will know of the famine which killed millions of the Ukrainians?

"Do you know how many died of hunger? Of belly-gripping starvation? How many parents ate their dead children to stay alive? How many were sent to Siberia? Or were shot by Comrades? Did anybody count? Two million, ten million?"

Kuibida had slumped to his chair. His face, rugged and time-etched around his eyes reddened by alcohol, was broken. His chest heaved and tears started from his eyes. He screwed them and wiped a balled fist hard across them. At the same time he was making sniffing noise, sucking mucous back from his nose. Witek passed him a dirty rag from the floor and he violently blew into it. He came up for air as though nothing had happened at all; control manifest in his smile.

"Ah, the Slav mind. The inscrutable Chinese element," Hanka breathed. She had a point. "Our beds are what's needed, early start and all that."

Kuibida nodded and took another large swig from his tankard, gulping hard, throat working, head back, emptying the contents before passing it to a trooper for another.

"And thank God, gentlemen, for anti-Bolshevik Poland! Because whilst the really bigwig Nationalist leaders headed for France or Switzerland, the real activists, those foot-sloggers like us, ran to Poland for shelter. And what did we outsiders do when we got there? We agitated the locals - not against the Soviets, no. But against the nearest target, the Poles and Jews. But I am running ahead of myself. Let me come first to men I admire. Men who are my idols. Petliura and Piłsudski. Piłsudski got the rag-tag Polish army together. It beat us nationalists fair and square in Galicia."

He pulled his moustache. "But Petliura was a Cossack, don't forget! He took on the Bolsheviks and the White Russians and the Romanians. Being no fool, he joined forces with 'Marshal', Piłsudski to get rid of the Bolsheviks once and for all in 1920. We were allies. I joined up in the forces of the Ukrainian People's Republic. I was there when we took Kiev. We were outnumbered and pushed back to the Vistula, fighting together like in the old Commonwealth days. We stopped those bloody Bolsheviks from rolling up the world. We stopped Lenin and the Comintern's objective of a Communist Europe. 'First cover the corpse of Poland' they said, 'then Germany, then France, all ripe for revolution." His bitterness was as acrid as my own.

By tacit consent we left shortly after. Despite the cold the air had that touch of warmth – no, not warmth, rather the scent of Spring that masqueraded as warmth. The air was in fact quite chill. We had a couple of hundred metres to walk, passing the troopers and their little street fires. Some still sang, some hummed, some rested on their greatcoats, some slept, some ate from mess tins or bowls, others smoked pipes and cigarettes. Faces shadowed by flickering light but a sense of quiet repose. Was it the calm before the storm? A few smiles came to us, some raised hands and fingers to acknowledge our passing. Comrades-in-arms for a few hours.

I felt sorry for these people. We could have been, should have been brothers-in-arms. Narrow nationalism built on borders killed the Ukraine. Yet here were people who had lived side by side for centuries in peace and war. In the distance a strange howling chorus wailed its way to us. A bleak sound that sent shivers down your back. Not a single sound but a combination of echoes that was unreal but real enough.

"The wolves in the Bieszczady," Kryszka grunted.

Hanka clutched my arm.

"That's where they will die," said Kryszka, nodding toward the troopers. "Caught between Poles, Russians and Czechs. That is where these heroes will die."

I was uncertain what he meant by heroes. Was he being sarcastic or complimentary? Either way I guessed he would be right. As in any war, it always depends upon who wins and who gets to write the history.

We clattered up the steps into the little apology for a *Dworek,* where lamps were lit and warmth beckoned. Our host had been burning furniture in the stoves. Determined not to leave it to anyone, even though outside a good wood-store was piled high under the eaves. As we passed noisily through the long passage-way, our 'host' heard us. He had had clearly been drinking too, and begged us to join him for a night cap. The drink had made him talkative, and maudlin.

As we sat together, his talk took a new turn. He told us of the atrocities the Ukrainian irregulars, the Banderistvi, had committed against their own people as well as Poles. "Horror stories, like something out of a medieval torture chamber. A young girl caught talking to a Polish boy had her legs forced apart. They tied her to two bent birch trees and pulled her asunder. One time they put a Catholic priest in a box, then sawed him apart." We were too fascinated to ask him to stop. What is that part of human nature which forces us to listen to the most grisly narratives? We listened in horrified awe to stories of cleavers and axes, blood and entrails, noses and breasts cut off, multiple rapes. Wives and daughters tortured before their husbands and brothers. Babies spiked on bayonets. Penises used as trophies, vaginas cut out. Even the old Tartar impalement, the stake, driven into the chest and the person raised to slowly suffocate. "The most merciful deaths were from machine-guns and bullets," the old man breathed sadly. "Did their deaths help the Ukrainian cause? Of course not! Does the world care or even know?"

We knew, and we knew that those in power knew. Both in the West and in the East. The old man shook his head. "These crimes were committed by bloody savages. They don't represent the Ukrainian people. Those who warned their Polish neighbours or sheltered their children and paid with their lives, those were the *true* Ukrainians. *Locals,* of any ethnicity, who belonged to the land and humanity. "

Hanka nodded. "Just a few days before you two arrived here, General Świerczewski, the deputy defence minister of Poland, was killed in an ambush by the Lemko Company of the Ukrainian Insurgent Army, commanded by Stepan Stebelsky , known as Khrin. You are seeing the results today. In the name of revenge, the Polish authorities have started Operation Wisła, in which the remaining Ukrainian population is being deported by force to the new territories of Poland."

"Not new territories, little butterfly, but recovered territories. We must get our words politically correct. They help to cover up unpleasant facts. Of course it is an inhuman crime," Kryszka added. "The Germans will blame us as inhuman, as we blame the Russians as being inhuman. Genocide, ethnic cleansing, we shall all be accused of it. But I bet not one whisper will be laid at the door of the real culprits. The inhuman beasts who think borders are more important than lives. Stalin, Roosevelt and Churchill, they willed all this horror and don't you forget it!" He spat out the last words. "The Lemkos did not kill Świerczewski, the Polish special forces did. A sniper from the rear got him. It was a political assassination by the Communists."

Witek swung around, but not before I said, "Wasn't he the one called Uncle Walter, one of the so-called heroes of the Spanish Civil War?"

"The same," said Kryszka, "but he was a drunken sot, an embarrassment. Bierut, the Polish President was under orders. They came direct from Beria and Stalin's right hand man here, Ivan Serov. He's the one who really runs the country. Said to get rid of him. Convenient excuse to move the Ukrainians too, as well as get rid of any Polish sentiment on their behalf."

"Like mine, you mean?" I added.

"Correct," Kryszka said in his monosyllabic way.

Witek was clearly disturbed. "How do you know this, Kryszka?"

"It is my job to know," came the reply.

Seeing the men eye each other I realised this was the first real challenge from either of us to Witek's authority,

Hanka saw it too and quietly suggested we set guard. With our host we decided who would keep watch and when to change our guard, just in case.

My watch was in the depths of night. As snores rolled around the rooms, I painted pictures in my mind of the impoverished gentry who might have lived and played here. I sat ladies in silk and feathers at the polished black grand piano, hands fluttering like little sparrows over notes set by Chopin. I set men in *kontusz* to drinking and carousing, wearing their wide sashes, bejewelled sabres and extravagant headgear. I even gave one or two a scalp lock and called them Cossacks. I saw how the mead flowed, their moustaches dripped.

And as I fantasised Hanka came to me, nestling against my back, softly breathing into my ear.

Leaning on my shoulder, Hanka slipped her hand inside my shirt. "Is this what you want?" She didn't wait for an answer, but immediately slid around me, soft, available, her warm lips wet. I held her close, pushing my hand to the small of her back, feeling her hips respond.

As I withdrew from her moments later, I felt desolate, my member excruciatingly sensitive as it shrank away.

"Should I have stayed away?" she asked quietly.

"No. You're wonderful." I kissed her long and slowly, open-lipped. But with no passion, just doubt.

Ours had been quick breaths and quiet, throat-catching pants. But she slipped away as quietly as she came, pressing her fingers to her lips and then to mine. "Adieu, my sweet cowboy."

I had failed to keep guard. I was excited by her. I was a man. But I fell to wondering why I felt no pleasure afterward. The little death, the French call it, that feeling of empty desolation. I did not love this girl; I had no knowledge of her. I was not even sure why we had made love. I had felt no need for it, but she must have. Was that her wanting me, or merely wanting to give what she thought I wanted? Was it lust? Born of fear of the future? Or simply the need for human togetherness?

Sex without love touches a need. For some it's like tobacco, becomes a drug. I smiled at my philosophising yet felt ashamed.

Morning came and ahead lay the long march for us all.

Outside the sun was up and the street bustling with activity. Cattle were lowing from barns and hens clucking as troopers rounded them up for the farmers either for the pot or the journey. The cooking fires were alight and troops queuing for food. Kukura had arrived and invited us to take breakfast with Kuibida. We walked down the dirt road as though we were on a holiday outing without a care in the world. Inside we were still tense, concerned about what we called the trouble makers, the red and blacks. Of them we saw no sign.

Kuibida was still in the barn and had set up and organised a number of trestles like a huge table. He sat like some latter-day Hetman at its head surrounded by his officers and NCOs with a few of the younger troops so adoring of him the night before. Kuibida was a character larger than life. The cooks or villagers had rustled up boiled eggs, sausage, some cottage and baked cheeses with good bread. It smelled delicious. The samovar was steaming but Kuibida was drinking from a foaming wooden tankard.

"Good morning my friends. Glad to see you still alive," he joked. "Come, come I have a place for you. I want to share food with you but also to finish what I was saying last night. You thought I was drunk but I was not. I feel destiny will not treat me well and I want to tell you things. I want you Poles to understand how we, how I got into this mess. Poles must understand." He muttered this last statement as an afterthought.

Kuibida tore a strip of bread and ate heartily. Clearly the grief of the previous night had passed. He started right in again but in a more relaxed manner. He seemed to settle on me as the main target for his speech.

"The Poles got their Treaty of Riga and with it West Ukraine. And we Ukrainians got nothing. And as for Petliura, well, he got a bullet in Paris. After Poland he went into exile in France where some Jewish Communist swine executed him, doing the Reds' dirty work in the name of Jewish vengeance for pogroms. All a Bolshevik fix-up, of course, to discredit Petliura, who was never anti-Jewish. The Reds have always been adept at using anti-Semitism as a weapon to stain reputations. They know New York Jews better than anyone and probably have their plants running the place."

For me it was time to leave, not sit here and listen. I blamed the damned mead from the night before for this new lecture. "You're losing me," I said.

The Cossack beamed at me. "So I am an educator for you too, yes? So I try to explain. The Ukrainian government went into exile in Poland and Petliura, operating from Tarnow, set about starting to build a government and army again. We had lost before because we could not raise enough troops. We were divided; many did not want the Polish alliance, especially those radicals now living in a free country. They were not in the Red Terror. And I suppose in fairness it was just beginning.

"The Reds set up a Ukrainian Soviet Socialist Republic and it was now right next door to Poland. The Bolshies kept pushing to have Petliura back, to try him and execute him. Of course the Poles were not having any of it, but they did intern the army at Kalisz. Petliura hopped it to Paris, as I said, and I hopped it home back over the border. I did not know what was to come, you see. I wasn't a politico, just a soldier. The Poles mostly looked the other way. They treated us well, so a number of us went over the wall one night when the guards were looking the other way."

Surprisingly Kryszka, who was normally silent, especially in the morning, interjected. "It all comes down to Versailles. The fall of Empires, too many politicians trying to draw borders in faraway places. They tried to use language as an arbiter, but Central Europe, most of which was at one time the Commonwealth, had been subject to Austria, Hungary, Russia, and Prussia. Those Imperial powers banned all native languages. So some people no longer spoke their 'ethnic' language. Each community had to fight their corner in the end. It was war. For example, towns were Polish and Jewish and the peasants were Ruthenian, so where did each belong? They fought to find out."

There was silence for a moment at this unexpected academic interruption from a man known to hold his counsel most of the time.

I added into the space my own thoughts "Here am I too, allegedly a Pole but with an ethnic Ukrainian, or should I say Ruthenian father, who had been a strong Polish nationalist. He considered himself pure Polish. He spoke Polish and to my knowledge no Ukrainian."

This interjection had rather thrown the expansive Cossack.

"Thank you for that, my friends. Now where was I?"

"You went back home from Poland after the Reds had settled in a bit."

"Ah yes, I went home to my *kulak* family. As I already told you, they were hard times boys, hard times. I lost my wife. I lost uncles and aunts, my mother, my brothers, my sisters." This morning Kuibida was in charge of his emotions. We were not to hear details, just events. "So I survived. I joined the Party."

There was a wave of surprise around the table. "Yes, I went to see the local commissar, said I wanted to join the Party. They were not stupid, so I was grilled about Petliura and my past and my daddy and his past and my family. I was asked who was a secret White. This was survival, you understand. I am ashamed to say I told them of the hoof-beats in the night, nightriders coming and going. I gave away neighbours to survive. I told them I wanted to join the army. So they sent me to Rostov-on-Don, where after some time being re-educated and indoctrinated with Communist and Socialist clap-trap, I became a rifleman in the 436th Infantry Regiment of the Red Army. So I saw the famines, I saw the people. As they say, 'I was there'. Then the purges began."

I straightened in my seat. Now Kuibida was on more familiar territory for me. Whenever I heard of the purges politics became personal. I believed the purges had something to do with the murder of my parents and my surrogate uncle, a hero of the American Kościuszko squadron, during the Polish Soviet war. Had my parents known something that represented a danger to Stalin?

When I was a junior air force attaché in Warsaw, just before the outbreak of the war, the purges had not long finished. I knew that in typical style Stalin's protégé Sergei Kirov, who publicly opposed and criticised Stalin in the Politburo, had been assassinated by a young Communist. Stalin had announced this as a Trotsky-organised murder.

It was Stalin who first began a purge of the Party, executing anyone he thought supported Trotsky. Old Party faithful like Smirnov, Kamenev, Zinoviev and others on the Central Committee were done to death. Two Jews and a Russian, I thought, plus Trotsky the Jew. And Genrikh Yagoda of course. The head of the NKVD, who had organised the Kirov assassination and had done Stalin's dirty work, beginning the purges of the old faithful. He was a Jew too. It was Yagoda who had organised the GULAG system and sent so many Jews, Poles, and Russians to their death in the slave camps.

Yagoda, and now Yezhov, I mused. Nikolai Yezhov, nicknamed 'The Bloody Dwarf'. Stalin had made him People's Commissar for Internal Affairs, the head of the NKVD. As for Yagoda, he had been shot. Stalin was ruthless.

I came back to the moment and found myself still listening to the Cossack. I doubted I had missed much. The Germans had invaded Poland by now and he had been part of the Red Army that had 'liberated' one half of Poland. "I was in the North," I heard him say, "up near, but east of, Wilno. For some god dam reason the Jews welcomed us. They turned out with flowers and food. That upset the local Poles for sure, the ones who recognised us as enemies. I guess the Jews saw us as their protectors from the Germans. Well, we soon had the task of clearing the Poles out. First the intelligentsia and then the forces, like the fire brigade and the police. The NKVD special units shipped them east and began giving their land to the Lithuanians, moving them in. Then the Bolsheviks began on the rest, anyone with a business or trade."

He had dropped the 'we', I noticed. It was back to 'the Bolsheviks'. "At this stage it began to dawn on the Jews that they were Poles too. Not only that, but many of them were classed as 'petty bourgeois, enemies of the people. Any Zionist was a 'counter-revolutionary'. It had been the wrong move to welcome the Soviets!" he said, turning to Hanka.

"I agree," she said. "My parents were patriots, we didn't welcome them. We were moved to the Warsaw ghetto forcibly."

Kuibida looked chastened. "So the war dragged on. The Allies, the Germans and the Russians fell out. Apart from Poland, most of Europe was pro-German and had either been invaded or had allied themselves with the Germans. It was only Poland, still with a big army, air force and navy, along with little England, against the world, with a few free French and a handful of Norwegians and Dutch."

"Don't forget the British Empire!" I chimed in.

"Oh yes, I had forgotten," he laughed. "I had forgotten."

"Well, the Reds were short of officers. They had kept killing them, so just before the war they sent me off to Frunze Military Academy and rushed me through, teaching me all about how Stalin was a genius and the concept of deep battle. Load of rubbish, my children."

"Did you have red boots?" some wag officer asked.

"No, I did not, sunshine, and I didn't have a Red mind either. But we, did have a Don Cossack, God bless them, in charge of the regiment. He was supposed to be real Red, a party member since 1927, and he had the Order of the Red Banner to boot. He was commander of our 436th Infantry Regiment of the 155th Soviet Infantry Division. That man spoke to us like I speak to you. And we the regiment decided that the 'Great Patriotic War' was not for us and that we wanted rid of Stalin. So in August 1941, when we were covering the Red Army retreat, the whole of our regiment went over to the Germans."

There were whistles and gasps of surprise. I had never heard of this and evidently neither had Witek, because he sat up and paid more attention. Previously he had appeared to be still half asleep. Since he was an historian, I had presumed knew all this stuff.

"So, children, I became a Cossack again. The Germans soon had us as the 120th Don Cossack Regiment. Our task was to begin raiding into Red territory, which we did with relish. We went for commissars and the local Soviets. In the North it was okay at first, the regular army treated us well enough. Then came the SS and the Gestapo. We were Slavs, *Untermenschen*, sub-humans, inferior beings. I had thought the Germans would throw the Bolsheviks out and help us set up a free Ukraine. Do not make the same mistakes *we* made," he said, inclining his head towards Kukura. "I realised that first it was to be the Jews, next the Poles. There were not so many Jews, so they were being dealt with first. The Poles could wait and meanwhile be worked to death. So I deserted and went to the woods and joined the partisans. Not the Soviets or the Poles but the god dam Ukrainian Insurgent Army. My enemies were still the Soviets, but now especially the Poles. Some of us did fight the Germans from time to time, but as I found out, our main job was simply terrorising the Poles. We had to get rid of the Poles, see? So let the Germans do the Jews whilst we do the Poles. Sick ain't it?

CHAPTER 7

# THE NEW BORDERLAND

I liked Przemyśl. Situated at the foot of the Carpathians, it lay close to the border with the Soviets, the Communist Russian Empire proper. Two years ago it had been in the Eastern heartland of the Second Republic. It had been in Poland.

The Russians had stolen half the country.

The lazy San River still wended its way through the town. This was the river the Poles had expected to shape a defensible front against the German invasion in '39. It was not to be. The Russians had invaded too, colluding with the Germans. So the San had divided the friendly conquerors. It was here to Przemyśl's east bank that many Jews had run for safety from the Germans. The river had not saved them. The Germans attacked their erstwhile friends and the Jews were subsequently exterminated. Six hundred Poles were caught assisting Jews and were martyred accordingly.

Though tired after our long march the town enchanted me with its unforgettable landscape of steeply rising, narrow streets connecting historical buildings and old churches whose towers climbed ever higher. The steeply sloping main square was quaintly beautiful too, with its castle and cathedral, monastery and convents and medieval walls. But there was no synagogue standing. The Germans had seen to that. The town was clearly recovering from the aftermath of war. Bombed out houses were still nothing more than windowless facades. Gaps in the street where buildings had been destroyed gaped like a row of bad teeth.

Reconstruction and building work was going on everywhere, bricks piled high and counted. The town, rebuilt after the total destruction of the First World War, once more required love and the spirit of its people to reconstruct its heart. Everything was run down, of course, and like everywhere else peoples' lives were turned upside down too. But the flower sellers had returned. *I could live in this town*, I thought, *when someone had sorted it out*. I liked its coat of arms, which bore a rather nice black bear. Silly things appeal to us in strange circumstances.

Witek had caught my gaze and interpreted it correctly. "You like this place, eh? The oldest city in Poland after Krakow. Now it's a dump and will become more of a dump."

"That's a bit harsh," Kryszka butted in. "I agree with Tadek. The town is beautiful. It has a fine square with some beautiful buildings."

"I agree, it has a few pretty buildings and lots of work to do on empty houses and where the Jews used to be. But half empty? Robbed of its people? It's a dump because people are dumped here! It's a dump for all those deportees transferred from over the border." His eyes twinkled as slowly his joke dawned on me. I'd noticed Witek liked to play with words, to use innuendo and double entendre. He chose words carefully, for their effect. Sometimes they seemed like nails driven into wood to secure an angle, driven in brutally to reach their purpose.

"There was the usual squabble between the Ukrainian nationalists and the Poles about whose town it was. Much like a mini Lwów. Polish citizens, including Jews, fighting the Ukrainians till the cavalry arrived, that sort of stuff."

"It's wrong of you to be so dismissive," Hanka shot at him." People died here for their beliefs, for their nations."

Witek's response to Hanka was sardonic and yet humorous at the same time. As we had drawn nearer to the city his mood had swung into this contra set of emotions, one moment cynical, sarcastic, the next informative and humorous. He seemed to pick on me as an outsider, which I was beginning to resent. The team was beginning to fracture. You could sense it.

"Always have done, my dear. Our proto-Canadian here will be interested to know that this is a real Polish city, in my opinion. No doubt about this one. Here lived the Lędzianie, the good old descendants of Lech, the original Pole! This is a city of Lechia, the alternative name for Poland. Sounds like Czechia, named for those other morose Slavs around Prague. Lechia and Czechia, two squabbling brothers."

Agents of the anti-communist Freedom and Sovereignty organisation WiN[1] were waiting for us in a shabby café. Gaunt looking men and women were drinking chicory and barley roasted to allegedly taste like coffee. Others sat at tables reading papers or sipping beer. A policeman strolled by, but no one took any notice. Not even when a man dressed in sports jacket and knee boots rose and came to our table, whispering something into Witek's ear. Witek joined another table. The three of us sat, feeling like birds in a cage, sensing we were surrounded whilst the tension mounted.

Witek rejoined us. "I've agreed we're to be separated into two groups; myself and Hanka and you, Tadek, with Kryszka. This separation will minimise the risk to people helping us set up our operation until we find Sikorski's daughter, if she's still alive. We need contacts and detail; Kryszka, that's your job. Tadek, you find any links to MI6, whether Britons, Poles or Russians."

I nodded. Such links probably existed. *But where were the traitors?*

At the end of the war the British had passed all they knew about clandestine Polish activities to the Soviets, as part of the 'Zones' of occupation deal. It was not seen as betrayal at the time, as the Soviets were Allies. It was however supremely stupid and had led to many deaths, even of those hidden from the established underground. In the Western zones the British and Americans were trying to piece together the Polish underground network in Germany. The French, suddenly back on the scene, remained aloof. As part of our mission I was to start some new links for the British. And just importantly try to record just who could be trusted for the exiled Polish government.

Kryszka and I were instructed to separate and follow a little old lady who carried two shopping bags. I was to go first and then Kryszka would follow after me. We sat in the café waiting, drinking barley coffee. Waiting, watching, exposed. Suddenly the man opposite signalled to me by lowering and folding his paper. A small dumpy lady walked past the café entrance. I got up and strode after her. She wore a long grey skirt that reached her midcalf. Broad of beam she rolled like a ship in a storm. Her legs were bowed and her feet slopped along in what appeared to be worn carpet slippers. I duly followed her, feeling like a greyhound forced to a crawl. I felt awkward, out of place but tried my best to look nonchalant.

We turned into Jan Matejko Street which still had some fine buildings. Some damaged, some in disrepair, but mostly the street was as it must have been before the war. I looked at the tired facades with their remnants of stucco mouldings, a mix of heraldry and Greco Roman motifs. *This will be a fine city again*, I thought.

The old lady toiled up the hill at a snail's pace. I felt conspicuous and vulnerable. After what seemed an eternity she turned into a large building through double, heavy doors. I followed into the cool darkness, wanting to glance back to see if Kryszka was behind. The hallway was typical of its kind. Well trodden concrete stairs worn to a polish with fancy iron balustrades coated in thick green many layered paint led upward. The walls were dowdy with peeling paint. It was cool and dark. The old lady toiled upward, the sound of her slopping slippers echoing with the sound of my boots, forming a bizarre jazz symphony. I followed upward, closing the gap now. Below I heard Kryszka enter.

She paused on the second floor where there were three doors. She rang a bell on the first door and for the first time she turned to me. Her face was that of a hard working peasant of indeterminate age. She could have been anything between forty and sixty. Her blue eyes contrasted with the brown of her sun wrinkled skin. She held her fingers to her lips indicating quietness. Kryszka caught up with us and stood close behind. The door opened outward and the old lady gestured us in. As we passed she whispered ,"God bless you Gentlemen." She must have pushed the outer door to as we went into the corridor of the apartment. The inner door was closed by a taller blonde woman who simply said "Welcome to my home. You will be safe here."

So it was here that we two settled. Here lived Aniela, our angel or messenger. We never saw the old lady again.

Aniela worked for one of the new government posts; she was an 'aparatczyk', and was being sponsored to join the Party. In 'real life', as she put it, she worked for the WiN to pass on details of those on the wanted list from a friend who worked in the office of the UB. She was a nationalist and she was brave. She was also very sweet. Well-dressed, exquisitely groomed, and every bit the embodiment of the pre-war Poland I had known and loved. Aniela wore her blonde hair shoulder-length, as well with that sultry look about her lips only Polish women can muster, that look of arrogant contempt flavoured with desire. She did not wear sensible shoes, despite the straitened times.

The apartment was spacious with high ceilings and wide views from the windows that opened onto the street. There was a large central room that served as dining hall lounge and music room. A small kitchen opened directly off this room. There were two bedrooms. Kryszka and I were assigned the larger as Aniela felt it right that she should give up her space to "two husky big men." Joy of joys there was a washroom and separate lavatory. A luxury indeed.

The furniture was an eclectic mix of family pieces, together with lots of photographs in various frames. Many were sepia but most black and white. One was a hand tinted colour print of an elegant elderly woman. "My mother", Aniela said. The rest were family of various ages and stages. The bed was comfortable and Kryszka decided we would sleep head to toe. There was no sign of a man or husband. We did not enquire.

Aniela had come through the war unscathed simply because she played the piano professionally. She was now our own personal angel because she played Chopin and she played him well, her emotions flitting over the upright piano keys like a butterfly. "Chopin," she declared the first night we met her, "should not be played with exaggerated pomp; hands raised like a sorcerer. Chopin was the master of the caress, the trickle of water over stone which gradually wears it away. Not the stomp of feet in well-cut leather boots!"

The Russians had enjoyed her playing, and then the Germans, and as she was part of the Polish underground she survived with most of her life intact. She had played in a couple of bars and officers functions, even a concert or two throughout the duration of the war. Like many civilians who supported the underground she passed on all the intelligence she gleaned.

Her view of the Russians and Germans was quite different. She described the Russians as brutes. "Boys in khaki who had never seen civilisation. Savages, who thought liberation meant licence to kill, pillage, rape. I was lucky; usually the class war meant death to anyone who could read music or play the piano. But I spoke some broken Russian and knew a few mournful songs that went well with the accordion. Then came the Germans. They at least understood classical music. And I was always in love with a Napoleonic uniform. I just adore men in tight trousers! It was war. You had to survive."

Aniela's face twisted for a moment, remembering something far away from us, a hurt, something perhaps beyond our comprehension. But within seconds she had straightened her back, and crossed her ankles to the other side, her feet dainty in the summer high heels she had blanco'd so beautifully.

She was still a privileged person, both for her music and through her work. Although her family had owned this apartment she could have expected to be informed it was too large for one person and have had a family assigned to live along aside her. We guessed she had a 'sponsor' somewhere. In this not so small apartment her most prized possession was a whopping big radiogram, just like the one my parents had bought so many years ago. It too was HMV, and stood in its own wonderful walnut cabinet. Aniela watched me run my hands over it, enjoying the smoothness of its polished veneer.

"London calling, London calling!" As she said the words, so familiar during the war she held her nose and made a sound like a duck before adding Beethoven's famous call sign, used by the BBC throughout the conflict. "Duh duh duh dumm, duh duh duh dumm." It had a strange hint of menace. She looked at me as though to say "We are not defeated."

Now began the same old waiting game, waiting for orders, arrangements to be made, boredom . We could not readily go out so we read and listened to the radio. And waited.

There was a go between, a courier who came to the apartment and shared food sourcing with Aniela. It would have been too obvious and have attracted too much attention if Aniela had started to buy for three. So each bought a little extra, to allow for us.

The courier's name was Elżbieta, Ela for short.

I was in love with her from the first moment I saw her.

Her first, breathless question to me was, "And what did you do in the war?" As I gave her a brief rundown of my exploits, I watched her, soaking up how wisely she nodded at each twist and turn of events. Was I even coherent as I spoke? I was so distracted, thinking just how lovely she was and how suddenly the world seemed rosier. Aniela looked on with slight amusement as we flirted becoming easier in each other's company by the minute.

She was not sensual in the obvious way Aniela was; Ela was much more subtle than that. I realised the first time I met her she had a sensational figure under her thick black coat and high-necked sweater. She wore black knitted gloves as I remember. Even inside Aniela's flat, she held on to them like grim death, in case she lost them. She wore her thick blonde hair in a short bob which emphasised the beautiful line of her jaw.

Ela was pretty beyond description. She had one of those faces, just the thought of which makes you happy. I liked the way her whole face smiled. That rounded, Polish face, where somehow the nose extends and curves too. She even had a nose that smiled, a Polish style nose. Her eyes and pert mouth were perpetually smiling. She was entirely kissable.

I liked the look of her instantly. The feelings of an instant have often been my downfall.

Elżbieta was two years younger than Aniela. And she was everything Aniela was not. Where Aniela was an angel, Ela was a pixie. She had a habit of looking at a person sideways, like she knew something you didn't. It was cute. I liked her clever conversation and the easy way she had with me from that first moment. I liked the way she boldly held my gaze until that indefinable second when she slipped away in a smile. I liked the way she used her hands to express herself. She liked to speak English and I liked the way she spoke it; she made it sound so bright and cheerful. I liked the way she flicked her hair. I liked the way she looked at the world in a practical, straight way. Being around her made me feel happy.

I fell in love in an instant.

Though she was so mischievous Ela had a very serious side too. Przemyśl had lost its Jews and 'Ukrainians', a large percentage of its population. So it had space for people. Expellees from the East were being resettled here. These were the surviving Poles from previous Russian ethnic cleansings of Eastern Poland, people who had been transported to the outposts of the Soviet Empire, those who would not accept Soviet passports imposed upon the destitute of a broken society. Along with them came the few remaining prisoners of war, men and women broken in body and spirit. These were the people she worked with.

That first night Ela spoke passionately about her efforts to help these people, particularly about the children. Families were coming back from the deportations of the early part of the war. The Soviets had especially targeted the intelligentsia, and especially Polish Army officers' families, intending to break the Polish military tradition once and for all. Children had been driven from their homes and cattle-trucked, simply because they were Polish, to Siberia or Kazakhstan or God knows where. Then the Soviets deported Poles for being Polish, for living in the section of Eastern Poland known as Kresy, annexed behind the Curzon Line.

"What a pathetic state they are in when they arrive,Tadek." Her bright eyes pleaded for understanding. "Not only have they lost parents and other relatives, they have witnessed the brutality, the murder, the rape and torture." The first night we met we talked long into the night. Ela wondered what had happened to the around two million Poles had been uprooted from their homes in the first two years of the war and sent east. Untold numbers had died. Hearing her talk I could understand why she worked such long hours, co-operating with a local Red Cross agency linking orphans with parents in the West. Especially as it was now being closed down by the Communist authorities. "Everything is tightening down, everything is being centralised and controlled by the Party. But some escaped south into Persia when Sikorski struck a deal with Stalin to form a Polish army," she told me hopefully. "Polish refugees, including many women and children, came together and formed the 'Anders' army, the Polish 2nd Corps."

I explained to her as gently as I could that they too were now 'refugees' or 'displaced persons'. The Polish army was no further use to the Allies. She looked at me disbelievingly as I told her of my travels through Germany where large camps of Poles were organised, Poles who refused to return to Poland despite threats even from the UNRRA agents who tried to force them to return.

"They will not go back," I told her, "because they know they will be arrested. People in the West they simply don't believe it. They didn't even accept the 'Purges' as a fact. The political Left seem blinded by the idea of a workers' paradise. The media are spellbound. But the Poles in Britain are certainly not lining up to return here, that's for sure. Why should they sign their own death warrant? The Exiled Polish Government in London has told everyone what's really happening, the arrests, the executions, how from the very beginning the Red Army behaved in a hostile manner to the AK. How once they occupied an area, they arrested the Home Army officers and men and transported them to the depths of Russia."

"I don't see them coming home now. They are lost to us, probably in a slave camp or shot if they are lucky." Ela shook her head. "Some of the transports stopped locally. Some went on to the New Territories in what used Germany, but a few stopped here. They children tell me such stories of slave labour, of death camps," she said sorrowfully. "One young girl told me how she and her mother, along with others, were simply dumped somewhere in the tundra. They built mud huts for shelter. She and her sister survived by catching and eating rats. No one must know about the *gulags*. But when they get here, the kids are emaciated, they look like sticks. They're as bad as anything you see on the films from the concentration camps, yet nobody gives a damn. Why is that?" she asked me.

I had no answer for her. "One of the greatest crimes ever committed against humanity, and no one wants to know. And in the future, no one will want to know either if this 'we must forget' message keeps getting broadcast."

"And all new returnees to Poland are told they must not talk about their experiences, otherwise they will be sent to prison. And people are so terrorised they need to forget. It is how the Soviet system works. So I guess I'll just keep on doing my bit."

When the conversation got too serious we played records on the radiogram. I taught her how to change the needle after she told me she'd been banned from touching the precious beast. Aniela was mad on the tango and we played her records over and over again. We moved the table and rolled back the carpet, smooching, body to body like the American films showed. She taught me the more elegant steps of the fox trot but there was not enough space so we ended up a heap of laughter.

Sensing my reluctance to try the tango properly she was determined to teach me the steps. She danced well. We practiced for hours, enjoying the pleasure of the rhythm in the closeness of our bodies. Here was a real woman. She had the feel of strength and solidity that transcends the slightness of girlhood. Her warmth and firmness satisfied me. It also led to passion. We both knew we wanted more and that more meant privacy. We needed time together. Ela proposed we risk cycling into the countryside alone. She assured me it would not be dangerous, with her alongside. She knew the ropes and the score.

The following day we took bicycles to a farm she knew and then rode horses at a walk up to Zniesienie Mountain to the Tartars' barrow. Legend says a Tartar Khan was buried there. The view is breathtaking. In the past it was a signal point to warn of invasions. A fire here would warn for miles around.

It was quiet apart from the sighing of the wind. The saddles creaked as the horses ambled around the summit. Occasionally they tossed their heads snuffling into the bit, snorting at the smell of fresh grass. We dismounted and let them crop the grass for a while as we chatted and rolled close together. Eventually we kissed, my hand resting lightly on her breast. We were willing partners but not today. There was a new level of love and respect that wanted to wait for the proper moment. This was pleasure of another kind, the oneness of a moment captured with the smell grasses, the good earth and the wind of change.

As we lay together Ela spoke for the first time of her younger sister Irena, who had been sent to relatives in Warsaw at the outbreak of war. A Girl Guide, she had acted as a courier in the 1944 Warsaw uprising. "After that we heard nothing. The authorities were not anxious to help find anyone who had 'been part of or associated with the AK in the Rising'", she said. "I just want to know if she survived. If she was in the official AK, maybe she did. They were supposed to be treated as Prisoners of War. It is the not knowing that hurts. It is like a sore, a nagging wound. I pray she is alive and perhaps in Germany or England."

I did all I could do. Held her close, let her weep. Until it was time to leave.

At the farm as we were returning the horses our easy afternoon together changed in an instant. Two militia men on bicycles turned off the road. We slipped into the barn and watched and waited. Ela's friends the farmers were waving their arms, but we couldn't pick up too much of the conversation. The militia men's backs were toward us. Eventually the police left, one clutching a chicken to his chest, trying to stop its frantic squalling. Ela and I giggled and held on to each other in relief. Clearly this was no more than a routine call – they were probably looking for an illicit still. The chicken was payment for not looking too closely.

As we cycled toward town a small foot patrol of soldiers were right in our path, toiling uphill toward the woods. They wore Polish uniforms at least, not Russian. Ela took the bull by the horns calling out "Killed any terrorists today, boys?" The officer was nonplussed, unsure whether this was sarcasm or genuine encouragement. "Papers," he demanded.

Ela turned to me, holding her hand out so she could pass our papers over together. I had to admire her bravado. In conversational tone she continued "We've just been out exercising the horses and saw a very funny sight, some militia men hunting vodka makers gathering chickens in exchange for 'free passes'. You should catch them on their bikes if you go on up that way. You can't miss them. They look like two comedians in a film!"

A couple of the troopers smiled. Clearly not one to miss an opportunity to gather information she smiled back and asked, "And what are you gentlemen up to today?"

"Best mind your own business, miss," the officer replied in a Ukrainian accent as he passed the documents back. He glanced at me enquiringly.

But Ela was already waving a kiss at the officer. "Enjoy your walk boys," she called to the troopers and I waved too as we shot off down the slope.

"Near miss," she said as we trundled over the rough ground as fast as we could. "Lucky he was from the Soviet Ukraine. Still a bit uncertain of Polish. If he was from Kresy, we might have had a problem. No matter. It's over now."

Kryszka furious when we got back and told him about the excursion. "That was so bloody stupid and foolhardy. Tadek, you bleeding idiot. You might have endangered the whole mission. What if you had been mistaken as partisans by security forces?" He almost fainted when we told him we had spent some time talking to a Ukrainian officer and troops in Polish uniforms.

"Being normal, Kryszka, is often the best disguise." Ela told him. He wasn't convinced. But I was in love, so what did I care what others thought? My every waking moment was filled with thoughts of her. It was a thrill to touch her, yet I found my self strangely restrained, not wanting my desire for her to show to others. She seemed to precious to be debased that way. She seemed so alive in a world that was drab. I loved the floral patterned frocks she wore, was fascinated by the way they outlined her figure. When I bought her nylon stockings on the black market Kryszka almost had a fit, even when I reassured him how careful I had been.

Within days Kryszka was in no position to throw any more stones. Aniela invited him to play the piano with him and they shared duets. I didn't know he played the piano so well. I watched what had happened to him happen to me. His liking for her turned to devotion which turned to something deeper.

"Fancy Kryszka, the man of iron, being in love!" I teased him, receiving a growl in return.

He was so attentive and Aniela loved it. We were all so happy and easy together. Shut in the apartment all we had was friendship, goodwill, love. An interval of sanity in a world building a new order of corruptive greed and jealousy, a society based on fear.

We played Aniela's records every evening. The voice of Pjotr Leshchenko swirled around the tiny apartment. Oh how those 'Dark Eyes' appealed to the the depths of my Slav being.*Tchernye Glaza* pulled my soul close to tears. *Pola Negri* even spun me around the floor with *Tango Notturna* as I held Ela in my arms. The German words somehow seemed not to matter any more. *Serce Matki,* a mother's heart, brought tears and a feeling of the coming end. We sang along with another her song of golden chrysanthemums in a crystal vase, soothing sorrow and regret. Felt with her as through silvery and misty tears she reached out her hands to them and whispered one question: *Why have you gone away?* Each night those words of Janusz Popławski stole deeper into our hearts. And every night 'Ordonka' sang her evergreen song, which I loved, *Love will forgive you everything.* It seemed to mean more to me, perhaps, because it came from the film called *A Spy in the Mask.* Her words, Ela softly told me, came from the pen of poet Julius Tuwim. For us it was more than a song.

> *"Love will forgive you everything,*
> *your sadness will turn into joy.*
> *Love can so easily explain*
> *a cheat, a sin and betray.*
> *Should you desperately curse him some day,*
> *that he is cruel or bad,*
> *love will forgive you everything,*

*because love, my darling, it's me."*

Aniela regaled us with stories of all the artists. She loved to tell us about Ordonka, who was married to Count Michał Tyszkiewicz. She knew every detail of the singer's life, how when living in Lithuania she was deported by the NKVD to Uzbekistan. How she escaped with the Anders army and ended up looking after Polish orphans. She had a collection of Rudolph Valentino photos too, which she kept in a shoe-box. 'Rudi' she called him. "Pola Negri always keeps this one by her beside," she said, pointing to a handsome studio portrait. Such banalities. The world is full of what we do say and what we should have said. I wish I had been honest. I wish I had told Ela how I felt.

We had so little time. And what we had we sometimes wasted talking of politics. She and I argued constantly about Mikołajczyk and whether he should or should not have joined the provisional government. I was scathing of his present position, how he had appeared to lose an election, which we all knew would be rigged. Ela, a Peasant Party activist, lost no time assuring me I didn't know what I was talking about. She reminded me sharply of the onslaught there had been against her Party. "Our meetings were broken up, party offices smashed up or buildings burned down. If you were a Peasant Party member you lost your job. And remember, nearly everything is now State-run, State-owned, so it's easy to be chucked out of your job. No job, no money. Many activists have been arrested, kidnapped. Some murdered. So how could we win? And how can you blame Mikołajczyk?" she asked.

"Easy," I replied, my feathers ruffled. "He sucked up to his Western masters, he was so naïve! The man should have stayed in England as Prime Minister of Free Poland, not come running back here as a Deputy Prime Minister alongside Gomułka to play footsie with the Reds about so called social democracy. Everyone knew the election would be rigged in. Mikołajczyk's party was hounded, persecuted, he should have pulled out in protest. The referendum the year before showed everyone the Communists were rigging the results. To go into the election was plain stupid, playing into Stalin's hands.

And then the final betrayal by the Americans. James Byrne, the US Secretary of State, stood up in Stuttgart and said the new German border with Poland was a unilateral decision of Stalin. What a downright lie! He said it to suck up to the Germans because Truman wants to draw a line across Europe. Byrnes even hinted the Germans might get back the territory given to Poland. What the hell did he think he was doing? He was driving the Poles towards the Russians. The ultimate betrayal of Poland by the past Allies."

"What has that got to do with Mikołajczyk?" Ela's question was as trenchant as ever.

"It would have been better if he had never come. He gave this whole charade a look of authenticity. The Western press will be convinced for a long time that this was a legitimate government. The events will not be remembered. They'll just quote the statistics – and that the Communists won."

Aniela was trying to be fair minded. "The Communist Gomułka has done some good things like continuing the pre-war policy of breaking up the big estates and giving the land to small farmers. At least he's a worker and not a total Soviet stooge". Such a remark, however fair, gave Ela and me the opportunity to ally ourselves against her. We were convinced we'd never see a good Communist, and so harmony returned.

Making up was always fun.

Kryszka broke his own rules and went with Aniela to the cinema the following evening, Ela and chiding him as they went out the door. Those few days were the happiest I'd known for a long time. I felt hope again for the first time too. The whole country seemed alive with people trying to rebuild their nation. The government too, whatever its complexities, was trying to reconstruct life. But it wasn't all so innocent and hopeful. I soon discovered why Ela had been forbidden from touching the radiogram. Buried within the HMV was Aniela's group radio for contact with London. At intervals set by her chief she tuned in, reporting our presence. She was given two addresses in Kiev where we would find the leads we needed. It took her some time with her code book to come up with the goods. We got word to Witek via one of Ela's repatriated waifs, a young girl nicknamed Jagoda, so called because she was as brown as a berry.

We were ready to go.

The night I told Ela we were leaving was painful. I hadn't felt such sorrow since my parents' death. I wanted to care for this woman.

Clearly she felt the same way about me. "Tadek, you know I do other work, underground work? For the Peasant Party? Because of my English, I have been asked to go away soon too. I'm to help get an important politician out of Poland to the West. If I am able I shall get out of Poland too. And I shall stay out. I want a life. Shall I go to America?" She looked me straight in the eye.

Snap decisions. I didn't want her to go to America.

"It is a big place. Perhaps I won't find you."

"You want to find me?"

"Of course I bloody do!" I said in English. "I want to marry you, Ela. Get to England somehow. Take a letter I am going to give you to my lawyer in London. He will guide you from there."

We embraced and we kissed gently. I had learned at last how good it was to be at the centre of my own happiness, not on the fringe of someone else's.

Immediately I wrote a letter to Messrs Redfern, Caper & McCulloch telling them that Miss Elżbieta Krupa, the bearer of the letter, upon identification should be given access to my property in Crown Street in Brighton.

Further she should be given an allowance of ten pounds per week until further notice. When I gave the letter to Ela she cried a little. Much later I realised she had not responded to my marriage proposal. I had made a statement, an assumption. But the question was never asked and the answer never given.

Aniela was in fine mood that night; she had found a chicken and potatoes and cabbage. As a treat, she played us some Chopin études. When the electricity failed as so often we listened to her by candlelight. Sitting with my arm around Ela In the darkened room I knew something like peace. Her dark eyes glittered – I could see the candle flames reflected in them.

The peace didn't last, of course. Within a few moments a comment of mine had offended Aniela.I simply said, "It will be a good thing when his Civil war in Poland is over one way or another." Entirely the wrong thing to say.

"How can it be a Civil War when only one side is Polish?" she said, standing up from the piano. "Do you think all these men running round in Polish uniforms are Polish?" She rummaged in a sideboard drawer, finally handing me a dog eared leaflet in triumph. I read holding the paper to the flickering light that cast shadows across the page:

> 'We are by no means a gang of bandits, as we are called by the traitors and villainous sons of our motherland. We are men of Polish cities and villages. We want for Poland to be governed by the Poles who are faithful to her, and chosen by the entire nation; for there are among us those who can't speak out, for fear of death and the clique of Soviet officers who are on the lookout to exterminate us. Therefore, we declared a fight to the death against those who – in return for money, decorations, or appointments from Soviet hands – are slaughtering the best of Poles, who demand freedom and justice.
>
> Major 'Lupaszka'

"This is not a Civil war, Tadek. It is a war to throw off the Soviet yoke, the invaders." She ran through the names of the Soviet staff officers 'Polonised' into 'Polish' security forces that she knew of.

"Okay, okay, I retract," I said. Of course she was right. Those left fighting - and there were many thousands - were fighting an invader. Only governments outside Poland had said the war was over. It was not over here, and would not be until the Communist usurpers were defeated.

Later that night we left on bicycles, one by one, careful to avoid the curfew patrols. We met Witek and Hanka at a small manor house, which was being turned into a Forest Ministry office. No builders were around. Our bicycles would be collected. The underground functioned well.

We walked into the woods to cross the border into the Soviet Union proper. Not far away was a weak point, a smuggling route not yet closed. It was dark. Very dark. The wind rustled through the trees so they groaned as though they were speaking to one another. As the gusts died away the pine needles whispered to each other, telling the tale of these humans trying to tread so softly across their forest floor. The night sky was black, moonless. The stars only served to show the tree-top edges stirring to and fro like the darkest swell of a sea. Whenever Witek stopped we all crouched and listened. When you listened you could hear the sound of our humanity, the blood circulating within our body, the thump of our heart, the white noise singing in our ears singing, the whistling intake of breath in our noses. What noisy creatures we are.

Where the track finished, at the edge of the trees, a dim light could be seen from a window. We were some kilometres north of the railhead at Medyka, deep in the forest. No dogs barked, no animals lowed. All we could see was a hut in a forest, close to the border, dark and sinister. Here before us was the ginger-bread house of Hansel and Gretel. Just a few days ago we had been in a similar circumstance, but this felt different. I did not feel the usual fear of anticipation. I felt a fear low-down in my gut, echoing back through my shoulders. A primal fear, a fear of religion, of ghosts, a fear of superstitions. Even Kryszka felt it, his fear sliding through his teeth: "I do not like this." His words summed up how we all felt. We had no option but to move forward. As we entered the clearing we started to fan out automatically, self-preservation training kicking in. As we did a door opened. Light escaped to reveal a small man in the doorway. We had made little or no sound but he known we were there.

He came forward, friendly enough, and waved us on. "Come, come, your honours. Welcome, welcome!"

We entered the hovel – for that's what it was. The hut still had corn stems wrapped thickly around its walls to provide insulation. The man himself had a face just as dirty a yellow, wrinkled like a prune, stubble escaping from his jaw in black dots as though he had been peppered with gunpowder. Perhaps he had. He had dragged his leather cap from his head and stood clutching it to his chest with his left hand. Now and then he'd bend himself almost double, muttering a welcome to the noble gentlemen. Hanka he referred to as 'milady' as he gestured to us to sit at the rough table. When we were seated a crone in long dress and shawl revealed herself, rising from her place on a chest in the corner. As he placed wooden mugs in front of us she poured some honey mead 'to warm us', she said.

We all lapsed into silence, our watchful eyes taking in the features of the room, whilst the strange couple sat in the corner on their wooden chest, watching us. There was a strong smell of damp, of horses, of wood-smoke and of human bodies. A single oil lamp placed in the centre of the table gave a steady glow, making our shadows dance like a theatre as we screwed our bodies round, taking in our surroundings. In one corner there was a stove with bedding above for sleeping. Skis hung in the open rafters. Wicker baskets hung on the wall, full of bundles of dried herbs. There was a small sled by the door and near the stove a pile of logs. Above it hung a variety of dried sausage and meat, the latter from deer, I guessed.

There was a curious collection of wooden figures too. On the wall several goblin faces were carved into the dark pine bark, the cinnamon-coloured under-bark giving a lifelike fluidity to the features. I stared at one in particular.

"You like Zaria?" the woman said. She spoke with a strange accent, made stranger by an obvious impairment to her mouth. At her question the others turned to look in the direction of my 'chosen' sculpture.

"Zaria, the Morning star. Heavenly bride, and protectress of warriors. Bright maiden, the goddess of beauty," the old crone cackled. Rising and coming forward, she stood where the light caught her, revealing her smashed mouth, its front teeth missing, some broken at the side. She held her jaw and I realised she was not old after all. Or ugly. Just worn out.

She had seen me looking at her mouth and came up close, without a trace of the obsequious manner of her husband, or was it her brother? She bared her teeth at me, only inches from my face. I smelt her animal warmth. It sent a strange tingling down my spine.

"Germans!" She spat the words. "Germans came here."

As she lent close her work-grimed red blouse gaped beneath her loose blue cardigan revealing the full, soft whiteness of her breasts, which she swung toward me. A dark green, stained, thin shawl covered her shoulders. She pulled it around her, like a screen from the others view. Her hands were curiously refined, the nails well tended, nonsensical in the surroundings. Her breath came to me again as her leg pressed against mine. Then she pulled away suddenly, cackling like a demented soul.

The man joined in with her cackling too. He sat crossed legged in his grubby sweater. His hands in contrast had black dirt grimed into every line, his nails cracked or broken. There was enough dirt there to grow potatoes. He kept pointing at his mouth too, showing a mixture of gums and broken stubs. Then pulling off his cap he pointed at an ugly red star shaped wound where hair should have been growing. Perhaps the result of a rifle butt smashed to his skull. "Germans too," he kept saying. "Germans too!"

Reaching behind the wooden chest he slowly drew out an MP40 Schmeisser, oiled, the magazine loaded. All of us had flinched and involuntarily reached for our handguns. The man, however, was merely caressing the weapon and had no interest in us. "We killed the Germans," he sang. "Chopped them proper." The strange woman was nodding vigorously. "We killed Germans," she echoed, still nodding and smiling her broken toothed grimace. She waved at the other images on the walls. I followed the directive of her hand. I believe the others did too. Kryszka I sensed was now coiled and ready for anything.

She pointed at two other carvings. "See her sisters. Your Zaria welcomes the sun chariot. Here is evening star. She closes the gates at night as the sun goes down. And this," she said, reaching up and taking down a carving, "is the mistress, the goddess of this moment, the midnight star. When the sun dies in her arms she rebirths him."

I thought of the maiden, mother and crone, of the ancient goddess of the Celtic Britons. Of my days in Glastonbury.

"You know these things," the woman said. "I see it in you. I know you want it. You know the magic in me and want to plant your seed. Yes, you may recoil, but you want."

All fortune tellers-know the signs of a potential customer, their interest. They sense it. They know how to ask the question that grants answers already perceived. She knew how to flatter, this one. I went along with it, if only to annoy Kryszka, who was so obviously spooked by this half-mad couple. And for Hanka, who had the look of the child listening to a story.

"The sisters keep the hound of hell from eating the little bear in the stars." The woman looked at me strangely, a look of almost flirtation playing around her lips. My eyes were beginning to play tricks on me. I rubbed them.

"See here," she said, now addressing Hanka and me, and the others if they cared. "Here my brother has carved Jarilo who leads us now, the war God. You are named for him," she called to Kryszka. "Jerzy, or Yuri. Not for the Roman saint, my dear one, my sweet. But for the old one."

"Shut your mouth, woman!" Kryszka spat at her. He was angry, very angry. Strange, I had never known his Christian name. Yet now he made no denial of her extraordinary claim. The woman ignored him, as did her brother, who had taken to whittling a small piece of bark in the gloom. "And this is Piorun the Thunderer, chief of Gods. See his symbol." She pointed at the small hexagram with its six-pointed star, stylised to resemble a flower.

Witek, the historian, made his first comment since coming into the room. "You see that symbol everywhere, high on gable ends. A pagan lightning protector, right under the noses of the black priests."

She smiled her awful grimace again when she saw me take in the other female carving. "You are a ladies' man." Again that fleeting, coquettish look at me, but then it passed, but as though it never happened. She returned to my focus. "Marzenna! Of course!" She clapped her hands like a delighted child.

"Who is burnt in effigy on the last day of winter, as every Polish child knows." Witek was well informed as ever.

"Burnt or drowned," growled Kryszka.

"Well, I didn't know that, and I was a Polish child once too, you know." Everyone laughed and I was glad to have given us a chance to relieve our tension whilst the odd couple looked on.

"Scratch a Catholic and he bleeds a Pagan," Witek commented as we returned to our mead. The woman brought out bread and broke it for us, giving each a piece and encouraging us to take more. As we ate she sidled up to me. "Sir, shall we look through the smoke? Shall I see what there is to see?"

"Oh Christ!" intoned Kryszka. "Shut your gob, you shining one, or else the *Domowije*[ii] will have you!" She flared and turned so quickly. I immediately thought of the Germans and the word they had used: 'chopped'.

She turned to me and crooked her finger under my chin. "You want to, don't you?" The wheedling, caressing voice with that strange accent pulled at my mind, my curiosity. I felt challenged. "You know how it is done?"

She pushed Hanka to one side of the bench where she was sitting and sat opposite me. Taking off her shawl she unpinned her hair, letting it fall down her back. Moving a shallow earthenware dish from the table she placed a candle in it. She started to look for a match but Witek was already leaning over with his lighter. After a couple of strikes he lit the candle wick. "Thank you, kind sir." Again, that odd look on her face.

She tilted the candle to allow two or three hot drops to splash into the flat-based dish, then placed the candle so that it would remain upright, held by the wax dropped in the dish. The candle flared between us and she moved the oil lamp to the chest, next to her brother. The light revealed him, still whittling, with no apparent interest in the proceedings.

We stared at each other through the steadily burning flame then held hands across the table for a moment or two, settling to each other. She relaxed and we released our hands. Reaching down into her blouse she pulled aside the top buttons of her dark blue cardigan and withdrew from between her breasts a *ladanki* attached to a leather thong. She half stood. Taking the herb bag over her head she wiped it across my brow, my lips and my nose. I could smell the sweetness of almonds. The bag was damp from the sweat of her breasts. The cloth not coarse, but smooth like lawn. I liked its feel and smell.

She leaned back, resuming her seat. Undoing the neck of the bag she withdrew a pinch of herbs, sprinkling the powder to the flame which flared up instantly. We stared at each other through the flame, pupil to pupil. I knew I had to hold the gaze, no blinking. My eyes water and I strained every nerve not to lose the gaze of this witch, this magician. Her face aged, falling away.

A thousand faces screamed. A young woman smiled at me, her face lengthening then shrinking. A halo of flowers began to spin around her head. Lips reached out to mine, wet with honey, red as rubies. My gaze held and I gained strength until I felt as though I could walk on water.

I blinked. The spell was broken. I was breathing heavily. The woman was still in trance. She looked directly at Witek and spat the words, fast and hard, in a voice not her own. "Whatever you have to do, do it quickly! Be gone, son of destruction!"

I glanced at Kryszka but there was no trace of recognition on his face. I remembered the words though, spoken by Christ to Judas at the Last Supper. I tried to think through its implications, but my mind was befuddled. Witek's whole demeanour changed however. White-faced he stuttered, "Quiet, you bitch!"

The woman hastily poured water into the shallow dish and up-ended the candle, letting the wax congeal in the cold water. She blew it out and returned the oil lamp to the table

Quietly she asked me, "What did you see?"

"I saw you age, like a hag. I saw you when you were young, with flowers in your hair. I saw your lust for the old ways. I saw a million faces screaming, moving. I saw darkness, a cold blackness I heard dogs snarling. I felt as well as saw. " The memories disturbed me. "And you?"

"I saw a bear. I saw your woman waving to a bear. Another bear took you to its lair. You grew thin and twisted and you struggled. Then I saw you old too, with white hair. You could not breathe, and then it was black."

A silence developed, interrupted by Hanka. "Well, go on then. What does it mean?"

"I don't know," I responded. "I was told these things are for us to ponder and perhaps remember, when it happens, like *déjà vu*."

The woman was looking at the wax. "You see a bear." Even Kryszka had the decency to grunt his acquiescence. His curiosity had gotten the better of him. She went on. "See here, there are two men. The bear is holding them." She picked up the wax and held it to the light. It was easy to see what she was saying. A little imagination, and you could see what you wanted. "You turn it over and see the men are free of the bear. There is a face, a round face with glasses."

"Let me see that," said Witek, grabbing at the wax. She tried to hold it from him but it collapsed, perhaps aided by the warmth from the oil lamp.

"Witek, really, how could you!" exclaimed Hanka, indignant.

"Sorry folks," he said lamely.

"We go now." I had almost forgotten the man in the corner. His whittling had stopped." Collect your things." His tone was different from the one he had used before. We gathered our gear as business people, party members, inspectors.

He held out his carving to Hanka. "For you, miss, a talisman. *Dziewona*, 'the maiden'. She is like your Diana, Lords." His old whining tone returning as he spoke to us three men. Did he hate us, I wondered? How was this peasant so educated as to know Diana the huntress? Taking down a hunting rifle from the wall, he checked it and slung it over his shoulder, smiling his broken-toothed grin.

His sister opened the door. "Go," she said. "Go now my brother will do his work, follow."

Her brother gestured us to follow. "We go now the time is right, the guards change."

We went. When I looked back she had closed the door.

We stumbled through the woods in the dark, keeping rather than seeing the person in front. Hanka brought up the rear. At the edge of the woods we stopped. The ground had been cleared for about two hundred metres width. Our guide whispered that when we left our cover we must move quickly and keep in his tracks. He gave us clear instructions. I could see the transformation; he had changed from a half crazed man to a wolf at one with the darkness and certain of his ways. "The ground is rough from truck tracks and the vegetation is growing back. There are criss-cross wires to alert the guards, so you need to step high and clear. There is barbed wire here too. Where we cross you will be able to roll under, not through or over. I have some sacking which I will lay down, to keep your clothes from becoming too muddy. This is a construction area. The Russians are building a proper border to keep their people in, not us out. They use foot patrols and dogs as well as sentries. Okay, let's move. If I freeze, keep flat to the ground."

At a crouching run we crossed the open area. We did as he had directed, being especially careful of the barbed wire and wooden 'horses'. Hearing Russian voices we all sank to the ground. A strong beamed flashlight pierced the dark, but it was a long way off. Sound carried here. Standing up we eased our limbs. At last we'd reached the shelter of the woods. The crossing had probably taken no more than ten minutes, but it had felt an hour.

Now we followed a more defined path, which threaded its way through the woods. At their edge we found cultivated fields.

"Here I leave you," our guide said. "Follow the field path. At the top of the grass bank you will find the dirt road which leads to the rail line. Turn left, keep following the tracks. The station halt is no more than half a kilometre away. There are houses the other side of the railway. You may see some early rising villagers aiming to catch the train for market before the main station. The Russians use the halt to do some last sorting of deportees from the East before the border. They don't use the station themselves as it might upset the natives," he guffawed. "Best of luck, my lords. May all the spirits be with you! I return now to my ancestors. You should be lucky;

tonight the frontier seems very quiet." With that, he vanished into the night like a cat.

We pressed on. Sure enough, at the top of the bank was the road. "Listen up," said Witek, "we do not know who will be at the halt. Maybe a policeman or two, or some villagers, as he said. I suggest we break up so as not to be so conspicuous. You two," he indicated Kryszka and I, "keep together. You look like officials, like inseparable twins. Plus you will get away with any questions from petty police or militia. Try to talk Russian less like a Romanov," he nodded at Kryszka.

"Hanka and I will cross to the village and come at the halt from different directions. We can meet up again once we're on the train. It's due in at ten, but it could be any time."

We had hours to wait and soon fell to silence.

The distant crack of a high-power rifle split the air, making us jump. The hairs on the back of my neck stood up. The echo of the single shot seemed to ricochet round and around the field edge like a bullet. Then silence.

"Perhaps he shot a deer," observed Kryszka, then shrugged his shoulders. We settled down in the cold to our own thoughts. Gradually the night sky separated into a band of indigo, brilliant blue and yellow. The morning star shone bright and beautiful. The day began to stir itself in home, farm, field and woodland. Sounds began to drift in the crisp early morning mist.

Time passed until finally Kryszka and I strolled down to the halt, where there was a stone and block station building. A couple of outbuildings stood to one side. One had a trail of rusting rails leading to it so I assumed it to be a derelict engine shed. A wide gravelled walkway, fighting with grass for dominance of the open space, indicated where the train stopped. Further on were the signals and a water tower. On the other side of the tracks the village with its houses sloped gently away, running eventually into Shehyni.

Witek was at the far end of the space. We settled close to the building which seemed to serve as a ticket point. A railway workman eyed us suspiciously. Several peasants stood around with bundles and baskets. They looked at us surreptitiously. We returned their glances with the haughty look of the party official, seeming like men in charge, untouchable by ordinary mortals. A horse and cart piled high with roots stood silently by. The horse, a beautiful chestnut with a honey-blonde mane, regarded us with complete disinterest. I marvelled at the way the peasant owner had added red trappings to its harness. This was not a special day, it was an 'every' day. I wondered if he took this extra time each morning to make his horse and harness look so well. Traditions were powerful.

Kryszka and I spoke idly of the strange couple we had met. They were not nationalist heroes; we had seen Witek pass money to the man. Perhaps they lived by people-smuggling or black market. Who could tell? There was a whole world of lost people.

"No Hanka yet," muttered Kryszka.

"She's cutting it fine," I agreed with the obvious. But my statement implied a question.

Far away a train whistled.

"Must have left the shunting yard and check point," muttered Kryszka.

"Come on, Hanka," I said to the air and stamped my feet to get some circulation going. I needed to pee.

Turning to find a wall or suitable tree, I saw Hanka come into view on our right, the other side of the track. She was haring down the village dirt road where it sloped away from the village, curving past the houses to cross the track close to the horse and cart. She was shouting and waving. Running at speed she left the road at the curve and bounded across the small field, straight at us.

We heard her shout – "Russians!" Almost simultaneously a group of khaki figures came into sight, in pursuit of Hanka. She was now only fifty metres away, the Russians about double that behind her. She stumbled, just as one of the troops stopped and loosed off a round. Without thinking I dropped to my knee. Steadying myself I took aim over my left arm. Too far for real accuracy, but the flash and crack might do some good and make them pause. As I sighted the pistol the blue caps of the advancing troops were clear. NKVD men, Special Interior troops.

I fired twice, aware of the hustle and shouts behind me, assuming Kryszka and Witek were taking up the fight. Perhaps the civilians had panicked. As my second shot went off a blow to my shoulder knocked me to the ground. As I fell, I part spun. A rifle butt was coming down to my right shoulder, its brass stock gleaming against the blue sky. It seemed to take an age to fall yet it came quicker than I could raise my pistol. Behind the stock I glimpsed a young face under a blue cap with its red star. I squirmed at the coming blow. Strong hands seized me, turning me face down on the gravel. There was a sharp stab in the top of my shoulder.

I screamed. "Dog's blood!" The words seemed to echo into a blackness so thick it stopped me from breathing. The pressure on my back eased. Far away I saw a pin-prick of light.

CHAPTER 8

# TERROR

The mind plays tricks and wanders to many places. I was not there when Aniela was arrested, but I know how it happened. It was the same for all. Those who survived had time to listen to each others' stories sitting together, backs to the cold cell walls. The stories were always the same. She would have told her story to a willing listener, saying something like this:-

"After the others were arrested, three motors came to a halt outside my apartment in Jan Matejko Street. I looked out of the window to see UB troops and some civilians jumping from their cars. 'Don't panic,' I thought to myself. 'Keep calm, they may not have come for you.' Even so, my heart was pounding. My breath coming in short bursts. You could hear the silence behind my neighbour's doors as their boots clattered up stairs. Smell the relief as the boots passed their doors.

They did not pass my door. Fists pounded and there was nothing else I could do but open to them, first the inner door and then the outer. Men pushed past me, ignoring me. Two men out of uniform, in suits and ties, brought up the rear.

"Aniela Radimirska?" one of them demanded

"Yes." Nothing else was said.

From the living-room came sounds of search and destruction. The breaking of glass and china. My wardrobe was pulled away from the wall and crashed to the ground. Drawers were pulled open, contents scattered. Photographs, books, clothes, underwear, all my personal things were trampled.

I could see it. The sacredness of a life now represented by detritus on the floor.

"Terrible. Like Nazis." I whispered it to myself but he heard me, the youngest one. Pleasant-looking if I'd seen him anywhere else, with deep brown eyes.

"Madam" he told me, "in comparison with the NKVD, the Gestapo methods were child's play."

"You're not the Polish UB then?" I asked him. Somehow it seemed important.

"One and the same, Madam, one and the same."

The older of the two turned me round, caught my wrists and handcuffed them behind my back. The pace of destruction slowed. A uniformed NCO saluted the older man.

"Nothing so far."

"Come!" the man said, roughly pushing me through the door. "Kratko, go ahead of her to make sure she doesn't throw herself downstairs or something stupid."

He held onto the cuffs at my wrist, propelling me awkwardly along the landing. As she started downstairs he pulled my arms up and back, controlling my every step. It hurt my arms and shoulders. Outside I was pushed into a car, a trooper either side. The harsh plain-clothes man sat in the front. His younger associate was gone. I felt so hopeless and panicky. He told the driver to come straight here, to the new headquarters of the UB. As I was driven away, curtains twitched and I could imagine the people in the other flats sigh in relief."

Kryszka and I knew more of how it worked. Knew more about who was watching and why. On Aniela's landing were two other flats. I could well imagine her next door neighbour Mr. Nowak placing a glass against the wall, to amplify the sound, listening to everything he could. What had he done when everything was quiet? When Aniela had gone?

The mind wanders. Sometimes I saw him in my imagination, picking up the phone, dialling an old friend. I could hear it ring. Hear the man's voice as it answered.

"Hello, Antek, this is Bartek. There has been an incident today and I feel a bit bothered. From the noise next door the place was wrecked. It was good to see our boys raiding such bandits, but it is disturbing all the same. I am going to bring a gramophone record over, is that ok with you?"

And the response. "Yes, certainly, do come. I'll expect you in an hour or so."

What had Mr. Nowak done then? If everything had gone to plan he'd taken a small suitcase from the top of his wardrobe. Found a couple of screwdrivers? Where would he have hidden the key? In his dead father's prized Stein? It was tall, fat, big and jolly with majolica decoration. I remembered. I could see him in my mind's eye, slipping out his door, closing it quietly. See him pause and listen. See how he opened Aniela's door and quickly close it behind him. Had he even noticed the destruction as he quickly crossed to the gramophone? Did he stand on broken tango records as he started to unscrew the precious radio from its wooden housing? It was a brilliant place to hide the obvious, I had to admit.

Hopefully the young woman who had moved into the flat below in recent weeks hadn't seen him leave. A returnee from the East, I had noticed her immediately, a bottle blonde, low class. I had no doubt she had been given the job of keeping the building 'clean'. As all private housing was becoming state-owned, such jobs were in the gift of the local authority. Her name was Dorota or something.

If she had seen Nowak go into the flat, if she'd seen him come out, she would have picked up the phone and dialled the number the UB had given her weeks before. No doubt she had some poor bastard of a husband deported somewhere. She would desperately want him home. If Nowak had been spotted, this was her chance. She would never tell what she had done.

Antek would be waiting for Nowak with the precious radio. He'd already know he was possibly compromised, though if Bartek had stuck to the plan the phone call would have sounded innocuous enough, even if the UB had been tapping his phone. There would already be another courier at his house, waiting to carry the vital radio to another operator.

Antek, as an officer in WiN, knew only too well the operational methods of the NKVD and its child, the Polish UB. The Communist State was slowly but surely in Poland, as well as in Soviet Russia, controlling every aspect of life from art to radio broadcasts, politics to theatre. Permeating everywhere, it weakened and demoralised people, creating a world of blackmailed informers and agents. He would know what to do.

*Dear God, let him have sent Jagoda to warn Ela.* Let him have sent her the message, 'Don't come back.'

It was in another world that word came to me from an eyewitness of what followed. I saw transcriptions too. I was able Kryska the bear facts. I would tell him no more. I recreated the scene. I had to, to purge myself.

Aniela would have been talkative. Nerves did that to some people. The talking helped them feel in control, even when they knew that they were powerless. I could imagine her joking that she was gasping for a cigarette. Anything to stop the fear, even for a second. I imagined how she felt, waiting in quiet dread. How did she feel when the silence of the cell was shattered? When she was quickly bundled us up the steps and into a bare reception room where she was left alone?

I played the scene over and over in my head, time and time again. Saw her take in the windows that had been whitewashed over, see the rough iron bars had been hastily set into the frame.

I saw every detail. How two women suddenly come into the room. The older and larger was dressed in the uniform of the UB, the younger and better looking one wore a smart black suit, white shirt and red tie. Secret Police. I could hear one of the officers barking at Aniela:

"You are Comrade Aniela Wanda Radimirska?"

She was plucky. That would be a good ploy, to show she was not afraid, to sound indignant. "Yes, I am Aniela Radimirska. Of what am I accused? Why am I here?"

"You are an enemy of the State and a Western lackey," the older of the two barked back in heavily accented, Russified Polish.

"Strip to your underwear!" the younger one said, by her speech a native Pole. "Do as I tell you, you stupid, stuck-up cow." The younger woman advanced face to face with Aniela, stabbing her finger into Aniela's chest with such force she was pushed across the room. "Now strip!"

Aniela undid her tweed skirt, letting it drop to the ground. "I bought this before the war," she said absentmindedly as she took it off. "The tailor told me it would last forever."

"Shoes!" barked the woman.

Next she slipped her blouse over her head. Cream, with little puffed short sleeves. Three or four buttons were set into the ruched top, darts fitting it to the waist. Aniela, so careful with her clothes, loved that blouse. She knew it gave her a good line, showed her figure. This left her in her under slip, a beige satin with brown lace trimming.

"Stockings and suspenders!" came the next bark. These stockings or 'nylons' were a treasured gift from a Kryszka. Aniela took them off carefully. She struggled with her French knickers; the suspender belt she wore under them had to come off. The whole episode was humiliating, two women watching her every movement.

"You may as well leave your knickers off, bitch," growled the big woman.

"That'll do," the younger one said. Aniela stood there as the two women picked up her clothes carefully looking at them. "Watch!" the big woman demanded and snatched at Aniela's wrist. She spotted Aniela's wedding ring too. A tussle began to get it off. For the first time Aniela showed emotion. She began to plead. "No, please, no!" But they took it anyway. The two women left and the door slammed.

We were left alone in the room. Aniela tried the door at the far side of the room but it was locked. She tried the other door but no luck either. She stood at the window and with her spit tried to rub a small hole in the whitewash but it would not budge. In the end she sat on the floor bringing her knees to her chin, arms wrapped around them for warmth. She waited.

The far door opened. A uniformed figure stood framed against the light. He walked in, hands behind his back. He walked around Aniela, deliberately looking her up and down. She turned as he walked around, trying to look at him eye to eye, to challenge him.

"Stand there!" he said, pointing to a place in front of a wooden table on which was a set of files. A uniformed woman sat down at another table. She had a sort of typewriter in front of her. The man placed his polished boots on the table and leant back in his chair, apparently examining his nails.

"My name is Kuczarek. You are here to be interrogated about your illegal activities against the Polish People's Republic. We know you have been serving as a radio operator for that gang of bandits in London pretending to be a government. Now I need to know your code name and your call sign." The officer spoke quietly, without looking at Aniela.

She came back at him. "I don't know what you are talking about. It is the present government which is illegal."

He sighed. He took his boots off the table and sat up. He just stared at her. "This is tiresome," he said. He got up and walked round to her, his face inches from hers. He suddenly grasped her jaw between fingers and thumb squeezing, twisting his hand, forcing into her throat. She gulped and gagged. He relaxed his grip, still staring eye to eye. Walking back to his seat he resumed his previous position. She swallowed hard feeling her bruised throat. She lifted her hand to feel the ligaments of her jaw. She was convinced they had been torn.

Quiet returned.

"See that wall?" He pointed at the wall to his left, where the young uniformed woman typist had begun typing.

"Go stand against the wall, facing it." Aniela did as she was told.

"Now reach upward, hands flat on the wall." Again, she did as she was told.

"Reach up, up, higher. On your toes. Flat against the wall."

She would have heard his footsteps coming close. Felt his breath on her neck. He moved back a little, allowing her to sense the space in between them then shoved a polished wooden baton between her legs. The baton end pushing into the wall, dragging her slip tight against her buttocks and thighs.

"Legs apart, Madam." Aniela shuffled, tightening the trapped slip against her legs. "Up, up," he softly crooned. The baton, held straight to the wall, was pushing up against her pubic bone.

"Up, up." She stretched upward, avoiding the pressure.

She let out a small gasp at the effort. The baton lowered slightly in response. Aniela relaxed slightly to the lessened pressure. Slowly the baton left the wall. She concentrated on every micro movement, fearing, sensing, listening. The air seemed electric. The baton moved backward, so very slowly, tracing the curve and clefts of Aniela's body. Drawing back it parted her buttocks. Her lips and throat were dry. The baton continued its journey backward. The angle changing as its head rose.

"Oh God, oh God!" Her fear was in each syllable.

The baton rose, forcing against the satin, causing pressure, relieved only as she flattened and drew higher to the wall. The baton followed to the point where she could go no further. Fearing the pain, Aniela shifted slightly, only to feel the baton slip higher. She arched slightly to receive its entry. The baton eased away. She waited and it returned more sharply. Aniela jerked with surprise but was forced to meet it. It was withdrawn slightly and came gently seeking again. Aniela did not want pain. She shifted to meet it. It came and went, never quite penetrating. It developed a rhythm and she followed, slowly sinking down the wall, inevitably lower, till flat on her feet and using the wall to support her she leant into the seeking baton. Hips raised, legs parted, receiving and responding to the rhythm of the baton. Suddenly, on the point she expected penetration, it stopped. She would heard footsteps walking away.

"Sit." He ordered quietly.

She moved from the wall, conscious of her slip caught within her cleft. Conscious of its wetness as she pulled it free. Caught between fear and shame, the shame of fear and its power to demoralise. She had given in. It was a battle.

"You see how easy it is, to become our creature? You already see how easy it to accept the inevitable. But as you have just seen, cooperating can alleviate suffering, stop pain and save time and trouble, comrades. I will leave you to think things over."

Some underclothes and a shift were thrown into her cell.

They came again in the night, in the cold before dawn. A desk, a light, a chair with straps in front. Another chair with a white enamel bowl of water. Steam rising from it. A white towel hung from its back. To the side of the door the woman officer in skirt and shirt. She sat at the desk with her stenographic machine.

And so the questions began. "You are a bandit and wish to end your crimes? You belong to a Fascist organisation and you communicate with British spies?" When Aniela refused to respond he pressed a buzzer and two troopers came into the room. One grasped her shoulders, forcing her to the chair, whilst the other strapped her hands to a chair. They then started on her legs. She struggled out of reflex, self-preservation, but she knew there was no point it was an involuntary reaction.

The troopers left. Silence for a while. Aniela had wet herself, the warm urine running down her legs. The questioning began again. He loomed over her, suddenly shouting loudly in her ear, the same questions over and over.

At first the slaps were gentle, but they increased in tempo and violence until they were bouncing her head from side to side. His questions were shouted in her ear.

A cuff across her face split her lip. Some of her teeth would be gone. She spat blood. There was a brief respite as the officer walked to the wash basin and rinsed his hands of blood. He wiped his hands on the towel, turning it pink.

"Yes," he said, "your blood."

He pressed the buzzer again. The troopers returned with a machine. Electrical terminals and dials. They plugged it in, trailing two wires toward her, each end of attached to a crocodile clip. He came around behind Aniela, gently lifting her slip straps over her shoulder exposing her brassiere. As the slip fell she saw that it was splattered with blood. He reached inside her bra, grasping and groping her breast. She tried to struggle as he grasped at a nipple and pinched, hard and long. For the first time Aniela screamed.

Then she wept.

"Just answer the questions. It will get worse," he said.

"Go to hell!" she gasped.

He nodded. A trooper came forward, pulling her bra up over her breasts. She whimpered. The crocodile clips were attached, forcing their teeth into the sensitive shrunken flesh. Aniela shouted and as the current was sent surging through the wires the shout turned to a long scream, her body convulsing with the current.

The flow stopped. Aniela breathed heavily, exhausted. The trooper undid the straps.

She heard someone say as though far away, "Enough." She could hardly walk and was supported as she staggered to a cell. At the doorway she felt someone force a bottle to her lips and she gulped water, spilling it over her front. She collapsed and passed out, slowly coming to an hour or so later.

That night the cell was cold. There was a miserable grey blanket.

"Not what you are used to, Aniela," she mumbled to herself when she awoke.

"I hope it doesn't have fleas," she joked out loud as a way of relief from pain and tension, needing to hear a human voice if only her own. Even in her present condition there was a battle between self-respect and survival and gave in to the necessity of the rough, grey duffle blanket. She gave in to the necessity of the rough grey duffle blanket.

My cheeks are throbbing. My chest hurts." Aniela spoke the words out loud into the cold cell light. She felt her ribs, checked her teeth gingerly with her tongue. She felt they must be loose but was relieved to find only one gap. The hole felt enormous and she snivelled at the thought of it. Gingerly she felt her split lip, now crusted with dried blood. She felt her nipples spitting on her fingers to give some healing comfort.

She slid into sleep but was woken by the sound of screaming and boots echoing down the corridor. The noise went on and on. She wondered how long she had been asleep. There was the sound of boots and doors slamming. The grill on the door was pushed open violently, then closed, more boots echoing, and the cell door was flung open.

"Out, out!" someone bellowed into the space, the sound magnified in the small cell.

Momentarily blinded by the light Aniela clutched her blanket, holding it like a talisman, but it was dragged from her. She was marched, shoved and pushed to the same office where, at the right hand desk the same stenographer was waiting, the same officer was waiting, smoking. The same bowl of water and white towel. But this time there was a stool, no chair. The officer came around the desk as Aniela sat on the stool, waiting. He stood over her.

She was trembling.

Her hair was pulled so hard she thought it would come out by the roots as he yanked her up right to her feet. For a second she was suspended but had no time to cry out as he roared in her ear, "Did I tell you to sit? You are a non-person, you are a worm. You do not exist. Fascist filth does not sit before their betters."

He punched her so hard in the stomach she convulsed, falling forward. As her head came down she caught the glint of the brass knuckle duster that smashed her cheek bone, jerking her up to a standing position. Her legs collapsed and she fell to the floor. His boot toe caught her in her private parts. She began to scream as the boot landed again. She vomited.

The stenographer winced with each thud. That session Aniela told her code name. Later that day, in another session of beatings, she gave her call sign. In yet another session she gave the names of Antek and Mr. Nowak. In the early hours of the morning, in yet another session, she said whatever they wanted. A form was pushed at her, which she signed. She had no idea what it said. She was now blind in one eye and whimpered when she was dragged from the room by two guards.

She was on her knees when the bullet exploded her skull. She had no sense of it happening, a moment of kindness, a blankness. Perhaps she was simply trying to remember where she remembered the smell from. The smell of faeces and fear that the cattle gave off when the butcher called to cull the cattle. The UB men checked she was dead, and each taking one arm dragged her outside to the concrete yard.

They left her body beside another prisoner, a half-dressed man who seemed to have his arms and legs set in a grotesque position like a broken puppet. She would never have recognised her Mr. Nowak now. They called to another trooper who was smoking, leaning nonchalantly against the wall in the bright sunshine, enjoying the warmth. They shared a joke: "Another one for the forest dump, Timofei." A Ukrainian name.

"Polish fertiliser," the trooper quipped. They laughed. Times were good for these men, after all. They had food, clothing, shelter, and their families were well provided for. And what is more, they had power, the power of the People!

The hatchet came down. The hands were tossed to one side, onto a growing pile.

"Leave the heads on. The saw is blunt" came a call. "No one is going to check. Give us a hand, boys, to move this shit. I need to get them up in the lorry."

The trooper carelessly threw aside his half-finished smoke. "God, this job is as bad as heaving potatoes on the farm," he observed as both bodies were heaved into the truck.

In the office the young woman stenographer was recording: 'Aniela Radimirska, Fascist bandit, shot while escaping.' Would it have given Aniela peace to know that later that night the same stenographer wrote up her report, passing it to a WiN trustee in the intelligence unit? That she recorded everyone who died that day? The names of the interrogators, the survivors, the stool pigeons, the dead. Naïve but brave, risking her own life, which was soon to end. But her record survived.

Many have seen her records. They exist. I Tadek Labycz read this account.

****

Kryszka shivered. His body was battered and bruised but he was alive for some reason. He stood in his cell facing an open window to the cool night air. He shrugged his bruised shoulders. The cell was too small to lie down in, just large enough for him to force his body down and knees up. The steel door or wall was cold against his back.

The bruised soles of his feet throbbed. He wondered if the cigarette burns on his chest would scar. He wondered why they had left the nails on his hands and chosen his toes. Perhaps they had a foot fetish. His penis was suppurating from the crocodile clips.

He had said nothing. Grinning through aching jaw, split lip and missing teeth he thought he must look like that half crazy guy who guided them over the border. He had given them two names. One in England and one here in Poland. Both men were good Communists, but now they would die as his interrogators had been convinced by him of their treachery to People's Poland. It was a way to take some with him, he thought.

He thought of Aniela all the time. It was her vision and those few happy days that gave him succour, support. Her name was safe with him deep in the recesses of his mind they would never find her name.

He liked being an animal. They had reduced him to being an animal. So he was as cunning as an animal, just like the man in the forest who was no longer as crazy as Kryszka at first had understood him to be but crippled in mind. *Just like me*, he thought.

He shuddered and shook at the thought of the stool. They had to force him to it at first but the second time he had gone to it like the animal he had become. The stool had a small spike which was shoved into the rectum. The victim was forced to sit on the stool to avoid a beating or worse. If the question was not answered sufficiently the stool was kicked from under you.

Kryszka thought in the third person. He could not put himself on the stool in his own mind.

The stool jagged into the rectum, splitting it and causing haemorrhaging.

It punched back into the prostate causing such a dull aching pain that you howled – not screamed. It hurt now, throbbing as Kryszka thought of these tortures. His buttocks clenched as he dismissed the thoughts, concentrating on a tango a long way away.

Still he had signed his confession and told them of his war record and, yes, he had told them many names of people in the Polish Air Force in Britain, but he knew most were still there, safe. He had spoken of his mission to find Sikorski's daughter. He could not puzzle out why they had not asked him about Tadek Labycz. He had given the name but they showed no interest. He still had secure his contacts here in Poland or Ukraine or wherever he was. The men whom he saw were both Poles and Russians.

He coughed and he tasted blood, but it was too dark to check.

They were coming for him now, he could hear them. He cried as he thought of Aniela.

*I am tired. I cannot go on.*

The door opened and he fell outward at the feet of the guards. In the light of the passage he briefly glimpsed what he thought was a chef, all in white. Then he passed out.

The hospital doctor adjusted his high white hat, and gave Kryszka an injection muttering, "He is critical".

The guards rolled him to a stretcher and followed behind the hurrying doctor.

# CHAPTER 9

# SLOWLY YOU DIE

There was the sound of engines far away in the distance, doors slamming. Nothingness, a train and the smell of straw, a rocking motion that sent me to a deep sleep. There were wide marshes and storks overflying my home, in another time.

I woke with a stinking headache. My temples throbbed, the back of my neck felt as though a sledge-hammer had hit it. My shoulder felt bruised and at the top of my shoulder I felt the ache from where the hypodermic had been stabbed into me. I was naked. I could see nothing. Slowly and delicately I moved my finger-tips around my torso, then my limbs, searching for further injury. With relief I found that I seemed sound enough.

It was pitch black and cold. I felt the floor. Rough-cast concrete. The walls were damp and curved up and inward beyond my reach. Water ran down the walls in some places. From the feel I guess they were moss-covered.

My throat was parched and tongue swollen. I could feel the damp air, deep in my lungs. I recognised the dryness of the anaesthetic. I licked the wall for water, too dehydrated to care about hygiene. For a while I lay there, reliving my last moments of consciousness. Then I called out, my voice echoing around the chamber. No response, so I assumed I was alone. As my mind cleared I shouted more loudly. In the echo I heard my voice, in English. I had expected to hear Polish, but the brain is a plaything to drug-gists. My brain told me to relax, that I wasn't functioning properly through the drug.

Eventually, as sense returned, I felt around the edges of the room. It was very long but quite narrow from side to side. I crawled around the rectangle on my hands and knees. In one corner was a hole, and, by the ordure on my hands and the smell, I guessed it to be a latrine or drain. I tried to wipe my hands clean on the wall. I was alone here now, but others had clearly gone before me, leaving their fear in the latrine and I guessed elsewhere. I sank to the ground, shivered and waited, knowing this waiting was part of the game to come.

A door slammed. I heard people. Though it was still black I felt the presence of others. Suddenly torches flashed at me, onto me, into my eyes, flashing continually on and off. I put my hands over my face as the lights strobed. Somewhere someone was banging hard on metal, making my ears ring as the noise echoed round the chamber. A jet of icy cold water threw me against the wall and then followed me as I twisted away from it. Water forced its way to my mouth. Its power sent me spinning to the floor and across the concrete. The lights dazzled me, the noise disoriented.

It stopped as suddenly as it began. A door slammed.

I lay there, wet, cold and, I realised, bloody hungry, which cheered me. At least hunger made me feel alive. My thoughts were not of terror but of hope; hope that the hosing had reached the latrine corner. I wondered if the mess had been cleared. I crawled in what I thought was the right direction but realised I had been taken by the water to the far end of the chamber. I crawled back along the chamber edge. And found the sink hole. It smelled fresher but I found solids that reeked as my hands searched. 'Well,' my brain teased me, 'let's take some good out of adversity. If I am to crawl in shit, let it be mine.' I heard myself chuckle, then giggle, a high pitched sound that eerily bounced back to me. I rolled over and wept, for everything. For the fact that I was on my own.

The waiting game began again, and again, and again, and again, and again...and again they came. Each time I crawled and scrabbled to the latrine corner, searching for mess. I swept the floor with my hands. I was an untouchable from India, a lavatory cleaning inspector. I began to talk to myself.

"You keep hosing this place down so I can eat off the floor! See, you bastards, you missed a bit. Huh? You think you have me, but you're just doing what I want, you filthy dog's blood mother fuckers!" I mumbled, sometimes I shouted. I asked myself if there were hidden microphones. I counted regularly between their coming and going, to see if they were clock-watching.

I knew this was a battle for my mind. A battle of deprivation, cold, hunger, fear, and a slow loss of physical strength. But they *wanted* something, I reasoned, so they would feed me something.

They came again. Before the door slammed a Russian voice seemed to call, "Food, pig!" Then silence, except for the ringing in my assaulted eardrums. I lay still for a moment, letting my senses settle and my brain calm. I got up on all fours and carried out my now established routine of shaking myself like a dog, then squeezing my hair as dry as possible. Next I would stand and slap my body with my hands to keep the blood circulating. I realised this cost energy, but I had taken a bet with the universe that they wanted me alive, so that if I keeled over they would want me enough to get me up again.

I was convinced I had heard the word 'food'. Or perhaps I dreamt it? I abandoned my latrine duties and frantically began a search of the floor. Perhaps there was a bowl or something. I stopped my search and thought it through. I began to sniff like a dog. I could smell something. It smelt 'warm', if that were possible.

I followed my nose, my hand sweeping in front of me. There was something on the floor. No plate, but a warm rough thing. I picked it, feeling the tough, warty skin. I tasted it. Potato. I wolfed it down. I found another. After a careful search, nothing else.

I must have slept. Because when they came again I was stunned by the hosing, the lights, the sound. This time there were dogs barking, and I could smell them. I cringed and whimpered. The hose fell to a trickle. I could feel the dogs' breath, inches from my face. I didn't want to be bitten on the face. I flapped my hands in front of me. The door slammed. I searched like a pig, nose to ground. No potato.

They were gaining. I was losing. I thought of those women and children, cooped up in cattle trucks for days. If they could hold out, so could I. At least I had water, they often they went days without. At least I was clean; they became louse-infested. They shared a hole or bucket with no privacy, I had my own en suite facilities. I was trained to resist interrogation, they were not. But then, of course, they were not to be interrogated. Just enslaved and/or worked to death. Or shot.

These contrasts were my resistance strategy. My mind had to remain mine. I knew my real enemy was panic and fear.

After another one of the 'events', which was the name I gave to them, I convinced myself I had heard the word 'food'. Sure enough, I found another two potatoes and some slimy stuff which, from the smell, might be cabbage but I ate it anyway. This time I ate slowly.

The worst part was the cold.

I had no idea how long I had been in the chamber. Was it a day? Days? I tried to remember how many 'water events' had taken place. But I could not.

"Oh, mother," I found myself whimpering, "I don't know why I am here. How did I get into this fight? I want to go home and fly again. I want to be normal."

I thought of Hanka and her fatalistic Jewish attitude to life. Should I just roll over too, accept what was coming? The door opened and I stood up, ready to 'fight'.

A voice barked, "Come here!" and a pool of light indicated the direction. Blinking, I staggered forward, following the dancing torch beam snaking a pathway on the floor. I was caught unawares as the rough sack was pulled over my head. My hands were grasped and handcuffed behind my back. I panicked and peed. Cold steel was roughly attached to my ankles and I realised I was being shackled too. I struggled but it was a waste. A blanket was hung over my shoulders, coarse but warming.

An order was barked. "Forward!" and I was shoved from behind. I shuffled forward. I couldn't see through the sack but it allowed in some light. I twisted my head around, to see if there were any gaps or more open weaves and received a clip round the head from the guard behind for my trouble. I hated this hood. It amplified yet muffled sound. Made my breath warm and moist, tickling my nose unbearably. The smallest things become torture when you are already suffering. I felt I was suffocating, even though my rational brain told me I had plenty of air.

We turned left and I realised we had entered another room.

"Kneel," came the order. This was impossible for me and I lost my balance, falling forward, banging my head against a wall. A guard pulled me up and back violently. My imagination ran riot. *Was this it? Bullet or garrotte?*

A voice barked some unintelligible Russian, followed by a voice in Polish.

"Prisoners, you will remain silent, upright, kneeling until called for. If you change your position you will be beaten."

I wondered if the others were there; Witek, Kryszka, Hanka? I tried to call through the sacking, 'Kryszka!' The soles of my feet were pummelled by a truncheon or something hard. I shut up.

Not quite silence. This quietness was not empty. It felt of humans. There were odd sounds of movement as prisoners eased their position slightly. Guards were present. Occasionally they walked up and down, their boots clomping along the line. I had to keep my brain alert. I calculated that the room would be about nine metres by six metres.

A door opened. Someone was dragged protesting from the room.

Someone groaned and a flurry of blows followed. "Up, you scum, up!" I guessed someone had given out and slumped.

It was agony, kneeling there. Already weak, I had that feeling of a sick emptiness in my stomach born of hunger. My head was thumping for lack of fuel. The small of my back was aching. My shoulders, pulled back by the cuffs, were throbbing, so I had to wriggle them, chafing my wrists. My knees were pierced by shooting pains. I eased myself toward the wall I knew to be in front of me.

'Whack!' My feet were hit again drawing an involuntary yelp from me. I concentrated my gaze on a chink of light in the weave and mesmerised myself to an inner stillness. I saw Ela again, her sunshine and warmth. She smiled at me and spoke, but I couldn't hear her words.

My turn came when time had slipped to myriad visions of colour and people I had hurt and things I should have done. Whilst I sought the refuge of stillness my mind disobeyed me, chattering time away. But I had survived. Guards hauled me roughly to my feet. Of course my legs gave way. Pain stabbed me from toe to groin. The guards kept moving, indifferent to my plight. Half stumbling, half dragged, I moved along passages and up steps. As the blood returned to my legs I became more aware and upright.

We entered a room. I was told to sit and was pushed to a chair.

I felt fingers fumbling at the back of my neck. The hood was pulled from my head. *Oh, blessed light.* At first I thought I had been blinded; my eyes wouldn't focus. But gradually my sight settled. Immediately in front of me was a wooden table with heavy graining, lime-washed like a kitchen table. Two worn, thick, black leather straps were attached to it by copper rivets or bolts. The buckles were encrusted with verdegris and menacingly attached to my side of the table. One bright bulb shone from a wide enamel shade, providing a pool of light. But the shade cast gloom to the recesses and across the table. A fog of cigarette smoke hung in the air, drifting towards me. To one side was a large stone sink and single, high brass faucet, also greened with age.

Behind the desk in the half-light were three figures in olive drab; one sitting, two standing. I remember how the central figure had a polished Sam-Browne belt. He leaned forward, both hands on the table. Fat, pudgy hands, swollen fingers. On his right hand was a brass knuckle duster, its rings glinting in the light. Further to the right of his hand was a Tokarev pistol. The menace so very obvious.

"NKVD?" I managed to speak although my words were slurred.

The man opposite replied. "You are a little dated, my friend, as are most Poles. Living in the past, connected to your so-called 'Exile Government', which no one recognises since Comrade Stalin our Great Leader trounced your spineless western leaders at Yalta."

He had said this in a very relaxed way, his words not matching the menace of the table. He continued. "This is an MGB office, secret police, you understand? In March 1946, all of the People's Commissariats were restructured as Ministries. The NKVD was renamed the MVD of the USSR, along with its former subordinate the NKGB, which became the MGB, the Ministry of State Security of the USSR. The NKVDs of all the Republics in the Union also became Ministries of Internal Affairs but, please note, subordinate to MVD of the USSR. This is your first political lesson. So no more NKVD please. You are, as they say, in the clutches of the MGB. Or of Viktor Semyonovich Abakumov." The final words had a twist of menace. His lips smiled the words but his eyes did not.

"Is that your name?" I asked ingenuously. Abakumov, the leader of the MGB, was well known and notoriously brutal.

All three laughed as though I had made a joke. "As a foreigner you might get to meet him some day, but pray you do not. He is our chief and he likes to do things himself." He tapped his knuckle duster.

I stared at what I could make out through the smoke and light. All I could see was uniforms. I had to concentrate. The first rule of interrogation, concentrate on details. Observe. Look at things. Occupy the mind, focus on cracks in the wall, anything to occupy the mind and keep it from the moment. It was important to me, for my survival, to focus on detail, however trivial.

The angle of the light highlighted uniforms and obscured faces, except that of the man opposite. This central figure wore a *kitel*, single-breasted and fastened with five large brass buttons which caught the light as he moved. It had a high collar, fastened, I assumed, with hook and eyes or poppers, as no buttons were evident. The *kitel* had two breast pockets with flaps. I wondered if that was where he kept his cigarettes. His left hand held a smoking cigarette. Occasionally he tipped the ash to the floor. The hand withdrew every now and again, beyond the pool of light, and a fog of smoke danced into the lamplight, curling through the halo of brightness as he inhaled before blowing the smoke in my direction. Royal blue piping surrounded the cuffs and his collar edges. The material seemed to be gabardine, the *kitel* colour a dark olive drab.

All three, I could see, wore dark blue breeches and black leather high boots. The central figure boasted shoulder service boards made of gold braid. Like the brass buttons they were catching the light and glittering through the gloom. Royal blue stripes and piping, with silver stars.

I assumed him to be a major. His companions standing more in the background were dressed differently. One wore an officer's *gymnastiorka*, that uniquely Russian style of pull-over shirt. The *gymnastiorka* had an opening extending about half-way down from the neck hole, fastened with three small brass buttons. It had, I knew, a high collar fastened with two more small brass buttons, but this was out of my vision. I could see his sleeves ending in cuffs fastened with two buttons each, with cuff piping in royal blue, contrasting with the khaki of his shirt. He displayed, as far as I could see when he moved to smoke, olive cloth shoulder boards with royal blue stripes and maroon rank bars. A junior officer I assumed.

The light reflecting from the table surface was dazzling me now.

The last man to the right of him also wore a *gymnastiorka* shirt. His was identical to the officer's field *gymnastiorka*, except that it had no breast pockets and no piping. It too was a khaki colour with buttons that did not shine. He too wore shoulder boards, but in plain dark maroon with the same royal blue piping. 'An enlisted man,' I caught myself thinking, 'but enlisted for what?'

The cigarette was thrown to one side. "Shall we begin?" The central figure slid the words across the table.

"Your name is Labycz, Tadeusz. Your father was Sławomir Ignacy Labycz. Your mother was Barbora Danuta Sowińska. Your immediate family home was Demidówka, although your father was born near Drohobycz in the village of Stare Sioło. Your mother was born in Warszawa near Błonie, more accurately. And you were born in Odessa. I wonder why?"

The question was rhetorical so I kept quiet.

The major now leaned forward. He had brown eyes, the pupils hiding in the darkness. They were soft and slightly slanted. His face was round, fresh, with expression lines that gave him a look of humour. He was a man that laughed. His eyebrows, one of which was raised in question, were black and thick but not bushy, just well-defined. The dome of his forehead was fighting with his receding hair, which was slicked back.

"Well, is this you? Your family? Am I correct?"

My throat was dry with anticipation. I croaked rather lamely, "Yes." I felt I should say more but there was nothing I could think of.

"You are, therefore, a Soviet citizen. The son of a notorious counter-revolutionary and associate of the executed criminal British spy, Sydney Reilly. Why are you here? Who sent you?"

"I am a Canadian of Polish origin and am still a serving officer of the Polish Air Force. I am certainly not and never have been a Soviet citizen. I cannot in any way be responsible for the 'sins' of my father, and I never knew the man whose name you just mentioned," was my rejoinder. But his words were so similar to those uttered just before the war when I was recruited to the British Secret Service I was disturbed. Standing for the first time in the office of the then Head of the Service, he had made an oblique reference to 'knowing my father' too. Why he had known him was still a mystery to me.

"You are what you are, Labycz. And you are what I tell you," came the officer's reply. It was said in a mild enough manner. "You will learn that soon enough," he added.

The second officer pulled up a chair to the far end of the table and sat down. From a briefcase he removed a brown manila file. It was fairly thick. I could see the edges of typewritten documents. When he opened it and began looking through it, I observed telegrams and letters. He found what he wanted and placed the paper to one side. Taking out a blue bound notebook he sharpened a pencil with a pocket knife and then glanced at the other officer. Speaking Russian he announced, "I'm ready."

My bowels told me so was I. The other man had moved behind me but slightly to my left side. I felt him rather than saw him.

"Why have you come to the Soviet Union?"

"I came to see if the daughter of General Sikorski was alive, to bring her back to the West, in order to solve the mystery of the murder of the Polish Prime Minister." I felt this much must be known, so could do no more harm.

"Who told you she was alive?"

"I was told by my department head."

"Who told you she was still alive? A name."

"I have no name."

There was a moment of silence as the officer received my reply. He stared at me for a moment, eye to eye. There was no challenge from him, just assessment. He sighed and snapped his fingers at the officer on the left.

"This is your confession as an American spy." A paper was slid across the table, just out of my reach.

"That's untrue!" I protested.

He nodded to the guard at my side. I flinched, which he noticed, and for a second a smile played around his lips. But the guard only undid my handcuffs. I stretched and rubbed my arms and wrists. Life and pain and power surged back into me. He smiled broadly.

"Feel better now?"

"Yes, thanks," I said, trying to be conciliatory, but suddenly realised I was thanking a man who responsible for my torture. All part of the psychology of the moment.

He leant forward, looking at me earnestly. "Degradation is a curve of endurance. It is only a matter of time. Sign the confession and all will be well. The Americans and British betrayed you, so why are you protecting them? Already they are refusing to honour their agreement to recognise the new Western boundary of Poland. Your only security is the Soviet Union. Truman is no friend; he is drawing a line across Europe because he's terrified of the working masses. The American Democrats have never really had a stomach for the right fight. They were happy to fight the German Socialists, the Nazis. In fact, they forgot that they were Socialists!" He gave a short laugh. "But they will not fight us Russian Socialists. We are too close to home." He smiled again. "Read."

I wondered at the implication of the last sentence. He passed the paper to me.

"But it is in Russian."

"No matter, it is all there. Just sign, you can see where."

I placed the document in front of me, both hands on the table, and glared at this absurd man and this situation. I missed the nod.

A fist with knuckle duster crashed on to my left hand. It was unexpected. I screamed. My right arm was wrenched backward as I tucked my bruised hand under my arm. I was too weak to resist. My arm was bound to the chair. My mind flew back to the Gestapo in Zakopane, to my first mission with Kryszka where something similar had happened. It heightened my fear.

"Put your hand on the table."

"No," I whined. But the guard grabbed it from my armpit and, wrenching me forward, slapped it onto the table. The other officer had now come around. Together, whilst I struggled and whimpered, they strapped my arm to the table. I had closed my eyes. I did not want to look at my hand. I recalled Ela, trying to regain that recent sensation of happiness. I did not want to be here. I wanted to be with her. I kept my eyes tightly closed, forcing every muscle to another place.

"You may open your eyes now." His quiet voice came across the table. These men were masters of their trade.

I felt no shame in showing my weakness. He was right, it was about endurance. I eyed the guard who was now smacking a rubber cosh into his hand.

"No!" I had seen it coming.

Later in my cell, naked apart from my blanket, cold and hungry, I nursed my swollen hand and wrist. I had not signed. I had not given a name. I did not know why I had held out, nor did I care. They kept me awake with loud noises. If I dropped off they prodded me. Made me run along the corridor. They kept me awake for so very long. 'Sleep, just let me sleep, damn you!'

Something was important but I could not remember what it was. 'My name is Tadek Labycz'. That was important, that and 'I must protect the King.' "I am the King!" I shouted and I heard myself laughing. Was that me? I crouched in my corner. I could not be sure. Maybe it was the White Queen, or no, the Red. "Yes, it was the Red Queen," I mumbled. Pleased at the sound of my voice I laughed. I had never liked Tweedle Dum or Tweedle Dee. They frightened me.

My mind played tricks. Did I sign the confession? I couldn't remember. The officer's face swam before me. He was very nice, not like the brute. Time, oh blessed time, sweeping through space like a cloud. I began to think he was right. About Truman and about all those other things he said. They were making sense. People's Poland was not so bad. Yes, I could go back to the West. Yes, I could do some work for them. I wanted to sleep but I could only see Mrs Simpson and her jet brooch. She was dead, the nice officer had said so. I could not understand why I saw her so clearly. Ela didn't come anymore. I felt she ought to and puzzled why she didn't. I ate some soup and then they took my blanket away so I cried. I had liked my blanket and now I was cold again.

They didn't like it when I kept saying Sikorski had not betrayed Poland and hadn't deserved to die. They did not like Sikorski and feared his name, even though he was dead. I held his name in my mind, screwing it tight. My talisman.

They kept asking me about names. I told them I loved Ela, but they didn't believe me when I said I didn't know where she was. The brute stuffed a cloth into my mouth so I couldn't breathe. He kept pushing it down. I could feel it near my lungs. Someone else was holding me. I heaved and twisted, then water was poured over me and onto the cloth. I was drowning and Mrs. Simpson was shining. Then it was pulled out, like a giant tape worm, leaving me heaving and retching.

I could breathe and I could see faces. They hauled me to the chair. My hands and legs were strapped. I was a puppet and I was nothing. I remember someone saying, "Thirsty?" My head was forced back. I gave in as a funnel was forced into my mouth. I gagged again. "Names!" a voice screamed. Then water, till I was drowning. My stomach bloated. I gurgled, spouting water as the rubber pole hit my stomach and I spewed fountains, and water ran through my bowels.

"Names!"

*I can hear you,* I thought through a golden haze.

"Names!"

"But I don't know any names, except Sydney, and I don't really know him at all."

"He's going." I fainted with a sigh of contentment. I wanted to float, float into the blue.

I woke in a bed. Everything was grey. A man was looking at me, sitting on the bed at my side. "Water," he said and I cowered.

"No, no, drink." I discovered I was thirsty but too weak to move. I saw a doctor in white, and a needle. I passed out.

When I came round the man told me I was in the prison hospital. I couldn't move but the doctor said it was only internal bruising and I would heal in time.

"Everything takes time here," the Doctor said. "We all have plenty of time."

My hand was bandaged. Day by day as it was dressed, it healed. The suppuration stopped and this bred hope. Gradually I could move my fingers and the doctor told me I should do this. I was too weak to get out of bed but was told my limbs were workable.

My companion, whom I discovered was a Czech, fed me. We had soup and bread and potato. Who cared if it was foul, watery or meagre, it kept us alive and we were better off than in a cell. Zbiniek, for that was his name, had a badly burned face and he had lost one eye. When I asked him how he got the wound he told me had fallen against a hot stove. That, he said, was the official version found in the hospital records. "The hospital records are full of hot and cold stove incidents. Dangerous things, stoves. They should be replaced."

We laughed at ourselves. But he never told me his full story any more than I told him mine. All I learned was that he was a bomber pilot in the RAF who had been brought down in the last few days of the war and landed on the wrong side of the Allied lines. Picked up by the Russians as a British spy he had been sentenced to fifteen years in prison at some bogus trial. He was unpopular with the guards. We played chess.

Officially he was a traitor, as of course the Czech government had capitulated or allowed the Germans to enter the country without a fight. Many Czechs had defied their government and fled to Poland to join forces to fight the Nazis. Eventually some ended up in Britain. A famous Czech squadron had taken part in the Battle of Britain. Whilst at that time the Germans were not officially allies of the Russians, tacitly they were. The official reality was not clearly seen until the invasion of Poland in September 1939. That was the month the Nazis met the Socialist Republics of the Soviet Union half way across the corpse of Poland. So in the warped mind of the NKVD my roommate was counter-revolutionary and an anti-Soviet. A dangerous man.

The hospital was divided into small rooms. Although we saw other prisoners from time to time we were never permitted to enter each other's rooms. There were guards in the corridors. Bored, they would occasionally poke their heads into our room but never conversed. Our doctor, unsurprisingly, turned out to be a German war prisoner. He did not expect to be treated under the terms of the Geneva Convention as a prisoner of war, as he had been found with his unit treating both German and Russian wounded. The latter, having been captured, could be considered dubious renegades or class enemies, surrendering rather than dying for Russia. Hence he was sentenced for aiding subversives. Of course his patients were shot.

For some time it was as though we were forgotten. But then one day they came for Zbiniek. We shook hands. His bed remained empty for two days before they came for me too.

I was given new clothing, a striped uniform with my number writ large on my chest. Ominously, a padded jacket and numbered cap were handed to me too. My hands were cuffed and chains were looped to ankle shackles. Shuffling, I left my cocoon of security to meet my fate. We passed along interminable corridors, doors closed to the world, always descending. To me this meant only one thing – more interrogation. A great feeling of tiredness overcame me. I did not want to go back to pain. I could not go on. I began to stumble, felt weak and dizzy. This world of unending doors and locks and bars and gates and electric lighting - it was my grave. Finally a heavy door swung open to reveal a wide courtyard. An icy blast of cold air hit me and I shivered in my thin prison clothes, despite the added jacket. I looked around me at the high, faceless windows. Black holes peering through iron bars. Around and around I turned, my dizziness increasing. I thought of the lives behind the windows. Here I was, reeling in the cold, but beneath a sky. Its air was fresh without the sourness of a thousand other breaths tainting it before my lungs could take in its life. I laughed without mirth.

The guards now consigned me to were some smart-looking Interior Troops. I was marched toward a small truck and told to clamber into the back. The truck was closed in and painted khaki green. I could see no markings or insignia. Inside the outer doors was a set of bars and a door. A guard swung back the doors and 'invited' me to enter. There were benches along each side. My cuffs were tethered by another chain to a parallel bar running the length of the small truck. He remained on the outside and locked the barred door. The truck door was shut. I was alone.

A sliver of light entered the truck from some slit windows high in the wall. Try as I might, I could not stand on the bench to catch even a glimpse of the outside world. Still, the light was enough for me to look around in the gloom. I looked hard for nozzles. I was convinced this was the kind of 'death' vehicle the Nazis had used to suffocate prisoners. I saw nothing, and once the truck had started, felt nothing. The truck ran on tarmac, and apart from the ruts and bumps in the road, the trip was uneventful. I settled down into an uneasy doze.

We stopped and the door was flung open. I could see guards smoking. Beyond them nothing but bleak countryside sprinkled with snow. Countryside with that black and white look of winter. Yet I had entered this mad Russian world in the late spring. How long had I been in that 'house', as I called the prison? The door closed again. I pondered this loss, my sense of time. I realised that I could calculate that we had travelled an hour, but it might have been ten. My disorientation was so complete I had no idea, and what was more, I had no care or interest in anything except food. I was thirsty, so I breathed on the steel walls to make condensation I could lick. How long had it taken me to come to become an animal again?

The truck restarted. We must have turned off the road as the truck began to lurch and bounce. I had to hold on to the rail, to stop myself being flung about. My wrists and ankles became bruised. We stopped and all was quiet. Nothing. I strained very nerve and thought I heard another engine, then voices. The door was opened and I was ushered out into the cold.

The landscape, the same as before, was as bleak as the cold. Tall, leafless birch trees reached to the sky. It seemed we had travelled through and to the edge of the wood. Ahead, on a slightly raised bank, stood a large black ZIL 110 saloon. There were six security MGB standing conversing, including my two immediate guards. The two furthest away I could see had different shoulder boards to those I was accustomed to.

My guards returned with two MGB men. I did not want to die here. It seemed such a shame. That's all I felt. I thought of all the officers murdered at Katyn. Is this blankness what they felt too? I hoped so, because to think of family or loved ones in that moment would be the worst kind of pain.

I was un-cuffed, the chains were removed and I was marched toward the two different security men.

"Comrade Prisoner Tadeusz Labycz?"

"Yes," I replied. I had long given up the painful game of being a Polish airman or soldier.

They ushered me toward the ZIL. I noticed two men in the front. A driver and, next to him some senior officer, from the gold braid. My wrists were seized and new cuffs put on, but this time at the front, not at the back. This I took to be a good sign. One of the guards opened the rear door, pushing me into the centre, and then climbed in beside me. The other came in by the other door. The car was spacious and warm. It felt deliciously luxurious, the feeling of leather, the smell of cigar and cologne.

To me this was a Packard 180, a typical Russian engineering feat of copy-cat. I spoke in English to avoid retribution. "You can't even design a car without copying the Yanks, can you?"

The officer spoke, without turning his head. "I am glad to find you are not too changed, Tadek. You are safe now."

"Witek!" I shouted his name, or perhaps I didn't. Perhaps it was just a noise in my head. The needle hit my neck. I saw trees and light and heard a mumble, which was me speaking to myself. I saw some gates, I saw the words, 'All Union Institute for Mental Disease and the Deaf and Blind, Moscow District'. Did I dream that? Loonies and the deaf and blind? How could that be? The Socialist mind, social planning, social engineering. Was that me giggling? Then sleep.

CHAPTER 10

# CHESS

I awoke in a cell with light and a window. True, there were bars but it was a window nonetheless. Outside it was snowing. There was a heavy iron radiator and it worked. There was a bed and blankets. Everything was cream, not grey. Grubby, but not filthy. I ached.

The door swung open and an officer entered. Behind him a guard.

"Comrade Prisoner Labycz, you are now transferred to this unit for recuperation and rehabilitation. You will be kept here in solitary confinement . You are forbidden to speak to other inmates. Is that clear? You may speak only when spoken to by guards. You will be fed and exercised."

"That's kind of you," I replied in English. "What am I then, some kind of freakin' animal to be fed and watered? Are you Commies so inhuman?"

"Speak Russian, please," he glared at me, guessing the nature of my remarks.

"I said thank you very much, comrade, but where is Witek?"

"I am sorry, comrade, I do not know who you mean. Who is this Witek?"

"The officer in the car. I heard him, damn you!"

I received a hard slap across my face for my trouble and a reprimand for insolence. Feeling my bruised lip I apologised.

"Who was that officer in the car?" I persisted.

"Colonel Grigoriy Alesandrevich Medvedev of the MVD, the Soviet Internal Affairs Ministry. Aide to Lavrentiy Pavlovich Beria himself. You are a lucky man to have such a patron."

Beria. The man Stalin introduced to Roosevelt at Yalta as 'our Himmler.' My mind shot back to the strange couple we had met the fateful night in the forest. The woman's prophecy about Witek talked of bears. *Medved* was the Russian word for bear. No wonder he had looked so rattled.

It took a while to settle in to the regime of the sanatorium. Some, from their white uniforms, were evidently nurses, both male and female, but they looked tough enough. Others wore white coats like doctors. The kitchen staff looked like civilians. But for me and a few others who were kept segregated from the mass, there were guards in MVD uniform.

Food was taken in a mess hall. Like some leper I was kept to a small table on my own at the back. A guard always kept close. I looked around at the other inmates. Some were blind, some deaf, some obviously off their rocker. They looked at me, I looked at them. About two metres to my left and right were other 'solitaries'. We did not have to queue for food but were served by guards. That kept us apart and gave us no opportunity for talk.

The same went for exercise. Daily I was taken for a walk. There was an exercise yard, but sometimes we went for a walk around the grounds. We passed other prisoners. The guards were not too bad. A passing prisoner might mutter his name as he passed. A number of the names were Polish.

On my first day when I was returned to my cell after exercise, I found several cigarettes on my bed. These I passed to my guard. As a reward I received snippets of conversations, in particular about this place. I was suspicious of this gift from an unknown donor, but had learned the hard way not to ignore providence in prison.

I asked my guard where he came from. His family worked on a cooperative farm in the Kazan region.

"Most of the inmates here are mad," he told me. "Intellectuals and writers and non-conformist artists. Clearly they needed help to understand the benefits of Soviet society and not upset people with their ravings. Others are political prisoners who could not be persuaded to learn more about the benefits of a truly Socialist state. Polish and Ukrainian political prisoners, who are traitors to true Communism, having been Party members. Perhaps their workload has been too much and made them unstable."

My guard had never heard the word 'naïve'. How funny people are.

To keep myself fit I walked up and down my 'cell' and talked to myself a lot. I used my leaning trick that I had practised in the prison house. I would stand in one spot and lean forward and backward to my extreme point of balance, hoping this would keep me supple. I did press-ups as my strength returned. I now tried to count the days and calculated that I had been in the sanatorium for one month, give or take the first drugged days.

I pondered Witek again and again. I was convinced it had been him in the car. I went over everything I could remember. The more I did, the more convinced I became that Colonel Medvedev and Witek were one and the same man. Some aspects of this truth made sense, others did not.

Then we met for the 'first' time.

I was not cuffed or bound. The sun was shining into the room I was taken to. As I entered the room, Colonel Medvedev stood and indicated a chair.

I paused for a moment. A guard at my back; what could I do? I sat and gave him my opener. "You shitty bastard!"

His rejoinder was open and not hostile. "As for the latter, I truly believe it to be true. It's probably why I sit here today."

To the guard he said, "Wait in the corridor and stop anyone entering this room. If anyone resists you, shoot them. Is that clear?"

"Yes, Comrade Colonel."

He looked at me. "My bodyguard is one of mine, a rare thing these days, loyal as far as he can be. His parents are in a *gulag*, alive and doing forestry work. They criticised the Great Patriotic War. It could be worse. A crime against the great man Stalin himself. Can't have that, can we?"

I was bemused and totally confused. This was the same old Witek talking, acting as though nothing had happened. I stared at him across the table. He looked back, as ever tapping and turning his cigarette lighter.

"Look, I am sorry about what happened. It was not meant to be. There was a mix-up. It's a long story. Will you give me time?" The conversation was taking an extraordinary turn.

I became deeply suspicious and concluded that keeping my mouth shut was the best policy. After all, what was there left to tell?

"Where is Kryszka?" The question came involuntarily.

"In Poland. He was handed back to the UB as a Polish citizen. We claimed you as a Soviet. I am trying to find out more and will tell you what I do find out, I promise you. But I have to be cautious. There is a war going on here, a power struggle between Abakumov and Beria, between the MGB and the MVD. The latter has control, in theory, of the MGB, but this is Soviet Russia. A world of new Boyars, new princes and tsars. *Who will replace Stalin when he dies* is the question in everyone's thoughts. And meanwhile, following in Lenin's revered footsteps, Stalin sets each man against the other. "

Tap, tap went the lighter. He shifted his bulk slightly. "If this conversation had been overheard, recorded, I would be a dead man. You were never meant to be put in Butyrka prison. That was an oversight, classic interference by the MGB in your case. You were meant to go to Lubyanka, where in effect you would have been under my control. The troops who seized you were MGB. I've had a devil of a job tracing you. That minor demon Abakumov knows something is up."

"That's more than I bloody do!" I shouted. "Am I losing my mind? I don't understand, Witek. What the hell is going on? Where is Hanka? What happened to her?"

"I don't know, Tadek, truly I don't. She ran, she fell. From what I saw she shot some trooper who went to bayonet he,. He fell, she ran back to the village and that was the last anyone saw of her. The village peasants were tight-lipped despite searches. That's it, all I can tell you. My operation was taken over, compromised."

"You were going to put us in the Lubyanka? Are you twisted, you creep?"

"For your own safety and good," he snapped back, riled for the first time. "And not in the basement," he added. Regaining his composure he smiled. "You know the old joke about the basement, you get the finest view of Siberia from down there? Butyrka is a hell hole, but I tell you, you were in good company, past and present. Only the famous and the dross are put there. The Streltsy were put there by Petr the First for their rebellion. You Poles went in there in your hundreds after the January Rising in '63. The Allied politicians just bullshitted Poland, I tell you. Believe me, you were in the best of company, did you but know it. The flower of anti-Communist thinking behind those bloody walls. Our dear old Cheka Comrade Felix Dzerzhinskiy managed to escape from there, the only person I've ever known to do so. On a more sombre note, your General Anders was imprisoned there, and like you, was badly tortured. Hitler's nephew was tortured to death there back in 1942. Sad to say, General Leopold Okulicki, the AK leader, was killed there last year." He paused momentarily. "Yes, the one who, along with the other fifteen Polish leaders, was guaranteed safe conduct, and with Western support."[iii]

He gestured with his hand as though cutting his throat.

"And now, Tadek, you have a million questions. I know that. We are going to meet regularly. There will be no torture, I assure you. So old-fashioned and it serves little purpose. True, people give away friends and secrets, and in the end agree to almost everything. But truth is not always the objective. Breaking a courageous man and woman is an objective. Creating a dog is often what is wanted. Courage is an affront to torturers, it makes them feel bad, which is why often we continue to suffer. Oh yes, I have been there too. For me life is simple. You have things I want, I have things you want. In the end, when we trust each other, even if we are on opposite sides, we shall cooperate. Think it over, Tadek. More especially so, as according to the records, the court sentenced you to death. You were shot last week as a Polish counter-revolutionary since they couldn't hang 'British spy' on you! The British Foreign Office objected. In other words, Tadek, you no longer exist."

With that parting remark he stood up, smiled at me, and left through the door at the rear.

It was all too much to take in. In a haze I was escorted back to the sanctuary of my cell and to my own thoughts, to distil what he'd said as best I could. The mind games had begun. Was he genuine? Was I really listed as dead? If so, how many other 'dead' people were still alive, and for what purpose? These were the fundamental questions.

Over the next few days a wealth of such questions passed through my mind. Once, on returning to my room after exercise, my guard indicated my bed. He said nothing, just pointed. I stopped and heard the lock click. On the bed was a blank lined notebook, a pencil, even a sharpener. More than some Soviet schoolchildren had ever owned.

And there too was Witek's notebook.

I tried to think it through. If found, they could be my death warrant. There was no place to hide them except under the mattress. Why had Witek – or Medvedev – passed his notebook to me? Did he mean me to keep a record? If so, of what? And why? I decided to do nothing with the papers.

Days passed. I watched the other prisoners. As you do, I got on nodding terms with my neighbours, and one managed to mutter his name, 'Sergey Korolyov'. It meant nothing to me.

When I was taken to my next fateful meeting I had already decided to be quiet and say as little as possible. Witek sat opposite and stared at me, his lighter turning everlastingly. Eventually he spoke.

"I am not your enemy, Tadek, as you will learn. Russia is not the enemy of Poland or indeed the West. Think of me as your mentor, your teacher. My intention here is to teach you how to survive and serve the best interests of your country. All I ask is that you listen, ask intelligent questions, and that you, like me, are honest. Or at least as honest as we can be. I want you to complete my notes. They are about Poland and rightfully belong to a Pole. I am Russian, not Soviet. A historian. I recorded what I saw in your country. Now you should record the end of the story while I write a new story of my own land. This is the reason I gave you my journal, which was returned to you. I was lucky; the MGB goons assumed it was yours. They were so busy torturing you that they did not give a second thought to how you had a wartime record of a conflict in which you did not participate. The MGB simply co-opted the evidence in the handover.

"I see now that Russia has to change. The MVD is trying to change. We cannot carry on with the bestiality of the past. It is counterproductive. We get the answers we want, but we know they are spurious. Times are slowly changing. We have new truth drugs, brain-washing techniques, softer approaches."

My face had evidently betrayed my cynicism and contemptuous dismissal of this 'defence' of the Soviet Secret Police system.

"Do not look at me with such contempt; these truth drugs are all American or Swiss-based, so don't come the Holy Joe with me! Be realistic," he went on. "You and I know all Intelligence services brutalise, kill, extort, manipulate, engineer and coerce people and events. Do you want to tell me that that no Pole has ever beaten the living daylights out of a German or Russian or Ukrainian? Tadek, we know the truth. You and your friend Kryszka interrogated two clandestine Communist Polish officers in London, remember? You two arranged for them to be returned to Poland, and when they landed you had arranged for their immediate execution by the AK. Still pretending innocence? "

I held my tongue. I was watching him, trying to determine the significance of this whole episode.

"The Left, the Socialists if you like, and I make no differentiation between National Socialists in Germany or the Soviet Communists or British Labour or even the Left of the American Democrats. They all share one common theme: 'We the enlightened know best.' Like any other religion they have a dogma. It states that the Socialist State is the Kingdom of God on earth and the Party leader is the risen Christ. The Politburo, or Cabinet, or whatever you call the inner cabal, are like the kings of the Book of Revelation who throw their crowns before the throne of God. This allows us to do whatever we like for the good of the people. We are the dictators of this theocracy. We may decide who is mad or sane, who should write and what about, who should live or die. We Socialists may be as subtle as they are in the West or hard as we are here. What we do not allow is Freedom or Self-Responsibility. Self-responsibility destroys cohesion. We know at the centre how people should be: equal. For example, if one is poor, we all should be poor. If one is dim-witted we should all reduce our excellence to make for a comfortable life. Central planning is the best way, not individuality. Become a Socialist and join the ideologue club."

There was a pause. He broke open a fresh pack of cigarettes and offered me one. I refused, but he said, "Don't be a fool. Take a few for trade." I took three and placed them in my top pocket. Witek leant back and inhaled deeply before blowing a stream of smoke upward into the air. We both watched the jet stream slow and turn to cloud and nothingness as it drifted toward the ceiling. There was a long pause whilst Witek continued to smoke. He stubbed the cigarette out, screwing it into the ash tray. The air stank of his harsh Russian tobacco.

"Did you know Lenin visited Pavlov and his dogs many times? Lenin believed of course that we are animals, a product of evolution and therefore trainable. In time we human animals can accept anything. The strongest must survive. So what if millions die to the benefit of the masses? The sacrifice of today must pay for tomorrow. Thankfully we are now educating children to accept our new world. Our Soviet authorities are no different to the Nazis, who had similar views. To me this makes the trials at Nuremburg absurd. Only Germans on trial – bizarre, no?"

"Senseless," I said. He had caught my attention. Trapped me into my first utterance. I thought about this later. That one word changed my life. Because one word leads to another.

"Stalin said that trying to bring Communism to Poland would be like saddling a cow. He had no real ambition in Poland, you know. It was really a Western betrayal. Of course he wanted revenge for the defeat in the East by you Poles in the 1920s, especially because he was Commissar down there when you threw the Soviets out and stopped the Red tide. That love of freedom is your Polish weakness. You play with equality and socialism, but from an aristocratic viewpoint. You level up, not down, and that is impossible. You enjoy cooperatives until someone takes your land and then it is yours, only yours. You like individuality, you like debate.

"I want you to know the facts, Tadek. I was a sleeper in Poland, a spy. So I *was* in the Home Army. Almost everything I told you about me was true. I was against the Germans from the beginning. In the old days I would have been called a Menshevik. I truly have great sympathy for Poland, her suffering. When I described my feelings to you the first time we met I meant every word. Like your hero Piłsudski I am a pan Slavicist. Like that Czech artist Mucha, who painted those huge murals on the Slav epic when he was not painting tobacco adverts.

"As a nation I am told Poles were born in summer, children of the sun. That woman we met in the forest would say your nation's birth sign is Gemini. God help any Jan born on the sacred seventh of June! Such a man would go slightly mad every Solstice. St Jan's Eve is still celebrated in every village in the Slav world. Pagandom survived a long time in field and forest; the church was wise to adapt rather than persecute the old ways. The Great Mother is still Queen of Poland. The Black Sophia casts her spell through Slavdom and for you, Tadek. The Mystic Rose, eh?"

"What are you babbling about?" I was trying to appear unrattled but I was thrown again by this weird change of subject.

"And you a Glastonbury buff. You don't know the Rose path to Kraków and Česky Krumlov? Aah, I see I have touched a nerve. So you see, Tadek, we have watched you for a long time. Blame your father and your uncle the pilot. And our old enemy Sydney Reilly, the British agent who nearly overthrew the Bolshevik revolution."

He had caught me off guard and he knew it.

"Would you like to join me in a game of chess?"

Of course I said yes. And so we played. Witek won. When we finished he asked if I'd like to practice, so he gave me the set but no board.

It was an extraordinary meeting with no clear path or message. Or not yet, at least. Of course there was a path, but one I had to think through. This was just another move in this slow, mind bending game. It would take time to consider it all.

As he stood to leave, having passed me the small box with the chess pieces, he gave me a bundle of newspapers. "Today's is on top," he said. Whatever my feelings towards the man I was grateful. Wasn't that part of the process, though, to make me feel grateful? What had I done to deserve this? What was I expected to do now? And what did he mean by offering to be my mentor?

As I entered the cell I slipped a cigarette to my permanent guard. He said nothing.

I looked avidly at the newspapers. There were a few back copies of the *Daily Worker*, mouthpiece for the British Communists. Carefully folded in the centre of the pack were two back copies, not so old, of the *News Chronicle,* my favourite paper. On top lay *Pravda*, the party propaganda organ, but it was the date I was after.

5$^{th}$ May 1949.

I had been in prison for two years.

So now I knew.

It took a moment to sink in.

Time is a notion, one that exists as a turning of the earth or as the hands on a clock. I had no sense of loss, just surprise that time would fly so strangely in a half circle, in a half life. Time had just slipped away from me. I had aged. Changed. Grown.

Now my own record would begin.

I vowed to begin my journal to finish his.

Over the weeks, poring over the papers supplied, even if a little behind the times, I discovered that Britain's Labour Foreign Secretary had proposed a league of countries to stand up to the Soviet Union, which was later to become NATO. A bit late, I thought, and quite ironic. The Communists had taken over Czechoslovakia. Truman had signed the Marshall plan, to help reconstruct Europe. Billions of dollars had been pledged to fix its destroyed economies. Stalin was set against it. The British were out of Palestine without dignity, having been pushed out by Israeli terrorists. I smiled at this, thinking of the many ex-Polish soldiers taking revenge for their lost country by founding a new one in Israel. And the Israelis had fought and won against the Arabs. I felt some sort of pride in this, although I was not a Zionist sympathiser by any means. There was Communist insurgency in Malaya. Berlin had been blockaded by the Soviets and the West had retaliated with an air-lift of supplies. *If only they had the guts in 1945* I thought and read on.

The establishment of a Committee of un-American Activities led by Senator McCarthy caught my eye. "They needed this back in the war," I said to myself. "I hope they find the bastards that ran Poland down and canoodled with the Reds. Bloody newsmakers and film people." The French, I discovered, were fighting a war in Indo-China against the Communists. In March mass deportations took place in the Baltic States: over one hundred thousand people were sent to God knows where and replaced by ethnic Russians. *The same policy as in Ukraine*, I thought. Ukrainians kicked out and ethnic Russians brought in, then a vote on sovereignty and an ethnic plebiscite. And now this month the Berlin blockade had been lifted. "Just shows that standing up to Stalin pays off," I muttered. A new West German State was created.

I played with the chess pieces, a beautiful set, carved and polished by some master craftsman before the Bolsheviks' time, I guessed. I examined each one carefully. Every pawn, every castle, searching for a join or seam. But they appeared solid.

Why no board? He would not have given me the set to practise without a board. I re-examined each piece minutely. By pressing on the base of the knight and simultaneously pushing its head down, the base unlocked, revealing a hollow space. There was one black 'messenger' and one white. Only a fractional difference in weight was detectable, and not a seam in sight when closed.

So much to absorb. I was in two minds about everything. At times I wondered if my nerves would survive. I started to shake uncontrollably at night. I sweated badly. Looking back at those times I was ill – or certainly not thinking straight. Sometimes I woke up at night screaming. Many times I contemplated suicide. The early hours of the morning were worst. I had to keep warm. If I got cold I would shake and become so ill the doctors and nurses had to take over. If I felt sick I used to sit up and walk around my room. Gradually time began to heal my body. From time to time I thought of Ela, but only when I was strong enough. I tried so hard to keep sane.

Witek helped me through it all. Sometimes he even held my hand.

I recorded many of the things he told me. I had so many questions for him and kept my notes religiously. I put pertinent facts into 'his' journal and my feelings into the exercise book. I wanted to know if our mission to find Zofia Leśniowska, General Sikorski's daughter, had been a waste. Witek did not know where she was but confirmed she had been taken by the NKVD. So Kobyliński had been right in spotting her. "Alas," said Witek, "he is no more. He tried to gather a group of AK members to mount a rescue operation. But of course you were familiar with this, and so was Kryszka. Do you think we did not know you were going to meet and link with them?"

That was a cruel blow.

Soviet agents were apparently on board the plane; all who had meant to die had done so *before* the crash. As for the surviving pilot, Prchal, Witek simply said, 'Use your common sense'. He returned to Czechoslovakia after the war and did quite well, despite Communism, but eventually opted for the USA. Loved by both parties, apparently. And quiet about Sikorski to the grave.

"What about Joyce Herring, the second pilot's wife. She swore that her husband phoned her the day after the crash?"

"You know the answer, Tadek. Was she some lunatic? Was she a spiritualist? No! Until warned off, she maintained her story. You also know that two of the others on board were British Secret Service? Look, the politics were clear. Sikorski had to go. The general perception was that he was 'the awkward squad'. He was in the way, upsetting Stalin, and Churchill badly needed the Soviets onside. Come on, Tadek, please. The Germans were rolling all over Stalin. It was not the West needing Stalin but the other way around. Without US vehicles and British Hurricane fighters – what? I see you didn't know this?"

"No, I did not," I admitted, thinking of those terrible times in September 1939, sitting waiting with my lost friend Bolek on the Romanian border. Waiting for the promised British Hurricane fighters, for the Polish Air Force. But they had never come.

"Indeed. For your notes, about three thousand Hurricanes were delivered to the Soviets. So let's cut the political manure, Tadek. Stalin is not a politician; he is a devious Georgian conspirator. Not a military genius, just a powerful dictator. Was he really going to throw his toys out of his pram over Katyń? He knew the truth. The Poles knew the truth. So did the British and the Americans. Was his position in jeopardy over it? Not really. After all, he had just been caught out murdering a few 'class enemies' and was quite capable of throwing a few NKVD officers to the wolves if he wanted to. The Western politicians already knew he was a mass murderer – the Purges, the Ukraine and so on. So what was new, please? Would the Poles go off and sulk and join the Germans? History said 'no'. They fought on, regardless of far worse betrayals. Here is something for your notebook. Have you heard of Vasili Mikhailovich Blokhin?"

I shook my head.

"Blokhin was the chief executioner. Handpicked by Stalin, back in 1926. He is a survivor purely because he knows too much. He has a special group of MGB men such as Lieutenant Andrei Rubanov around him. Their sole role is to execute people. Every country has to have an executioner, I suppose. But is he blameless? No.

"He is your Katyń murderer, Tadek. He is the one who killed your officers. The man who massacred POWs against all the rules, and on Stalin's direct orders. Not for any particular policy but on a whim of personal revenge. Stalin does not like fear, and he fears Polish officers and intelligentsia. So all the prisoners at Kozelsk were shot, every night two hundred and fifty officers. Each evening Blokhin would don his leather butcher's apron and shoulder length gloves and go to work. The prisoner would enter the Lenin room, painted all over red. An identity check would be made and then kaput. The prisoner would be handcuffed and led into the next room. This room was specially designed, with padded walls for soundproofing, a sloping concrete floor with a drain and hose, and a log wall for the prisoners to stand against. Blokhin would push the prisoner against the wall. A bullet in the head finished the job.

"By the way, from the beginning it was intended to be a German crime. I think this, too, is what riled Stalin, being caught out. He is an emotional man, Tadek. The pistols used were all German Walther PPKs, kindly supplied by the NKVD."

The statement Witek was making was all the more shocking because it was said so matter of factly.

"What about the others, at Starobelsk and Ostakhov camps, and those from West Belarus and Ukraine?"

"So few mention them, just Katyń. They were murdered too, Tadek. Notice I did not say executed. Most went to their deaths at the NKVD prison at Kharhov or Kalinin. Some were put on rafts and set adrift in the ice-cold waters of the White Sea. The numbers were too great." He mused for a moment then leant across the table, staring hard at me. "That man shot six thousand people in twenty-eight days in April 1940. But all the Allies talk of are Nazis and Jews and little else at Nuremburg. Bitter? Yes, I am bitter too, Tadek, but for different reasons to you. We of the Soviet Union..." He paused and reached inside his uniform for a small notebook, which he consulted. "We of the Soviet Union killed at the least twenty-two thousand, four hundred and thirty-six Polish prisoners of war officers and NCOs. That is the official count."

He tore out the page from his book. This was his new notebook, in which he was accumulating facts and figures about the brutality of the Soviet system. "Official records are what we in the MVD say happened. But I record the truth."

"For you," he said, handing me the ripped page. "You know I like details. So from Sikorski's daughter, I have brought you to the murder of the flower of the Polish military. Its head, Sikorski disappeared. Supposedly killed in an accident. Sikorski's stubborn determination that Stalin should accept responsibility was not liked by the Allies. Why?

"The party line was because it made Soviet Russia look bad. We are bad, Tadek! God, don't we know it! Stalin could not care less what the world thinks of him. He has a simple, uncomplicated domestic life. Anyone here who speaks against him is shot. But the Communist International *does* worry. The subversive Communist state, the trendy Lefties, the Western Socialists, these are the ones who cannot stomach the truth. In wartime why should we care about them? It does not make sense, does it?"

As he spoke I thought about the system itself, not inherently bad. What was bad was the people who ran it, the goons who went too far. Even I had to acknowledge that Russia had grown. "Communism has worked for some," I interjected. "At least you won the war."

"Let me make my point," he retorted. "The real reason Sikorski had to go was a much grander affair. It resulted in interference in the internal affairs of Poland by the West, who leaned toward a stable Europe dominated by two powers, the US and Russia, leaving Britain to rule its waves.

"Sikorski had the measure of Stalin. In the West it will seem far-fetched to future generations to think that Stalin was afraid of Sikorski. Indeed, Stalin was afraid of Poland, Polish Generals in particular; he had an aversion to them. Stalin was afraid of the Polish army.

"I hear the British Foreign Office laughing, but then they would, wouldn't they? So many of our men have infiltrated their information services! They believe what we tell them. The British Foreign Office still lives in the Victorian era. They have no sense whatsoever of Central and Eastern Politics or indeed of Russia. They are still at the Great Game. Never got over the Charge of the Light Brigade. This is why Churchill was so comfortable with a deal with Stalin to invade and divide Persia. Oh yes the British understand oil. International law was simply put aside. Blood brothers, Stalin and Churchill. Amusing, no?" He laughed abruptly. A sardonic laugh.

"The Poles beat the Reds fair and square just twenty-five years ago, Tadek. The Americans did not even know about it in the White House. Roosevelt had no interest in Poland whatsoever, make no mistake. Churchill had been told by his intelligence services that Stalin had started secret negotiations with Germany, using the Bulgarians as intermediaries. That he wanted peace with Germany. Churchill was desperate to keep the Soviets in the war. He had always been supportive of Sikorski's government in public, especially when he needed Polish troops and airmen. But now Russia as an ally was a bigger prize. So in secret consultations with Roosevelt he put forward that some territorial concessions could be offered to Stalin on the Eastern Polish border. Notice, Tadek, which way round this occurred. Churchill was the man who made this suggestion. And behind Sikorski's back. It was impossible with Sikorski alive, and Stalin knew it."

Witek wagged his finger at me.

"So Sikorski had to go. Only four months after Sikorski's death, in the Teheran conference, Churchill and Roosevelt agreed with Stalin that the whole of eastern Poland would be ceded to the Soviets. This was on Churchill's initiative, not Stalin's demand. What price your Atlantic Charter now, Tadek? Who gave the intelligence to Churchill in the first place? Some of your old pals back in London, I believe. Did Churchill really think that Germany would give Stalin peace? How ludicrous, and a total misunderstanding of the Nazi mind and of Soviet Espionage. But then, the Foreign Office civil servants are so out of touch with reality. One and a half million Poles sent to the NKVD-run camps at Vortuka, Kolyma, Kaluga, Donbas, Kamchatka and Diagelvo. Do the Germans seem so bad now?"

He left the remark hanging in the air. I was invited by the silence to consider it. Then he restarted his monologue. "Was it so surprising that Stefan Rowecki, the commander of your Home Army, was betrayed and arrested by the Gestapo just a couple of months later? He was held in such high regard that Himmler himself met with him. Rowecki was offered the opportunity, by the Germans, to bring the Home Army onside with the Germans and jointly attack Russia. Think of that, my friend. If Poland had done to the West what they had done to Poland?

"This is precisely what Stalin was afraid of. He knew that Sikorski, like Pilsudski before him, could have joined Ukrainians, Balts and dissident Russians into a Promethean force that would oust Communism, or at the very least Stalin. That would have been a possibility, even in 1945. Zhukov was spent. Berling would have turned, and the Russians were more than ready to oust Stalin. The Americans wanted the Russians onside against the Japanese. Stalin kept his promise, made at Yalta, to end his neutrality pact with Japan and so invaded Manchuria in Operation August Storm. The Soviets conquered Inner Mongolia, as well as northern Korea, southern Sakhalin, and the Kuril Islands. They had every intention of going for Hokkaido, but the atomic bomb fell and Japan surrendered to the Americans.

"It was a stunning Soviet victory, Tadek, won by Russian troops who wanted to go home. One and a half million Red Army men far from home in a war they did not want. Soviet Russia was now tied down by the need to sort out China. Many of the troops were from 'Western Ukraine'. Think about that, laddie. Large numbers of Polish *kulaks* who wanted to go home to their families, to a plot of land, to a democratic Poland which no longer existed. It was a golden moment for a stand against Stalin and a deal with Russia. But the West had no stomach for a fight; even if they were just bystanders. Anyone could see it was the moment to finish the fight. It appears to me the West was in love both with Stalin and with their own clever treaties and power. So today Communism sits at the West German border, courtesy of the West. Make no mistake, Churchill completely misjudged Stalin. Both Western leaders actually believed him.

"As for Rowecki, he remained loyal. Died in a concentration camp in Sachsenhausen. Before his arrest, General Ignacy Oziewicz was also picked up by the Gestapo. As commander of the National Armed Forces, the NSZ, he was a real catch for the Nazis. My friend, Tadek, you lost your three top Generals in a matter of weeks. Does that seem like carelessness? Does that not disturb you? And to add fuel to your fire, I might add that two of the Polish betrayers of Rowecki are alive and well and agents of the new Polish UB, the secret Police. Wheels within wheels, my friend. Does this answer your question?"

It did. And in many similar conversations I was able to tease out the politics from the honour, the betrayals from the heroism. Discover what liars the men who run our lives were. Men of grandeur, with egos that we, the little people, never understand. Yet we thrive on their empty speeches, hoping always for a better world.

On one occasion I remember, when the birds were singing outside and the sweet fresh air of freedom sighed through the window in a zephyr-like breeze, Witek cornered me.

"Now, I ask you a question, Tadek. When you went to the US last year, and you spoke with Karol Rozmarek, the Polonia leader, why did you not ask your American pals – and the Central Intelligence Group after all became your buddies – why they suppressed the Katyń story in the press? Why did they forbid its publication? Real censorship, in America!

"Did you not ask why the report on Katyń compiled by Lieutenant Commander George Earle at the behest of the President was rejected? Earle was Roosevelt's special trusted emissary to the Balkans, a career politician, ex-governor of Pennsylvania, a trusted man. Why then did Roosevelt insist it was a German crime, when he knew full well it was not? Why did he allow the view of Elmer Davis, head of the US Office of War Information, a news hack, to prevail? When it was well known he had clear Leftist sympathies? Why was the American public not trusted with the facts? Roosevelt ordered Earle directly not to publish his findings. For his trouble Earle ended up in Western Samoa for the duration of the war."

Again Witek consulted his notebook before tearing out another page and handing it to me. I was aghast at what I read.

*Secret communication from US Ambassador Moscow. Polish government described as 'a group of aristocrats looking to America and Britain to restore their position in Poland and their landed properties and feudal system.'*

"Is this true? Is this what Roosevelt believed?"

"You know Roosevelt promised the Poles anything they wanted back home. He needed their votes. Once he had the election in the bag and the backing of American Poles he had no further interest in Poland, believe me. The Teheran conference of the 'Big Three' was, in actual fact, the meeting of the Big Two. Roosevelt tried as hard as he could to cosy up to Stalin. You remember that Mikołajczyk, the then Polish Prime Minister of Poland, had asked both Churchill and Roosevelt to be present when the Polish borders were discussed. He was told no. What they really said was 'Bugger off and mind your own business'. Which, by the way, he did. Well, I can tell you that when the Polish borders came up, Roosevelt said he was tired and took himself into a corner and pretended to sleep. How would *that* have gone down in the American elections if it had got out? He said it was an Anglo-Russian affair. So, Tadek, don't put your faith in America, especially the Democrats. That's how you lost Eastern Poland and millions lost their lives. That's how the Poles lost their land and homes. How a civil war started. How Stalin got away with murder."

One afternoon I questioned Witek fully about the White Cossack we had met, and learned of the stain of Operation Vistula.

"Down there in the east, in the wilds as you know, remnants of the Home Army, NSZ and others were fighting it out, or sometimes cooperating with the Ukrainian partisans. Stalin sent ten regiments of NKVD or MVD troops against the six thousand or so Poles and roughly four thousand Ukrainian insurgents. The partisans were crushed and the Ukrainians slaughtered. The civilian remnants were packed off to the 'newly created districts' of Warmia and Mazury. Polish forces took the lead in this 'crime', Tadek, alongside their Soviet friends. The area was simply denuded of people."

Another time I quizzed him about the Soviet use of torture. "Why is it that you keep people alive forever? Questioning them till they confess even to crimes they did not commit?"

Witek had flashed one of his disarming grins. "We have a simple belief: whoever disagrees with us must be mad. The dictatorship of the proletariat does not allow for any dogma other than ours. It is the way, the path of truth. The Left always uses this moralistic tone of political correctness. Therefore we have to justify our actions. The Nazis viewed us Slavs as sub human, which allowed them to kill us quickly – just get the information then *kaput*. We need to convert the mind in order to win the game. It's like the Inquisition, you understand. We are in a battle for souls, for hearts and minds. Once you are whipped into true belief you are free to go – either to the good earth or back to society."

And so it continued, week after week, my education in politics and facts. I learned, just as I had done as a child, to observe, to think. I had become too emotional, allowed myself to be driven by a sense of injustice. Witek knew I could kill without compassion. He knew I had a rage which sometimes overtook me. His intention was to train my dispassionate side to better understand the very phrase 'God, Honour and Fatherland', writ so often on Polish sabres.

After a while, I began to win at chess.

# CHAPTER 11

# THINKING OUT LOUD

Colonel Grigoriy Alesandrevich Medvedev, known by some as 'the Bear', puffed smoke at across the table at me, watching for the slightest trace of irritation fleeting across my eyes.

"Good, Tadek Labycz, very good."

"What?" I responded, one eyebrow raised enquiringly.

The Colonel paused before answering. He had just given me a compliment. The truth was he had trained me well. The British were amateurs, he had told me. Just threw lads into the water and watched to see if they could swim. Medvedev had shown me over recent weeks how to use and control my face. How to bully, how to threaten, how to push one's face close, how to smile, to relax, to raise an eyebrow like now in full innocence. How to scowl, how to deceive. I had learned well, but would never admit it.

"You are a natural observer and mimic, Tadek. You should have gone on the stage."

He liked me, which was part of the trouble. That was why he had taken such care, making me repeat movements again and again until my eyes could twinkle or screech like an angry owl at will. Taught me how to give my eyes that look of nothingness which provoked fear. He'd had me practice on the female nurses in the prison hospital. Taught me how to use my lips, which he joked were 'sensual and soft like a woman's'. I'd practiced on them until all the women around were in love with me, or at least desired me. The nurses were, of course, all informers, some of them MVD agents. At least two were MGB, although they thought they had covered their tracks. Nevertheless, I knew the consensus amongst the women was that Labycz had kissable lips. I'd overheard one of them commenting on my hair colour, how when I was younger with true blonde hair I must have looked the part of the dashing airman.

Medvedev smiled. I watched him, this man I had come to know so well in recent weeks. I knew how he ticked. I knew now that he felt he should speak. The time lag was too long. He didn't want to give his opponent an opening. And so before I could take the conversation further, establishing its flow, he continued: "I was thinking about the past, that is all." Before the obvious question he knew would come back from me, he added, "Which is not for you to know." He smoked and blew the smoke as he wished.

In order to win my trust, Medvedev had shared a little of himself. Recollections swam back to mind of conversations we had had. He had endured a hard life. Though he had never admitted it I knew it had felt good to unburden himself. Witek/Medvedev was a man searching for reasons.

*"My problem was that my father was a Tsarist, a bourgeois petty official, actually in the Okhrana, the Secret Police. We lived in Krosno where he organised some pogroms against Jews. I was little; I remember only scraps, images. Then the Revolution; my father joined the Reds. He was Russian and my mother Polish, which is why I'm fluent in both languages. My father died somewhere, I suppose."* He had tapped the ash from his cigarette. *"My mother and I had a tough time. We were not popular from any side, but she got some work as a railway clerk and then she remarried. At school I was a 'bloody Russian, a Red'. My history teacher encouraged me to study more with him and I went to his home often. It was here I recall reading Marx and Lenin. Thanks to his influence I became a Communist, a full-blown Party member in a proscribed organisation. It was secret, a great bloody secret. One day he had asked if I could obtain details of some trains due to move troops. He told me my mother would know. That is, I suppose, how easily I became a 'fifth columnist'. I enjoyed the secrecy; it gave me a sense of power, superiority even, over my contemporaries. When my teacher asked if I would like to go to Moscow to university, I did. Left home with one bag and a one-way ticket. Scrawled a note for my mother."*

He had inhaled deeply, thinking of those Moscow days.

*"The university was genuine, in the sense that I obtained perhaps was granted a degree in history. My love for the subject is genuine, Tadek. But my real role at university was training- a few students of my own age drawn from a number of countries. I found I was sponsored by the Communist International; it was their 'schooling' that I attended. I remember particularly a young Frenchman - but then, we were all young, malleable at least, if not gullible. There were even a couple of Americans, which surprised me. Some Poles, Czechs and so on. One I recall well – Bolełsaw Bierut. Even then a turd and arse-licker. Now the President of Poland and well and truly under Serov's thumb. Serov the executioner of the Generals, the Ukrainian Commissar of the NKVD and the man who cleared out millions from their homes to languish God knows where. If Khrushchev is the butcher of the Ukraine then Serov must be the slaughter man, the bastard.*

*"I never really intended to become an agent or sleeper. It just happened. I learned, as I have taught you, Tadek, to manipulate others, to let them do the work. To infiltrate and manipulate. To create a set of circumstances which others must follow, a pattern they cannot avoid; a trap which they create for themselves. A certain weakness for a woman, a homosexual experience for a man. Mostly it was money or opium, they were much the*

*same. Then blackmail. Morality opens a possible powder keg. Any weakness could be powerful in the large game. Just think how Stalin played Roosevelt over Poland. The Polish vote was in the bag at home, so who needed Poland? Soon Roosevelt was describing Poland, his most loyal ally, as the 'Polish Headache'.*

The lighter continued to tap as Medvedev reminisced. *"I learned the art of coding, the best dead letter-box techniques, how to use firearms. I learned how to be dead to humanity, to hump a fellow student for lust. I learned a strange history of the working class and the dreaded capitalists. I was shown the need to exterminate vermin. Then I was packed off back to Poland 'to get a job'. In reality I was a junior officer in the NKVD on leave!*

Colonel Grigoriy Alesandrevich Medvedev paused, watching me intently.

Today was the day, I felt convinced of that: after months of careful picking and prodding, of exchanges on both sides, each of us knew a point in time would come. And this was it. This was the test. I knew if I responded the wrong way now I would have failed. If I sat and remained neutral, come what may. I would have won.

Still the Colonel waited.

I sat and watched the older man, waiting for whatever it was that was about to happen. This thing that was about to take shape. He knew it. I knew it. This was not the moment to speak. This was not his show, I thought. Let Medvedev call the tune, lay out the score.

He stubbed out his cigarette, screwing it into the saucer used as an ashtray. "This is how it all happened. I have been remembering. Some things you already know. The war came. I was called up to the Polish Army. As you know I escaped to the woods. Then word came to me through a Jewish partisan group that I was needed. I met up with a senior NKVD man, who gave me the job of infiltrating and eventually helping destroy the Polish Home Army in whatever form that might take. Shocked, Tadek? I even worked for a while under the direction of General Serov.

"Serov is an expert in deportation and mass exterminations. Ukrainians, Lithuanians, Latvians, Estonians, Crimean Tartars and so on. And now he had been assigned to crush the Polish Home Army. Does this astonish you?"

"No," I replied evenly, "for we have been enemies." The next sentence was very carefully worded. "My enemies' enemy is my ally, not my friend. This I have learned. How you came to be what you are is not my concern."

Satisfied, Medvedev carried on. "So now I fight the so-called 'cursed soldiers', the Polish resistance to Communism or, more accurately, Russification or Sovietisation. Those partisans betrayed by everyone in the West. I see that, Tadek. I understand them and admire them. But my father was Russian. I see the Russian perspective. The way I see it, Tadek, you and I are not unalike. But you made a choice for Poland and I for Russia.

"In 1939 the Russians invaded Poland on the side of Hitler. I found this surprising. Hitler persecuted Communists. So why were we allies? You Poles fought like tigers against the Soviet liberator, gave us a drubbing in small, unequal fights. I saw this so clearly. Why did you fight, we wondered? You were peasants, farmers, workers, teachers, rich and poor. Why did you fight us? You fought because you were all Poles, whether Jews, Lithuanians, Ukrainians...you were Polish citizens. You had a cause stronger than mine, a republic with ideals stronger than mine.

"In contrast, our Political Commissars had schooled the lads in our Russian regiments to enter Polish homes and say, 'We lack nothing in the workers' paradise. We have everything we need.' Then of course the boys went on the rampage, searching for anything from soap to clothes to send home. But they had said what they were ordered to say. I was not a fool. I asked myself why had we invaded Poland?' To free workers? Of course not. To liberate Ukrainians? How absurd, considering the millions we had starved, deported and replaced with ethnic Russians. The truth was that Stalin wanted personal revenge for defeat in the recent Russo-Polish war. He was winning in this second round, but what he really wanted was to stop the Germans having the oil fields in Poland and Romania. *That* was what it was all about.

"Over the war years I reported back to my superiors that there would be nothing but trouble from the Poles. The big Communist idea was to establish a puppet Communist government and ignore the legal government in exile, and all with the connivance of the West. That happened.

"Stalingrad, my friend. Were you there? No. Was anyone there from the West? No. So we all suck up the Communist propaganda filth of an heroic army that saved the world. Boys without guns. We do not talk of the madmen in the NKVD who shot them in the back if they refused to run forward. 'Pick up a rifle from a dead Comrade. Forward!' Heroism, yes, as well as heroism from the Germans and Rumanians on the other side. Russian might in numbers, cannon fodder as in 1914. But Russia won, the Great Red Army alone withstood the might of Germany. And then on to Kursk. Churchill no longer needed what had been the third largest Allied force against Germany Poland. They were relegated to number four. He now had Russia. Emotional man, your Churchill."

"Not my Churchill, Medvedev. You know I met him. We did not take kindly to each other," I interjected. "He was ruthless, as ruthless as you need to be in a war. And he was the free world leader at the time."

Medvedev cut in: "Yes, ruthless, but prone to an irrational emotional conscience also. In a way he was very similar to Stalin – his sentiments ruled him. But he didn't have the system to back him up.

"Please do not look at me as though I am mad, boy. Politicians, the élite of our world, use power in what they see as an objective way, devoid of emotion. A million deaths mean nothing, but a *personal* loss, ah, that means everything. Hence Stalin never forgave the Poles for his defeat in the twenties, because in the south he was the responsible Commissar. If Stalingrad was Kirovgrad he would have run. If Stalingrad fell, he fell. If he fell, Churchill knew, as did Sikorski and the Polish Generals, that the Soviet Union would disintegrate. Communism would be finished. Russia would fight on, of course, but Hitler knew the Rumanians would desert him, leaving the Ukrainians at his back. It would be a different world. Churchill saw Stalin as a safe pair of hands. He and FDR kept the war going."

Medvedev beamed at me as though he were five years old. "You do not believe me, do you? Do you still believe everything you read in the papers? Do you not remember that every single word in this Workers' Paradise is state controlled and sponsored? Do you really believe that Stalingrad could have been won without Churchill, or that Stalin could have won without American aid? It was not tanks that won the war but American trucks and supplies. A State secret, my friend. Churchill needed to dump the Poles, as he had betrayed them at Teheran by promising their country to Stalin. He needed to get the British public onside with a victory, so he could persuade them to conveniently forget Stalin's alliance with Hitler and the alliance the British had with the Poles. Churchill had his secret weapon: Beaverbrook and his press. Massive aid, Tadek! To all historians and tacticians, Stalingrad became the key to capturing the Soviet Union. That was always the story we told. More important than Moscow, we said. Pah!" He brushed the air as though swatting a fly. "Pah! What does the West know of the Russian mind? Of Holy Mother Russia? It is not in the Caucasus. I do not care about the Soviet Union. I am a Russian.

"Sure, the city was a centre of both rail and river communications, but it was not the centre of the Russian world. It was close to Georgia, Stalin's home, which is why the city was named for him."

He wagged his finger at me across the table. I hid my rising impatience. What was the reason behind this intense discussion?

"Stalin ordered factory workers to die, but pleaded for Allied armaments. Winston Churchill made sure he got them. Without that support – kaput! Did you read about this in the newspapers? Read about massive aid up the Persian Gulf through Iran? And the remainder across the Pacific to Vladivostok? Or across the North Atlantic to Murmansk? We would have won without the aid and tied the Germans down, but we could not have moved so far west. And the Allies of the West would have taken Berlin, not the Russians.

"Stalin simply pushed his luck at Teheran over Poland. Roosevelt was not interested. Churchill was a pussy cat and surprised Stalin by offering

Poland on a plate, a gift. Your Sikorski would no doubt have settled with Stalin for Lwów, Brest, Litovsk and Grodno. Wilno might have been a sticking point. Churchill and his staff proposed the Curzon line, which Stalin[iv] had not even heard of. As it coincided neatly with his pact with the Nazis he went for it like a dog at a meaty bone. Stalin was cunning as usual. He used Katyn as a bargaining chip. He knew the British did not have the balls to back the Poles. Churchill was mesmerised by a kindred spirit, but Churchill did not realise the crucial difference in their emotions. Stalin's deviousness led him to good humour, whereas Churchill's cunning led him to remorse and tears.

"Sikorski and his Generals were prepared to tough it out, and if needed fight it out. Stalin knew he would have to compromise with them. The Poles knew they would have to surrender territory. Stalin played a game of 'bluff the British and sod the Americans' – who had no interest in Polish borders.

"Take that on board, Tadek. Believe me, you are going to meet some of the characters that betrayed your country. The Politicians, Tadek, the politicians."

I took quiet note of this remark. Typical of 'the bear' opposite, the remark appeared to come from an animated Medvedev. This was a posture, just like the old Witek was a posture. It was what the man himself had taught me – a ruse; a play to watch the reaction. It was a pawn advanced, to see if the gambit would be taken. In my mind I moved my king one square to the side, sheltering it from attack.

The last few weeks had not been in vain. By now I could almost read his mind. 'So *far so good,*' he'd be thinking. '*He is watching me carefully. I know he noted that last supposed slip of the tongue, but he voiced no whisper, no hint of acceptance. Good man. He still does not trust me, but he believes me.*'

I knew that he would be watching me carefully as he made his next play. If I stayed still, gave no indication, he might make his move. He believed I was isolated and malleable enough to be useful and do whatever job he had in mind for me.

Medvedev spoke again, weighing every word. "Sikorski and the Generals did not want the Home Army to 'surface' if the Russians got to Poland before the West. Sikorski, as you know, wanted to go in through the backdoor, from the east. Stalin did a deal with Churchill which you have stumbled upon. Churchill also feted the Polish civilian leaders in London, especially the Left-leaning Mikołajczyk, who in turn soft-soaped Korbo?ski in Poland. And voilà, the Home Army is given up by its own politicians to stupid and inhuman orders to 'aid' – meaning 'surrender to' – the Soviets. Sikorski's death we all know about, but Churchill's friend or protégé in the Polish Exile government, Mikołajczyk, also side-lined General Kukiel.

Crucially he got rid of, to virtual internment in Canada, Chief of the Polish army General, Sosnkowski a man of honour, a true old-time aristocrat. All this happened exactly as Stalin requested or demanded. And as directly ordered by Churchill to Mikołajczyk. Was it right that little Mik did as he was told by a foreign head of state? The price was a main job in the new government, the story line that he chose to put faith in Western promises for free and unfettered elections. Oh, come on Tadek, please. Such stupidity makes me feel ill. How could he believe that? Unless he was motivated by pride or greed? For Christ's sake, how many men died through Mikołajczyk's and Korboński's naivety? And, I might add, are still being killed today! Stalin ran Poland from the day little Mik gave way to Churchill.

"That was the end. Stalin had what he wanted; there were no more Polish generals. The ones he feared had gone, and the remainder would not lead a war against Russia. All the people he feared were gone. I saw this clearly too. We, the Soviets, had won. The Romanians, Czechs, Slovaks, Bulgarians, Hungarians, Italians, Croats, Ukrainians, Latvians, Lithuanians, Estonians, Tartars and arguably the Finns all fought with Germany. They are legitimate areas of Soviet interest. Poland never deserted the West. Poland should never have been betrayed.

"It was agreed with Churchill that under Mikołajczyk all the Polish forces would become subject to a supreme Allied or British command. So gradually the mavericks, the loyalists like Anders and Sosabowski, were side-lined and discredited. Anders was lucky he didn't end up with a bullet. Poor old Sosabowski got the blame for the Arnhem tragedy. Whilst Browning scarpered, forgetting to mention that the Brits dropped the Poles on top of the Germans, who conveniently shot the troops up as they parachuted in. But then they were meant to be used at Warsaw, Tadek, weren't they? You know all about that! So Warsaw was left to die."

I was not as dumb-struck as I would have been even a few months earlier. Every day of this confinement had a purpose, I knew that. All roads had led to this point, but what was the end game? I wondered.

"Some Allied planes did try to get through from Italy, and some drops were carried out," I countered.

"Oh come, come laddie! Are we siding now with the Soviets who sat on the other side of the river watching the Home Army die? Those Soviet Allies who 'unexpectedly' refused landing rights to relief aircraft? You know that SOE acted against specific orders when they carried out those relief drops. And orders from whom? Stalin's new chums, of course. Those at the top, those behind the closed doors, the ones who do not tell the troops the truth."

Medvedev took out another cigarette, lighting it from his ever turning chrome lighter. For a moment he was silent, taking took two more puffs before drawing in deeply. He shifted his position to a more relaxed pose, crossing his legs and leaning back in his chair. His boots glinted in the sun. The piping almost glowed. Then he began again.

"I want you to know more, otherwise what happens in the next months or years will make no sense. I intend to play a role in those events and I'm inviting you to do the same."

This was the moment. My response had to be just right. "I hear you. Now explain."

"When WiN was established I helped to infiltrate it. It is now heavily penetrated by my MVD men. There was an American Operation called Sunrise. This operation was a reformation or reorganisation, a cooperative venture using the old Nazi Army Intelligence Service. The Americans set it up under Reinhardt Gehlen. Remember him?"

"He was the German Major General in charge of Intelligence in the East, in particular the Soviet Union and Poland."

"Correct," Medvedev continued. "Gehlen has set up a spy ring with American backing, using old friends and officers. They call these new agents 'V men'. I suppose ex-Nazis need employment of some kind."

We both laughed. It was sort of funny after all.

"Politicians, Tadek. *Realpolitik*. This puppet Gehlen organisation is now the eyes and ears of the CIA. They are in contact with and supply money to it. They think they run the agents. But we, the MVD, supply mis-information. The Germans have always been hopeless at being spies. I will give you a name: Stefan Sienko. Remember this name.

"You should be aware, Tadek, that most of the money coming from America to support WiN goes to us. Can you imagine it, American money going to the MVD! We operate it virtually as a scam. The Polish UB run it, as proxies for me. For example, when the Polish government gave an amnesty in 1947, over sixty thousand troopers came out of the woods. The amnesty was a ruse. Gomułka was shit scared of the AK and he made it quite clear. To quote him exactly, "Soldiers of the AK are a hostile element which must be removed without mercy." In the Polish Central Committee, Roman Zambrowski has said that the AK has to be 'exterminated'. We cherry picked who was a foot soldier and who should die. It was easy."

My face was set like stone, but my stomach churned at this news. Thousands had been arrested, and many deported, imprisoned or shot. Gone were the early days when Berling's 1st Polish Army, the one set up by the Communists, went over to the AK in droves. Whole units deserted, disappearing into the forest and the remnants of the Home Army. The generals had been so right and the politicians so wrong.

"I must confess, I did not think Gomułka would renege on the amnesty in such a massive way," Medvedev said. "That, however, is war and I am an officer. My job now, Tadek, is to destroy the remnants of the Narodowy Siły

Zbrojne, your National Army Forces, the NSZ. The group which I think you favour and which you have aided. These have always been the tough guys, the hard-core anti-communists.

"If I do this, I am above suspicion. The policy is to turn them into bandits. As I speak we are staging bank robberies to discredit them, a few rapes here, a few killings there, even a train hold-up. The radio and press will highlight the atrocities as crimes against their own people. It is our intention to isolate them from the 'reasonable' WiN soldiers and turn them into terrorists, pro-fascist allies of the Ukrainians. It will not be so difficult to squeeze them like a pimple. They need food and money. So in time they will *become* real bandits. The children will see to that, as our schools' re-education programme rolls forward. Give them time, they will hang themselves. Like wolves in a trap they will snarl louder, alienating themselves from the people. People want peace now. They want to get on with their lives. We have them so deprived they have to work. They have no time for fighting. Sad, isn't it?"

I did not reply to what seemed a rhetorical question. But yes, it was sad, very sad.

"Then of course we shall push hard the anti-Semitic card, which worked so well in the elections. Kielce, Tadek, Kielce! Surely you have worked out that Stalin ordered a collision course between Poles and Jews? He needed to divert American public opinion from favouring Poland after all. What better way than to have a mini-pogrom? As you know, we had already started pushing Jews into the secret police, which did not endear them to the local Poles. In Kielce Jews were attacked by local workers from the nearby steel mill, all orchestrated by the local Party of course. The security forces stood by and did nothing, on direct orders from Warsaw. Our local troops did the same, on orders from Moscow. It was 'unfortunate' that these particular Jews were seeking shelter. They were returnees from camp deportations. Some having been saved from the Germans by good Poles were now being hunted by shitty Poles. At least that was the news story we put out. Well, there was some truth in it. Forty-two people were murdered, including women and children. Wounded Jews were even beaten on the way to hospital.

"I remember now. As I recall, for a few months children had mysteriously gone missing. That day someone had gone to the police to say Jews were stealing children, to use their blood for rituals."

There was a shift in intensity as he answered. Clearly he felt it was time to get his reasons for all these 'confessions' across to me; he was ready to move the conversation forward.

"A little boy made the claim he had been kidnapped, and that all the bodies of the missing children were in the cellar of a local kibbutz house. All hell broke loose. Hard to imagine that people believe such stories. I am always amazed what Roman Catholics will swallow when it comes to super-stition. Of course we had the old story of anti-Semitism in Poland all over the American headlines. That cut money to the political parties when they needed it, and helped the Polish security forces get over the beatings they were handing out to opposition party workers. Now the Security Police became Jew saviours.

"The point is, Tadek, all your friends are coming to their end. If they can, they should get out. Bierut is now both President of Poland and General Secretary of the Polish United Workers Party, so be sure that apart from the secret trials and murders you are already familiar with that a new set of show trials is imminent. All the surviving opposition leaders and partisans will go. Mikołajczyk and Korboński were wise to do a runner when they could. Of course, you realise we did a deal with Churchill to 'let' this happen under the noses of the Polish Security forces and the MGB?"

Immediately I thought of Ela, how close she must have been to this escape. I prayed she had made it. All this time I held her image in my mind like a sacred jewel, never to be acknowledged or divulged. The vision of her, the memory, had kept me sane. Schooling my features I allowed Medvedev to continue his virtual monologue.

"Bierut intends to follow in Stalin's footsteps. About ninety or so Polish officers will go to show trials, some those who have returned from London. But also many political enemies, both Communist and anti-Communist. A typical purge, Tadek. Typical Stalinism." He rubbed his forehead. "So now to you and me."

"You are to be exchanged - for one of ours. A German we would like back for services rendered during the war. The British MI5 want you back because someone has tried to kill you twice now. They do not know who or why, but it seems you ought to be dead. Not so surprising, Tadek. Even MI5 have worked out that someone over there in their own department wants you deceased. So you are back to being a pawn. You are sort of going home; Menzies wants you back for his mole-hunting in SIS. We have talked.

"But I hope you will be my knight too. I have a task for you. Eventually you will come back here. You are to assist myself and Comrade Beria to eliminate Stalin."

Despite all the schooling I'd received I was stunned, shifting uncomfort-ably in my seat.

Medvedev continued: "If we are caught, Beria will escape. And let us pray you and I have time for the cyanide capsule! Beria wants to know who Abakumov is running in London. He needs him or them out of the way before he makes his move here. Now it's all about who succeeds Stalin. Beria wants the Marshall Plan for Russia. He wants reforms, an end to some of the repression, and he wants his enemies dead. All very Russian.

"I want you to convey this message to the right American people. Make sure it does not go through British channels, except direct to Menzies, otherwise it will endanger the reformists here. Eden's right hand man in the Foreign Office was always a Soviet fellow traveller, for example. You now understand us and our ways. We share certain aims. Beria wants a secure Poland. And an anti-German ally on his doorstep, one which is not pro-Western, though not a puppet. A balancing weight, if you like, whilst Russia restructures. "

I forced myself to stay calm.

"He knows, as do you, that when Germany and Russia are friends Poland suffers. The inevitable fallout is always in the cockpit of Europe, Poland. So a strong Poland stops that fall-out. Beria is not a fool. The Union *will* break up at some point.

"Shortly there will be two dangerous German States: one, filthy rich and aggressive, to dominate the political scene in Europe with American money and American military power. The other, a Stalinist puppet that will terrify the West with a new Stalinist military and prove what a healthy workers' paradise can really look like. And this East Germany will look over their backside at the part of Germany the Big Three gave the Poles, will always be a threat to keep the Poles quiet."

"Do I have a choice?" I asked, playing for time as I tried to take on board this breathtaking tumble of words. I was to be a pawn. Messenger and actor both. My emotions were torn between the obvious desire for freedom and doubt for the future. I wanted to be out of this place with its sterile air, its institutionalised atmosphere. The guards, the talks with Medvedev, all would be gone. I wanted free air. Yet was what was being offered with this freedom? I was not free of myself, my obligations, my debts to people and indeed my own honour and self esteem.

All I knew was that I wanted to be free at any price. I would sort my head out later.

"A choice?" Medvedev replied. "None."

"Do you really think the West will listen?" I asked. "Beria is known to be a pervert and a criminal." I already knew the answer, of course, and was not looking for a response. The question was more of a comment. If Stalin could get away with murder, why not Beria? After all, he was only a lieutenant. And to think there wasn't one Russian on trial at Nuremburg.

"If you speak well of Beria people will listen in the Security Services. The politicians are another matter, they are almost entirely corrupt. The working class politician is always greedy. Think of me as Russian. I am not an Imperialist; I believe the Revolution was betrayed by the Bolsheviks. Beria is a Georgian. Unbelievably, neither of us is a 'Soviet' man, that faceless, classless, sexless person of the Soviet art style. When you have had time to think all these things through you will agree that abnormal times breed abnormal people who do abnormal things. Was it right to bomb open cities in Poland in 1939? No. But was it right to bomb and create firestorms in 1944? Yes, because the times were abnormal and we had adjusted to events. Pragmatism, Tadek, pragmatism. As I see it we are essentially nationalists - with a tendency to live and let live with our neighbours."

"As well as murderers and thieves," I challenged.

CHAPTER 12

# IRENA

"One more thing," Medvedev said. "Your friend Kryszka is alive, though I can't say he's well. He is to join you. I have arranged this and negotiated it with the Turks acting for money. The Britisher Menzies is behind the scene. I hope his life, which I give to you, will keep my life safe with you when needed. You understand?"

"I do." I realise here, of course, that Witek thinks he can play me like a fish. Yet I do admire the man. He knows Kryszka and I have a strange bond that I will honour.

He also knows that he, Witek, can rely on as me as I can rely on him in return. Yet I will be free and do what I want. I will beat him, as he will beat me from time to time. We just acknowledge that it is the same game. We are the same team.

"Good. Then here is how it will be. You will be flown south to Poland. Your friend will, along with others, be sprung from jail. The NSZ, with our assistance, will carry out the action and hand Kryszka on to you. In Krosno you will meet up with a new NSZ team. What and how much you tell Kryszka is then up to you. He is a very loyal man, both to his country and friends.

"Aniela's killer, Kuczarek, is in the Special Bureau, and also, on paper, a Major in the Polish UB. The NSZ wish to remove him. I wish to remove him. You will organise matters for Kryszka to remove him. I do not want you involved, as you have other work to do."

"So I work for you now?"

"You work for whom you want, Tadek. You are one of those free soldiers. You took an oath to the British. They broke that sacred trust when they tried to eliminate you. You took an oath as a Polish airman to the Republic. But it no longer exists, at least as far as most of the world is concerned. You can work for whichever side you like; for the moment you have become indispensible to us all. You are, as you told us under interrogation, a Z man, an anti-Communist sleeper within the SIS. Set in play by Sinclair."

"Did I really tell you all that?" I asked.

Medvedev smiled. "Drugs, Tadek, drugs. As I said, there is no need for sadistic brutality. We are masters with drugs and poisons.

"My friend, you are about to become a hero. A returned prodigal. It is arranged for you to steal a Polish plane and fly with two or three partisans back to the Free world. The press will love you. You will become a national hero, which means we Reds will have to leave you alone, at least until the dust settles. The UB will never forgive you, of course. They will come after you. But once Kryszka has completed our deal, eliminated Major Kuczarek, and our man is in his place, we can tip you off at every turn once. Always a life for a life.

"Of course, it will not be the real you splashed across the papers for public consumption. We don't want your picture or real name known. So on arrival, the Polish Exile government has arranged for some local hero to take your place. A similar story to your own will be invented. It will take the UB a few months to work out that they were duped, by persons unknown and for reasons obscure."

He looked very smug at that point. His face lit up as he dreamed of the puppet Polish Counter-Intelligence trying to work out what happened. "The double blind should work, depending on how much your friend Kryszka talked about you when he was drugged or beaten. Time will tell."

This was the moment to make my stand. "Remember one thing, my friend. My service is the protection of the State. I was brought up to protect its freedoms and values. For now that State still lies in London with the Exiles." The next remark was addressed to Medvedev in a sincere way. "I feel sorry for you." And I did. I felt genuine sorrow for this man I had known for a short while as Witek.

"Believe me, Tadek, I weep for whoever I am too," Medvedev replied, sensing the drift of my thoughts. "I too am trapped; I love Russia and am fond of Poland. So I fight my own fight. If I am caught I shall be strung up with piano wire."

It was time to point out an obvious flaw in Witek's plan. "What about my time here? If I escape, you will be fingered, surely?"

"I have one ally here. Volkhov, who as you know, stands outside the door. I also have one faithful driver, Mishkin. Both Russian patriots and good Communists. I have never officially been seen here. Your transfer was an administrative mistake by a man who has long enjoyed his subsequent posting to the sunny Crimea."

"And my special guard?" I thought of the young man who had been as decent as he could be to a special prisoner.

Medvedev looked hard into my eyes, holding my gaze unwaveringly.

"The moment you leave here he will be arrested. He will escape, and by accurate fire receive a bullet in his brain. His relatives will be rounded up and despatched to a *gulag*. There will be no interrogation. It is usual in these circumstances. The hospital director will lose his job but not his life. The two MGB nurses who were aware a special prisoner existed will simply disappear. One of their bodies will be discovered on the border of the American zone in Germany. People will make of that what they will."

"What a cold, calculating bastard you are!"

"Pot calling kettle black," rejoined Medvedev, but I could see I had touched on a nerve. He shivered. "Let's get on. The operation name for your heroic escape is Irena. It's irrelevant, really, but I thought a man like you would want to know. Being resolute, I am sure you will acquire a radio if you do not meet with an accident or a bullet. I want one year of quiet from you, Tadek. Yes, one year. We need to consolidate our position in the Army. It is our weakest link. I do not trust that preening parrot Zhukov. The politics are secure here, but we must also have American backing in particular. Time is on our side. Stalin ages and is ill. Perhaps we will not have to shoot him." He laughed, but was immediately right back to business. "When you have your radio, use this frequency." And he handed me a note.

"This will take you directly to the MVD system. We will be listening, as will the GB, and as will the Americans and the British and God knows who else. Everyone will ask themselves, 'Who is this? And who is he talking to?' So be very careful. When you want to be contacted, use the call sign 'Goose boy'. If I am alive I shall answer with, 'Plum Brandy'. You reply, 'Toast' and then I reply, 'Yellow Candle'. Here in my second notebook is a series of call signs and responses. Always use them in sequence, never using the same one twice except for the original call sign. The shoes you are given have a place in the sole for this list; I hope the British do not take your shoes away. If they do, then your first message must make that clear. I have one man in London I can trust. Here is his face. Remember it well. If this man finds you, trust him. I will not give you a name as we have not yet decided on it and it may change."

And so it was that I turned up in a square in Krosno, in the autumn of 1949.

Whilst the world watched Korea, waiting for the conflict that should have been in Poland, I walked around the large square, exploring the concept of proxy wars. Was this how it was to be, I wondered? Wars between East and West, fought elsewhere, because the Bomb precluded war in Europe? I agreed with Witek, as I called him. Strange that; in prison, he was Medvedev, but out here he was Witek once more. For the first time since my arrival back in Poland I fully realised the trust this odd Russian patriot had placed in me. I held his life in my mind and will.

The airfield I had recently landed at had been a flying school. Now it was a Soviet base. Krosno, that sweet town known as Little Krakow, was still beautiful in the late September sun. Kryszka and I sat in the shade. Not so far away was the famous Dukla pass, the road to Hungary. The Soviets and Germans had pounded the area till the end. The surviving Lemkos, categorised as Ukrainians, whatever that meant, were shipped off to the Soviet side, to Khrushchev's playground. Presumably these people would replace those he had murdered. I hoped they enjoyed being Ukrainian and smiled at my own sarcasm.

Kryszka was lost in his own thoughts. He had become even quieter than before. He had always spoken little but now he seemed taciturn. I noticed that when he held a cup or cigarette his hands shook a little. He was not in good physical shape and had adopted a slight stoop. I wondered how he saw me. He would see me changed too, I supposed. Whilst I was in reasonable physical shape, he was not.

Both of us were shot to pieces in our heads, of that I was sure.

I had arrived by plane in the clothes supplied by Witek. To all ostensible purposes and to any observer I was a civilian, though perhaps smarter looking than the average. He had also provided me with a bag, in which were a set of more workaday clothes for later use.

Our parting had been a strange affair. Witek had tears in his eyes and had called me his son. I did not respond because I felt nothing for the man. Or perhaps because I did.

"Here, Tadek, my gifts to you," he had said and passed me a Polish Air Force 'wings' badge. This had been my talisman from the war, something I had kept, a form of personal identification not to a third person but for myself. It reminded me of where I had come from. Next was his leatherbound journal, his notes on the war. More than a diary, it was a legacy of facts and figures, opinions and orders. Later, as I thumbed through it, I realised that he had added to it in neat script right up to the point of our capture, when Witek mutated into Medvedev.

All entries after that were in some form of code. Just symbols, no letters or numbers.

"You will work it out," he assured me, but he gave me no clue, except to say, "Is being a Jew a question of ethnicity or religion? You enjoy history; start with the Khazars."

The Khazars were an ethnic Turkic people, who had converted to Judaism. They had once had an 'empire', like the mysterious Sarmatians and Alens who occupied the Caucasus. The Khazars were thought to have ended up in Poland, in that border area called Ukraine. Some historians claimed these converts to be the true ancestors of the Jews of the Slav world, rather than the results of a Jewish migration from German lands. The clue to the code lay in the language.

Lastly Witek had passed to me my faithful Radom Vis semi-automatic pistol. Cleaned and oiled. One of the finest hand-guns ever made, the Germans had kept it in production as one of their standard weapons. Mine had been an original Polish version. Sure enough, there were the nicks I had made in the butt to identify it as my own. I checked the weapon. The clip had its full complement of eight rounds. He slid a small box towards me. Spare cartridges, just in case. I could have shot him then.

As it was, we shook hands at the Soviet airfield.

His last words to me were, "Remember, Tadek, there is no honour amongst politicians. Never trust them. They steal our lives."

I climbed into the Russian version of the Dakota, alongside a number of other military passengers, mostly, but not all, Security troops and officers. I had a row to myself. No one seemed keen to talk to me. At the Krosno end, once the steps had been wheeled to the side, I was shown some deference in priority, exiting behind a fully-fledged colonel.

As I walked onto the grass a car drew up. The driver got out and saluted. No questions were asked and no papers required, although I had been given some form of *Sprawka* or travel document. The driver held the rear door open and we drove off, watched surreptitiously by some of my fellow passengers as they tramped across the field. As we drove I noted a small transport craft being refuelled. The bowser and tractor were close up to it, so I couldn't identify the type, but it had Polish markings rather than the red star of the USSR. It was tucked close by the side of the nearest hangar. I guessed this was the plane destined for our escape.

I also saw MiG 3 fighters.

We drove off the field, through the lower part of town. A lot of construction had started. From what I could see, the Germans or Soviets had done a lot of damage. I asked the driver whether the glass works had been reopened. His reticence on the subject stopped my questioning further.

We crossed the railway that led up to Jasło passing along Grodzka Street. Near the top, before the main square, turning right into a street of substantial, older, wooden houses the driver told me to get out and to walk down the road. "Take the first right, and then knock at the first house, the one painted ochre. Ask for Irena."

I followed his instructions but could see no 'twitching' curtains. This was a Catholic country and the old people felt obliged to tell the priest what they saw. It would be interesting to see who won the battle of the spies. Materialism, I reasoned, would beat God. I reached the house which had been painted yellowish-brown at some time. Now the paint peeled to show wood planking aged grey. The door opened without me having to knock. I was expected.

There was no hello or welcome from the middle-aged woman at the door. Her sleeveless blue dress was old, but pressed and clean. It revealed plump arms with the tell-tale hang-down flesh of later middle age. Her faded blonde hair was streaked white. Her face was a little haggard, with the lined look of the people in this country, yet her skin was thick enough to maintain a certain roundness that spoke of vitality.

"Irena?" I said.

"Obviously," came the curt reply. "Follow me."

The large house was clearly divided into flats. She obviously wanted to hustle me through the divides that separated people living here. We went through a door that opened into a large living area. Large double-glazed windows gave a wonderful view of an overgrown garden with fruit trees. I walked over, drawn by the freshness of the green. Wasps were busy tackling over-ripe pears. There was a pleasing feel to the house, as there so often is from wooden houses. I wondered what had happened to the owners. Ethnic Pole or Jew? I doubted they would have survived. Wrong race, wrong religion, wrong politics...even the wrong eye contact with the wrong person was sufficient.

She ushered me into a small box-room with a chest lining the length of one wall. On top was a pile of blankets or rugs laid out like a bed. "You stay in here." I put my bag down and thanked her. She turned and left.

I decided to change, blend in with the crowd, though I'd yet to see one. The street was quiet like the grave. Serene. No sense of expectancy. This was strange to my stretched nerves, but pleasing. I felt like a boy scout on holiday as I carefully took off my 'fine' clothes and donned a clearly second-hand set of baggy serge trousers and a thick shirt. The pants felt ten sizes too big. I had a sleeveless pullover with a couple of moth holes, and a grey jacket, from the mixed flecks made from shoddy. My boots were of the work type, with laces to my ankles. No socks. Lastly, a flat cap and I was the perfect Soviet citizen. I hoped I would fit in here in the New Poland.

Should I venture out into 'Irena' territory, I wondered? I was in need of a pee and desperately wanted a wash. I had three bars of highly scented soap as 'currency' from Witek. He had told me to give it to people when I wanted to be ingratiating. He had also supplied me with three packs of American cigarettes or 'Bribes'. Some of the new Polish money had come with the clothes too, just a few zlotys to tide me over. As Witek had said, the new Communist money was worthless anyway. Owners of the old currency had not been able to exchange it for the new currency above a pittance, so all their savings were wiped out. A black market in currency already existed. Witek had supplied me with fifty US dollars – 'genuine', he had assured me- now nestling in my boot. I was rich.

Used to the direct command of the prison hospital, I pondered her directive, and then decided to venture out. This freedom was strange. Everything felt out of focus. After so long surrounded by the muted inhabitants of the sanatorium people seemed abnormal to me, not quite right, a little overblown and excitable, larger than life should be. It was taking time to adjust. Sudden sounds made me jump. I felt less related to people, uninterested in them. I simply felt harder, tougher, detached.

Walking along the narrow dark corridor toward the large room. I passed another door near to my own. The room was larger than mine. I glimpsed a mattress laid on the floor.

Irena I found in the large room, slicing bread. She ignored me I wandered over to the open window. She had changed into a thin cotton floral print dress. It dawned that the best dress had been taken off and hung back up straight away. She had prepared herself for me, the smart new arrival.

Without talking I went back to my room and picked up the three soaps. Back in the main room I placed the three soaps on the large kitchen table.

"I have already been paid," she snapped.

"These are my gifts for you," I replied, thinking how like Witek I sounded. I moved back to the window. "The clothes and the bag will be left in the spare room. You can sell them when I've gone. My other boots are worth something." They were beautiful, brown leather Polish cavalry boots. I had wondered from whom they had been taken and when.

"Do you have a lavatory?" I asked.

She answered so brightly and warmly I was taken by surprise. "I do." I have the only private lavatory and bathroom in the building. Everyone else here has to use the communal lavatory outside. But I have a splendid bathroom. Everything works. Would you like to wash or shave?"

I was taken aback by this string of information. She really was proud of that bathroom.

"I'd love to clean up."

I was shown to a door obscured by some curtaining. And there it was, with a Victorian-style bath and well-worn brass taps and faucet. The bath's enamel had been removed by years of scrubbing with abrasives. A green stained line ran down the tap end. Above the bath, attached to the wall, a gas geezer pointed its spout to the plug-hole beneath. And next to the bath was a lavatory, complete with dark mahogany seat. Irena handed me a well-worn striped towel and a bar of soap. Lastly, she gave me a bath-plug of the universal type. "This is worth a lot of money," she said, placing it into my hand as though it were a piece of good jewellery.

"I understand," I said, remembering the prison hospital where there were no plugs. We had stuffed torn-up strips of Pravda into pulp to stop the water running away.

Refreshed I sat opposite her and ate the bread and cheese she had provided. We drank tea in silence. Finally my curiosity couldn't stand the quiet any longer.

"Do you live alone?" I asked.

"No, I have a son."

"Is he at school?"

"Yes, he is now, but he will be staying with a friend whilst you are for the next two nights."

"What happens after two nights?"

"Obviously you will go wherever fortune takes you. Your contact will arrive here at seven."

"This is still a big place for just the two of you." I was fishing to see if my seven o'clock appointment was her husband.

"I am a Party member and a good Communist. So I deserve more than those who fought against us."

"Do I fight against you?" My question was aimed at trying to understand this situation. She had been hostile at the beginning, so just who did she work for?

"I am a journalist," she offered. "I like to speak the truth. I know we did not win the election and I know that what we have now is not what I fought for; this is not Polish Communism. One day we will have Polish Communism and then you will see how well it works. For now I ally myself with my class enemies."

"Am I a class enemy?" I asked mildly.

"I have no idea. I know you are playing a game with my enemies, the NSZ, and that I have to cooperate with them sometimes. We shall smash them, but for the moment they are useful. I write pieces for the paper, make sure we cast such slurs on them that no one will support them. You smell nice." She shot me a disarming smile and we laughed both at the turn she had taken. It was a signal that the real conversation was over.

"I left the soap in the bathroom, I assure you."

At seven the evening had drawn in. My hostess lit an oil lamp. "The electricity is still not as it will be," she apologised. Always with Reds, I had noticed this practice of surmounting practical issues by projecting a rosy future.

She watched the garden from the window. "Time to go. Just follow the stairs down. Instead of heading for the front, turn left, then go out the back door. Go straight ahead, under the trees. You see the point of his lit cigarette? He is waiting for you there at the back gate."

"What if I am seen? Won't you be reported?"

"Not after dark. My neighbours think I open my legs sometimes for strangers or party officials."

I said nothing, but thought how matter-of-factly she had explained her situation. Another life mixed up and lost.

Padding through the warm air I headed towards the red glow. As I approached I saw in faint silhouette, a man. Seeing me he stubbed the cigarette on the wall and then pocketed it. A professional, I thought. No trace of butts on the ground.

'Polak?' This was my code name for Operation Irena.

"Yes," I whispered. back.

"I am Mazurek. Follow me about ten metres behind. If I stop, you stop. Have you got a gun?"

I nodded.

"Don't hesitate to use it." A chilling reminder of the times we lived in.

We headed uphill into the old town, slipping through side streets. He turned under the bell tower into the precinct of the Franciscan Fathers' Church. We slipped into a side building.

"Okay, we wait. You know where this is?"

I shook my head.

"This is the place of Anna and Stanisław, the Polish Abelard and Eloise. Unrequited love and all that. They had to get permission from the Pope to marry. Poor man died on his way to Rome. Well, we may as well pass the time. Smoke?"

"No thanks," I replied, "for some reason I never started."

"I won't then either. It's just nerves, you know, something to do."

We heard approaching footsteps and tensed, both of us with weapons at the ready. The door creaked opened. We saw two shadows. Code names were exchanged and the two NSZ soldiers embraced. The second man held back, still in the shadows, but I recognised the body shape. It was Kryszka.

"Mazurek," I whispered quietly, "lend me your lighter." He passed it over to me and I struck the flint, the small flame catching and illuminating the small space. I held the light close to my face and turned to Kryszka.

"Tadek! Christ's shit! You bloody moron!" We fell on each other, embracing hard, cheek to cheek. We laughed then coughed down our emotion. There was nothing to say really. We parted, patting each others' arms. Kryszka kept muttering, "Bloody hell!" In English, of all things.

"I thought you were dead!" he said at last.

I had the advantage of him. "I was lucky. They told me you were alive."

We had a lot to catch up on and a lot to do.

So here we were, the old team, sitting on the *Rynek*, Krosno's market square on a warm September day, sitting enjoying the sun and watching the world go by. Black tea. No lemon, an impossible luxury. We did have good bread though. Krosno was famous for its bread, and despite the shortages what we had was different and delicious. Baked on the premises, the owner had said. "We are too small to close down." The big bakeries had been nationalised.

It was good to see that industry, private or state, was taking hold again. Life was indeed returning to some form of normality. True, there was building work everywhere. This handsome square with its medieval buildings was more than the worse for wear. But the people were alive and clearly

intended to rebuild their shattered city. The old seventeenth century tene-
ments were once again occupied by the wealthy, the élite of the town. But
this time Party and Security officials had been given apartments in these
ancient buildings.

I looked across the square to the old town house which had been built
by a Scotsman in the 16th century. He had been named Portius for some reason, according to my town guide of last night, Mazurek. The food market
had been operating today and the peasants had come in to sell their wares.
There were 'no hungry peasants', at least this had always been the cry. So
although the State did not yet dare to collectivise Polish farms everywhere,
the farmers still had to meet quotas and sell at State prices calculated to
make life difficult. These local markets were a lifeline to town dweller as
well as farmer. Kryszka and I had bought some carrots, apples and sausage,
both for sustenance and ease of transport.

We had spent the night planning today and sharing our experiences.
Talk of Aniela was off limits. He just clammed up when I tried to raise her
name, or ask him about his loss.

Carefully we listened to the plans laid out by Mazurek and his number
two. Our role was to be the hit men; we were the insurance that we had the
right man. Mazurek's team would relay the information to Witek's men. It
was an uncomplicated dead letterbox job. But as the two NSZ men said,
Krosno was not the metropolis of Warsaw so news would spread. Their planning was meticulous, and included a fall-back situation should things go
wrong. It was a joint operation between NSZ men and WiN partisans. The
latter would provide escape routes and pre-attack services and any immediate support. WiN was still strong in this part of the sub-Carpathians.

Mazurek's number two, the guy taking care of Kryszka was code-named
Łoś. Elk – it suited him. He was the local WiN leader and was to be one of
our passengers on the flight out. "I'm told you are the one who can nail the
traitors in WiN," he said, pumping my hand. "Well, my job is to get you to
the West. Every blasted leader we had in the Kraków and Rzeszów district
was rounded up last year. Adam Lazarowicz, Mieczysław Kawalec, Józef
Rzepka, Franciszek Błażej, Józef Batory, Łukasz Ciepliński and Karol
Chmiel. That was not coincidence. They are all in Mokotów in Warsaw. The
UB are slowly killing them and us."[1]

Kryszka growled. "I was there too. I met and know some of those men."
he muttered. "Błażej is so badly beaten he is eaten with gangrene. He stinks
and rots. Commie bastards."

Those Łoś had named were all local heroes, mostly caught in
Krakówand Rzeszów. I knew the names and more from 'Irena', who that
morning had shown me some of the articles she had written. When caught,
the 'bandits' had their identity and code names published in full so that

everyone, either legitimate or clandestine, was aware of the Security Police success. She was especially proud of the capture of Ciepliński, who had attacked but failed to capture Rzeszów castle in an attempt to release over four hundred AK soldiers from the Soviets. Irena had deemed this a rebellious act when it happened in 1944; now she was not so sure, having seeing the actions of the NKVD, now the MVB and the UB over the years. She was ambivalent about many things, but this man had tried to inform Western Capitalist Allies of events in Poland and of the potential for a rising here in the South East. This she felt sure was the act of a traitor. No amount of reasoning with her changed this view. We agreed to differ.

Her justification was that what we saw around us was not Communism but Stalinism. The fact that Stalin was implementing fundamental Communism and following in the footsteps of Lenin made no difference to her at all. There are none so blind as those who will not see.

Our debate had begun in the morning over breakfast. She had gone to some trouble, laying out cold food. She asked if I had slept well, all the usual polite enquiries of the morning. I told her that being perched high above the floor on a narrow cupboard had felt like being in a bunk at sea. When I asked her how she'd slept, she said well, 'Apart from the cockroaches, which is why my son sleeps on top. Me, I don't mind so much." But evidently she did, as she shuddered.

"Have you filled in the gap between the wall edge and the floor?" I asked. "I saw some putty in the bathroom. Let me try filling in some cracks, I have nothing else to do until late this afternoon," I volunteered. I was glad of something to do. The waiting alone would have driven up my adrenalin and I would have had a bad time worrying. As it was, I was sweating at the thought of what was going to happen. I needed to be calm. The team was not due to meet up until three in the afternoon in the *Rynek* area. All was planned. It was just a matter of being in the right place and a few casual nods to the people we knew.

"Okaaay," she answered, drawing out the word. "See what you can do. I will be back at two o'clock. Will you still be here?"

"I expect to be. Here, take this for the extra food. It's maybe capitalist but it won't bite." I passed over a five dollar bill, a gesture of goodwill. I did not know how far I could trust this woman; this was an 'ingratiating' experiment. I understood neither her politics nor her position in all this.

Kryszka and I had been told we were to stay out of trouble until the market started to close down about four; it was then we were to strike. The target was expected to have a Soviet visitor and to be taking tea. We would see. 'Be at the market place at three. Acknowledge the two of us. Cross the square at precisely four and follow us in. You wait and take tea at the *Chłopska* Café.'

I spent the morning kneading putty and packing old newspaper into the crack between skirting board and floor in the bedroom. The board was set firm to the wall but there was a gap at the bottom. The oilcloth or linoleum had been pushed under the skirting so that it took up some space. I used a kitchen knife to push the putty in and seal edges. Of course I knew it wouldn't last long, it would dry out and crack, but at least it kept me occupied. Occasionally I saw the antennae of the roaches flicker out from their hiding place. "Got you, you little buggers!" I muttered, drawing immense satisfaction from the fact that they would be entombed like an Egyptian scarab beetle.

It was a game, to keep me steady. Subconsciously I heard every movement in the house, flinched at every voice, every sound. Once I thought I heard an English voice on a radio, but the sound was quickly lost. The Soviets were jamming the BBC and American stations.

In the room there was a mattress on the floor. Bed linen and cover had been folded and lay piled to one side. An old wardrobe with a large mirror stood to one side. It was made from dark wood and belonged to another age. The silvering of the mirror on the bottom edges was flaking. I pulled the door open. At the base were three drawers in light wood. One contained underwear, another blouses and tops, the last bits and pieces of makeup, some tawdry jewellery and some photographs. There was a photograph of a group of partisans. Three men, two kneeling and one sitting in the middle. Each held a rifle. Nothing but the forest in the background. On the back was scribbled 'Zbiszek, died August 1941. Forever mine.' A red lipstick kiss had now faded to brown.

"So he was with the Communist partisans." Talking to myself broke the oppressing silence that increased with the heat. It was getting hot.

On the rails above the drawers was yesterday's blue dress, a couple of skirts, a top coat, and a couple more print dresses. This morning she had worn a black pencil skirt and white blouse with matching black and white court shoes and a loose lightweight blue jacket draped over her shoulders. In the corner of the wardrobe was an untidy pile of shoes and boots, probably six or seven pairs. You could see what she valued. At the far end, under a white cover, was a silk ball-gown in emerald green, pushed to one side, hanging all alone. My mind went back to Manci, the Marta Hari of my University days. She had taught me how to love a woman in more pleasant times before the war. Pleasant but dangerous; I had been too romantic to realise what was happening around me. Quoting Manci I said, "Blondes should never wear this green, it drains their colour." Chuckling I went and tidied up, washing my hands, cleaning the putty knife.

Afterwards I checked my pistol again and again. I emptied the box of spare cartridges into my pocket and put my – or Witek's – notebook inside my jacket pocket. As always I kept my Air Force badge in a side jacket pocket so I was ready to go. Going back to the bedroom I sat on the floor. It was quiet in here and had a different feeling, a different scent. By the wall near the window there was an upright wooden chair. It was too uncomfortable to sit on for long, so I lay flat, letting the cool of the lino drift to my back. And I waited.

She came back at two, as she'd said. I heard the clip-clop of her high heels. The latch turned but she did not call out. The sounds had broken my reverie, thoughts had turned to dozing. I felt slightly silly in there, like a child caught some place out of bounds. Irena opened the door, smiled and came across to the chair. I made room for her to sit down. She crossed her legs, rubbing one hand up and down the right one as though it was tired. She glanced around the room skirting. "Good job!" she allowed.

I hadn't moved except my arms, to make room for her. Now I found myself slightly uncomfortable, sitting at an awkward angle inches from her knee. I realised that all her leg rubbing had been to draw my attention to her stockings. She saw me finally register them.

"Black market. Real American, with real dollars. Thank yoooo!" As she elongated the 'you', she uncrossed her legs. Touching her fingers to her lips she leant forward, pressing the fingers to my upturned forehead. Her blouse gaped and I caught a glimpse of silk bra, the kind I had seen when peeking through her things. She leaned back and giggled like a girl.

We made eye contact. She had good legs. Wide, strong knees, muscular calves. One ankle was tucked now behind the other, one foot half out of the black and white court shoe. She eased herself a fraction toward me, allowing the skirt to slip above the knee. We held each other's gaze for a moment. Only our breathing could be heard. Conscious her knees were parting I leaned back slightly, seeing the stretch of skirt tight over rounded thighs, the dark stockings with their dark tops emphasising the milk white flesh that would feel soft to the touch, softer than the feel even of eiderdown. And then I saw the wedge of white, covering her pubic area. I licked my lips, my mouth dry. A pathway to lust.

I looked at her again. She sat expectantly, waiting for my move. Placing one hand firmly on her knee I heaved myself up from the floor. "Must be getting old," I quipped. We laughed, the tension broken. "Shall we have a cup of tea before I go?"

"Yes, let's." And so it was that we spent the last half hour before the finale of Operation Irena talking about her lost husband, her son and her ambitions.

As I left I thanked her warmly.

"No, thank you," she replied and we kissed on the doorstep for the benefit of any spying neighbour. Pulling me close she whispered in my ear, "I mean it. Thank you for your kindness."

The clock crept to four in the *Chłopska* Café. We spotted the other two and moved after them. It was a pleasure to see that despite hardships the flower-sellers did a good trade. We passed close to two bored militia men, part of the secondary police force. Some Russian soldiers, we guessed on leave, were hanging around a bar at the other end of the square. Voices were raised and an argument was developing between the locals and the troopers. The militia men headed that way. As we followed our two under the portico, I glanced up at the façade of the building we were about to enter. A man who had been attending to some guttering from a ladder leant over from his perch, and I saw him cut the telephone wires. Two young men fell in behind us.

Mazurek and Łoś went straight through the open door and into the cool dark interior. A young UB guard sat at a desk just inside. Confronted by two pistols he rose and raised his hands, glancing at his machine pistol to one side. Mazurek lifted the machine pistol and slung it over his shoulder.

"Turn around," he told the boy, who did as he was told. Mazurek brought his pistol down on the back of the guard's head. He dropped like a stone.

"Shoot him if he comes round and gives any trouble," he said to one of 'our' youngsters. "He should be out for a while. Another team member was lashing the boy's feet and cuffing his wrists with cuffs he had found on the guard.

"Keep your eyes open," the first young partisan was commanded. He saluted Mazurek.

A young woman had silently joined us, carrying a bunch of flowers. As quietly as we could we went upstairs, but our boots echoed. Each floor had two apartments, each with a steel-reinforced door and spy-hole. One of the lads peeled off, with the instruction to shoot anyone who came out. Elk took the next floor, leaving four of us, including the girl, for the final floor.

We three men stood to one side. Mazurek would cover this floor whilst Kryszka and I would go in. Kryszka had the only weapon with a silencer. We had thought of blowing the door, but this way seemed cleaner, safer.

The girl pushed the buzzer and thumped the door and stood back. There was the sound of footsteps. Someone paused, looking through the spy-hole. "Oh flowers, how lovely!" we heard a woman say. Bolts were drawn and the door opened.

The girl fled as we two burst through the doorway, throwing it wide and pushing the inner door back on the woman. Kryszka headed straight down the passage whilst I swung the doors to, giving the startled woman a heavy slap across her mouth and hissing for her to shut up. Her lip split. I saw tears and terror mix as I pushed her ahead of me. She did not resist but scurried forward. As we entered the dining-room she slipped the other side of a beautiful modern highly-polished mahogany table. The whole room was newly decorated and filled with modern furniture.

The Russian was already dead, slumped back in his chair with a neat hole in his forehead.

The woman clutched two children to her. One, a boy, I reckoned to be about seven. The girl, a pretty blonde in a pink party dress, was around ten. Wide eyes were fixed on Kryszka who was pointing his pistol at the UB man. There was a moment of suspension, of absolute silence, of astonishment. Kryszka was transfixed, motionless, staring at his target, Aniela's killer. Kuczarek was still holding his teacup in his right hand. His left was out of sight. He should have been dead by now, like the Russian, but Kryszka was motionless.

I sensed rather than saw a movement, the merest shadow to my left, in the glass-panelled door. As I turned I saw a uniform and a machine pistol nozzle and fired three rounds. The noise was shattering as the glass disintegrated. A uniformed guard I guessed to be a bodyguard was blown backward into the next room. This was not the plan. Intelligence had not spotted the extra guard.

The woman set up a wail loud enough to waken the dead. I reached over and hit her hard in the mouth again. She settled into sobs.

Kryszka was now leaning on the table with both hands. He was sobbing too.

"Why are you going to kill my daddy?" the little girl asked, without any sense of emotion.

This was turning into a madhouse, but I felt a need to answer.

"Your daddy is being executed. That means he has done a lot of wrong things. The law says he should die. Your mummy will explain some day."

"My daddy is a hero of the Soviet Union. I will kill you when I grow up!" the brave little girl came back at me.

"Well, lass, let me tell you, I am a Polish officer in the legal Air Force of this country. Your father is in Polish uniform and subject to our law!" My tone was bitter with sheer anger and frustration.

She stuck her tongue out at me and in that same second I blasted her father to perdition. His left arm had been rising slowly, so slowly, to a firing position. I guessed he would have initially fired through the table and then fired off at us for his life. As it was, my two bullets took him in the chest and had thrown him back against the wall. I pushed around the table and put a third one in his brain for good luck. Grabbing his weapon I kicked the girl who was now clutching at my trousers and kicking me off my leg. I threw her hard against the wall, winding her. I watched her slide down the wall with a surprised look on her face. She had hit the back of her head hard.

"Pain hurts, doesn't it?" I yelled. "Ask your bloody mother who your father really was, you spoiled little brat! Ask your mother for the truth and be thankful you are alive!" Grabbing Kryszka, I pulled him along the corridor onto the stairs. He seemed to wake up from his trance in the cooler air and started mumbling apologies. "That can wait" I snapped. "Deed's done."

Mazurek was waiting, straining like a greyhound on a leash. We turned and fled down the stairs, jumping the flights. We collected our men. On the ground floor Mazurek turned and sprayed bullets upward at the landings. Every apartment was a UB officer's home. They would have tried the phone and found it dead. Maybe they had a radio. Whatever the contact they may have made, they would now be armed and ready for a shoot-out. Mazurek's warning gunfire would make them cautious for a few more precious seconds.

On the square people were running away, or just standing in groups, unsure what to do. They had heard gunfire but the echoes did not identify where it had come from. We scooted out, going our separate ways. The two militia men I'd seen earlier started running at one of the boys. A window was open somewhere above us. I guessed someone from one of the apartments was shouting and pointing at the lad. A fusillade of shots rang out. People dived to the floor or started to really run. I could not see what was going on for milling people, but clearly a partisan had opened up on the militia, from the sound with a Sten gun. The militia men went down in front of me to the left. The lad ran on. The shots had come from the other side of the square, clearly from a covering party.

I grabbed Kryszka's arm. "You make sure you get on that plane, old buddy. I tell you, if you are not at the rendezvous I will come for you, whatever it takes." He gripped my arm and we parted.

I saw Mazurek drop his weapon into the basket of a little old lady flower-seller, serenely wandering across the square despite the hubbub. One of the boys barged a woman carrying a paper folded under her arm, who then eagerly left the scene. It was well organised.

I ran to the corner and down a side street. A horse and cart were waiting for me. The farmer whipped his horse and I sat back on a pile of beetroot as though content with our sales at the market. The horse was a beautiful roan, all its red tassels dangling for market day. The farmer said nothing, just turned, and winked. I scrabbled in the sacks, realising that if stopped my face would look white compared to his. A bit of dirt and beetroot might help.

Not so far out of town we headed to his farm. It was a small affair but close to the airfield. The militia would turn the town upside down but would presume the 'fighting' party would have come from the forest, not from the direction in which we were headed, which was a Soviet base. Our horse and cart were passed by some trucks coming up from the airfield, full of troops to help the militia and local UB mount a search. The hardcore UB men would come down from Rzesów and be in Krosno, we reckoned, around midnight.

For the moment I was safe. By the time we arrived at the farm I had fallen into conversation with my rescuer, the owner of the horse and cart. He turned out to be a Lemko.

"Well, how about that!" I said. "I thought you were all supposed to be deported, off becoming good Soviet citizens."

"They forgot me," he explained. "The Polish Reds came and said, 'You can take one cow and two bags. Everything else must stay for the new people. They were so busy clearing out the villages that, because my farm is this side of the airfield, they forgot me. They never came to round me up and I wasn't going to move on my own. I went up to the *biuro* to sort out my papers. The man in the office knew my son, who had gone to the war in '39. This man was not a true Red, he was handing out papers to help people. He registered me as coming from the East. So I live here still."

"And your son?

"The same man at the office told me he is in England, alive. I had a letter from the Red Cross but I need someone to read it. He has been with the Polish Army all the time and survived. I have written to him," the farmer said. "The Polish man wrote down what I said and said he would get it through the censors. Everything sent abroad is read by the secret police. He told me this."

"If in England I meet him, would you like me to say how well you are?"

He replied that he would like that very much, and would it be possible for him to come to England to meet his son before he died? Would his son like the farm, did I think, if the Communists hadn't stolen it by then? I gave him a few dollars, for which he was genuinely grateful. So far in Poland I had no need of bribes. He stowed away his dollars, knowing it was the first of the hard currency he would need for his fare, if ever he could get a passport out of the country.

His son was called Bohdan Hudak he told me. His own name, I learned, was Nykyfor Hudak, but he was now known as Jan Kowalski. Equivalent to John Smith in English.

Sitting in his kitchen I asked him about his neighbours. "Why wouldn't they shop you?"

"Oh, we have all learned that for the moment we are all Poles. People around here hated the Russians, and now they hate the Polish Reds. Pity we didn't have time to sort it all out before the war. We get along now. It will take time to get rid of the memories, the killing and the fighting. My neighbours see me as taking a stand against the Reds, so I am one of them now."

His dog pricked up its ears and growled. Whilst talking to the old man, I had cleaned and rearmed the Radom. I reached for it now and moved to the side of the door.

"Jan, Jan, it's Mazurek." A gentle knock on the door. The dog rose and growled, baring its teeth. The old man ran his hand along its back, calming him. He ruffled its neck and it stretched and yawned, thinking its job done. It sank to the floor, muzzle between its paws. The old man opened the door and Mazurek pushed in.

"Time to go," he said as I stepped aside from the shadows, pocketing the pistol.

Outside the door the flower-girl stood in the twilight, shadowed by the linden trees close up to the farm cottage. She offered a tentative smile which I did not return, preoccupied with my own thoughts. The adrenalin had drained. I felt both numb and sick. My mind raced, turning over and over the events in the room. *What had I done? How could I have been so callous? I recognised a new, almost pathological coldness in myself. What had I turned into?* The thoughts raced endlessly around my tired mind. I had appeared so cool, so together and completely unmoved in that room. And in the moment I was. It had been as though I were in shock. Now I felt drained, ill. Yet we had still another trial to undergo.

We walked in a line, separated by about twenty metres to limit the possibility of ambush. Sticking to the unmade consolidated mud road, deeply rutted from trucks and farm carts, we cut across a narrow field, disturbing some tethered goats which sent their fractious bleats into the air. But no human stirred. We passed through a small wood, the ground soft and spongy underfoot. At the edge of the wood we paused. The moonlight was clear, throwing its luminous silvering over the farmland and the open ground which ran up to the perimeter fence.

Mazurek cupped his hand and blew between his thumbs, giving a good impression of an owl hoot. An answering 'twik, twik' returned to him from not so far away and he answered again. Shortly we heard rustling and the rest of the party joined us: Kryszka, Elk, and two other men I had not seen or met before. The two new men were better dressed than us. The older one carried a briefcase.

Clutching my hand he thanked me for 'shooting that bloody bastard!' The other man held back in the shadows. Across the divide from the wood, we watched the perimeter wire, to see if the guards were alert or if dogs were loose or on leash with foot patrols. Nothing. "They must all be tied up in town with the search," I volunteered.

The wire gleamed silver in the light. I thought of the film *Dangerous Moonlight*. How apt that title was to this moment.

"Are we ready? And what about the girl? Is she going back now?" I whispered to Mazurek. I had assumed she was some sort of guide or courier.

"She's going with us," Mazurek whispered back.

I was fast losing patience. "That wasn't the deal, Mazurek. We only have room for six of us." My voice was rising. "The plane cannot take seven people to the American zone. It won't make it. It doesn't have the range. God knows, we're not even sure if it's been set up or even has fuel!"

"She is my wife," Mazurek hissed at me, "and she goes."

"So fuck us all for your wife!" I came back at him.

Kryszka and Elk crawled up to us, hearing our raised voices.

"Problem?" Kryszka questioned.

"No, not at all. Except now we're having a family outing as well as an escape." Tersely I outlined the situation.

"Are you sure there is a real problem with the fuel?" Elk asked. I reminded him he knew nothing about aircraft.

Kryszka quietly explained that even if we tore out every seat and ditched all the ballast we could, we'd still be on the edge of the range of the craft, even with six people.

I felt sorry for Mazurek. Squashed together on the ground as we were I could feel him trembling beside me. "Sorry, my friend, it's not personal. I am wound up, that's all. But we do have a problem. Who are the other two guys?"

One it seemed was a courier with WiN and headed for the Americans. The other was a Peasant Party politician big-wig, someone who had opposed Mikołajczyk's complicity in the Provisional Government. As a result he was now on the Communists' death list.

"That's it, they are on the passenger list, whatever," I said. "Mazurek, you have to face facts. You have a job to do in the Resettlement camps. You are a sworn soldier, under oath. You have to go, she does not. We'll try and get her out later, another time."

"No need," Elk interjected. "It has only been assumed that I was coming. I can stay. Things will get hot here. The boys will welcome a steady hand; the repercussions and arrests after the execution will be tough on the local WiN or NSZ people. You all go. I am staying. No argument. My decision, my choice. Shut up and don't argue!" To emphasise the point he rolled away from us.

As I dithered, put out by this sudden turn, Kryszka, who seemed recovered from his breakdown, said, "Okay, let's get on with it." He broke cover with the wire-cutters and headed for the perimeter fence. Cutting the wire he went through, taking up a firing position the other side of the wire. One by one we broke cover, the two new men first, then me, then Mazurek. We crouched low and ran like rabbits for the wire. The girl was last to be covered by Elk. Mazurek went through the gap and then held the barbed wire high enough for me to scramble through. As I twisted I could see the girl and Elk standing together where we had hidden. They had the colour of ghosts, and they were embracing. As I watched, they parted like lovers, her outstretched arm lingering to his last finger-tip touch.

"His sister," Mazurek said.

I turned and ran for the Yak 6 parked about a hundred metres away by a rudimentary hangar. Kryszka followed then the two VIP passengers. They hit the ground at fifty metres to cover me. Mazurek and his wife stayed flat at the wire. We were prepared to fight if we had to. The moon shone its brilliant light. Who knew what the shadows held.

I raced on toward the twin-engine aircraft. Its drab olive had been transformed into a coating of icing sugar by the moon. Breathless with anticipation, I heaved myself onto the wing and through the hatch. There it was, that old familiar smell of oil and metal, even though this plane was mainly of wood construction. I pushed forward to the cockpit. No hidden enemy. Strapping myself into the pilot's seat I sat for a moment looking at the controls. Witek had drilled me from a photograph. A photo is one thing, reality another. I flipped some switches and the controls smouldered dull yellow. No doubt the others could see the cabin glow. The needles began slowly to edge round their dials. The needle flickered and settled - a full fuel tank. My chest was still tight. Still no alarm.

I pressed the starter button for the right side engine and the propeller wheezed into life. A short sputter and it was alive, a blur. The aircraft started shaking as the engine picked up. The rest scuttled to the plane. Vaguely aware of bodies piling in behind me, I started the left engine, which seemed to take an eternity of coughing and wheezing. Kryszka was waving from the front, the chocks were away. I eased the throttle. We began to move forward very slowly. I saw Kryszka run around the wing. The side hatch was slammed. He squeezed forward and slid in beside me. We exchanged grins. "Get us out, Mr Navigator!" I said and he gripped my arm in response.

We bumped across the grass. I felt calm and alive. Already I loved the feel of this little aircraft. It was real. I switched on the forward light to give us a clear view of the take-off point. As we turned to line up for our run we looked left and right. Lights were coming on in the wooden huts and blockhouse the other side of the engineering hangar. No lights spilled from doors and no shots followed us that we were aware of. We passed three of the elderly MiG 3s lined up to our right.

Then we saw him. An officer of the MVD, in a greatcoat and full uniform. I knew every detail of that uniform. We expected a shower of bullets or vehicles racing to block our path. But nothing. He just lifted his hand, as though bidding us farewell. We looked at each other and wondered. This whole escape was engineered, filled with its own mystery. I turned the craft and applied full throttle, the engines roaring to an angry buzz. I let the brakes go and we bounced across the field. Suddenly there was no more bounce - we were in the air. I pulled the nose up and around and the red and white chequer board identification marks flashed for a second in the moonlight.

Below us light spilled and we felt we could hear a klaxon braying. I shuddered at the thought of the three fighters. They may have been war vintage, but I knew these were late versions and well able to shoot us out of the sky. We would travel at about 100 mph whilst they could reach 400 mph. I smiled to myself. I was already converting back to British standards, leaving the metric world behind. These were outdated craft, so probably some sort of reserve. The MiG 3 was suited to chasing high altitude bombers. We, on the other hand, were going to hug the ground. I began to worry about other pursuit craft. Supposing we bumped into a flock of MiG 9 jet fighters? It would be the end of us if we did.

The undercarriage locked home with a comforting crash.

As the drone of the Yak faded into the distance the base would be alive with people milling about the accommodation huts. The Poles would be upset they had lost a plane. I smiled at that thought then thought of Elk, quietly slipping away. 'For your freedom and ours' – the motto of the Polish Army in his mind, I hoped. He had probably sacrificed his life for his sister.

"I hope you make it," I cried out loud to the moon. Still looking up, I spoke to the heavens again. "You bloody bastard, haven't you had enough blood yet?"

But God never answered. He never did.

He left the talking to the priests who knew his agenda.

# CHAPTER 13

# THE WELCOME HOME

The twin-engine aircraft flew on toward Germany and the American air base near Regensburg. I kept the plane to a modest hundred miles per hour, flying low and hopefully below most radar. Tracking the roads clearly visible in the moonlight I prayed the weather would hold. We had to pass through the Beskid mountain region and then turn northwest across Czechoslovakia.

First Kryszka organised everyone, dumping through the hatch anything that was loose and could be easily jettisoned. A toolbox went, some parachute sacks, fire extinguisher, interior cladding... everything that they could rip out or tear off went through the hatch. The open hatch made a racket and a storm of air roared into the plane, yawing the aircraft from side to side. The girl, Wanda, began to panic and had to be calmed by Mazurek.

Finally Kryszka eased himself into the co-pilot position and became busy with his maps by the light of a torch. He would be the navigator once across the border. He was also the ears of the trip, tuning and listening out for any aircraft radio that indicated our flight interception. The engines roared and the passengers settled to a shouted conversation led by the volatile Wanda. "Perhaps we'll be welcomed by a committee," she exclaimed. "A welcoming committee of ladies sparkling with jewels and Polish nobles dressed in traditional silk and fur with sabres at their sides and heron crests in their hats. A gypsy band should be playing when we arrive. Vodka, mead and champagne will be on offer..." she laughed. We all joined in the game, adding to our guest list the rich and famous of a Poland, from long ago.

The excitement settled as the adrenalin drained. Everyone slept except Kryszka and I. We weaved and bobbed the Yak through the mountains at tree-top height, following the road as best we could. It was a nice plane to fly, light and responsive to the controls. We flew over a sleeping countryside. Light was beginning to creep in from the east. We were now nearing the newly created West German border.

"Only sixty miles to go," Kryszka informed me. I decided to gain a little height. Light was coming in fast now, clearer as we gained height. I wanted Western radar to see us. We did not know what reception might await us. We presumed friendly but we were reliant on Witek's intelligence. Suddenly the plane rocked and a jet fighter shot by us. It gleamed silver in the morning light, sliding ahead of us, leaving a vapour trail as it climbed and wheeled and came at us. I slammed the throttle wide open and dived, keeping my narrowest side toward the front of the oncoming craft.

The passengers were awake and started shouting. Kryszka bellowed at them," Shut up and strap in." He began to send on the open radio: "May Day, May Day! We are a refugee unarmed Polish aircraft heading to Regensburg American Air Base. We shall cross the border in eight minutes. We have civilians on board and we need landing permission, I repeat...."

The jet slid alongside, the pilot clearly visible. The fighter was sleek, with the pilot set back and above the jet engine. Its wings were straight, not swept back. It was snub-nosed and its roundels of red, white and blue showed it to be a Czech fighter.

"Yak-23," one of the politicals called out, "lightweight fighter."

"Heavy enough for us," growled Kryszka.

The fighter veered away from us and shot up, lifting effortlessly above and around us. Wheeling away and coming at us again, it fired its two cannon across our front. We saw the orange-red twinkling flashes and tracer dash across our front.

"Hold on everyone, I shall try to make a race for the frontier when he comes at us again. Everyone hold on tight!"

Kryszka began to call again on the radio, this time giving the call sign Witek had supplied.

The fighter again appeared at our side, this time on my starboard. With disbelief I realised he was smiling and gesturing 'follow me' signs. He indicated to go down. So I did. He stayed above and began to buzz us, but there was no more gunfire.

"One minute to the border," Kryszka intoned.

The Czech fighter shot ahead of us, wheeled and peeled away at what must have been the ground border then, rolling over us, settled by our side. The pilot made the thumbs up sign and raced ahead, waggling his wings in the well-known victory sign as he climbed away.

Thanks seemed inadequate for such an act of kindness or defiant bravery from a fellow pilot. Thank God they had not scrambled a Soviet plane. Perhaps he would face a court martial; who would ever know?

Kryszka sighed and the tension drained from us.

"It's the Yanks," Kryszka said, and began talking into his radio and guiding me in.

The reception committee waited. Not the one Wanda expected or had dreamt about.

As the plane taxied to a halt, a swarm of jeeps and military personnel surrounded the plane. We were ordered to lie face down on the concrete apron, hands behind our heads, whilst the plane was searched.

Eventually we were ordered to stand and were separated. I was searched, handcuffed and placed in one of the jeeps. The morning was chilly and low cloud was coming in from the west. The sunshine was fading. Wanda was wailing and kicking out when she was separated from Mazurek. He called out, "Thanks, guys. See you in London!" Kryszka was as morose as ever, saying nothing. The politicals seem to have fared better, presenting some papers from briefcases. I noticed they were not handcuffed. The jeep started with a jerk.

They transferred me to a cell and I was interviewed by a young air Force officer. Requesting he contact the US embassy and notify them of my presence, I gave him my full name. I was well treated and given a medical checkover. No one would tell me what was going on, but I had a radio and papers and good food.

On the morning of the second day Chuck Beavers arrived from the US embassy. He was big, dark hair with a crew cut. Brown eyed and bronzed, with a wide, open face. His handshake was firm. The guy was reputedly some second consul, but in reality he was the head honcho of the CIA. We had never met before but instantly felt at home with each other. My personal possessions were returned with apologies, including my Polish eagle mascot, my Radom pistol and the box of chess pieces Witek had given me. Best of all, Kryszka and I were reunited.

Chuck had information. "The British are spitting blood that you broke the rules and came here, you crafty son of a bitch. They were sitting up north waiting for you to fly in over the Baltic. So now they're hot-footing it down here to find out what the hell you have been monkeying round with us Yanks for. They will be here tomorrow for their debriefing. They smell a big rat."

"What about Mazurek and the girl?" Kryszka asked.

"They've been turned over to the Red Cross and will go to a Polish displaced persons camp. There are zillions of them over here. For Chrissakes, the politicians thought they would all go home as soon as the war was over. But people didn't fancy swapping Nazis for Reds so they stayed put, and now they are a fucking nuisance to the politicians. I expect most will end up in the good old US of A and England, but time will tell. The United Nations Relief and Rehabilitation Administration got itself a bad name for forcing people back home into the arms of the Communists. So they ain't trusted. The Big Three agreed at Yalta that all the folks had to go home, like it or not. Stalin especially insisted and his two lickspittles agreed. Didn't reckon on people though, did they?

"We ain't all fucking hard-hearted like they think, so the Germans here supported them, and public opinion sees them as refugees, especially as Germany is now split up. God knows how many just slipped into the European economy. Good time to disappear but the Soviet citizens, including many of you Poles" – here he gestured at Kryszka, for I was a Canadian in his mind (*whoever would want to be a Pole?*) – "especially from the part we gave away, UNRRA sent them back to be killed. Decent of them. They've got Jews, Poles, Czechs, Estonians, Latvians, Lithuanians, Croats, Slovenes, Slovaks, Slovenes and Uncle Tom Cobley and all to settle. It's all a bit of a bring-down.

"By the way, your political friends were whisked away. They had documents from London and Washington. So by now they are the other side of the world, I guess. I can find out if you want," he offered.

"No, don't trouble yourself, Chuck. I never knew them till they got on the plane." This was true, but I also knew our paths would have to cross again.

"It's my turn to pop for the doughnuts," Chuck volunteered, already heading for the camp canteen. "You two wanna talk over some things about me, I guess? See whether you can trust me?"

"No really, Chuck, that's ok," I replied quickly. I liked this guy.

"C'mon, don't try a snow-job on me, buddy, I know the score here. You two have to hang tough on whatever decision you made back in Polak land." With that he left us alone.

So who could we trust with Witek's message? Could we trust Truman even? The scheming of Roosevelt and his inept handling of Stalin would have precluded this. Both his administration and Intelligence had been shot through with Reds of various persuasions, as well as some NKVD sleepers. We wondered if Truman had the courage to sweep up. It was he who had ordered the disbandment of the war time OSS. Due to its personnel, the new Central Intelligence Agency could only be split, as before, between pro-British and French sections and those more inclined to nationalist causes.

Eventually the three of us sat down over coffee and doughnuts to discuss what to do. Chuck, as his very name implied, was not an 'admin' type but a field man. He knew 'what was what', as he put it. He had been at Yalta as one of the Security types, close to Allen Dulles and Stewart Menzies, the head of MI6.

Chuck was keen to tell us about Yalta. How he'd seen and heard the politicians wrangling and haggling over Europe. "Poland was like a dressed chicken," he said. Stalin wanted Dresden bombed. "So it happened – and for what?" Chuck asked. "Dresden had no strategic value at the time. It went something like this: 'You have ninety percent influence in Romania. Swap us with Greece, and we'll split up Yugoslavia fifty-fifty as well as Hungary. Then you take seventy-five percent of Bulgaria.' Believe me, man, that's how it happened.

"Menzies told Dulles that England had always resisted a single dominating European power, but now Russia was just that. In intelligence terms a new war was on. Britain was the first target and then the US. I'm told that just before he died Roosevelt croaked, 'We can't do business with Stalin.'"

"Shit and more shit," Kryszka shoved into the conversation.

To lighten the conversation I added, "Talking of Stewart Menzies, let's have a drink of whisky kindly supplied by the station commander in honour of our escape. His family are whisky barons. So let's drink to the old soak!"

In the next hour or so we debated going to the top man, the Director, Roscoe Henry Hillenkoetter. Until Chuck assured me he was more interested in Flying Saucers and alien landings and Koreans than Soviets. We ran through other people Chuck knew. There was Arthur Goldberg, a prominent labour lawyer who had been with the European section of the OSS. I couldn't trust such a Left-leaning activist. In the end we listened to Chuck's recommendation and settled on John Ford, the film director, as our go-between.

"So John Ford is ex-OSS and still a CIA man?" I said. "What a turn up for the books!"

"Yeah, on paper he did film work for the navy, but he was a top advisor to Wild Bill Donovan, the head of OSS, and he still has his ear. So if I can get you to Ford, which I think I can, then he can get you to Wild Bill, and then you and he can decide what to do next.

"Bill Donovan, although thought to be 'out of the scene', is chairman of the newly-founded American Committee on United Europe, which is supposed to counter the new Communist threat by promoting European political unity. The European Movement was created in October last year, when the Joint International Committee for European Unity changed its name. Some big names joined the gang. Duncan Sandys was elected President. Léon Blum of France, Winston Churchill, Alcide De Gasperi of Italy and Paul-Henri Spaak from Belgium were elected as Honorary Presidents. US policy is to promote a United States of Europe, and to this end the American committee is used to discreetly funnel CIA funds to European pro-federalists. Believe me, we are spending a million dollars a year on the project. So Wild Bill is not out of the game by any means. He and Ford are your guys."

Ford was a hero to us all. We spent time chatting about his films, *The Lost Patrol, Stagecoach* and *Drums along the Mohawk*. Kryszka revealed how he had fallen for Claudette Colbert, whilst Chuck and I felt more akin to John Wayne and Henry Fonda. I hadn't enjoyed the film *Grapes of Wrath;* though Chuck and I agreed on the importance of Steinbeck's novel, we could fall out over the film. Kryszka had neither read the classic nor seen the film, so he acted as referee.

Then Chuck cut to the chase. "Okaaay. So let's see what ya got to show me, let's cut the yap and get the cash."

I set up a chess board and took out the pieces Witek had given me, setting them up as though for a game. This was no game however. Like Japanese Hakone puzzle boxes, a number of the pieces could be taken apart by a combination of twists and movements. Inside each chamber was a roll of microfilm and a small glass vial of acid. If the pieces had been smashed open the film would have melted.

"It took me weeks to learn the tricks," I commented quite proudly. Witek had never told me the movement combinations. Even now I wondered if there were more than the three I had discovered.

Chuck and Kryszka both admired the workmanship.

I knew what the film contained. Beria, I explained, was prepared to concede the New Russian Empire for a set of peaceful proposals to redevelop Russia and assist its people to better living conditions. He proposed that allies of Germany should still suffer and provide reparation, as should Germany itself, but not the Poles and Czechs, who should be allowed to form their own new alliances, hopefully, with a more 'sensible' Russia.

The sting in the tale was clear. How to get rid of Stalin? And would the West help?

And the final sting? Just the tiniest detail, of course. I had a list of Soviet spies and was to be given assistance to find any and all moles in Britain and the US run by Abakumov of the MGB.

"Jesus wept." Chuck whistled between his teeth. "Well, little buddy, we best get you out of the hands of the British as soon as we can."

"Tomorrow morning they arrive to collect you and we will have to hand you over. But I reckon you will spend September in Washington. The 'Polish' pilot who stole the plane has turned up. He will give 'his' story to the free press. The Polish exile Government lot gave him to us. He's from Scotland. The two politicos you brought out are supposed to be the reason for the whole show here – we hope the Soviets will buy it. At the moment only Witek knows the real facts as well as we three. One of our crew went all over the Yak. Not one hair, not one fingerprint from you two remains, even though we have no intention of ever giving the plane back. And we're going to buy the guy and gal off with a home in the Promised Land. So it's a wrap. Let's crack that Scotch again!"

The next day dawned to a typically German rain sky. Grey from horizon to horizon with a steady drizzle. The British contingent arrived in an RAF transport. We watched it come in and taxi close to the station hangars, away from prying eyes. "The new Vickers Valetta," muttered Chuck. "Brought the British weather too."

We were in no mood for banter, so stayed quiet.

The British party clambered down the steps. A couple of RAF types and five civilians. Two of the civvies were clearly goons, looking around them as though they expected the Apaches to attack the wagon train at any moment. Kryszka and I looked at each other and smiled.

"Brawny, ain't they!" Chuck observed.

The landed party was hustled away from our sight. Chuck set off with us down some corridors, past the canteen where metal trays being washed from breakfast were making a racket. The Americans didn't use plates but a tray with pressed depressions for every item. "Slick and quick," Chuck called it. We had eaten like kings in the canteen and slept between sheets in a central-heated room with washing facilities. The West was already hammering out a new commercial world. I thought of the poor bastards in the forest, grubbing and begging a living from the peasants. Witek was right, we had become bandits.

"Here it is, guys," Chuck said. "Best of luck. See you in Washington later this month." He shook hands and patted us on the back. "I respect you guys. You make it out of here, right? Okay, buddies, so long!" Chuck was quite emotional.

All I wanted now was to get out of here now. Briefings and debriefings and one secret service laying off another was not my idea of getting out of the Soviet Union. I was desperate to see Ela.

The door sign simply said, 'Interview Room'. We looked at each other and knocked.

"Come in."

Three chairs were set out in a triangle away from the central table. Standing against the window was a tall man peering through closed venetian blinds. He had his back to us. I noticed his expensive chalk-stripe dark grey flannel suit and that his blonde hair was overlong for the military. Turning he said," Hello, Teddy, long time no see!"

My God, it was Rupert. My old university roommate, my mentor in all things English ways and in upper class pronunciation, the man who had introduced me to glorious Somerset and its ways. The man from the Foreign Office.

"You have been a very naughty boy." He smiled broadly. Turning to Kryszka he patted him on the back. "And Kryszka, we meet again. You, my man, have aided and abetted a deserter from the RAF! So you two had better behave for the next five minutes.

"I don't know what you have been up to with our American cousins, but apparently we need you to help sort out some house-cleaning which would be embarrassing to us if it turned out to be dirty linen that would upset the public."

"Typical British oblique speak, Rupert. Are we friends, enemies or what?"

"Well, as I said, old boy, apparently needed, but as to friend or foe I don't yet know. On a personal note, however, definitely friend, which is why I think I have been chosen to come like the Angel Gabriel with tidings of good cheer. Not, of course, that you two are virgins, but in matters of espionage I am angelic."

185

We shook hands, smiling into each other's eyes. Rupert asked us to sit. "Thought a table between us would have given the wrong message," he explained. "Sitting here like three children makes us equals, I believe. My job is to deliver you securely and safely to Britain, without Guy Liddell of MI5 tumbling that you are the exchange. Mr Kryszka, you are apparently the fall guy, although nothing more will come of it than a few unpleasant stories of Polish complicity in a spy ring etc. The thrust of it will be that the Soviets sent you back to jail in exchange for one of theirs. You are, however, a free man, I can assure you. The press are anti-Polish anyway so it won't hurt the domestic exile Poles much. You should all go home to be shot, apparently. The British Left is nothing if not naïve on the one hand and blood red on the other.

"I have here a gift from HMG, Teddy: your Canadian passport, an American passport, and of course, a British passport. And for you, Mr Kryszka, an American passport should you ever need it, a gift from your new friend Chuck, and an alien's registration card from HMG allowing you to stay in Great Britain. Unlike the Americans we still don't trust Johnny Foreigner, you see. Anyway, I'm sure your Exile people can fix you up with whatever you need, better than we can."

Kryszka just grunted. Being second class came naturally.

It emerged that Rupert was certainly something in the Foreign Office - "Best left undefined." He had left the Somerset at the end of the war. Stewart Menzies had interviewed him about a year ago, explaining that he was to "assist in getting you out of Russia. My own Foreign Office sources thought you were dead, killed on some wild adventure. Anyway, Menzies is not a man to cross or deny, so my career hangs on you getting out to meet him. He simply told me to tell you that it is time to clear out the Gripper mess and that it's wise to put the big fish with the Americans. Do you know what he means?"

"I suppose I do," I answered. Gripper, once my immediate superior, had been killed because he found out who the moles in the Service were.

We were given new clothes and some money. The RAF Valetta was not to be our transport out. The goons and Rupert would return today. We unseen civilians would be 'given a lift' by another RAF transport due in with some British Forces mail and returning personnel, RAF and USAF boys. We were to be dropped off at Shoreham, hopefully without arousing curiosity, as returning engineers. The plane would then fly on to Wiltshire or wherever.

England was as green as ever as the aircraft turned in to the airfield over the river Adur. The South Downs have a special beauty. Swathes of sheep-fed turf running into the Great Yew forest. We could see the scarp ridge with its tree ring at Chanctonbury and the great hill fort of Cissbury. There was Lancing College, and over to the left Arundel Castle, home to the Catholic

Howards. 'This England, Green and Pleasant Land'. We touched down on the grass field. Walking up to the main road there were no customs or passport checks so we walked to the rear of the terminal building, to the RAF section and a nod from the conscript guards. Returned to civilian use, the airfield still served as an Air Sea Rescue base. The war was well and truly over.

The terminal building was an Art Deco masterpiece, shining white in the sun now breaking through the clouds. We went straight to search out a taxi or transport to Brighton. In the end we caught a Southdown bus into the Pool Valley terminus. A quick walk round Old Steine, where the fountain was being repainted, then up North Street, along Western road, and there was Crown Street. My home, my retreat, my Ela.

All throughout my nightmare her face had been my only constancy. She was my angel, my talisman, her name my mantra. The image of her had kept me sane through pain and cold and hunger and desperation. Whenever the fear or agony was too great she was always there waiting. We had lost two years together, but I had no doubt we could recover those moments we shared in the hills, that we could laugh together again and be happy. She would come with me to America or Canada, to a new life. Have children. Live on the farm, whatever she wanted.

As we walked, Kryszka and I debated what to say and do. Should we get the key from the lady next door, the one who used to have the Airedale dogs? Were those curs still alive? Hopefully they'd been eaten when rationing was bad, I was always wary of dogs. Should we just knock on the door and fall into each other's arms. I knew I would be tongue-tied. Part of me feared I would cry – there was so much within me that needed to be let out. We walked quickly, pausing only at the bottom of the hill. I was sweating, nervous and agitated. At the top of the Street a new building blocked off the cul-de-sac of what was otherwise Queen Anne terraced houses. I had chosen the street just for this reason. To get to me people could only come in at the bottom of the street – one way in and no way out. The house I had chosen because it had an extension with a flat roof that would let me out onto the roofs and the next street, west or north, should that be necessary.

We opted to knock on the door. As we stood by the little Queen Anne bay I looked around. The newer building now seemed to be a sweet wholesale business with the business name of Peter Panto, which sounded rather jolly.

"Here goes," I said as I twisted the bell, sounding a mechanical 'Brrr'. We heard footsteps coming downstairs, then along a short passage.

The door opened and there she was. All my words had left me. All I could do was smile at my Ela. She had not changed.

"Tadek," she burst out. "I thought you were dead! My God, you are alive!"

A Polish voice called out from along the corridor, "Who's that, Ela?"

"Old friends," she called back. "That's Antek..." she whispered in explanation, "...my husband."

My world turned upside down.

Kryszka gripped my arm as a man arrived, looking over her shoulder, eyeing us up and down with typical Polish suspiciousness. Immediately taking over the conversation, he asked, "What do you want?"

Blind rage replaced shock. I was ice-cold now. "I want you out of my house."

Ela went white. Antek paled too but stood his ground, shielding her from us. "Fuck off or I'll push your face in dog's blood!"

"Wrong answer, my friend." Kryszka spoke up. "I suggest you quieten down till this is sorted out."

Ela was desperately trying to explain. "I...I thought you were dead, Tadek! We have a young baby. We have nowhere to go."

"What the hell is going on?" Antek was besides himself.

"Sod you all!" I cried. "Take everything, get out. Just get out of my house and stay out. Are you working? " I directed my question at Antek.

Caught off guard the man answered truthfully, "No, finding work is difficult for a Pole."

"Then that makes me the man you're living off, and that stops now."

Ela began to sob. "Please, Tadek, give us a chance, let us stay until we find somewhere else. We have nothing!"

"Compared to where I have just came from you have *everything*. You made a life choice, Ela, now go live it. What did you expect? Pack up and go. Go, be a refugee like most of our people. I want you out of here by tomorrow night."

I turned to Antek and said quite quietly, "And as for you, don't threaten me again or else you'll get a bullet in the head. Is that understood?"

He did not respond but just looked at me.

I grabbed Kryszka's arm. "Let's go."

We walked down the street. I did not look back and no cries came after us.

Eventually Kryszka spoke. "I have never seen you lose your temper like that before. You can be human after all, Tadek. But was that wise or necessary? She knows what you are, who you are. The wrong word from her and your cover is blown to 5."

"That's rich coming from you," I shot back. "You risked as much with Aniela, taking her dancing. You took risks too." It was a stupid and childish jibe.

But he was right, of course.

We ended up on the sea front with the bright light in our faces , being blown by an onshore breeze. Clouds were scudding across the sky. The sea swelled navy blue to sea green. On the beach the pebbles sang their song of surge and retreat. Under the West Pier some boys were throwing stones at pigeons sheltering in the iron struts. When we shouted at them to stop they ran off, I guessed back to the slums just north of the Esplanade.

We sat down on the pebbles, cleared now of barbed wire and mines. Kryszka threw stones to allow me some privacy. My shoulders shook as I wept. Great waves of dry, racking sobs. Snivelling, wiping snot with the back of my hand, choking with emotions. I wept for myself and for a multitude of people I could hardly remember, whose lives I had touched. Lives I had ruined by my pride and ambition or sheer selfishness. People who had loved me but whom I had never really loved. What a bastard I had been.

Kryszka came to sit with me, then just held his arm round my shoulder, saying nothing. There was nothing to say. He had frozen in Krosno for the same reason I was weeping now. We knew each other well.

He was right, of course. How to extricate myself from the situation was the problem. I could not use my bank account. Any movement on it would alert 5, who would have a permanent watch on my bank. Redfern, Caper & McCulloch, my lawyers, handled the allowance to Ela. It would raise suspicion if that stopped. The worst part was that their offices were on Curzon Street too.

Eventually I asked Kryszka to return to my house to Crown Street. I told him how to find my stash of cash. He was to give Antek and Ela fifty pounds and explain that the allowance would continue for another eighteen months and then stop. This would give Antek time to get on his feet. But they were still to leave the house.

"What's this, expediency or kindness?" Kryszka wanted to know.

"I have no idea," was my reply. He smiled quietly and shrugged his shoulders.

"I'll book us into a hotel in Regent's Square and meet you back here by the pier in a couple of hours, Kryszka. Agreed?"

"Agreed," he said and walked briskly away.

I went and sat back on the beach.

CHAPTER 14

# INTERLUDE

Kryszka was as good as his word. He had made a phone call after his visit to Crown Street to break the news to my 'tenants'. The message he brought back was one of sorrow and regrets. He had a report of a different kind too. Ela's husband Antek Sobczak, his informant in London told him, was a 2nd Corps man from what had been Eastern Poland, now incorporated into the Soviet Union. "He was in Italy and fought the campaign. Sad times, Tadek, you know this. Nowhere to go, you see, so you become a hero."

"Sobczak accepts the money for the child's sake but he is a proud man and will pay you back. I believe him. He is not so bad," Kryszka offered. "I guess they will go to a resettlement camp or move to London with your money. He could set up as a watchmaker, he says, as he was before the war. Do clock repairs and suchlike. Ela is distraught. Her world has turned upside down too, Tadek."

I chewed on this but I was hurting too much to respond.

We stayed away two days. They had given their keys to Kryszka. The house was as I remembered. They had cleaned up, left everything like a new pin. There was a note for me, in Ela's handwriting. I did not open it then. It still remains with me as a treasure today, unopened.

At night the dreams returned. I wanted to get out. I was tired, so tired. Everything about me hurt. I wanted to go home. I wanted security. I felt ill, as though I couldn't cope with life. The sunshine was an insult, darkness a place of concealment. Why should I go on giving, being sucked dry by life? Why should the child I was be brought to this insanity?

My mind was breaking down.

There was no time for me to settle in my thoughts. Stewart Menzies was due down for a meeting with me tomorrow. We had arranged to meet at the Brighton Museum near the Corn Exchange. He assured me there was a room with a couple of skeletons and an amber cup from the Baltic. "Beaker people, you see. Must be your ancestors from the Baltic, trading with the Celts and making their fortune."

We met as arranged. "Comfortable journey on the Brighton Belle. Pullman Express, you know." I did, as I had travelled it pre-war.

"Why ever did you buy a bolt-hole down here in this land of queers, pimps, theatricals, spivs and Jews?" he wanted to know.

"I suppose, sir, because it is cosmopolitan, not very judgemental, and just a little seedy. I like it."

"How is Poland these days? Rough, I suppose?" Menzies asked with more than polite concern. "I always admired the Poles. They had a rough deal. Warsaw had a bad time, ninety per cent destroyed, bugger all the yapping about Dresden. Warsaw was a beautiful city."

I knew that in July 1939 Menzies had gone to Warsaw to help bring back the Enigma coding device. On his return to Britain he had been made Director General of MI6. We had even met once, briefly, at the Embassy. I guess he remembered this, although he made no mention of our meeting.

"I am here to see *Private Lives* at the Theatre Royal. My secretary has come down with me. So your cover is not compromised." He winked at me, which seemed unexpected and out of character.

"Best to get out of the country whilst you can, my man. 5 will still be after you and they will not own up that one of ours tipped them off. We know from our cousins that we have a code leak. Something we learned from you Poles, all about codes. We get pieces of information, no pattern. The Americans call it Operation Venona and point to us as a source. Nothing concrete, just a feeling these code boys have.

"Will you take the work? Find out who or what is leaking? Is it women, boys, money or – God forbid – idealism?"

"Yes sir."

"I have taken the liberty of booking theatre tickets for you and your Polish Masters in the Exile Government. Go nowhere near Queen Anne's Gate. Just about every Security Service has it staked out. Phone this number from a call box if you need help or have information. It is your friend Rupert's number. Whoever it is will sit on your left. The rest is up to you. Officially I don't want to know."

The evening came. The theatre lights dimmed as the orchestra struck its final chords. A well-dressed woman squeezed into the seat next to me just three seats in from the aisle. The curtain pulled back and the woman took off her right glove and extended her hand to me. Leaning over she whispered, "Krystyna Skarbek, but you may call me Krysia." The play began.

Still whispering in my ear she murmured, "Brighton loves its Dolphins."

I intoned, "No, they belong to Hove."

She giggled. "I'm glad you are the right one, and that you are so handsome, darlink." She emphasised the word like a German film star. "It's like a comic book, isn't it? All this cloak and dagger? "

During the Interlude, in the bar, we chatted over drinks. Krysia handed me a large manila envelope, sealed and taped. I opened it. As I had suspected from its feel and weight, it was Witek's notebook. I had consigned it to one of our fellow political travellers and he had sworn to take it to

Department Two in London, marked for my attention. I had been sure, had I kept it on me, that the Americans would have confiscated it, Chuck or no Chuck. My common sense had paid off. There was no way to know if it had been read or the code broken. A mass of interesting war detail and a hidden group of names lay therein.

I learned my pretty bright companion was no other than 'Christine Granville', Churchill's favourite spy. Now she was stateless, like so many other Poles, the British would not give her naturalisation papers. She did bar work, or any work she could get to get by. She had been living this way since leaving Cairo, where she had been marooned at the end of the war.

Krysia excused herself quite early, saying she was meeting up with a friend, Ian Fleming. The name instantly raised my guard. Ian would know me at once. I was glad I had spun a yarn about my life and given her a false name. She, of course, had cottoned on though. She was very well trained. "I will keep you out of it, have no fear. I have no love for the British. Apart from the sex, he's intent on keeping tabs on us. You know, spy and counter-spy. The British wanted to set up a new spy system within Poland in '45. Even I was scheduled to go back. But the scheme fell apart because the Reds knew what we were doing before we did. Fleming thinks I am a double agent – which I suppose is true, since my loyalty is to Poland. He pays the bills, hence I need him. And that's my secret, so don't tell."

"Are you travelling back with him?" I asked.

"As a matter of fact, no. He motored down and has to go over to Shoreham. He says there was some funny business the other day at the airport. I am not invited. He usually takes me to a place down in Dover, the Granville Hotel. Isn't that twee?"

"Good that he is busy. I will put my report above pillar number three underneath the West Pier, counting from the east on the shore side. There are ledges used by pigeons. I didn't bring it tonight just in case. Can you pick up safely before eleven?"

"Yes I can. You can trust me," she said.

"Thanks for the warning about Fleming. Clearly Menzies is not as watertight as he likes to think."

She smiled. "We exiles have to watch our backs. I suppose we know too much. We shall all end up with a knife in our back if we aren't careful."

"Or our heads in a bag in a UB office," I added.

"Ah, you know their trademark," she cooed.

When the final curtain came down we went out, arm in arm, to find a nightcap. "Did you have a bad time in France?" I found myself keen to prolong the conversation. Extra time with a fellow loser.

"No, not compared to others. I was awarded the *Croix de Guerre*, but was kicked out of France by de Gaulle like all the other SOE British girls.

Like you, I sort of became part of the RAF. I was a WAAF!"

"I had heard you were in the Womens' Transport Service, a FANY?" I said.

"That too! I think I was the only one from SOE to make both! I guess that's why I got the different gongs. The bureaucrats got me in twice." Krystyna smiled impishly. An impulse made me catch her hand and kiss her finger-tips.

"They don't hand out the George medal and an OBE for nothing. Most of the other SOE people only ever made it to MBE. So did you become a secret colonel or something?

"No, but I did make it to Flight Officer. I called myself a navigator." That impish smile again.

"I reckon you got up to no good in Cairo. That's what it was all about, you were somebody's favourite!" I teased her.

"Ah, Cairo!" she sighed. "Groppis and the pashas, the roof-top restaurant under the night stars at the Continental Savoy... and of course, my happy times at the Muhammad Ali Club. I never got an invite though to the British Gezira Sports Club. Even though Polish troops were fighting in Tobruk we were not quite yet 'equals' in the officers' clubs. Anyway, our beloved General Kopański did not consider me quite kosher. My mother was Jewish and dad was a banker." She said this with a hint of sarcasm. "Anyway, my life has turned into one bloody awful mess. Too many loves, too many loyalties. And no damned money!"

"Was that because you became involved with everybody?" The question was impertinent.

She stared at me hard. "Try being a woman in Cairo in wartime. With everyone wanting to be in your knickers and expecting you to pass on pillow talk."

I had touched a nerve. I tried to calm the sudden tension. "Wasn't your latest admirer involved in the Rudolph Hess fiasco? When Hess was tempted to fly over to Scotland to 'come to terms' with the British?"

She accepted the peace offering. "I believe so."

"Cairo was the centre of SOE for the Balkans as well as the Middle East, wasn't it?" I volunteered. "Was it all belly dancers, hookahs and clandestine meetings with handsome, dark-eyed men?"

"Oh yes," she said, "Once I stripped naked and danced under the moon for one of the Egyptian princelings. You foolish man, you are a typical romantic!" And she leaned close to my face, eyes now twinkling, red lips slightly parted inches from my own. She ran her finger under my chin.

"Cairo!" She sighed in that special way, as she had done five minutes before. "It was tough. The British SOE agents were all at each others' throats, interested only in position and rank. The Americans were just coming in then. The OSS was new and thought the British stuffy and rather bad to the Arabs. There was a little American Colonel called Harold Hopkins, who really got up the Brits' nose. He was convinced that the Arabs liked the Americans better because the Americans weren't imperialists and the British were!"

In the bar we found she was happy to keep sharing. "Up in the North, a Polish major with Intelligence told me that the Americans had set up a School of Oriental Research in Jerusalem, run by a German Jewish Rabbi called Glueck or something. He was an archaeologist and was digging up stuff all over Transjordan." We giggled at what we thought was a pun, and I sipped my White Russian and she her Black and Tan. I noticed she was wearing a French perfume.

"Anyway, the Jews were trying to buy off the British over their home-land issues by being tough guys for SOE in the Balkans and doing 'derring-do' stuff for the British. The Zionists thought that being brave would help their case. Many of the fighters were Polish citizens who got out of the *gulags* but ran for cover rather than the Polish 2nd Corps. Some are desert-ers who have the benefit of the blind eye.

"As for us Poles, well, it was a hotbed of unrest. Katyń was not forgiv-en and Sikorski was not the favourite in the East, in Cairo, as people like to think now. Being dead often breeds legends!"

"He was in Cairo just before his so-called accident, wasn't he?" I asked, innocently enough.

"You know damned well he was!" she shot back at me. "Who do you think you're kidding? Never kid a kidder, and that was damned clumsy. I know you have an interest in Sikorski's death.

"You tell me who you report to and maybe someday I'll chat with you over tea somewhere nice. It would have to be classy. A deal, as the Americans say?"

"Okay, a deal. You know I report to the London Polish government and you will have all the details in my report." I smiled as sweetly as I could .

"Don't leer at me like that, it makes me feel uncomfortable. So you are on. Sikorski gossip for tea at the Ritz. And yes, it's clear you can be trusted because you got your book back via a very sexy lady, me. But if you report only to London then I am the Queen of Sheba."

"And I'm Solomon," I heard my own reply. "With eyes and a body like yours you could well be the Queen of Washington, London and Moscow combined for me."

"Touché," she answered. Veering away from the subject, she continued. "I liked Cairo, I couldn't help it. The place is like a drug. Our Mr Churchill likes that part of the world too, North Africa. He has a weakness for kings and princes such as Farouk, even with his peculiarities and sexual penchant.

"And what about Greece? Wasn't that run from Cairo too?" I asked, changing to what I felt was safe territory.

"It was, but the Yanks and the British fell out over that too. SOE and the American OSS were at loggerheads. Churchill, of course, wanted the exiled King George back in charge, whilst the Americans, being good Democrats, wanted the Communists in control. But they hadn't really worked out in the White House that they were Reds. After all, they were Greeks, not Russians! The Yanks are so un-European. Hence the well-armed civil war in '44 – OSS versus SOE, Communists versus Royalists."

"And the British won and had to put down the Communists."

"And Churchill fell in love and then out with young King Peter of Yugoslavia," she pouted.

"Ah, the Chetniks. I once heard the BBC actually say that the Chetniks were the first organised guerrilla army in Europe. What a bloody cheek, when we Poles had been at it since 1939! What is it about Poland and the British consciousness, Kryszia? Why do they have such trouble recognising Poland?"

"Good question," she said, "I have a theory." She wagged her finger at me and winked. "I think they like to be top dog. Like old Churchill in the war, all that bulldog and Empire stuff. Whilst he liked Sikorski, just as with de Gaulle, he couldn't face Republicans. He is, after all, the descendant of a magnate family. I bet he didn't like Oliver Cromwell either.

"You see, Poland in the past was an advanced political society, fairly democratic for its time. It didn't have a cousin or offspring of Queen Victoria or the Kaiser or The Romanovs or the Hapsburgs at its helm. Rather it had some generals and a different democratic and republican tradition. The British don't like foreigners without a decent monarchy and a bit of British blood. That's what I reckon Churchill thinks. And on the British Socialist side, well, we beat the Russians in the twenties, so we are the bad guys!"

"No, no, that's too simplistic," I said, "Churchill is as ruthless and as crafty as a cartload of monkeys. You are right to some extent, but fundamentally he is an Empire man. Eden and Macmillan are just as bad, but not so Empire-mad. As for this Labour lot, as a Party they have no love for the Poles. And Attlee is just dumb. Nationalise this and nationalise that, it's all he cares about, allowing his Left wing to run riot, stirring up class war and causing community breakdown led by Communist Trades Unions. " I grinned at my own – naturally unbiased – commentary.

"Fan of the Labour party then?" The question was rhetorical. "Don't you feel we need health care for all, free at the point of delivery? Aren't you proud of the new National Health Service that came in last year?" she chided me.

"It's not the free part I bother about, it's the lunatic idea that the health of the nation will so improve that it will pay for itself in a few years and cost the country nothing. That's just plain lunacy One day it will bankrupt Britain!"

"Shush, shush my little fascist, you are upsetting the neighbours." She touched my hair gently. She wiped her finger on the table mat. "Too much Brylcreem, my sweet." For all her joking she was right; it was clear that the bar had its fair share of tweedy intellectuals as well as a couple of poofs who were earwigging close by and scowling in my direction. I had heard one earlier extolling the virtues of nationalised railways.

"Maybe I should buy a flat cap to show solidarity," I shot back, and then we really laughed together. Just to annoy our listeners.

"As I was saying," she went on, "lots of Poles got stuck in transit in '39 and '40 and went into the Chetnik resistance. The Chetnik leader was a King Peter man, through and through. But in come the Americans with Rough Rider Roosevelt making promises. Eventually he starts arming the Partisans, Red Communists led by Tito and opposed to the Chetniks. So all American resources headed the Partisan way and the Chetniks became side-lined. The Reds kept up pressure on the Germans, earning themselves brownie points. The Chetniks did attack the Germans but their strategy was like the Poles - wait for the right moment for a national rising. The Allies wanted instant action.

"The upshot was that Tito, the Communist leader, got the Allies to drop the Chetniks. He exploited the Croat versus Serb ethnicity problem. Roosevelt and Churchill wooed him but he outwitted them. With Stalin's personal backing he invited the Red Army in right, under the nose of the SOE and OSS. Stalin must have laughed himself silly. The Poles and the Yugoslavs given away by the brilliant demigods, C & R Incorporated!"

"What happened to King Peter?" I asked.

"Churchill had bullied him into deserting the Chetniks and denouncing them. They were mainly Serb, by the way, and strongly anti-Communist. So they were reported as being collaborators with the Germans. Same old story as in the Ukraine. Churchill stuck in a puppet, ignored King Peter, and in the end the poor boy was deposed. Yugoslavia went Red and all thanks to the Big Two. What a cock up!

"So some advice for you as a fellow drifter. You must be careful now with the Polish Exile government , deciding whose side you take. The French were the first to 'derecognise' our government. Is that a proper word? Followed by the British and the Americans. Only Spain, Ireland and the Vatican still recognise the Polish Government in Exile. All good Catholics together.

"So now, not unnaturally, the government has begun to split. The Socialists against the Conservatives. Or the Generals, the Second Corps boys and General Anders against the old guard and the Air Force and so on. It will end in more tears. Solutions will need tenacity and courage. Here endeth my lesson," she intoned.

We tailed off into private and quiet thought.

I touched her hand. "I do trust you, Krysia, by the way. I recognise your record and frankly am honoured to meet you," I decided to say. "You come from a good blood line, unlike me!"

"Oh, you are sweetie. Let's have that tea at the Ritz sometime. I have a lot up here," she tapped her head, "I'm sure you know what I mean, and I feel I can open up to you. In a strange way it has been a magic moment, a release. There is just so much to tell."

She touched her fingers to her lips and pressed them to my lips. We laughed and parted. She to her paramour and money, and I to my bed.

That night I lay in my own bed at last. Clean sheets at last, but no peace of mind. I left the curtains open, staring at the night sky and silhouetted chimney pots opposite. Sleep would not come to my tired brain as it struggled with the past hours, the past years. I was bitterly unhappy at the way I had acted towards Ela. I had felt so blown about my emotions, so out of control. Now she was gone I felt there was nothing left. I was nothing but a common assassin. It felt as though all goodness had been drained from me, as though there was no morality left in me. I felt lonely, unwanted and I hated my own feelings of self pity. I no longer knew myself, I felt so uncertain of who I had become. I missed mum and dad. I missed my childhood and Mrs Simpson. Where had my 'child self 'gone, my soul? What would my mother think of me now? Everyone had gone except for me. I felt impotent, knowing I hadn't planned any of this. Call of duty and country had led me to this dark vortex. I needed to find myself. I needed to be calm to rid myself of such destructive fast fits of anger. I needed to go home, I realised. Besides, I had a year to kill.

The sea surged on the Brighton pebbles with its slow, even wish which preceded the return of every wave. The sea sent a constant rhythm; I tried to match it with my breathing. The thud, thud of a fishing boat engine far off shore beat into my mind.

I kept seeing Ela's face. Crumpled, thin, those tortured eyes darting at mine, searching for love, for hope. I had seen in her a sense of tragedy. Not betrayal or even hurt, just deep loss, deep pain, pain beyond even mine. Was it really love she had lost? Was that tormented look from the heart? I realised that the tragedy had come not only with the circumstances, the shock, but through the realisation that an end had come. Her eyes had been first pleading then dull. I realised I had not heard the words she said.

What I had seen was the look of heartbreak.

I wept for my callousness, for my divided mind.

What was I doing?

Whom was I serving?

So many decisions.

Krystyna Skarbek, with her sensuality and hidden secrets, came to me in dream time. She was right; the West had become an Anglo-American empire. Roosevelt had liked that idea. A Democrat could not have an American empire, but jump over the British and there you have it. As for the British Imperialists, they knew the world had changed. The days of Empire were over, without the Americans, so they would settle for second best. And Stalin had gotten his Empire too. So now we had a stable world of Empires, back to how it was before the First World War.

But a world of confrontational Empires, Reds versus the West, a conflict to be played out around the world. Churchill, Roosevelt and Stalin and their war games. They created an Iron Curtain, it had been hung with the betrayal of Poland and the death of Sikorski. *What else did Kryszia know*?

My mind wandered on and on. I had never meant to become an assassin. Was I one? What was I fighting for? All I knew was that I was eaten up with a desire for vengeance. Mrs Simpson's voice echoed down the years from the good book. 'Vengeance is mine, saith the Lord of Hosts'. At some point in the turmoil I slept, but my mind was awake. I woke to another day.

During an early morning seafront walk to stow my package for Kryszia safely amongst the pigeon droppings, I resolved to head briefly for Canada and then to the USA in order to complete my mission for Witek. The London Poles would take some actions about WiN and the Communist infiltration before I could talk to the Americans. As always there was a short term and a long term.

When I phoned Rupert we agreed I should sail on the MS Stockholm, the Swedish American liner sailing out of Copenhagen. He thought it better I disembark in Halifax, Canada, not New York. A circuitous route, but a safe one. Rupert advised me the boat had a reputation for rolling about in Atlantic storms. "She's too small for the Atlantic really," he said, describing her as "more like a yacht than a regular liner, sleek and modern". I must confess to being excited at the prospect. Apparently the ship was fast and new, her maiden voyage having been only last year.

"You are to travel tourist class, so as to be inconspicuous." I could have flown and would love to have done so but it was too observable. From Halifax I would take the train right across the country to Calgary and my remaining family, the Smolletts. Hopefully the travel would give me time to think. To sort myself out.

I asked Kryszka to come with me, but he refused, saying if I had no objection he would "stay in England, here in Crown Street". Sensing my friend needed a quiet place to heal too, I saw no problem except with money.

My bank was still in moth-balls, so to speak. Kryszka surprised me as ever, told me he had already spoken to the owner of the sweet wholesaler at the end of the road, who could use security duties and caretaking after hours. Apparently with sweet rationing still on there was a "constant risk of break-ins."

"Little money, but it is a start," he said. The owner's grandfather was a Jew from Lwów, "so he felt sorry for me."

Rationing was still in place in England in the post-war years. It had been a shock to me. Petrol and sugar were both subject to restrictions, worse even than in war time. The excuse given was the need to feed Europe and its broken agriculture. I felt it more likely to be down to the love of control by a centralising Labour government.

So life was settled for the immediate moment.

I travelled by ferry and train to Copenhagen, where I boarded the Stockholm. I found myself elated at the prospect of getting out of Europe. I was going away. I was going home.

At the same time as I set sail, Kim Philby was heading to Washington, D.C. to take up a post as First Secretary to the British Embassy. He was to act as liaison between the British Embassy and the newly formed CIA.

I had packed what I had, which was minimal. I'd had a few things stowed away in the cottage but not much. Clothes I could buy in Canada or the US where there was no rationing and I could spend money.

Austerity Britain and shattered Europe would be far away.

Bleeding Poland would be a fading dream.

Or so I thought.

# CHAPTER 15

# LAND OF THE FREE

Travelling tourist class was no hardship on this Atlantic crossing. Despite the dire warnings from Rupert, the ocean was kind and the journey smooth. I spent a lot of time on the veranda deck, reading in the comfortable wicker chairs. Before setting sail I had accumulated a set of novels I had missed over the past years. By chance I seemed to have packed two books about race. My nose was soon stuck into *Cry the Beloved Country* by Alan Paton, which I followed with *Last of the Conquerors*, the story of a black GI who marries a white German girl. The moral of the narrative was clearly that Nazi Germany was less racist than parts of America. Naturally the book provoked some deep thinking, so deep at times I was grateful for distraction in the form of *Picture Goer, Life, Harpers Bazaar Magazine* and *Vogue*. Even complimentary copies from the liner or waifs and strays from other passengers.

Gradually I felt my spirit calm. Just looking out of the window, watching the swell of the sea, basking in the warmth of the sun was soothing. In the evening, rather than mixing in the Lounge, I took myself off to the writing and reading room to catch up on my heavyweight novels and to spend quiet time. I also wrote up my own thoughts and notes in Witek's brown book.

Too soon we cruised into Halifax, which had played such a major part in the Allies' war effort, as the only Canadian Atlantic port. Before the war it had been a depressed area. I was told by one of the pursers that, back in 1945, there had been riots in the town because wartime prosperity looked as though it would ebb away. Strange benefits of a war so far away.

I planned to leave Halifax immediately. There was nothing in the city for me.

We sailed into the Ocean Terminal, at the south end of the city. I had no problem on entry as I arrived as myself, a Canadian citizen returning home. Thanks to Rupert, all my papers were in order.

My plan was simple. From Halifax I would board a train up to Quebec and then on to Ottawa, where I would meet my old mentor, the General. From there I would head westward out over the plains to Calgary, but I would fly.

One quick reverse charge trunk call from the quayside to my uncle Jack Smollett changed my plans. My idea of a long trip over the plains, courtesy of Canadian Pacific, was blown away; the Smolletts had arranged for a pick-up by a small air charter company delivering parts to Montreal. A short hop and they could pick me up at the Uplands airport. I felt a surge of joy at being in a free country where enterprise counted. For the first time in years the burden of war began to fall away.

I had to be at Uplands in exactly twelve days. So I went straight to the rail station and caught the first train out. First I needed a bank, shops, and some new clothes. I needed to feel *myself*. I decided to skip Montreal, just do the necessities and then press on to the capital, Ottawa. Montreal I remembered as the French heartland of the country. I recalled how its mayor had resisted conscription in the war and encouraged young Quebecois not to register and enlist. I was still in no mood for such ideas. The train took me on to Ottawa, which was all new to me. I felt excited, like a kid let out of school. Arriving at Union Station late I headed for the best hotel in town. It was set right next door to the Parliament Buildings and the landmark *Château Laurier* hotel. Taking a cab from the station, I discovered Ottawa was not what I expected. It was beautiful, clean, and for the most part modern.

What struck me most was that it was not Europe.

My hotel turned out to be a magnificent limestone edifice with turrets and masonry reminiscent of a French château. Rooms were available. I booked in for ten nights. Now I had the luxury of becoming a tourist for a few days. The Parliament building seemed more impressive than London's. I spent time around the Irish and French area in ByWard market and visited Notre Dame Cathedral. Slowly I began to realise just how new this country was. Even the magnificent old buildings were relatively new. The country was driving forward, thrusting itself into prosperity. But underneath the facade it was clear that the working classes faced the same issues as in Europe. It was a different type of instability, but it was there just the same. This war had changed people, changed lives.

I bought a camera and took lots of photographs when I was in public places. I was, after all, a tourist. I found a shopkeeper who could develop my film overnight and over a period of three days studied the photographs I had taken, very carefully, using a magnifying glass. I was searching for any faces that recurred, any figures turning away. I checked clothes and features and postures. Eventually satisfied I was not being followed, I contacted my mentor General Sosnkowski, who along with Kryszka, had been my saviour in the British plot to eliminate me back in 1946.

Naturally the General's phone was tapped. His movements were being watched. Stalin had so convinced the British and the Americans of his danger to the Allies that Churchill had demanded his removal as Polish Army Commander. Mikołajczyk was bullied into agreement and the General sent to virtual internment in Canada. Even now requests for travel were refused. He was not welcome in the USA although his only crime was that he opposed Stalin. He was, as a result of this antagonism, a hero of American

Polonia, that Diaspora of Polish emigration.

To me the General was the *Szef*, the Chief. Others called him *Baca* or the 'Shepherd'.

I sent him an innocuous postcard, open to being read and signed it Tadpole with three kisses and a squiggle, possibly a tadpole. The card made some rambling references to visiting the family, trying to sound as feminine as possible. I gave the hotel address, a date and time to meet. Being open is the best disguise.

On the appointed day I explained to the head receptionist that my sister's uncle was arriving and that he would ask for me. On arrival, the clerk was to pass a sealed envelope to the old man. A sum of money equal to the job was paid over. The clerk, I was happy to learn, was called Jankowski, which he pronounced, being Canadian, with a 'Y'. This is how assimilation works and roots are lost. Reassured by the Polishness of his name, I gave the name of the General, Kazimierz Sosnkowski, the last of Stalin's *bête noirs*. Not a trace of recognition passed his eyes. The man's Polishness had long gone.

My envelope gave instructions to the General to head straight up Rideau Street, turn left at William Street, and then drop back into ByWard market. I explained I would shadow him until he was clear of followers and then we would talk. I had already made contact with an Irish Nationalist guy running a small eatery nearby. His anti-English attitude meant there would be no problem finding a quiet table, far from prying eyes.

The time came and I shadowed the General as he walked from the hotel. Sosnkowski still had that military bearing one would expect. Before we reached Dan Kirwan's bar and dining-house, I walked past him, muttering, "Follow me." Hastening my step I slipped ahead of him by three yards before gliding into the bar door. He followed me in and shook my hand warmly before our host Daniel Kirwan took us "through to the back, where the boys meet". Where we were promised we would not be disturbed.

Pleasantries over, the old man and I sat at the oil-cloth covered table facing each other. He listened silently as I poured out my whole story, from the debacle on the border, to the meetings with Witek, including his astonishing plan to assassinate Stalin. I spoke of my own personal predicament too. I was, after all, under orders from this man. But as I explained, in *ad hoc* terms, I was also under orders to the British, the Americans and the Russians.

"No mean feat," he responded drily. "You have become a quadruple agent!"

I was not amused.

He knew me of old. "Think about it like a chess game. It's just a question of laying everything out. It may be boring at times, but to see the picture we have to look at the players and the pieces. You and I are not concerned about the British or the Soviets, only insofar as they move on *our* board, which is Poland. They move on our board because we have something they want. We need to identify what that is.

"So let us start at the beginning. If ever you write your memoirs always tell your readers that it is the boring bits, the table-laying, the scene-setting that makes the story. The reader has to observe the plot to see what is not obvious, otherwise it is no substance."

I looked at this shrewd man. He and General Sikorski had not been the best of friends. Comrades-in-arms, yes, but Sikorski knew Sosnkowski's power base of was the military, both in Poland and in exile. Sosnkowski had been with the old Marshal, Piłsudski, from the beginning. He was an old-time Socialist, one of the founding fathers of the Republic. Sikorski and Piłsudski had been at loggerheads for years. The forces had always been right behind Sosnkowski, but he was not the 'diplomat' Sikorski was. Perhaps that was why the common man liked him.

He seemed to have read my mind. "The old generation, my generation, the old Socialists, of every colour from pink to red, were all *connected*. Someone always knew somebody else. It was how we organised ourselves, into cells. So in a strange way we all knew of each other. Pi?sudski was a very distant 'cousin' of Stalin if you like! The important point is that each had some knowledge or measure of each other. Teddy, you will be surprised how much Big Politics is about personality.

"Stalin is, as his pseudonym suggests, a man of steel. He is a Georgian, therefore from a minority, so always paranoid, suspicious, cunning. He is also without normal feelings, a psychopath. He insulates himself from emotion with a sea of 'toadies' and butchers. Like Lenin, he is a man who views other humans as vessels for his will. That will is Communism, the breaking of freedom, of expression and thought of others. So his *modus operandi* has been terror and absolute power. He killed all his generals and officers in the Purges. He has killed millions, using Khrushchev, in the Ukraine. He killed *kulaks* by the thousand in his farm collectivisation programme. He starved the population to extermination and then resettled the depopulated Ukrainian land with ethnic Russians. To be Ukrainian in the Don basin today is to be a Russian. He cowed the surviving Cossacks and murdered the Tartars. So the massacre of our officers at Katyn was nothing special to him – officers and leaders were killed as a matter of course. To him many Poles were what he thought of as Whites. They deserved to die.

"Roosevelt and Churchill knew all this. Yet he blinded them. If we look at the reasons for the war, both the underlying and the obvious, the Allies had no victory because Stalin out-manoeuvred them at every stage. How? First, he had a network of agents in every country dedicated to penetrate and manipulate the Intelligence services of the West. Second, he had corps of Soviet sympathisers, based on propaganda, about the equality of the working classes and improving their lot. Third, he had the support of national Communist parties, who had a role to play in influencing, by infiltration, left leaning and liberal organisations in the West, whether that be trade union, political party or a newspaper. They were all directed by the Comintern.

He paused, sipping Guinness, which our host assured us was the genuine stuff made only with water from the river Liffey. I was disappointed as always that such a creamy, delicious-looking head did not taste like the clotted cream it looked it should be.

"The aim of the Communist International movement was simply stated: 'To fight by all available means, including armed force, for the overthrow of the international bourgeoisie and for the creation of an international Soviet republic as a transition stage to the complete abolition of the State.' That was their position in 1919 and it did not change under Stalin. Whatever Communist leaders may say, Stalin ran the Comintern. He purged it then packed it with NKVD agents at home and abroad. Yes, it is finished today, but only because the tool has worn out. Stalin has replaced it with the Cominform, a simple propaganda machine intended to re-educate the satellite countries by rewriting their history and soft-soaping the West. He has learned the power of the media! By the way, Teddy, did you know Roosevelt had to apologise to Stalin for the insult he felt at being called Uncle Joe? Stalin considered it a slur.

"How all our lives are affected by these demigods. Poland defeated the Communist invasion of Europe with no help from anyone except some French advisors. Stalin knew then, in 1944, that he had to remove Poland from the scene if the planned revolutions in France, Italy, Yugoslavia and Germany were to succeed. He needed to avoid an alliance of Poland with the Ukraine and Lithuania at all costs. He had to *break* the Poles, so he used the West to do it.

"So how do we explain the American, with their professed love of freedom, joining with a mass murderer? How do we explain the shrewd war-loving Churchill being out-foxed? How do move forward now? Use what we know to obtain a free Poland? These are interesting questions. The West totally misjudged Stalin. In Roosevelt's case he acted for personal electoral gain, no more, no less. Europe did not interest him as much as the Far East. Soviet agents and left-leaning, perhaps partly blinded Liberals are at the heart of all this. Roosevelt was misinformed about Europe by his staff, which was riddled with left-leaning philosophers sympathetic to the Soviet system. And also by a military intelligence service who not only gave wrong information about the Reds' strengths and weaknesses, but actively armed the Communists who then fought against their own Allies from China to the Balkans. Truman, to give him credit, is trying to put this right with his new CIA. But the damage has been done. As for Poland, Roosevelt gave his famous 'Poland is an inspiration to the world' speech and then left our country to Stalin's mercies. He did not conceive the danger that would follow in Europe. I doubt he care. He simply wanted his troops out as quickly as possible. He actually thought they could leave Germany in two years. As a result of his blinded policy I predict they will be there for years to come.

"Just now things in the USA are swinging the other way. A certain senator from Wisconsin is upsetting the boat now. Have you heard of Joseph McCarthy?"

I confessed I had not.

"That man is destined either for a bullet or to be smeared out of history because he is gunning for the Communists in the USA. Broadly speaking he is telling the truth and Truman knows it. But if this truth comes out it could wreck the Democrats, so Truman will not go very far with his reforms. The Kremlin knows America. McCarthy's end will be girls, drugs and drink, or failing that a car accident – as happened to your parents, I believe. Knowing the Americans, McCarthy will be given a five-minute witch-hunt with fall guys and then there will be a cover-up. Too many writers and theatricals, Teddy. Too many Liberals who didn't know they were duped. Too many reputations to fall."

The reference to my parents showed on my face. Their death was a continually motivating factor in my life. "The long hand of the Soviets."

"What about Churchill and Poland? Why did he betray Britain's most faithful ally? The code breakers, the technologists, mine detector experts, all those hardened troops and expert flyers... why did he betray them?"

"Churchill wanted Russia in the war and cemented the Alliance. He overestimated the prowess of the British and the strength of the Empire. So he gave Poland away, initially swapping a bit in the East for a bit of Germany in the West. In other words, he matched Stalin's complete lack of morality or care for Polish humanity. In his way he was just as ruthless as Stalin. No doubt he felt once Stalin was in the camp he could charm him with rhetoric and regain ground. Sikorski had indicated he would sacrifice *some* territory in the East, but again Churchill misjudged the little he could give.

"Sikorski's position did not please many Polonians this side of the Atlantic. He met with British Foreign Secretary Anthony Eden in January 1942 to discuss Poland's future. Sikorski proposed the creation of a new Polish-Lithuanian union; it was to have as head of state an English prince. "

I was a little dumbstruck by such a thought, which would have been a rather beautiful arrangement and an astute political move.

"Such an idea was appealing to Churchill but anathema to Stalin. What is intriguing was how Stalin found out about it. And now, Teddy Labden, you may remember the first of our strange accidents. Prince George, the Duke of Kent, was killed in the late summer of 1942, in a plane crash at

Eagle's Rock, near Dunbeath in Caithness. He was in a Sunderland, a particularly safe aircraft, as you will recall. The following November, right here in Montreal there was another attempt to sabotage Sikorski's plane. Both engines of his plane to Washington stopped working. Sikorski accused the British of trying to kill him. His aide-de-camp, Captain Główczyński, recalled Sikorski saying to Frederick Bowhill, British Air Marshal, who had congratulated him on his survival: 'If you could accompany me on the way to Washington tomorrow, I would feel safe.'

"Sikorski was flying to meet with Roosevelt, hoping that the results of the future peace conference would ensure Poland received not only eastern territory, but western as well. This time he got nothing more than the expression of best wishes for Poland and the Poles. I tell you that Sikorski explicitly blackmailed the President, dangling the possibility of a Polish-German agreement.

"They didn't finally get him till July 1943 in Gibraltar. Due to special VIP treatment got, no one really knew exactly who was on board Sikorski's plane when it went down. I certainly do not. The exact cargo manifest is unknown. Neither does anyone really know who was on Maisky's plane, parked next door so to speak. The identity of the bodies recovered from the crash site was always uncertain. Some bodies, including that of Sikorski's daughter, Zofia, were never found. How convenient that there was a special British Intelligence operation opposite, managed, I am told, by a man called Kim Philby. Perhaps it was he who organised the boat pickups observed from both shores? You should find out, my boy.

"What we should dismiss is a planned coup by me or other generals. Sikorski dealt with this in Cairo. Of course, there was opposition to his plan on the eastern frontier, but the cities were always secure – Lwów and Grodno, for example. I did not know his mind on Wilno except that he, like Piłsudski, proposed a union.

"Poor Ludwik Lubieński had the unhappy position of being at the site of the crash, being head of the Polish military mission in Gibraltar. I am even told he had to undo the pilot's Mae West. The poor man must have been almost in shock at what had happened. And even more astonished the next day when the pilot told him he was not wearing a life jacket.

"Let us be generous to Churchill. The Russians assassinated Sikorski because the Poles in alliance with other Slavs and anti-Soviet elements in the Soviet Union could overthrow him. Quite straightforward. He was scared Sikorski might even do a deal with a reconstructed anti-Nazi Germany. So Churchill, when requested, turned a blind eye to his own intelligence services, who connived with the Russians, resulting in Sikorski's death.

"After the event and as part of the programme the Poles were emasculated. I myself was becoming a victim by Churchill's express command to our so-called leader Mikołajczyk. But at least I am alive. I am the last survivor. Anders and his allies are alive too, but their power, their legitimacy was taken away by the British.

"You must view Churchill first and foremost as an orator. He was no general. He was an actor providing a performance which he lived. Afterwards he'd go home and cry to his wife. Yes, Churchill wept bitter tears over Sikorski. After creating Poland's doom in '45, he even went to the trouble of asking the Chiefs of Staff to explore the possibility of the West invading Russia to free Poland. He actually put forward the idea of dropping an atom bomb on selected Russian cities, using German troops. 'Operation Unthinkable' they called it.

"Of course, the Chiefs said 'impossible' because they were pumped full of lies about the state of the Soviet Union, which had been constantly portrayed as invincible. How could the Americans do a *volte-face* with Uncle Joe? Let the American public know that the Red terror dwarfed the Nazis, and that they, the people, had been kept in the dark about it by their own government?

"I believe Churchill salved his conscience. His Chiefs said no, but he had tried and he had cried. Emotions played such huge role in this last war.

"Everything was falling apart. The Russians got further west quicker than expected. The Italian campaign was botched at the end, with the Communists being given orders in France, Italy, Greece and Yugoslavia to defeat the Germans. They were told to be uncooperative with the Allies and slow them down. Once the boys had crawled off Omaha beach and the tanks rolled on from Sword and Juno, everything else was a sideshow, a supporting act. No one took a great interest in what the Reds were up to. We were all one happy family winning in Normandy. But look at what happened. How narrow was de Gaulle's escape from assassination on his entry to Paris?"

Abruptly the General changed tack.

"And now you sit here before me with this conundrum. Why are you here, Teddy? Do you want me to sanction your assassination of Stalin? Do you think it will help Poland?"

I had thought long and hard about this. "If it is a Polish venture, then no. That will only bring about another round of vengeance. Will it reduce the pressure on the survivors of the Home Army and their relatives? Yes. The Stalinists would be replaced at some point, just as the Soviet Politburo will change. If the replacement for Stalin is the man we believe to be his successor, then Poland will gain territory in the East to some extent, certainly the towns. Will Poland be free of Communists? I do not know. Will the world be a better place? Undoubtedly."

"Not good enough, Teddy. There are too many uncertainties. I cannot order or sanction such an escapade. If you want to go ahead with it, then you must either go it alone or with the assistance of the Americans. We exiled Poles, I agree, are all officially still in the Army, awaiting our moment. So if this moment comes as a result of your actions, then as always we will be the first to fight. For this immediate event you are planning we must watch our backs. I wonder, too, if you really have the makings of an assassin."

I blinked back the tears that came to my eyes. "Sir, I am no assassin. I will not allow myself be called that. What I am doing is taking revenge. My parents were killed, my friends were killed, and my country was betrayed because of one man's megalomania. This is totally personal. I understand and accept your position, but I will not be defeated. This is war. I consider this an execution, not an assassination."

"As you wish," the General replied. "You understand my position. I will, however, give you the same order as Menzies: break the Soviet spy ring that brought about our demise. I will advise President Zaleski and Prime Minister Bór-Komorowski, as well as General Anders in London to square the circle. London and the remaining underground in Poland will assist you, but no more than that."

"Thank you, sir. I understand," I replied.

"Canada is a strange place. Sections of it have a distinctly British tinge, especially amongst the Security and Police Force. "

"The Mounties always get their man, sir!"

"I wish that were so. But they can be slow on the uptake. As an example, let me tell you of Igor Gouzenko, an important Soviet cipher clerk. He went to the police right here in Ottawa with over one hundred secret documents revealing a massive Soviet spy ring. First the police would not even handle the documents – why? Because it was September 1945 and they thought as the Russians were allies they should hand him and the documents back. The man hid, and went to the papers, which as you know are Beaverbrook dominated. As you might guess they did not want the story. Back Gouzenko went to the police, who eventually passed on the news to the Americans. They discovered the Russians were working on their atom bomb but were a long way behind them. It allowed them to check for leaks. Unbelievable but true. Naivety? Or sympathetic Communists? It was the same for your parents. The police cannot conceive foreign spies and nasty killers from Russia. It's 'not cricket'. Thank God the Americans play baseball."

We dined on a rich Irish stew and soda bread, exchanging news and views. He listened sympathetically to my tales of the anti-Communist underground. I was glad to hear that the traitors Witek had identified and the siphoning off of money to WiN were being stopped. Mikołajczyk had not been well received in America, he told me, having being seen as a traitor for joining the Provisional Government. A view I had always shared. Nevertheless, Mikołajczyk and Korboński had been on a charm offensive.

They had spoken here in Canada, in Toronto and Hamilton to the Polish Canadian Congress. Stefan Korboński was, according to the General, a much more genuine man than Mikołajczyk. "After all, he was in Poland and not part of the Exile government. He generously defended Mikołajczyk from too much criticism, but with fighting still going on in Poland he is hard to defend. Someone described the events in Poland as a civil war, which had caused some heated exchanges between the majority and brave few Communist sympathisers." The General shook his head. "Of course, it is not a civil war. The combatants represent on one side the only legal government, the one in London. The enemy is a foreign power reliant on many foreign occupying troops. So the Canadian Poles would seem to have the matter precisely right. Korboński was given a little tour of Canadian Polonia and was surprised by how strongly the Polish community felt, how well informed they were about current affairs."

I had a theory on that. "The Canadian Poles are newer. America has a much older community with quite disparate roots from us Canadians. In a way we are closer to home than many of our American brothers and sisters." That being said, I knew American Polonia had risen and was rising to give every form of assistance possible to the old country. "Just a shame they voted Democrat!" I added.

The General laughed.

Later in my hotel I looked back on what had been for me a very uncomfortable conversation at times. Without the General's support I was not destined to be a Polish patriot. Rather an unknown maverick, if things went wrong. Perhaps, I concluded, this was the best way. This way I could also keep things personal.

As I replayed our conversation in my head I thought back particularly to the General's warning:

"Be very careful, Teddy. You are a marked man. This very moment in Moscow Comrade Abakumov could be picking up the phone to Mikhail Ryumin, the Deputy Head of the MGB. He will let his overseas network know that Teddy Labycz has somehow walked from the prison at Butyrka. He won't like that, Teddy. So he'll order that everyone involved in your 'care' at Butyrka is dealt with. He'll have all the suspects sent to Sukhanovka prison, where they know how to make prisoners sing.

"By now he will suspect that his friends in the MVD are hiding something. He'll be very sure to talk to Comrade Beria about you.

"But before that, Teddy, he will give the order that you are to be eliminated."

CHAPTER 16
# STARTING OVER

It's always good to be home. Those first exciting moments when everyone says they love you. Smiling faces surround you. Hands are shaken, hugs exchanged – you greet people you have known from another time. Everyone says you look well, no matter the truth. The places you have known all look as different as they are familiar.

The traveller returns as a centre of curiosity. The exciting one who has seen and done things ordinary mortals have never done. The returning soul now has experiences, an understanding of life, has known the losses and exchanges of war. Life has been lived at a different pace, in a different way, from those who stay at home.

I looked down as our Dakota wheeled and came in to land at Smollett field, excitement tinged with fear.

Everything was different. There was a new concrete apron with hangars to one side. A building stood where huts had been. Its many sky-lighted roof seemed to cover an acre. This must be the new factory. About the only familiar thing was the plane itself, which had shuddered and heaved itself into the air. Its two aircrew were ex-Canadian Air Force, now running a small transport company from the field here. They'd had to borrow to buy it, they told me, but the 'kite' seemed in good condition, having one new engine on the right with only 250 hours since Major Overhaul. The left had just over 600.

I could see two Liberators parked up, painted camouflage green. "Used as drill aircraft for training fire crews. Sad, really, to see the old ladies retired so early," one of the crew shouted back in response to my enquiry.

These work horses never had the 'glamour' of the Flying Fortresses the USAAF had used to bomb the life out of Germany. Yet with their long range it had been in these craft that a few brave RAF and SAAF men had flown all the way to Warsaw and back during the Rising. A motley collection of South African, Polish and British airmen had flown up from North Italy, up over Hungary, across Czechoslovakia, over the Carpathian Mountains, across Poland and into the burning hell of Warsaw. They dropped down to a few hundred feet counting the seconds to the drop, and then canisters away. And how many made it back through the searchlights, the flak, the night fighters or even the weather? Only half the flights ever returned. Sombre thoughts for a home-coming.

Further proof that for me war was still waging within me, but not for these people.

Crash! We were down, the engines' revving woke me from my reverie. We taxied close to a hangar with its sign emblazoned across the front. *Canadian Hawk Transport Services.* Large blue letters on a white background. Inappropriate, I thought, for a Dakota. But we all have our dreams. Acknowledging my nervous anticipation I deliberately took note of details. They kept my mind occupied till the moment I had to face all those people I could see waving at the plane. They were standing outside the white-painted single-storey offices, which I presumed were the offices of the two-man band. They had told me they had a mechanic secretary and a secretary who made the coffee.

There, parked up by the office, was a shiny beige Packard 22 series. The pilot had called it a 'Woody Wagon'. Its huge gleaming chrome bumpers, shiny wood-trim side doors and panelling were shining in the sun. Running toward the side hatch was Aunt Jean, holding on to her hat for dear life, white gloves waving frantically. Uncle Jack leaned nonchalantly against the car, legs crossed, holding up his hat. I felt so shy, I felt sick.

"Here's our boy, Jack!" Aunt Jean declared. Jack unwound me from her hugs and kisses, grasping my hand which he pumped up and down. "Good to see you, son. Welcome home!"

There were more grooves in Jack's face. Jean had a few more wrinkles. Jack's hair was whiter, not the steel dust I remembered. Jean's was dyed a different colour. Otherwise they seemed the same. I climbed into the back of the car and settled into the red leather. The car started and we were on the last leg home. Though the station wagon swayed over the field till it hit the road, the interior was quiet after the roar of the plane. Auntie Jean screwed round on the front bench seat and immediately started to talk, telling me all her news. I saw her reddened lips moving, heard names of people who had been in my life, twelve or even twenty years before. I heard Jack say, "Leave off, Jean. Let the boy settle."

"No it's okay, I like to hear."

"See," she said, "the boy wants to catch up. Don't you, Teddy?"

"I sure do, Auntie, and you're the one for all the news, not Unc!" We laughed at my familiar name for Jack, which I probably hadn't used since I was ten. As Jean talked I dreamt my way through a torrent of words, catching the odd name or event. Their past washed over me like the tide, rising slowly, bringing me into their world, of which I had remained so much a part. So much love. The thought made me depressed. I was tired as Jack said, but coming to understand that the tiredness was more than physical.

We detoured a little, in order to pass my parents' old house, the one which had held so much promise for our family. We slowed down in order to crawl past and I realised it held no emotional memories for me. The property had gone up for sale, the proceeds had been invested. "Most of the personal stuff is at the spread," Jean reassured me. The Smolletts' place was closer to 'home', was where I had grown up.

In some ways the old place had not changed. Other changes were evident. The farmland was long gone, sold as part of the early oil boom. The old barn was still there, but the 'burbs', the bungalows of land development, had crept ever closer.

"Everyone wants a home of their own now," Auntie Jean explained. "And we women want a modern, scientific kitchen." That part of the spread had certainly changed. Gone were the old pine dressers. Everything was cream-coloured, sweeping built-in cupboards with chrome handles and some sort of plastic resin work surface called formica. There was a big refrigerator that defrosted itself, apparently very new in 'appliances'. A 'deep freeze' stood in the 'utility' room, which I used to call the scullery. It was 'swish' and new, but clinical and Spartan to my way of thinking.

Then they showed me into the room they had set aside for me.

I was overwhelmed. The room was large, furnished with possessions from my parents' home. There was a large dressing-table in walnut with a huge cloud-shaped mirror, a matching double wardrobe and a smaller man's robe complete with cufflink trays and tie rails. There was my own single bed, with its patchwork cover made by Mrs Simpson. Either side of the bed were two side tables my dad had insisted on calling wine tables. On the tables were two side-lamps, typically Art Nouveau, each boasting a Tiffany shade. The big triple-glazed window had a view out over the windswept prairie. Underneath were a small, comfortable leather Chesterfield sofa, and a library of my books. The polished wood floor was overlaid with a large Indian carpet and the scatter rugs of eastern design called *kulim*. These rugs were traditionally Polish.

In the corner, looking a bit lost in gleaming mahogany and in contrast to the warm walnut, was my mother's pride and joy: the HMV radiogram cabinet.

To the left hand side of the bed a door led into a small box-room. Uncle Jack indicated I should have a look. Inside were a number of tea chests and picture frames wrapped in hessian, along with a couple of trunks and cardboard boxes, full of books and records.

I was lost for words. Instead I hugged Auntie Jean and thanked Unc by shaking his hand.

"Come on, Jean, let's leave the boy to unpack for a while."

"Dinner will be at seven sharp," my aunt said, and then mercifully I was alone. It was very quiet in the big house. The wind whistled just as I remembered. Out there on the prairie in the middle were nodding donkeys from the oil wells and no cattle or sheep.

Without taking my shoes off I lay on the bed and breathed in and out, slowly and regularly, thinking things over. Thought turned to dreaming and I fell asleep. I must have dozed off for a couple of hours. When I woke the light had changed and the dark was coming in. I looked at my watch. It was half-past five. I was beginning to feel hungry.

Jean had laid out towels on the bed, which I hadn't disturbed in my slumber, so I must have been dead to the world. I began to unpack my suitcase and hang up the few clothes I had bought in Ottawa. I picked up the Radom and looked for the best place to keep it. I didn't want to make it obvious to the Smolletts or any cleaner they might employ. I settled for the top drawer of the small wardrobe, laying it there, along with spare ammunition.

To the right of the room was another door that opened into a small washroom. I had a good all-over wash. There was running hot water, supplied, I guessed, by an oil-fired boiler. Then I looked at my meagre wardrobe, which to some would be wealth. I had bought the requisite grey flannel suit and a dark blue business suit. Not what I wanted right now. I needed to be comfortable. So I put on a western-style shirt and pair of slacks and slipped on my new loafers.

Next I explored the box-room. Aunt Jean had saved a number of paintings including the Janis works and a Mucha poster sketch I had sent home in the first few days of the war. I remembered buying them from some Jewish people selling up. For the life of me I couldn't remember if it was in Poland or later in Rumania. In war there are winners and losers. Now, some ten years on, I felt more than a twinge of guilt at my purchase. My parents' paintings from the house were there too, a scene of horse trading, an old man in winter time with horse and sledge, and a pastel of a young woman in peasant costume. I found my mother's tea-cup and saucer set in royal blue and white porcelain, the one which had belonged to the Sowinski family. The Smolletts had been exactly right in their choice of souvenirs when they had packed up my parents' belongings.

Jean had cooked a roast chicken with all the trimmings, followed by good old rice pudding with nutmeg, which she knew I loved. We chatted over the meal about something and nothing and everything, all at the same time. "I really appreciate the way you did up the room. It's certainly been a prodigal's welcome," I said to Jean, squeezing her hand.

"You should know we've changed our mind about selling the house here, Teddy," she replied. "We're still going to Miami though. We'll be spending the Canadian winter there and summer here."

"But we want you to have a home in Canada, a bolt-hole this side of the pond," Jack assured me. He went on to explain that they were arranging to settle the house on me, to avoid tax.

After dinner I helped with the washing-up and we all settled down, Jean to her knitting as always, needles clacking deftly between her fingers. I knew her hobby kept her hands supple and free from rheumatism. Unc and I settled for a brandy and we fell to talking about business. Jack knew I didn't want to run the family business. We soon agreed that selling up was the best deal.

"The Fairchild Corporation has made an offer for the field and the factory, lock, stock and barrel," Jack informed me. We had run a machine tool parts service and reconditioning centre during the war, and as Jack said, "made a mint out of the misery of others." On one level I knew he felt bitter, remembering his own son's death in World War One. But Jack accepted the reality of life and was keen to remind me we were not war profiteers. It was clear that the American economy was war-driven and fortunes were being made. Unlike Europe, North America was in boom time. The War had been good for business this side of the Atlantic; obscene but true.

The Smolletts had found oil on the land early on, but about four years ago they had leased off the last part of their land, all but the five acres immediately around the central farm buildings and the house. The leased drilling concessions had been to some big players. The oil had "gushed cash", Jean chipped in. So as a shareholder in the 'family', Jack asked if I was happy to sell to Fairchild.

First I asked about Bowness, the original airfield to the west of the city.

"It's long gone in favour of the present site, McCall Field, over in the north east, and had just now given back to the City of Calgary by the government. There was no longer a war, so the four runways and all the hangars had been given to the civilian authorities. There seemed no sense in us holding on to our field even for sports or light craft, so I agreed to the deal," Jack answered.

Hearing Fairchild intended to continue to operate a landing strip for their executives to use if they came in from the east or from the US, I suggested we negotiate landing rights for ourselves and even for Canadian Hawk. Jack didn't see a problem and was glad I was thinking forward.

Later that evening I spent time going through my parents' record assortment. The Andrews Sisters seemed to have been their favourite. I found Bill Holliday, Glenn Miller and my favourite Anne Shelton. There were more classical records than popular music, mostly Gigli and Caruso opera pieces and a lot of Tango music. The latter sent me into a black mood. The last time I had heard it was in Przemyśl.

Most of my parents' music was in the older shellac 78 rpm form. Jean and Jack had moved on to the new vinyl microgroove recordings and a portable machine that played at the new speeds, both twelve inch and seven inch recordings. I vowed this would be my bigger first purchase. It was time to move on, I kept telling myself. I was determined to wash the past away.

I'd buy myself an elegant, modern wardrobe. I'd go to the city and hunt for new clothes. I needed a way to feel more a part of civilian life.

Calgary was beginning to boom. Its tallest building, the Palliser Hotel, was about to be outstripped by a new office building. The oil boom meant new office blocks. Downtown Calgary had changed forever from the cowboy town of my youth. I easily found the check sports coat I wanted and a couple of lightweight wool jackets. Cardigan sweaters were in vogue, the sales assistant told me, and so a couple were added to my purchases. I found some polo shirts and three brightly-coloured short-sleeve ones Auntie Jean thought 'quite revolting and so American'. *Good*, I thought. I indulged in some cuff-links and a variety of handkerchiefs and neck ties, though I realised that unless the occasion was formal they were becoming less popular.

I realised I was lucky; I had money and a lot of it. I could buy distractions. So I wallowed in the cinema, playing catch-up with pleasure. I carefully studied Rock Hudson, Cary Grant and Gregory Peck, the clothes they wore and the way they handled themselves. I went back to reading Cowboy comics for men and abandoned the two classics from the ship part read. I joined the MAC, the Movie and Actors Club, a group of business people who staged plays and excerpts from musicals in the old Isis movie house. But at night, no matter how hard I worked at distracting myself during the day a black mood would descend. I could no longer fight the memories.

Sometimes when I got the shakes at night I would sit in a chair and read, just hoping my mind would still. I felt so cold, cold *inside*. I could hear my organs working; they were so loud I thought others might hear. The more I listened the more my heart pounded, squeaking in my ear with the pressure like a rusted pump. Try as I might I couldn't seem to think of the future. It was just too much trouble; it took too much effort. I found it difficult enjoy ordinary things even though I tried. Worst of all I became afraid of sleep in case a nightmare came. Unable to sleep I was listless during the day.

Aunt Jean began asking questions. She knew from my bed linen that I had the night shakes and occasionally she'd hear me call out at night. When this happened I was always drenched with sweat. To calm myself down I'd get up, take out my pistol and strip it down, oiling and checking it. I felt a strange comfort in the weight and the familiar feel of the butt.

Worried, Auntie Jean suggested I go speak to a doctor in town who specialised in this new disease people called depression, which she said was about 'black moods'. Uncle Jack suggested I could be suffering from 'shell shock' just like soldiers did in the Great War.

To ease their worry about me I met with Dr Klaus Weiss – once. A psychotherapist, his aim, he said, was to aid patients with problems of living. Psychotherapists, he told me, employed a range of techniques based on experiential relationship building, talking, and behaviour changes designed to improve the mental health of the patient.

There was nothing wrong with my mental health, I told him. It was the rest of the world that had gone mad.

I did not visit him again.

Uncle Jack laughed when I relayed my experience. "Though your idea that all the world is mad except you and possibly Kryszka is probably the first sign of madness," he smiled. I told a concerned Auntie Jean that a good priest and confession would do a better job for me. Jean, still determined to cheer me up, did her best by me, organising a series of dinners and parties. Week after week I was paraded past a variety of young women of the local 'good' families. Touched, I enquired of Lucy, my first girl friend from way back when. But they were long gone.

In the end what really helped was the thought of others and being taken out of myself. Jack was having Union trouble at the factory in the run up to the Fairchild takeover. He asked me to go down there with him, to talk over the plans Fairchild had offered with some of the Union officials. They were dubious that those plans did not include redundancies.

I wasn't sure I was the best person to help and said so. "I don't think they're going to listen to a rich Polak made good off the back of Canucks, Unc," I said. These old time Canadians still look on us new immigrants as incomers, stealing the dirt that is their heritage.

"In one way you're right," he agreed, "but you talk straight and hard, whereas I try to compromise. Maybe your approach will make one or two think on." So we tried it.

Initially I wasn't a success, because I wasn't prepared to soft soap them. I told them that the world, including Jack and I did, not owe them a living. I was honest, said we had wheedled out of Fairchild a deal that protected them, but that we in all sincerity we couldn't say whether Fairchild would honour it in five years' time. I told them straight that the world was changing, that the economic good times brought on by the war were over. Most of them, as skilled workers, had been in protected or reserved jobs, so had done well on other men's sacrifice. After I had spoken Unc explained the deal again. This time the vote went in favour, by six to four; the Union would recommend acceptance to the workers.

As we left the canteen the loudest of the opponents, a skilled pattern-maker, made a V sign at me then slid his finger across his throat. In gentlemanly manner I returned with a finger salute. As we walked away another man detached himself from the small group. He was dark-skinned with black hair.

"Howdy, Teddy. You don't remember me, do you? Billy Two Rivers?"

"My God, Billy! I would never have recognised you. You were a little skinny brat when I last saw you."

"And you were a ragged-arsed Polak who used to chase the girls," he came back at me. "And now look at you!"

Instantly Billy and I were right back where we had left off. Sensing it, Uncle Jack left us to our reminiscing. The next day I borrowed his car to drive out for the evening to see Billy's place and meet his family. It was clear to me that Billy was very proud of his new home. It was typical of the standardised building going up everywhere. Outside it was plain, as featureless as the surrounding country. Inside it was modern and welcoming, open plan, with a large basement. Billy's wife Celine was of French Canadian stock. So both their children, a small boy and girl, were dark and swarthy from both sides of the gene pool. I was introduced to the kids as a war hero and was made to tell them tales of dog fights, Spitfires and Hurricanes, Mosquitoes and Tornadoes. Marie, the youngest, seemed the most blood-thirsty.

"Gets it from her papa," Billy's petite wife observed.

Over a beer Billy told me he had been sponsored by a teacher at school. That he had gone on to technical training, ending up a specialist machine-tool operator specialising in aircraft, mainly Liberator components. He had spent most of the war repairing and refurbishing damaged parts of salvaged craft shipped back over the Atlantic. After the kids had gone to bed, at their invitation, I told Billy and Celine openly about my experiences. They listened with surprise and sympathy. "We had no idea what has been happening – not even that the Poles were excluded from the victory parades because the British did not want to upset the Russians." Billy was appalled.

"Despicable!" Cecile said.

"What's even more despicable," Billy said, "is that all this was kept from us and is still being kept from us. Teddy, how about you coming over one evening to give a talk to the Union about your experience of Communism? I think it will be a shock to some, and really effective, especially as you're a local."

"Won't that cause trouble?" I asked.

"You still got the jitters, man. This is a free country; if I found what you said informative then so will others. We got our fair share of Commies, but most of us ain't even political. We just want our jobs. So you come tell them what you told us. I'll fix it." Cecile was keen to help too, offering to organise some fund-raising and gather clothes to send to Europe. Something in me stirred back to life. I suggested the help should go to the DPs, the displaced persons in Germany and Britain, rather than direct to Communist Poland, where any aid was likely to be siphoned off by the Reds.

We talked too about happier times. 'For old times' sake Billy and Cecile asked if I was free the next day, saying they wanted to take me over to the reservation at Morley, home of Billy's grandfather Running Deer. The old man remembered me well, they said. Looking back, I can tell that these good people sensed my pain and wanted to help.

We had to travel about fifty miles toward the reservation. I wondered why. "In my day I was I able to sit in tepees just down the road from the Smolletts, Billy. Not this far out of town."

"When we were youngsters there was more animosity between races and tribes and different groups of immigrants, but also a strange tolerance, Teddy. We all kept ourselves to ourselves, whatever we were, in our little enclaves. Remember your Tommy Riley, from that bog Irish family, and his sister Lucy? They belonged to the Irish enclave. Remember all that talk of their superiority over you Polaks, all that love and hate? Back in those days we were on Smollett land and the whites – your daddy, Jack Smollett and old Mr Simpson - got on well with us. We hunted the land and kept down vermin and helped out with the cattle sometimes. So the elders just carried on as the ancestors had done. Nowadays we aren't allowed to move around. We've been 'settled' and land rights more or less resolved. It suits the likes of us progressive youngsters but not the elders, like my grandfather. They still hanker to go and do what they want, where they want."

Pondering this 'solution', I watched the country roll by, and spent time getting to know Billy's kids, They talked about school and asked all the questions kids ask, like why there was no television yet in Calgary when nearly everyone else in the country had it. I told them I hadn't seen a television in England yet either, although more and more people were getting them. That mollified them a bit. "Radio's better for your imagination anyway," I assured them. "One day TV will be so big it'll tell us all what to believe. People will use its power to stop us thinking and writing and having our own opinion."

The reservation, when we got there, was not that different to the 'burbs'. There were bungalows here too, in amongst the shacks and cabins. Like anywhere else, the local environment depended upon people, their habits, cleanliness, their pride in themselves. These things aren't a matter of economics.

Billy's grandfather lived alone in a small, wooden, two-room cabin with a traditional sod roof. The old man welcomed me into his house with quiet chant then offered me the traditional pipe. Running Deer was just as I remembered him, dressed in a clean western shirt and jeans, his long, grey hair caught at the back with a red ribbon. After welcoming me he sat down in his rocking-chair, whilst the rest of us made do with stools and the floor. The children were sent out to play in the yard with the chickens and the goats. Gradually the room became Indian quiet, settled and relaxed.

Eventually the old man spoke, recalling times long ago. I listened respectfully as he reminded me that the Stoney nation was a branch of the Sioux nation from the Great Plains. For a moment he gently chided Billy for leaving the nation, but Billy ignored him, not contradicting his elder in the

Indian way. There were long silences which I tried to fill by asking lots of questions about land rights and Indian law and oil and gas in the area of the reservation. I had my questions answered, but mostly by Billy.

Running Deer shuffled off into the other room, to bring back three items. Two were photographs. One was of Queen Victoria, the other a group of Indians in full ceremonial dress. Some wore headdresses of eagle feathers. Others had bare heads or single feathers. Two Mounties were in the picture too. Running Deer pulled the group photograph close to his eyes, squinting hard. He pointed to a figure at the back.

"Here I am," he said, "I remember who I am." He cast a mournful eye at Billy. Turning to me he said, "When you came as a young boy I called you Laughing Coyote. You were a prankster, always joking. Now I see a large hole in your heart and a deep sadness in your sky eyes. This is the look of a warrior who has seen much and knows the loss of his people."

I looked into the old man's watery eyes and saw compassion and understanding. A great sense of tiredness, almost relief overtook me. His words, spoken in his typical sing-song fashion made me feel peaceful, at home, as though he were lifting some unseen weight from my shoulders.

"A nation ceases to exist when it loses its history, its pathway. White leaders try to lose their peoples' history in lies. Every day there is news in print, and now news in the waves of the air. This White news becomes history so quickly and is no news. I listen and hear gossip and opinion. We, the Stoney nation, tell things as they have been, not as we would have liked them to be. We keep our ancestors alive in song and dance. It was a big fight at the Little Big Horn, but not big enough. The Ghost dance did not work for us, but we told the story anyway.

"Laughing Coyote, you must remember your history and tell the story of your people. Tell your young people where you have come from, what journey you have taken. You know a little of the ways of our nation. You know that the White Eyes always broke their treaties with us too. They did not think that we 'savages' had honour and truly believed in words made as promises. They saw our land as empty and stole our hunting grounds for gold and cattle. They left us no hope, except in our selves. Laughing Coyote, you have lost hope. Do not hope for an outcome, this leads to disappointment. Hope that in any outcome you will be true to who you are and will act with courage. You have suffered pain in your heart for other people, you have been carrying their burden. You cannot do this. It is their weight to carry. You must look to your own. Only then can your courage help them and the future be changed."

The old man sighed. "I wish I could invite you to a ceremony in the old ways. But the dances are no more. The Department of Indian Affairs say our medicine dances are not lawful. The grass dance, the sun dance, all gone.

But one day they will return. Our power will be shared again."

Rising, he put around my neck a small, beaded buckskin bag, coloured brown by wood smoke. Inside I knew there would be a few stones, perhaps a bone and some herbs. I recognised it as a medicine bag. "For power, to make you strong in your battle against evil spirits and men," Running Deer said.

We sat for a while in silence and then the old man rose again. "I am tired," he said and shuffled to the next room, closing the door behind him.

We collected the children. Outside the sky was beautiful with that evening luminosity which enhances the clouds hanging low over the far mountains. It was getting cold. The snow was already deep on the mountains. And it was getting dark. As we drove home, from somewhere deep in my own thoughts, I questioned Billy's son. "I'm Polish. What are you, Jake?"

"I'm Assiniboine from the Stoney tribe, like my dad. We are a tribe who cooks with stones." Jake made this statement with that enigmatic elegance of stance that Native Americans can display. A sense of pride, of knowing to whom they belong.

Sensing where I was coming from, Billy laughed loudly. "Attaboy, Jake, you just scored a real goal!"

The day helped, gave me back some perspective. And Billy helped in other ways too. He was as good as his word; a meeting was fixed. I had expected a small union hut but instead I was taken to Calgary City Hall, a sandstone building from the previous century. Quite an honour, I realised. The new mayor, Donald Mackay, had obviously thought it a good idea for a son of the city to explain what was happening in Europe. I was pleased for one reason only – it would hopefully raise funds for the Polish refugee charities.

I spoke to Jack and Jean about how to handle the talk. Jack was all for explaining details, all the betrayals and double dealings. Jean's attitude was more prosaic. "Teddy, a lot of your audience will be women who will fall asleep if you give them all of Jack's arguments for and against. And of course there are bound to be a few hecklers and then it will go wrong. Why don't you just tell them what *life* is like in the workers' paradise in Poland? Give them your first-hand experience?"

So that's what I did.

The hall was packed with, I was later told, upward of three hundred people. Billy introduced me and there I stood on a public platform for the first time in my life. Looking out at the audience I tried to remember the tips I'd been given by Billy, who did a lot of public speaking in his Union work. "Pick out a few friendly faces in different parts of the audience," he'd said. "Talk to those people, not a blank audience. Before you start, breathe deeply. Modulate your voice, speak slowly. Don't hang on to the podium, use gestures. Above all, smile and take your time."

I was grateful that his wise words flooded back to me now as I stood looking down at a sea of expectant faces. There were some reporters in the front row with their notebooks, even a flash photographer I guessed to be from the local rag. My heart pounded, making squeaking noises in my ear. My throat dried up and I felt a desperate urge to grab the glass of water and take a large gulp. I resisted, knowing it would make me look an amateur. I felt as if a tight band was squeezing the breath out of me. Checking my notes a final time I swept the auditorium with a broad smile and began to speak.

"Ladies and gentlemen, let me begin my telling you that in Poland an event like this could not take place."

Someone near the back of the hall immediately challenged my assertion. Luckily Billy had prepared me for such an event.

"I am happy to take questions at the end of my talk, but perhaps I should remind all members of the audience that people have come here to listen to me tell my experience of Poland as it is now. They have not come here to listen to others air their opinions." I got no further. Bursts of clapping broke out and a number of men turned to the antagonistic questioner, saying "Shaaarup!"

"Thank you." I gestured with my arms for the crowd to settle. Curiously the interruption had settled me and given me confidence so I went on.

"Gentlemen of the press, when you write a story you are allowed to tell it how it is. Maybe your paper has a bias. You compete with other papers and your editor wants you to tell it a certain way. However, you can argue with him and talk of the freedom of the press. Eventually a compromise is reached and some truth is told. In Poland it doesn't matter what paper you buy, all the news is censored. The paper has to tell the Party line. Your paper is only there to tell the population how good government policy is, how bad America is, how benign Comrade Stalin is, and how he is like a father to the Polish nation. Your paper is a propaganda tool, not a news sheet. It is there to mould the population, especially the young.

"You would be told to report how many bricks have been made and how many houses have been built. How many bandits have been rounded up, how many workers have won an order of merit for working longer hours unpaid than they should. How these 'voluntary' workers are always happy to contribute fraternal donations from their wages to the children in Uzbekistan. You would not mention the secret police agents that you saw at the rally, noting names down. Because if you differed or disagreed, gentlemen, you could simply disappear. No one would ask where you are or where you have gone because everyone would know.

"In Poland you worry that your next-door neighbour heard you call the local Party leader incompetent. You worry that your son at school has been asked to write down what books you read. You worry that you did not attend the rally for fraternal friendship with Latvia because your mother was ill. You worry there is no bread in the house because you did not have time to queue. You worry that the parcel sent by your cousin in America was opened and that something was taken from it that was forbidden, like a book or newspaper or dollars."

On it went, my litany of the daily fears and anxieties faced by the Polish people. I told them of the struggles of the remnants of the Home Army against the Soviet occupation, keeping things simple, not explaining unit names and factions. I spoke of the life and death struggle the West had barely registered and not bothered to tell their people about. I saw from faces in the audience that my listeners were shocked and surprised. I was aware of the press scribbling notes and hoped they would print it all, especially my comments about the Hot War being ignored in the West.

But for the most part I focussed on the daily inconveniences and injustices. "If you want to visit your relatives in a nearby town, you have to have your identity papers, like an internal passport, certified by the mayor's office. The same office may have to certify that you have relatives in the other town, and you may have to have a letter inviting you to go there. If they happen to live near by the coast then you could be in big trouble, because the coast is an insecure border and you might be up to no good. Woe betide you if you have had contact with foreigners. You might, according to your age, also have to have military documents to show you have been in the army, otherwise you will be considered a deserter by nomination. No residency makes you a tramp and illegal. Which way you have travelled and how you got there will be noted. Every road is controlled, every car noted, times of arrival and departure filed. Every time you leave your apartment you know the doorman or caretaker will note what you do, what bags you carry, the time you leave, when you arrive back. If you are late to work for a few times you might be classified as a saboteur and sent to a labour camp. If you want to shop...." And so my story went on, for an hour.

At the end there were no questions, but I received strong applause, bravos and whistles as I sat down. A few people began to stand up, still clapping, and then the rest of the audience stood. I had to stand and bow my thanks again.

Afterwards, people came up to me and we spoke privately about events. A young communist and I fell into a discussion about the difference between his utopian ideals and Stalinism versus Marxism. Because of his entrenched positions it rapidly became a sterile intellectual debate. He had entirely missed the point of free democracies and the simple fact that Europe had been divided by force of arms and the political will of three men.

Thankfully I was rescued by a Czech man who had recently arrived in

Canada from a camp in Germany. "I am from that country everyone forgets," he said. "No one talks of us. It is always Yalta or Potsdam. The Munich betrayal is never mentioned anymore." The Czech had come to Poland over the border in June 1939 to join the Czechoslovak troops fighting to restore the independence of their homeland. Modelled in the style of the Legions of the First World War, they had battled alongside the Poles in the September campaign. So they also bore the dignity of being 'First to Fight'. General Lev Prchal had led them. Now he was stuck in Britain.

I listened to the man's adventures sympathetically and at length. I felt I owed him the time. As he said, who else was interested in the Czechs' and Slovaks' experiences? He remembered vividly September the 17th, when his column arrived at Horodyszcze, and the move to the village of Pidhaitsi the next day, where they ran into the advancing Red Army. They were destined for internment – and not as prisoners of war. Officially the Czechs were part of the Reich and the Russians, the Allies of the Nazis. Realising their predicament, he had joined a group led by a Captain Fanty, who managed to avoid internment. Marching to Tremblowa, then to Kopychyntsi and Husiatyn, they crossed into Romania. He was with the Czech battalion at Tobruk and in the Italian campaign. His experience there was the old story between France and Britain. "The fucking French and British didn't come after fourteen days as they promised and as the treaty said. We held the fall-back line whilst they just sat there on the German border, making a token gesture and dropping leaflets, whilst the Germans dropped bombs." Captured, he was eventually sent to a displaced persons' camp because he refused to go back to a Red-conquered Czechoslovakia. "Millions died. Many, many British, Poles, Americans and Empire troops all died when we could have taken them from both sides. The Germans had nothing in the West to stop an attack. They either gambled on the French having no stomach for a fight, or knew that they would not attack. Was there a secret deal? What do you think?"

I answered truthfully. "I know now they never intended to live up to their promise."

It was not only the Poles who had a bad time. I agreed with his parting comment which was: "That's the way politics are, my friend. Forget the past, make a new life."

*Good advice, so why couldn't I take it?*

Auntie Jean was in charge of the fund-raising for the event. Though the money that had come in was substantial, she set about arranging a 'honey auction' to raise more money. This turned out to be a dinner club event where eligible young men, mostly wealthy business people, were bid for as dinner partners for an evening. The motives of the bidders were many and varied, from business mentoring to 'bed eyes', as Jean put it. I hated the idea, but as Jean said, "You are the star prize!"

When the time came I was auctioned to a mother and daughter consortium. I went for the princely sum of $500 dollars. Poor Uncle Jack only made $25, and that was a put-up job by Jean's friend acting as proxy for her. "It's your own fault, Jack. This is the only way I can get you to take me to dinner. A lot of money was raised and sent to the Canadian Polish Association for Refugees and Displaced Person Relief Fund. Mother and daughter spent the evening listening to my Polish adventures over a dinner paid for by the restaurant as part of the donation. I spent the whole of the meal trying to ascertain whether the stocking'd feet running up and down my trouser legs belonged to mother or daughter or both.

My body was recovering quickly now after a slow start. I had started to do some early morning running and was doing some weight-training to get into better shape. My mind was taking longer to heal. Sometimes, without warning, a memory would return. When recalling certain beatings I would have to turn away from the task in hand and pull myself together.

My name started to crop up in the local papers. I declined a couple of radio slots. This upset Jack and Jean, who were working hard to raise money. They were owed more of an explanation other than that I did not enjoy the growing prominence I was achieving. I could not live this lifestyle, and I couldn't pull these two much-loved people into my clandestine world.

It was time to talk to Jack and Jean.

The firelight flickered and the lights were low. Winter had come and it was a good time to tell. We sat down together and these kind people listened with infinite patience and compassion as I explained what had really happened in the intervening years since I had last seen them.

It was a cathartic experience. I spoke for a long time. They sat and simply listened, Unc smoking his pipe, watching me intently. Auntie Jean, her knitting in her lap, watched me with eyes full of love. At the end, Unc said, "My poor old son. We knew you were up to something. I had guessed intelligence work, but we had no idea."

Auntie Jean went to make coffee. I could hear her crying for me in the kitchen. When she came back, dry-eyed, she spent time tut-tutting about governments and politicians having no honour. "People can love each other," she concluded, "but politicians do not love their people really. They love ideals and ideas which crucify people or destroy nations for their own sense of rightness. Like your friend Billy says," she said, "we lend them our power through the vote or the military and they abuse us, lie to us and cheat us. It is all just words at election time, promises never kept." She smiled at me. "That's my soapbox over for today."

I smiled back, glad to be part of a 'belonging' that was so warm and uncomplicated.

"So, what's next for you?" Jack asked, ever the pragmatist.

I had not explained the aim of my mission to the Smolletts, just revisited the past without making links to future events. I had realised I was frightened of being caught by an inevitability in me, a fate. But somewhere, sometime I had made up my mind what to do. It had not been a conscious decision, no sitting down and going over pro's and con's. It was a decision made in the back of my brain, which had slipped in as a certainty yet without conscious reason.

"I'm going to go down to Washington and tie up some loose ends. I need to speak to some people in Chicago and New York and then head back to England. I think I'll settle there for a while. I have some loose ends to tie up in order to be released from my duty as a soldier." I omitted to say that I would be trying to expose a Soviet spy ring at the heart of American and British Intelligence. And that my plans further included the execution of Stalin. What they didn't know would not hurt them.

"Will you come back to Canada and eventually settle down with us?" Jean's eyes were hopeful.

"Perhaps, Aunt." I said this with as much sincerity as I could muster; I wanted to very much, the gremlin at the back of my mind was saying, 'I don't think so'.

Unc offered me an interview with the Boeing down in Seattle. He knew some of the people there. The company was concentrating on building civilian aircraft like the new Stratocruiser, a luxury long-distance airliner. I pretended to think about it, but it was a no go. How could I turn my back on my people? People still hounded in the forests by the security forces? People who slunk through the streets after dark?

There were business affairs to be tied up before I left. Investment management, stocks and bonds, insurances and such like. I wanted to separate my British money and affairs, still handled by my long-time lawyers in London, and this new money in Canada. I also wanted to make one last call into the past.

I went to meet old man Goretchko, the father of my boyhood enemy. The man whose son had caused my parents' deaths at the hands of the Soviets. I had never fully understood the animosity or the ferocity the younger Goretchko displayed towards me. All I knew was that our fathers had struck up some sort of camaraderie as a result of our feud. I wondered if the old cavalry officer might have some information about my parents' life in Poland before Canada. I also felt I owed him some kind of story about his son and the Bolsheviks. I had no clearer reason for going than a sense of obligation. I felt it to be an emotional duty, not a rational on. Just something I had to do.

I phoned him and was glad when he agreed to meet. Goretchko senior lived in one of the new 'burbs', Thorncliffe, in a plain-looking bungalow. As I drew up in the car I had borrowed for the day he had already opened the door and stood waiting. I felt nervous, not knowing how to handle the awkwardness. He was older, of course, and frail-looking, though he still had that look of military uprightness. That soldierly bearing must have been causing him pain, as he walked with a stick. As I walked up the short path, an elderly liver and white spaniel poked his head between the old man's legs.

He held out his hand. "Welcome, Tadek, it is good to see you. Please come in. Do you mind dogs?"

A good start. "No sir, I don't," I said, pushing the spaniel away and at the same time giving its floppy ears a good tousling. It not only wagged its tail in happiness at seeing a friendly stranger but half its body as well as its tail, slobbering joyfully. I squeezed past the dog and followed the old man into the open-plan living-room. It was cold and smelled of dog, damp and wood smoke. He indicated a seat and I sat down on a comfortable but worn armchair. Goretchko sat opposite on a matching chair and the dog clambered onto a third, which was covered by a blanket. The dog sat expectantly, looking eagerly from one to the other. Goretchko threw him a biscuit which he snapped in mid-air, and immediately settled down, head between paws, eyes still darting, clearly thinking 'something's up'.

Before I could say anything, Goretchko started to speak, breaking the ice. "In a moment I will offer you a drink, but first I want to formally offer you my condolences and regret at the death of your parents and your friend Ivan. I am fully aware of my son's responsibility. Since he has continued in the Bolshevik cause I have disowned him, and he me. When I realised his sin I confronted him, and we have never communicated since. It is my way. He may return as a prodigal, he is my son, but not as an unrepentant Bolshevik. I want to assure you I had no knowledge of his betrayal of you; I still do not know if it was stupidity or bravado. Please, I beg you before all the saints and the Holy Mother, to forgive me." He bowed his head and held out a hand across the divide.

I had never expected this. Taken completely by surprise I took his hand. "We have all suffered. Lives have been stolen from us all. There is nothing to forgive."

The old man wiped away a tear. "Thank you, thank you, thank you, my son." It was another affecting moment. I felt tears too but would not let them come, holding the emotion in my throat. To break the tension I said, "I heard you like a whisky, a wee dram," and I handed over the brown bag I had bought, a ten-year old malt, in case I needed a peace offering. He got up stiffly, using his stick as a solid point of stability, saying he would fetch some glasses. The dog came over to me, putting his nose on my knees and stared at me, clearly asking where his peace offering was. Goretchko filled the glasses and surreptitiously palmed me a biscuit. You cannot fool a spaniel's nose. It disappeared in one gulp.

"Chair, Bulba!" the old man called, and the dog bounded back to his station.

Now it was my turn to explain why I had felt the need to come. I told him at length of my meetings with many Ukrainians, what I had observed about the way Poles and Ukrainians felt about each other and how they both felt about Jews. I told him about my father being a loyal Pole, and how his son had always seen me as a traitor to the Ukrainian cause.

Goretchko dismissed his son's remarks as 'historically unsound' and said that my father, whatever his true ethnicity, probably as mixed as anyone in the borderlands, was simply following the custom of any educated or landed Ukrainian in claiming Polish citizenship. As we had land, our family had probably been loyal to the Polish crown for centuries, "as was my own family," he said. "Loyal registered Cossacks. Unfortunately my son has been infected by a narrow twentieth century nationalism as well as Bolshevism.

"A lot of Ukrainians have moved into Calgary in recent times from the old homesteads scattered around Alberta. To be honest, Tadek, all they want is a prosperous life. The 'old country' now only means colourful costumes for the children and dances, a few knees up, nothing more, it is the best way. Even the orthodox religion is fading. Prosperity and education are the key to most differences, as it would eventually have been in Poland. Your father and I used to talk about such things. We had a lot in common."

This surprised me. "After your run-in with my son we met up. We discovered we had shared some experiences in Europe. We used to meet once every two weeks over a drink." I had never known this.

"The second Republic," he went on, "and the Civil War were confused times. I fought with the Whites and your daddy, first as liaison for the Whites and then liaison with the British Secret Service. He then worked directly with Sydney Reilly."

There it was, that name again.

"Reilly, who was a most effective British spy, drew him into his ring in Moscow. They plotted to overthrow Lenin and install Savinkov or maybe even Reilly himself as some sort of dictator. Who knows now... The price of his service was you and your mothers' free passage to Canada, courtesy of the British."

I was astounded at this bit of history but it made sense. No one had ever really explained how I had gotten from Odessa to Canada before.

"Your father and I were both Mensheviks. I was more a supporter of Alexander Kerensky. Your father was more inclined to Boris Savinkov and Lev Kornilov than I. As you know, Kornilov tried a coup that failed. He insisted Lenin should be hanged even before the Bolshevik revolution. To cut the story short Kornilov ended up in the Civil War leading the Don

Cossacks against the Reds. I was with that Volunteer Army. Your father joined the Polish Odessa Legion. So our paths nearly crossed."

"I know very little of my father's past," I told the old man. "It was a closed book, apparently for my own preservation. I now wish he had told me more."

"And what of you and the Smolletts?" came the shrewd observation. "Have you told them everything? Or have you held back certain things you have been doing? I am an Easterner. I know how things are over there, so you do not fool me." His eyes twinkled with friendly humour. "Least said; I am not asking."

"Why was my father such a Polish nationalist?" I asked. "If he was a socialist of sorts, how did he become so involved with Piłsudski and the Legions?"

"To be frank, there is no simple answer," he intoned.

I butted in. "Is anything ever simple in Eastern Europe?"

"Let us blame it all on the Hapsburgs, then. It all began with the fall of the Empires. The Hapsburgs ruled a medieval-style empire full of different ethnic minorities and Christian faiths. You could say they were the inheritors of the Byzantine Holy Roman Empire. Many of their subjects were Slavs, but the hub was German-speaking Austria and the Magyars of Hungary. The Magyars caused a lot of trouble in the middle of the 19th century because they wanted equality with the German speakers. The Magyar Hungarians were utterly opposed to what we would call Pan Slavism, led by Russia, using Serbia. Here you see the origin of the First World War. Poland had been partitioned, neutered, back in 1795 by Austria, Russia and Prussia, to keep the Poles in check with their ideas of liberal constitutions and keep democracy at bay. Russia and Prussia used force to quell the Poles, who were in a constant state of revolt. Then along came Napoleon, and perhaps one of the golden ages of Polish militarism, in support of the French who promised a reinstated Poland."

"And we all know what happened there," I chimed in. "My dad always said we should never trust the French." I had become intrigued by the way Goretchko was talking. I had never really seriously discussed such issues with a survivor of the Russian Civil War. That war, brushed aside these days as some event far away, held the key to the origins of the Second World War. The Civil War had created my existence here in Canada. I began to realise it had been an outgrowth of the nationalism of the Poles and Czechs that infected other ethnic groups. I began to realise too that the broad brush of Socialism originally meant nothing more than being anti-Imperialist to many people. Goretchko was providing the links event by event to the consequences of today, the cold war.

I was beginning to see myself with an *inheritance* of revolution, one that gave me the resolve to carry matters through, unfinished business passed from father to son. It was a matter of freedom. The Second Republic was destroyed and Poland was back under the heel of a Soviet Empire. Now it was my duty to carry on the fight whatever I felt.

Goretchko evidently wanted to finish his story.

"The Poles had many uprisings; against the Russians in 1830, against the Prussians in 1848, against the Russians again in 1863. Where did they happen? In the former territory of the Polish Lithuanian Commonwealth. Not in some confined area of the Versailles treaty, territories of the Second Republic. No, the risings took place in what we today call Poland, Lithuania, Belarus, Latvia, northern Ukraine and western Russia. Were these totally ethnic Polish insurrections?"

The question was both historic and informative. I understood its meaning only too well. The implied answer was that being 'Polish' meant living anywhere or everywhere in these old Commonwealth territories. It was a matter of shared culture and civilisation. People joined the so called ethnic Poles as Commonwealth citizens. Nationalism, as I understood it right now, today, simply did not exist then. They were revolutions of the landowners, the intelligentsia and the students. Whilst the peasants did join the colours many remained aloof until given an identity based on an invented nation state which politicians promoted as the 'return of land' to the poor peasant.

The old man was talking into the distance as though I did not exist. He became animated as he recalled ideas and events of so long ago, before he became frail, before arthritis robbed him of his quickness and led to his present life of unremitting pain. "In the same territories, never underestimate the contribution the 'Poles', and now I mean all sorts of so-called peoples, made to the 1905 Russian revolution. I could argue that it became a Polish revolution too. An uprising against the Russians. Today we talk of Communist deportations but they are nothing new. We must never forget that the Tsarist authorities moved large numbers of Jews into Poland in the East, after the 1905 Revolution. But I digress, Tadek, we should be talking of the Ukraine. Much of which was under the control of Austria and Hungary. The Austrians did not have the balls of the Hungarians to fight their Socialists and Nationalists, so they used more subtle tactics. Using law and bribery they set one group against the other, Pole against Ruthenian, Ruthenian against Jew. It was their policy. So it was the Austrians who first encouraged a Ukrainian national concept, which in reality never existed.

"Once the genie of nationalism was out of the pot, like with land ownership reform, the trouble began. There were very diverse attitudes from the Ukrainians toward the Poles. The most strongly anti-Polish feeling was stirred up by the Communist Party of Western Ukraine. It sought to incorporate the eastern borderlands into Soviet Ukraine. The nationalist Ukrainian

Military Organization, the UOW, strove to create an independent Ukrainian state. The aspirations of a free Ukraine were supported by the Greek Catholic clergy of the Church, the Uniates, rather than the Orthodox. On the other hand the more moderate Social Democratic Party cooperated with the Polish Socialist Party. It was this road which most Ukrainians followed. Of course, cooperation with the Poles led to other groupings, including the moderate Ukrainian National-Democratic Federation, but all the democratic bloc were too weak, too political, perhaps too democratic to restrict certain of the radical nationalist groups from causing trouble."

"You keep mentioning land reform as being so important? What part did it play in the politics and hatreds that grew up in the whole are of the Western Ukraine?" I had witnessed this ethnic hatred or known of its consequences since the fall of the Republic in September 1939. Sitting here listening to an ordinary man who had lived through the times that gave birth to such events was worth the time. I asked the questions because I wanted answers, wanted to know why humans behave toward each other with such savagery.

Mr. Goretchko paused, raising his hands to his nose as though in prayer. There was a long pause before he answered. As he took his hands away from his mouth I noticed they shook a little, a sign of age.

"All the so-called ethnic conflict was compounded by conflicts of an economic and social nature. The fact was that the majority of the Ukrainian population were uneducated peasants. The larger landowners were mainly, but not exclusively, Poles. Hence, the Ukrainians often went into battle with the slogan of 'revenge on the Polish *Pans'*. This problem could only be resolved by radical land reform. In 1925 some reforms were made, but not enough to please anyone, neither Pole nor Ukrainian. The Republic needed time, Tadek. It was a new nation. The minorities were hungry for education, land reform, economic generation. The country needed money and support but it received very little. The rest you know. Communist agitation, resettlement of Poles into Ukrainian areas, education in Polish, the failure to set up a federal system. That was the world your father grew up in. He was a federalist like Pi?sudski and he was in a hurry. For him time ran out. He ended up here in Calgary with you and your mother and through sheer hard work made something of himself and you."

I thanked him for his insights. We talked for hours of Calgary, of people his son and I had known. Remembering his age and health, I eventually made a move to leave.

I had learned so much and yet so frustratingly little. I had a bigger picture of my parents' world but knew little else about them. Yet I was coming away with a new sense of continuity. I found this strengthening. I knew my parents would approve of my conduct now whatever it looked like from outside. Thinking over Goretchko's words I decided it was not courage I lacked but determination, the will and the patience to carry things through to the end, whatever the consequences. To help me gain that perseverance I could choose from many role models from the past.

Goretchko eyed me succinctly. "I know you will go back. I also know you are on opposite sides, but if ever you meet my son, please remember me to him and say that I failed him. Tell him he is still my son."

I promised I would.

One last act remained, one I had avoided since my return. I visited the graves of my parents, of old Mr Simpson, Ivan Patterson, and lastly Mrs Simpson. I left flowers at them all, as a token of respect. I looked at the headstones, the white marble kerbstones and green marble chippings. I wondered what I was supposed to feel. I felt cold, my loss was long gone. Only at Mrs Simpson's grave did I go through a simple ceremony. Opening the last pages of the Bible I read out loud, about how there would be no more pain or suffering or death, for all things would be made new. I had thought long and hard over the years about those words and all the lives I had seen ended.

As I turned them over in my mind they turned to ashes. I looked at the sky but there was no response, save the greyness of leaden cloud.

I oiled my Radom.

I said my goodbyes.

I left for Washington.

# CHAPTER 17

# RED AMERICA

Western Canadian Airlines got me as far as Montreal, and then Trans Canada took me over the border to Chicago, my first stop. Chicago has been called the second city of Poland. Landing at Chicago Midway Airport, I headed to Polonia Triangle in West Town, the centre of Polish Downtown, the 'Polish patch'. Chicago Polonia began in 1837, when some November insurrection survivors led by Captain Jan Napieralski settled in the city. Every major Polish American institution or organisation was based here or had representation in the area.

I had been warned that the Poles hereabouts had developed a language of their own, called 'Poglish' by the non-Polish locals, a *mélange* of both languages incomprehensible to others. I found a boarding-house which had been recommended by one of Calgary's Polonians, close by the Chopin Theatre in North Noble Street. The small hotel was run by a family who had come to Chicago in 1910. Through sheer hard work in the cattle-yards and later steel-works they had build themselves up to claim ownership of this small but thriving business. The Daszewski family, the owners, specialised in 'theatricals', visiting artists and writers, and had developed a reputation for good clean home-from-home service. Round and about were eating houses and restaurants specialising in Polish, Ukrainian, Jewish and Italian fare. It was a good working-class environment.

I was there specifically to make contact with Karol Rozmarek, president of the Polish National Alliance. The organisation continued to support the Polish Government in exile. In 1944 Rozmarek had organised and led the Polish American Congress, the all-Polonia political action federation. The PAC was working towards the realization of the hopes of generations of PNA members,uniting Polonia's energies in support of a free Poland. I wanted to discuss relief funding for Poland, to which I would contribute. My core aim however was to reinforce to him, face to face, the way the Communists had infiltrated WiN and were misappropriating money.

Running Deer's challenge ringing in my ears, I was frantic to tell him of the desperate struggle the remnants of the partisans were facing. Men and women were still being betrayed or let down by the West or – perhaps worse – ignored. I wanted Rozmarek to consider means of aiding the armed struggle and how we could maintain defiance against the Reds. I wanted to counter the views being expressed by Mikołajczyk and his allies about events in Poland. Mikołajczyk had never openly supported the fighters and still did not give them recognition. Rather he pursued the narrow Peasant Party line which had been so disruptive in the London government, leading directly to the sanctioning of the Communist regime. He was still Churchill's puppy dog.

Rozmarek and I met at a Greek restaurant called Vosnos, outside the community. It was discreet, out of sight of questioning eyes. He wore his hair slicked back above a strong, clean-cut face. Wearing a formal suit and tie Rozmarek looked every bit a lawyer. The man had an aura of charm and strength about him and he spoke with conviction tempered with empathy. After formalities and a discussion of the menu, he explained that his main focus was special legislation to allow for Poles, especially the displaced and refugees, to enter the USA and be allowed to rebuild their lives. His wife Wanda, too, was very active in support of refugees.

I was anxious to explain myself: my new-found wealth and my desire to associate myself by donating to the PNA was neither a political move nor for personal gain. Without mentioning the Witek plot, I revealed the penetration of the intelligence services in the USA and Britain, as well as my assignment to help uncover the moles. In return, Rozmarek outlined how Communist Polish security forces were working to undermine and sow discord within Polonia. That in particular, they opposed resettlement in the USA and were portraying the new Polish regime as legitimate and progressive. "They have a black propaganda campaign against any people like you, who have experience of real life in Communist Poland," he said.

I shared my bitterness that the Home Army, its allies and now its remnants, had never been properly armed. He was stunned at the figures I gave him for the support British SOE had given; to Greek partisans 6,000 tons of supplies; to France and Yugoslavia over 10,000 tons; to Yugoslavia, with the addition of US aid, another 8,000 tons while for Poland just 600 tons. He was shocked by the disproportion.

Even at this stage I wanted to find a way to get arms into Poland for the forlorn hope, and thought it was perhaps possible via some ex-Polish Air Force people. Rozmarek promised to introduce me to some arms dealers. The best weapons would be German or Russian, he said, to allow continuity of supply and also obscure any American connection. "It is a dark world you are entering, Teddy. I cannot help you except at extreme arm's length, but I will introduce you to our counter-espionage group and then you can take it from there. Expect contact from a certain Teresa Sawicka in Washington."

After this brief but successful interlude I took a plane to my destiny in Washington. There I opted for a room at the Hamilton Hotel. It seemed a compromise between the trendy Fairfax or the President's second home at the Carlton. The Hamilton had seen better days but was still a good choice.

Hugely popular throughout the 1930s and 1940s, it had hosted one of Franklin D. Roosevelt's inaugural balls and Hollywood's singing cowboy Gene Autry and his horse, Champion. That fact alone was enough to make my decision. The Beaux Arts structure featured a stately entrance with an arched stained-glass window, and vaulted ceilings which I loved. Chuck had agreed it as a good place. Only five blocks from the White House and not far from the Capitol, museums and the National Theatre, but not overpopulated by the British diplomatic service.

I had hardly settled in when the phone rang. Chuck's cheery voice sounded in my ear.

"Hey, buddy, wanna meet? 10.30 tomorrow morning for a culture shock? Say the Freer Gallery, 12th and Jefferson? Quiet place. You'll find me looking at Korean teapots."

"And the purpose of the meet?"

"I'm your handler, buddy. Someone's gotta watch out for your butt in this den of thieves," he joked.

"Am I relegated to dog status then, to needing a handler?"

"Nope, but we gotta have the chat just to sound serious!" He laughed at his own joke. "See ya tomorrow!" and he rang off.

Next day, after a giant American breakfast in a nearby diner, I got a cab to one of the monstrous edifices demonstrating the might of the American dollar, in this case the gallery buying up the best of the world's art. I found Chuck staring at the most exquisite ceramics.

"Is the fight worth it, I wonder, when you look at what we humans can do when at peace? Joseon Dynasty stuff. Just look at this white porcelain jar." Chuck hardly glanced at me. The jar was richly ornamented with animal and plant motifs in a single brown tone over white. "It's dated around 1500 CE. Can you imagine such skill, at that time? And now we're at war with the bastards and more American boys are dying."

I took my opportunity for a barbed comment. "Having shoved Poland up its own arse. You didn't learn the lesson, did you, when you fucked the Koreans at Potsdam, carving it into two parts without bothering to ask its people? You gave half of Korea to Stalin at Yalta, and seriously expected the Soviets to stop as agreed at the 38th parallel! Roosevelt was off his head. Or else in love with Stalin."

"Watch it, cowboy. FDR was our hero," Chuck countered.

I knew him to be a staunch Republican so pushed on. "When you Yanks finally comprehended the disaster you'd caused in Europe, you tried to make up for it in Korea by having elections in your zone, promptly allowing and creating a North Korean Communist government manufactured by the Russians."

"We backed our strongman Syngman Ree against Stalin's Kim Il Sung.

Both want a unified Korea, but the Russkis armed the Northerners and we didn't arm the South till it was too late. There was one hell of an invasion and we were in the shit up to our necks. I don't need you to tell me it's East Europe all over again. I agree, FDR was a Soviet lovebird." At which point Chuck clapped me on the back and said, "Time for coffee."

Sipping the black stuff, sitting opposite each other, Chuck confided he had recently lost a great 'compadre'. A CIA agent had been killed entering Tibet in search of intelligence on Soviet nuclear tests in Kazakhstan. "I was on China station with him early in 1950. Douglas and I got wind that Chinese and North Korean intelligence were forecasting a summer KPA[vi] invasion of the South. Nowadays they're saying we had two weeks' notice of the invasion, but we didn't." Chuck looked glumly into his coffee then stirred himself. "Anyway, buddy, I'm here to sort out how you lie with us, the CIA. If you're kosher, and I have no reason to think you ain't, I want your help finding out which Brits we can trust and which we can't. So how do you wanna play it? Do we pay you as an independent or do you come on staff?"

"Look, Chuck, as far as I am concerned I am a Polish officer in the Intelligence section and still on active service. For me the war will not be over until two things happen: one, the Soviet occupiers leave. And two, there are free and unfettered elections. In effect, I am still at war. I know it sounds proud, but that's how it is for me."

Chuck's demeanour changed and he discarded his flamboyant rogue character for a moment. "Teddy, I'm with you, man. I can't be proud of the US treatment of Poland, and I know that the disbanded army was, and is, ready to pick up the fight anytime. But we have our own operation in Poland now and we want you to help us do some much needed weeding.

"For a start I wanna show you some goodwill, a gesture. So I'm telling you that it's a gentleman named Guy Liddell who wants your head. This is the same man who decided to destroy all the intelligence records the Poles handed over to the British, thereby destroying our and British ability to pick up intelligence networks and assets."

"Not forgetting," I added, "a list of suspected Communist traitors and subversives in and outside Poland – as well as cutting the lifeline to the Underground. Thanks for the tip off. So what do you want me to do?"

"Well, we gotta wait while upstairs in the firm – the CIA – decides whether your Beria character is kosher or worth the bet. Our side tells us the Poles will never forgive Katyń. And he was the guy who organised it all. Not a pretty pal to play with. So Truman would want to know why you think he is worth backing. He would want your opinion, Teddy."

"I am no politician. How can my opinion help? This is statecraft, Chuck. The Truman Doctrine is his invention, not mine. He and Acheson, together

ll, say they want the end of Communism, and that America is
' the free world, supporting democracy. So let them lead. They
ppy with Stalin for umpteen years. The old bugger is going to
die someday anyway. So surely to God they have worked out which of the
bloody executioners left they prefer to sleep with?

I was becoming more vehement by the minute. "For Christ's sake,
Chuck. You're asking if I can recommend the man who destroyed the flower
of Polish intelligentsia? I tell you how I can justify it! I will do anything that
will give me a free Poland and the East back. Just like Sikorski, who would
treat with the devil to fight for his country. Just like Churchill, who would
do anything to save the Empire, including the murder of his friends." I spat
out the last words leaving them to hang in the air.

"Easy, sunshine, down boy. They want to know who would wear what,
that's all." Chuck raised his finger to his lips to quieten me.

"Forget the Germans," I said, "concentrate on the Russians. They
annexed half of Poland and the Baltic States in 1939. Latvia, Estonia,
Lithuania – they all disappeared with hardly a whisper. All eyes were on
Poland. All this was part of the Molotov Ribbentrop pact. You know the
story, mass deportations, arrests, torture, murder. The Balts suffered badly,
so when Barbarossa[vii] happened, it was hardly surprising that they aided the
Germans. They learned their lesson, though, along with Białorussia, when
they were turned into the Reichskommissariat Ostland, in effect a German
colony.

"The confusion was that the Balts fought with the Germans to stop the
Soviets taking them over again in 1944. Of course, the Allies had already
sold them down the river to the Reds, just as they had Poland. They actually
believed you Yanks believed in democracy and would help them get their
country back! Only the bloody Finns got away with it with the West. How
come they could fight against the Russians, in effect you Allies? First the
Winter War, and then with the Germans until the end? What is it with
Finland? Have they got something you want?"

"I don't give a fuck about the Balts or the soddin' Finns, my job was
simply to ask if the Poles would cooperate with a Beria government!" said
Chuck.

Angry now, I told him the best way was to ask the legitimate government in London. "You know, Chuck, the one you dumped in favour of your
Red friends and dear, sweet, Uncle Joe?"

"You know we can't be seen to do that," he replied evenly. "That's your
job. You took it on, so damn well do it, buddy. Always the same, you
whingeing Poles." He clapped me on the back as a mollifying gesture. "Let's
get on with the job."

"Okay," I said, calming down. "The whole damn Russian affair is a mystery to me, a giant cock-up from day one, caused by the British Foreign Office arrogance in not listening. I don't blame Churchill but I do blame Roosevelt. He knew his intelligence was flawed; it was his ego trip that stole all those millions of lives away.

"On Beria I feel in two minds. Witek showed me a copy of his memo about Katyn. Everything comes back to that place, even Sikorski's death. What I saw was not an order but a recommendation. Stalin had requested a 'solution' to the Polish intelligentsia, especially the officer corps. The NKVD put forward what he wanted and the memorandum was signed, Witek told me by Stalin. But there were other signatories; Marshal Voroshilov, he of the Great Purge fame, then Foreign Minister Molotov, then Minister Mikoyan, a Khrushchev pawn, then Lazar Kaganovich, the architect of collectivization and the famine in the Ukraine, another Khrushchev crony. Last to sign was Comrade Kalinin known as *Dedushka* – 'Grandpa' in English. The whole motley bunch put their name on that document *except for* Beria, who signed it as the reporter or originator only, seeking instruction. So who was the Devil? Easy to blame Beria, I suppose. Only Khrushchev seems to have escaped the noose. Probably because he was too busy murdering Ukrainians. Putting it that way, as a Pole I could live with it in the sense that I am anti-Soviet, full stop. If you like I shall ask in London."

"Good man," said Chuck. "So you'll be off across the pond soon then? Let me fix that up. That way it will be quieter. Meanwhile, you need to look at some lists, some names. Thanks to Harry T. you haven't had to take a loyalty oath. But best keep a zipper or you may end up with a bullet on some sunny sidewalk." He slapped me on the back again, his way of softening the jocularly pronounced, but clearly meant threat.

I joined in his deadly humour. "I didn't think the CIA went in for assassination."

"We don't. We prefer to use outside contractors like you, Sonny Boy!" His smile was mirthless.

I left it at that. Chuck said he'd be back in a couple of days and that I should keep a low profile, particularly staying away from British diplomats. So I spent the next couple of days sightseeing, all the usual stuff, the White House, Lincoln Memorial, the Old Town area and China Town. I kept my head down and stayed in the hotel to eat in the evening and then drifted to one of the hotel bars. Bars can be pretty lonely places. They're a place to meet or drown your sorrows.

Drinking alone isn't much fun. I was sitting on a high stool staring at my White Russian, idly speculating on how long the ice in my glass would take to melt. Moments before I had been in dispute with the barman about my drink, in the nicest possible, inane way. I had been expecting Kahlua, vodka and fresh milk. He had served a Cuban version, with my happy consent. The bar was far from full, so we spent time discussing the merits of roasted Arabica coffee beans, vanilla, purest cane spirit and rum coming together to make this delicious concoction.

As the evening drew on, I had sampled the vodka versus rum version perhaps more often than was sensible. The bar had filled and the barman got busier, leaving me to my solitary devices. Memories come unannounced. The brain wanders, especially when its recesses are fuelled by alcohol. I was wondering whether there was a point in time where memory suddenly exists in a different way. When we're young we're filling our memory. We have no experience. Experience then becomes a part of memory. You share experience, so was memory shared? Or even passed on as a folk echo somewhere in the brain? I had just reached the conclusion that memory was more important to me now than in my youth, as it made me more cautious, when I heard a feminine voice beside me, saying, "Hello."

I turned to see a middle-aged woman, smart, well-dressed, sliding onto the stool next to me. She was perhaps ten years older than me, but a 'looker'. Brunette, with wide-set eyes and a full mouth with a full quota of red lipstick. As she slid onto the stool just a hint of stocking top was revealed underneath her pencil skirt, which her shapely but not too slim legs filled to a tightness as revealing as it was interesting.

"That looks appealing," she said, pointing at what was fast becoming melted milk soup in my glass.

"A White Russian for the lady," I called to the bartender. It appeared, but before I could intervene she asked for it to be put on her bill.

"I didn't ask for a drink, I just wanted to try the same as you," she purred. "But that was sweet, thanks anyway. My name is Lee, and yours?"

"Gibbs," I replied, "Frank Gibbs."

"It looks as though I have been stood up, Frank. And you?"

"Not me, I'm afraid. Just here for a conference."

"Not a politician then?" she asked.

"Fraid not. I'm from Canada. Don't know the political scene here in Washington."

"Shame," she said. "I live and love politics. I love politicians too; they're so corrupt and fun." She turned to me, crossing her legs. The skirt slipped a little higher, and yet she made no attempt to pull it down. This was no show; she was evidently just easy within herself and her own sexuality. I wasn't quite sure how to handle this and was beginning to wish I'd had less of the drink. The question was, was she genuine? Or a hooker?

She sipped her drink, making observations about politics. "Of course, it's all corruption now. You know, contracts and perks. The Democrats have been in power for twenty years and the election is going to be mudslinging all the way. Brigadier General Harry Vaughan, the President's ever-present sidekick, and influence peddler James Hunt are up to their necks in Government contract swindles. Hunt is Mister Five Percenter. The whole administration is on the take, from loan-rigging to tax frauds. Truman is on the way out I tell you. His cronies are looking for their next gravy train!" She paused, lighting a cigarette. "Smoke?" she asked.

"No thanks," I replied.

"Good boy." She smiled, inhaling deeply then, turning from me she blew out a cloud of smoke. "Either I don't appeal to you or you're a man of iron nerve, Teddy Labden. Shall we cut the crap? I'm Teresa Sawicka. You can buy me that drink now and I'll have the same. Get yourself a whisky or something."

I didn't bat an eyelid. I was just glad the fencing was over, the set laid out.

"I'm told I can trust you, Teddy. Can I trust you?"

"Isn't it the other way around – me giving you money and you delivering the goods?"

"Oh, I can deliver," she whispered, "exactly what you want. What do you want, Teddy? I mean, right now?" She leaned close to me. I could feel the warmth of her breath against my cheek, sending a small shiver down my spine. "I know what I want," she said.

"And do you always get what you want?" I asked, prolonging the chase and letting my hand rest on her knee at last. I had placed it very carefully, holding and moulding, caressing and lingering. I saw the recognition in her eyes. As I withdrew my hand she leaned even closer and whispered, "Let's go to my room. This is America, the country where you can kill a man, soak yourself in alcohol, but not kiss your girlfriend in public." She laughed teasingly and caught my hand. We headed to the lift.

"Good night," the barman called.

In the elevator we kissed. Mouths open, hungrily working our lips. She pushed up hard against me, rocking her pelvis so that I could feel her soft belly demanding satisfaction. We stumbled along the corridor, not quite steady on our feet, not so much driven by alcohol as by the passion of the moment. My memories of that night tell me that the abandonment that followed was heightened by a lack of sentimental emotion other than lust or the desire for satiation, that there was healing through the insignificance of the moment of intercourse. What appealed to our nature was of no importance, except in its own fulfilment. This was no affair, no prostitution, but passion born of the brevity we both understood in that moment. I recall her flushed face, how she lay open-mouthed, eyes staring into another world. I recall the sensation of her cool white thighs, devoid of their black stockings, pressed against my roughness, entwining, forcing. The soft fullness of her breasts swaying above me with the urgency of her need. I can feel still the roundness of her buttocks pressed against me and the release as we came together.

Or has memory passed to imagination?

In truth I have a hazy recollection of afterwards, of a half-lit room, a ghost whispering of events. I remember a need for the bathroom, of returning and seeing Teresa turned on her side facing away from me. Her hair had tumbled forward and she was leaning on one elbow as though looking at something. Did she regret it? I sat on the bed and ran my hands over her body, softly caressing her, following the shapes and folds. I trailed my fingers along her back, down her arms, and then I swung onto the bed, kissing her shoulder, smelling her fresh sweat. I pulled her hindquarters to mine and reached around her, running my hand as far as I could, until she eased her thighs open. "And again," I heard her whisper.

She raised herself, pushing back at me. Now she was on all fours and I was behind her, thrusting my hand between the legs which had parted for me. The rhythm of my foreplay was matched by her intensity and occasional gasped breath. I mounted her and thrust forward, penetrating deeper than I had ever experienced before. The ambrosia of orgasm gushed by me and down our legs. Not the oil of entry, this, but the emission of completion. We both lay back to our thoughts.

I drifted off in a reverie of ideas based around the male capacity for quick, multiple orgasms, deciding that such ideas were nonsense. When I woke I found I had been covered by a sheet. Teresa was sitting close to the bed looking at me. The make-up was gone, the glamour had gone, but the room was warm.

"Awake?" she asked.

"Yes," I answered uncertainly.

She stared at me. I held her gaze with mine until she dropped her eyes. I grasped her hand in mine, gently stoking her skin with my thumb. I rolled to my side, resting my head on my hand, elbow to the mattress getting more comfortable so I could see her better. I reached over and took her hand again, reassuring her by touch.

"Do you like me?" She asked.

"I would have hoped I had already shown you that," I replied.

"I wonder how you'll feel about me when I tell you this," she smiled sadly and began her story.

"In 1939 I was a schoolteacher in a mixed village of Poles and Ukrainians. We had some Jews in the village too. Most were farmers who had new land handed out from the government when a large local estate was broken up under the pre-war land reform act. My daddy was the local postmaster. Mum was a housewife of the old school, keeping the usual cow and some chickens. Our family had lived there forever. Some of the new land went to Poles resettled from the army. I married one and had a son, Tadek.

"When the war came my husband was called up. I moved back to my parents with Tadek for more security. We did not expect the Germans to get that far east. My husband had said we had no western natural frontiers to hold, so we Poles would fall back, defending what we could in the west to a defensive line not far from our home.

"You know the story. We did not expect the Russians to come but they did. Most of the local lads had been called to the front, so the village was mostly women, children and older men. The Soviet Political Commissar told us the facts of life, but since my husband was not an officer I was to be allowed to stay. The village elders and pro-Polish officials were thrown out, and new Communist appointees sent in. We did not expect that some of the Ukrainians would act against the State. One day some Ukrainian Nationalists came, wearing the red and black arm bands of the Bandera faction. There was going to be some big meeting. The Ukrainians had been given the job of security for the local population.

"The first we knew there was something wrong was when we heard gunfire. People ran into the street. Then we heard the Germans were coming. A Ukrainian neighbour was led into the street further down and was shot in the head. We heard people shouting 'Pole lover'. So we ran back into the house. They beat on the door and must have kicked it in. I heard daddy shouting and mummy screaming. Then she suddenly stopped. I heard her being strangled. There was a croaking noise. Tadek and I were in the parlour. When they came in I held him. Then they screamed at me that as a schoolteacher I had beaten Ukrainian children. So they took Tadek." Her voice was low and absolutely leaden. No modulation, no stress, a monotone. She was staring at me, but without sight. "I screamed but they held my arms and held my face forward. I had to watch him being clubbed with their rifles, again and again. He didn't scream, but I heard his last whisper. When he had become a blood-stained heap they took me. There were four of them. They weren't from our village. I was scared and hysterical. They didn't have to do much; I gave them what they wanted. They threw me in the corner and I crawled to Tadek and held his little smashed body to mine.

"They started to take things then, putting our valuables in a sack. I think they were drunk. They whispered together then pulled Tadek from me. When they grabbed me again I started screaming, so they punched me till I shut up. Two of them dragged me outside. The other two carried out a small table. They forced me face down onto the surface and tied my knees and ankles to it. Then they pulled my skirts up and over my waist and bound me to the table by my waist. My arms were tied with longer rope to the other corners. They forced an old lady, our next-door neighbour, to sit next to me, saying loudly, 'Polish whore for free'. She kept whispering to me, 'They have my husband.' The way my face was turned I could see a crowd of them, along with some Russian NKVD units cheering as my Daddy was hoisted up a telegraph pole by his ankles. As he hung there the soldiers made the villagers run past and hit him. Then the same soldiers came for me. Some did what you expect, but then the Germans came and they sat down with the Commissar and I was left in peace.

"When it was time to go, the German officer said to untie me. The Reds objected. There was an argument. I heard the German soldiers slip their safety catches on their guns. I couldn't see by then and I was barely conscious. I found out later our village street was right on the dividing line between the German and Soviet zone. The Russian said I couldn't go with the Germans because I was now a Soviet citizen as Poland no longer existed. The German insisted I was on his side of the road. The Russians laughed, as they do, but the German took me. He gave me his coat and took me to a field hospital. I never saw him again.

"As I had been brought in by a German officer I was assumed to be 'someone', so I was taken to Krakow. I was given a job as an interpreter for the Germans in the new General Government. As a 'collaborator' I was given special digs. And then I found a sugar daddy who, in exchange for occasional sex with me and his friends, said I could live in his quarters right on Rynek market square. He was a 'fixer' for the SS and Frank. He collected heirlooms and art from the Polish State and from individuals, both Poles and Jews. As the time drew near the end, he was responsible for arranging forged papers and arms. I fled with him from Kraków to Berlin.

"Before you ask, yes, I did get arms to the AK and no, I did not betray my country. I gave what help I could to the underground. I am sure he knew this.

"With the advance of the Russians, just before they entered Berlin, we fled west and met the Americans. He had papers, you see. He knew things they wanted to know about SS men, who they really needed to pick up, like arms experts. So we got away and ended up in Lebanon, in the French zone. He began to trade in arms for the Arabs and I for the Jews. We made a lot of money. I met a lot of people and soon realised the world of politics was dirtier than the military. The Yanks armed the Arabs whilst publicly supporting the Jews, whilst the British assisted the Jews whilst publicly supporting the Arabs. And all the while young men died."

"And how did you get here?" I asked.

"Eric was shot. I believe by a Red Jew. I fled, and my Jewish friends helped me get into Egypt where I collected all of Eric's assets, including his agents etc. I set myself up as the agent for a number of arms companies, both legitimate and illegitimate. It was arranged that I marry a kindly, ancient Jewish New Yorker so I can live in America and supply arms to the right people. The CIA tolerates me and I survive. Do you know of Meyer Lansky?" she asked abruptly.

"Sorry, no I don't," I had to confess. "Should I?" I asked.

"He might help you," she said. "Outside the law, of course. His full name is Meyer Suchomlanski from Grodno. He is rapidly becoming Mr Cuba, running various clubs and things. I will mention you to him. When you are done being a hero he could use someone like you." Finished, she smiled. "And now you know. You are amongst the few who know why and how. You know why I behave as I do."

"Teresa, can you get guns into the hands of the Underground in Poland for me? Into the hands of the *Narodowe Siły Zbrojne*, the National Armed Forces, even though the NSZ is accused of chauvinism and anti-Semitism?" I asked straightforwardly, watching her eyes.

"There are always idiots everywhere. We are not so stupid as not to know the difference between propaganda and truth. I know what Lieutenant Colonel Kasznica was like, poor bastard, an honourable man, "Wąsowski" was his pseudonym if I remember correctly. He was one-time commander of the NSZ. They called him anti-Semitic. The Soviet propaganda machine did for his reputation. The political group that birthed the NSZ had an anti-Zionist position, not one of anti-Semitism. The two are far from synonymous but in the public mind they can be made the same. This new generation are going to die too; you know that, don't you? There is no hope. The US will not assist them."

"So why do you think they still fight?" I asked her.

"Because, like you, they are full of hate and have nowhere to go, except a downward spiral. Until they shed their blood for Poland in some back-street, where it will be washed away by people who call them thugs. That's the way of death for idealists and lunatics. We are all the same. Hamsters on a tread-mill. We cannot escape. I am no different."

We did a deal, there and then. Small arms, modern, portable, usable with captured ammunition. Money out of untraceable Swiss accounts.

"How will it travel?" I asked.

"Not for you to know, but it will come from Egypt to Bulgaria and then into Poland as something it is not. There it will be consigned to people I know who will make sure it goes in small packages to the right dispersal point, which you have supplied. That is your end of the deal. I will deliver to the location you indicated. It is all about money in the end. Money or sex," and she winked.

The phone rang. She answered it with a few monosyllabic yeses.

"You can go back to your room now. My men assure me you are clean. We have put every piece of paper back, including your precious note book which everyone is so keen to lay their hands on. Please be sure we have taken nothing. But we had to be sure of you too. And don't worry," she added almost coquettishly, "we replaced the hair you put across the door too.

So sweetly old fashioned, Teddy, but I admit, very effective. And your Radom on top of the wardrobe, so obvious. Now go. We will let you know when delivery happens. It will be quick. Your people have no time left."

I was not angry; it was simply what should have been done.

But there was Chuck to face next morning. "So you met up with our gangster gal? You still got your balls on? You look like shit!"

I admitted they ached a bit.

"Wears off with age, as does the urge, boy. So what's the deal?"

"Truthfully, none of your business, so shut the fuck up!"

"Tetchy, tetchy! We got work to do, and we got transport outside. So how was she? I think she likes it like a dog. You a dog, Teddy? Guess you needed a knot inside her to keep her happy and joined."I was not a dog-owner, so it was years later that I understood what he was talking about. Maybe it would have suited her better. After all, what damage had been done to her mind and body? I could not contemplate it. All I managed I did manage a feeble, "Lay off, Chuck. You shouldn't judge what you don't know. That's the trouble with you Yanks. You moralise when you got shed loads of shit in your own yard. Just lay off her and accept she is useful and plays the game straight."

That said, I worried about how the last act had been played out. And I couldn't forget the image of her bound to that table. Masochism or release? I changed the subject, telling him that as we had stumbled along the corridor Teresa had mentioned that Guy Burgess had been sitting in the lounge. I wondered if he had spotted me.

What she'd actually said was, 'Watch out for that queer', and that he had been keen to watch me, but had kept himself out of my sight. "Behind a potted palm, sweetie. Such a showman. And he has more twists than a monkey's tail. Very British, though. I think he's creepy."

Chuck sobered. "I wonder what she meant by that? It was clearly some sort of a warning. We don't want you near any Brits on this outing." He asked the driver to pull over near a diner and went to make a call. When he got back in he said, "Looks like the death throes of the Labour government. Burgess is over here in the Embassy, making himself a drunken nuisance. To keep him on the straight and narrow the Brits keep him in the company of a man called Philby. He's even forced to share an apartment with him. Let's hope he was too drunk to really notice you."

We headed down East Street, coming to a large brick building partly hidden behind a tree scape. The car swung into a short drive bordered by a chain-link fence and topped by a couple of strands of barbed wire. Sure enough, there was a modest plaque indicating 2430 E Street. The same plaque bore a round blue circle bearing the words, 'Central Intelligence Agency'. We were ushered into an inner office. "Soundproof," Chuck volunteered "the inner sanctum of the Directorate of Operations."

Two men entered the room and we both stood.

"Gentlemen, please sit," the taller of the two men said. "I know who you are, but you, Captain Labycz, you do not know us, I assume." I noted his clear and positive intention to give me my proper name and acknowledge my rank. This seemed a promising start.

"I am General Walter Beddell Smith, Director of this establishment, and this is my colleague Allen Dulles."

Beddell Smith had a gaunt look, a narrow head with a large cleft chin and slightly sunken cheeks. I judged him to be around sixty. His colleague looked little different in age but was more rounded, less the military type.

"We have invited you here to help us unravel some of the issues surrounding Operation Venona[viii]. Venona is a listening station, let us call it, monitoring Soviet intercepts of cable and radio signals. We have a Soviet agent, perhaps more, working at Arlington Hall, the Signals HQ for the military. He alerted the Soviets to what we were up to. The codes changed. We are now working on them as we can crack a code and they cannot stop the signals. We can't nail him, the traitor, because he knows too much, so he has been suspended and he is out of the running. But Operation Venona is compromised. We know he was sending information to a British mole in the Embassy. We suspect Burgess. That's the story so far."

It seemed to me that if we were listening to the Reds, then they were also listening to us.

"Now the British must know all this because at Eastcote they have the same intercepts though different methods, and we do share the information. So the question is: Why do they, the British, not act? You require this answer, as it is your assignment from Menzies. There is more than one mole, we can be sure of that from our experience. We have the same problem as the British – what to do when we find the moles. We have Reds under every bed as McCarthy is making obvious, but we are after the MGB and MVD people, not sympathisers, idealists and foot-soldiers."

Dulles cut in. "So we want you to look at some intercepts, Captain Labycz, to see if they mean anything to you. But you need to understand that we have no idea who is loyal to us, so your 'Witek' plan is in jeopardy from the start. We have kept it under wraps here in this office. Only the four of us are aware of it. We cannot send it to the White House yet as, incredibly, we are sure the plan will be either ignored or 'lost'."

Disturbed I was keen to know more. Beddell Smith and Dulles looked at each other. Dulles nodded to Chuck, who began to talk as though they had pulled a string on a puppet. I supposed in any fall-out Chuck would be the fall guy.

"We don't even know who amongst those around the President are informers, agents or sympathisers. The whole Democratic Party seems to be confused between Liberalism and Communism. The Alger Hiss affair certainly showed us that, a Soviet spy in the State Department helping set up the United Nations. He certainly demonstrated that the Harvard Club means more than America to some in the party and the press. They have gotten quite hysterical about McCarthy and seem intent on discrediting him. Hiss was a spy, no doubt, and the administration, even Roosevelt, knew of him right back in 1939. But they did nothing except promote him and his brother. Even Daladier in France warned he was a Soviet agent. Nothing happened. He moulded US policy in the State Department, virtually created the United Nations structure, and turned up in Yalta as an advisor over the carve-up of Europe.

"We are not even sure about Harry Hopkins, God rest his Soul. We now feel he was instrumental in helping the Soviets win the war by not only giving massive aid to the Soviets, but also going along with this 'Soviet sphere of influence' policy. Harry was at all the key conferences as Roosevelt's closest advisor. He even lived at the White House. Harry knew every Russian worth knowing, and before Harry died, Truman even sent him back to Moscow.

"We know that there was an agent called simply '19' at the big conferences, and that information was passed to the Reds of private conversations between Churchill and Roosevelt where Hopkins was the only other person present."

I noticed Chuck had dropped his gung-ho American West phrasing for a more serious tone in front of his superiors, who were watching me intently. Chuck continued.

"I suggest you have to look no further than those two to find out how you lost Poland. Now whilst it's true they are now out of the way, Venona is still turning up hundreds of intercepts with reference to different departments. The Liberals just cannot accept that the Reds are the bad guys here. Soviet spies in the administration are still in place, and McCarthy is not fighting windmills. The Democratic Party still seems to think this is all a figment of the imagination. It is not, as you know. Communists are described as 'Agrarian Reformers', which lets butcher Khrushchev off the hook. There is an 'inevitability' theory that states certain countries should be allowed to go Communist and so on. That's our background, so no way can we let the Witek plan outside this room."

"It already is. You know that. I have fully reported to the London Polish Government," I replied.

"We realise that, son," said Beddell Smith, "but those people have never let us down before – why should they now? And that's the opinion of Menzies across the water too. We think the operation is still tight, secure."

A sheaf of paper was passed across the table by Dulles. "See here, we have picked out code names and related them to specific trains of information. This group, for example, always go to this unidentified handler. Any ideas?"

I looked at the series of cables, all directly about policy, not military information. "This would all go to Izaak Ahkmerov and then direct to Stalin, bypassing both the MVD and MGB. You won't find records of who and what in the files unless Stalin wants it known. Ahkmerov bypasses the Politburo and Beria. Stalin keeps his secrets close, especially the big fish."

"So the bastard is still at work!" responded Chuck. "He was here in the US during the war and ran most of the agents. He was the big cheese. He left the dirty work to a guy called Katz, who ran Elizabeth Bentley, who eventually exposed eighty other agents. And Truman still will not listen!"

"I have heard of a Katz. Was his first name Józef?"

"Yeah," replied Chuck, "Joseph. He ran a glove-making company set up by the Soviets as a front."

"Same one, then. He was the agent who set up the assassination of Walter Krivitsky."

"You don't buy the suicide theory then? You feel he didn't kill himself?"

"Oh come on, man! Trotsky was done to death. No, Krivitsky was killed, believe me. My own parents were bumped off."

"Didn't realise that, Teddy. Commie bums."

I let the subject drop. I didn't want to open up the story of my parents and tread into the area of personal revenge.

Chuck and I were left to work through the papers. They were mostly identified and exposed groups, but, though the legs had been cut off, could they or had they re-grown? There was the Victor Perlo group, the Silvermaster group, the Myrna group, the Sound group, the Buben group and many more. I was unsurprised to see the depth of penetration of the OSS and the many GRU[ix] agents embedded in that service. No wonder Stalin was one step ahead. No wonder Eastern Europe was swallowed up.

It had been a difficult and long day. We had tried to match up some codes and names from Witek's notes, and managed about three from a hundred or so ciphers. I apologised that I had not been much help.

"At least we are certain about these three now. I guess if we try to sort them out, the Washington Post will go crazy again and tell the public we got paranoia and are digging up dirt to curb their freedoms," Chuck volunteered.

The three I had uncovered were all newspaper men. This hardly surprised me. It struck me, as in Britain, half the media men and half the authors seemed to be ex-Secret Service, or had been or still were in Intelligence. I chuckled on the way back to the hotel.

"What's funny?" Chuck asked.

"Perhaps I should write a book."

"Maybe you should," he replied. "If anyone reads it they won't believe it, the whole business has been such a farce."

"Even If they did believe it, the press would discredit it anyway," I mumbled.

"On orders from Moscow," Chuck countered. And we both laughed.

I was dog-tired as I left the hotel elevator. The corridor seemed endless. I was too tired to eat and too tired to face a noisy bar. I had a headache and felt strangely depressed by the day. My eyes were sore from squinting in the gloom. Dark work needs subdued light, I had concluded. The place had been air-conditioned. I was dry as a bone. My skin felt uncomfortable and drawn.

The thick red and cream of the carpet unrolled before me like a runway as I padded toward my room. At the door I paused and looked for my markers, a small piece of grit wedged in the bottom left hand hinge, a tiny sliver of match on the other side. Neither was present.

I stood for a moment, thinking. Had I made a noise coming along the corridor? No, although I had been dragging my feet it was in the mental sense. My feet had been quiet along the carpet, walking normally. Could it have been the maid? I had asked for my room not to be cleaned. It was possible, even so.

If there was anyone inside they were not friendly Indians, I decided, unless they were perhaps Teresa Sawicka's people. I considered my options. I could walk away. I could call Chuck from a house phone, but then if it had been housekeeping I would look a fool. Anyway, Chuck was not my nursemaid and the CIA had gotten all they needed from me. I was now expendable.

Chuck being the grand American he was, sure that everything stateside was the best in the world, had bought me a present a couple of days back. Convinced my Radom was too bulky he'd decided a small calibre lightweight hand-gun would suit me better for self defence purposes. So I had become the proud owner of a Ruger, point 22. The little gun looked like a small German Luger service pistol. I had to admit it was lighter, and Chuck assured me it was simple and reliable. "A point 22 rimfire blowback-operated semi-automatic pistol with a distinctive slim-tapered short barrel," he had said as he produced it from the box and waved it under my nose.

I had toyed with it, stripped it, but never handled it or fired it. Now I wished I had and that I hadn't been so churlish when he'd offered me a practice shoot on a CIA range. I had carried the Ruger to please him, more than anything else. "Gun law here in the US varies, Sonny Boy, but for sure this country ain't London with very nice bobbies. Never mind the Russkis, we got our fair share of bad guys that want your purse. You can't tout that tonweight service pistol about but you'll get arrested!" he had guffawed.

I retrieved the Ruger from my waistband at my back, slipping off the safety catch, aware that my life might now depend upon an untried weapon. The pistol was blued steel with the bolt 'in the white', unfinished. I held it momentarily, weighing it mentally, extending it as part of my hand, wondering what the recoil would be like.

I thought the room through. Possibly two people. There was a luggage area behind the door. One of them would be there. That would mean the other would be in front of me, either to distract me or take a shot, whatever their intention was. He would have to be at the foot of the bed or behind the bed, as the dressing-table and drawer units were against the left-hand wall. If they were professionals and not robbers they would have seen my markers. They would be expecting me. What would they not expect or prepare for?

I sat on the floor, praying no civilian would appear. Pushing my left shoulder hard against the door frame I brought my knees up to the other side, pushing against the door slightly. Awkwardly I reached up with my left hand and inserted and turned the key, pushing slightly. I turned the handle. The moment I felt the door give I pushed it violently with all my power, turning into the room flat, thrusting my legs as hard as I could against the door which swung violently with a comforting rebound against the body hiding there.

A figure opposite, slightly to the right behind the bed, stood with weapon raised, the silencer pointed where my torso should have been. I saw the flash from the silencer and watched the barrel lower as I loosed off two rounds that went home. The other guy had pushed back and stumbled from behind the door. He too had expected a standing person. The Ruger barked twice and he fell slowly to the ground, still partly trapped by the door.

Four shots, four thunder claps, four backfires or had the carpet and the corridor muffled the sound? I did not wait to see if any doors opened but quickly closed mine. I hoped the wall opposite was not made of plasterboard as the bullet meant for me must have embedded itself opposite or perhaps gone straight through. I paused, listening. Nothing.

Still holding the Ruger forward I felt for a pulse, but there was nothing from my 'doorman'. What about the guy in the bedroom? Was he down and out or lying doggo? Still holding the pistol extended, ready for any movement, I edged toward the bed. I could see blood.

I heard nothing. There was just a sense of danger before a third figure standing this side of the bed, backed up against the bathroom, sprung onto my back. I felt a slight scratch on my left shoulder as we fell violently to the floor. All the training in the world does not help; we struggled, sweated, clawed and twisted. My muscles strained as I felt my head being wrenched. Something was caught high up in my jacket. I felt a sensation of wetness on my shoulder. My assailant was trying to do something up there. I reached backward and back, tangling with the hand. As we rolled and twisted something dropped away, and then a deadlier game began. Fingers sought nerve endings. Arms and wrists twisted. I was heavier, so as we half-kneeled I managed to swing down violently, crashing my opponent's head into the dressing-table edge. There was a slight lessening of grip. The same move once more brought for me the welcome sound of flesh and bone or teeth as my opposite's face was smashed. Throwing my adversary to the side I chopped down hard on the exposed neck. I heard a slight click in the sudden quiet. The body slumped.

My breathing was coming in short bursts. I looked around the room, picking up the Ruger. My hands were shaking, not with fear but strain. I felt sick and sat on the bed for a moment, allowing the shock to pass and the adrenalin to drain. For long seconds I sat and breathed into my stomach, just as my dad had taught me. I counted the breaths in and out. When I felt able I went to the bathroom and rinsed my face and hands with cold water. There wasn't much blood, but angry friction marks showed across my cheeks and neck. I stripped to the waist and tried to see the scratch which was stinging. I managed to reach it with a cold flannel before getting dressed again and rewashing my face. I ran cold water over my hands to reduce the swelling.

And then I picked up the phone to Chuck.

"Jees –uz! I'll be right over and I'll get a clear-up team organised."

As I waited I refilled the Ruger magazine. Next I retrieved my Radom from the top of the wardrobe. Then I went from body to body, looking for identification. I was surprised to discover that my last assailant was a woman. I found the weapon she had used on me, the one that had snagged in my jacket and saved my life. It was a heavy metal syringe. Clearly they had meant to take me alive. The guy by the bed had used a dart gun, so the first shot had not been meant to kill. The 'door' guy had been the backup killer, if needed.

I was meant to open the door, take the dart, stagger in or out and then be trussed up. I thought about the man with the dart. He must have known I could have dropped him, and that I would have been expecting him to see him right where I had guessed him to be. For a moment I respected his bravery. Or was it insolence? Staggering, I would have been pulled in like a drunk. That's when the woman would have administered the drug. From then I would have been crated up and shipped out, straight back to the arms of the MGB. I shuddered at the thought.

"Neatly done, neatly done," said Chuck, handing me a strange dart with blue flight feathers. "It left just a small stain on the wall opposite," he added. "This is Agent Morton. He'll clean up and get you checked out, bill paid all courtesy of Uncle Sam. Can't have our friends being shot at without compensation."

I shook hands with Morton, who looked around the room.

"You were lucky," he observed.

"Just careful," cut in Chuck. "The Ruger, I guess, from the little damage?"

"Yup," I answered, "right on the nail."

"Leave all this here, buddy. Let's get you to a safe house."

"I'm packed and ready, let's move it."

Slipping into Chuck's Buick, I realised this meant goodbye to America for the moment.

"Well, who was it, buddy? Sawicka or Burgess?" Chuck's meaning was obvious.

"She has too much to lose. Anyway, I'm convinced she's for real. She mentioned Burgess. I now take that to have been a warning." I let out a sigh. This was a turning point, I realised. At last I had something concrete to go on.

Chuck, in sombre mood, began making observations. He kept pulling at his chin and pushing his hair back. This was the first time I had seen any sign of discomfiture in the man. "Three deaths are going to show up something. I will let our brother Ivans know tomorrow that their operatives have gone to Soviet Valhalla and to get out the Order of the Red Banner for the relatives. I shall enjoy that.

"The proof will be to see who starts checking on you here. I wonder who Burgess tipped off? I doubt he went round the Russian embassy. Why should he be concerned about you unless someone told him to be? Did he tell MI5? He might have known they are on your tail? Did a leak come from there? The British end should know that. We will contact Menzies direct, for him to chase that particular hare to ground," he ruminated.

We arrived at the new address.

Within another eighteen hours I was on a very big Boeing super dumbo, a fortress variant used usually for air-sea rescue. It was full of equipment destined for a USAAF base in Britain, in Bentwater, Suffolk. When I was invited up front I marvelled at the bank of controls.

"Flies itself," the pilot said.

"The RAF vacated it earlier this year," Chuck explained. "It's being brought up to scratch now and not yet operational. Ideal for you to slip in and quietly meet up with your man Rupert."

I settled to a troubled sleep in an observer's seat, a rather wonderful USAAF armchair.

It was a long flight.

# CHAPTER 18

# SOCIALS IN ENGLAND

Rupert was waiting as the giant taxied toward a group of hangars currently being refurbished. He cut a small figure, his raincoat flapping from the draft of our propellers. I waved but doubted he could see me. Thanking the crew I scrambled down the exit ladder, slinging my holdall ahead of me and hoping my well-wrapped alarm clock would survive, as well as the malt wrapped in copious shirts and sweaters. Nothing chinked and there was no whisky smell as I grabbed it and headed for my old friend.

He was as resplendent as ever in bowler hat and dark grey raincoat. I could even see a chalk-stripe underneath. We shook hands warmly and he ushered me to a black Wolseley 6/80, complete with driver.

"Gone up in the world, Rupert, driver and all. By the way, you look every inch ex-Guards." We had settled into the comfortable, brown leather seats. He tweaked his tie. "Somerset's, old boy, you know that only too well! The light Bobs and all that."

"With a bit of the Intelligence Corps thrown in, I guess," I added.

"No formalities here, by the way. Are you carrying a weapon?" Rupert asked as we swept through the American gates, two MPs saluting.

"I sure am, buddy. Two, as a matter of fact."

"You can cut that Yank accent right now, Mister," Rupert said. "I had enough of it down the telephone from your friend Chuck. What a name!"

"Well, he is sort of a cowboy, Rupert. It suits him."

"That cowboy image just about fits the CIA altogether, they're only one up from that crazy OSS outfit! I'd settle for the FBI over that lot any day." Rupert sighed as he passed this last remark, leaving me slightly deflated and feeling well and truly back in the land of English arrogance. As the driver drove fast down country roads I peered out of the v-shaped split windscreen. I had got used to space and the wide roads of North America.

"Is this your assigned car?" I asked.

"Good God, no!" Rupert exclaimed. "This is in your honour, one of the old Z people, a British, well okay, Polish sort of Canadian sleeper. A rare breed indeed, forgotten in the annals of the new SIS, thank God!

"I would like to buy a Rover 75 but I can't run to it. What I'd really like is a Bristol 2 litre. In fact, however, I am reduced to a Ford Consul; family and all that."

"So you had to give up on that MG WA Tickford?" I asked, knowing the gleaming cherry red sports car used to be his pride and joy. A great car, a drophead coupé with sumptuous cream leather interior. "Given up your beloved sports cars, then?" I asked, trying to regain some of our old camaraderie.

"It was all a long time ago, Teddy, the world has changed. We can't even make good steel. Modern cars are rust buckets. Buy an old one if you need one," he muttered, reaching for his wallet buried in a suit pocket.

I had no real idea that he had a family. From his wallet he produced photos of an English wife with a typically long 'county' face, big teeth with lips drawn back, like a horse the French would have said. One baby and another toddler. I exclaimed fulsomely. "If people like you don't get me killed I shall look forward to a good pension and my garden too."

"The old guard from SIS are gone and the old firm is full of journalists, book writers and BBC commentators and hacks. Mostly Labour scribblers, trying to share out everybody's wealth except their own book rights. Menzies is on his way out, you know. He doesn't see eye to eye with the Labour government, which he considers responsible for damaging every-thing from the economy to allowing the Soviets to infiltrate SIS! He knows you from old Admiral Sinclair days. Only last week he was saying that Queck's[X] Z group which he had formed has been eliminated. Either died on active service in SOE or like you gone to ground. Z was intended to stop the Soviets seizing power. So Menzies realises you were empowered to act for the British independently, to maintain our sovereignty against the extreme Left.

"Despite this new Cold War, the Labour dictum is 'we must not be nasty to the Soviets'. We can get on with the Bolshies once Stalin has gone. Rajani Palme Dutt, with the pro Stalinist line he pushes within the British Communist Party, stands no chance of ever being elected, so people like Rajani's wife, Salme, who was his Comintern go-between with Moscow, serve the useful purpose of keeping the British public thinking that there are no Reds in Labour as they would all join the Communist Party. People are so naïve sometimes. Rajani Palme Dutt is a Stalinist of the old school. Harry Pollitt, the other leading light, nearly made it to MP in Rhondda East in '45."

"I believe Salme was an Estonian or Latvian. I met her once. She was quite open that she was a Comintern agent, sent here by Lenin," I comment-ed, digesting some of Britain's current politics and remembering what had gone before. Nuances from my parent's discussions came floating back to me. "Is that the same Pollitt who joined Sylvia Pankhurst's Workers Socialist Federation?" I asked.

"Don't really know, old boy," Rupert replied. "But her party was amal-gamated or federated – you know what these Left organisations are like, always changing or arguing – into the Communist Party as we know it here today."

I started to talk about Soviet infiltration of political parties but Rupert wagged his finger and pointed at the driver. Instead we talked of friends and family and reminisced about Cambridge. Arriving in London I opted for a stay at the Tavistock, my usual pre-war haunt. The driver was dismissed. We entered the foyer and Rupert cautioned me for a moment. Taking me by the arm he took me back through the chromed doors to the pavement and promptly hired a cab. "Thought we should stick you in the Connaught, to get you reacclimatised to England. It's quiet, more private house style, you'll love it."

"Sounds good, but why the cloak and dagger stuff?"

"New driver, old boy. Who knows whom he knows?" Rupert answered. "Anyway, we meet Menzies at ten a.m. sharp. You come over to the Foreign and Commonwealth Office. Ask for me and then we'll descend into one of the dodgy tunnels under the City and arrive at the Admiral Citadel. We're tunnelling everywhere these days, in case of a nuclear attack. All very hush hush, except everyone knows. All the Post Office Telephone tunnels are really communication tunnels. They pop up all over the place. I dare say you can get from Downing Street to Trafalgar Square quicker than taking a cab! The Admiralty Citadel is a monstrosity, hardly used now the war is over, but you can't miss it, old boy. Except you have to get in it from underground. Designed like Hitler's bunker, to be defended."

The following morning Stewart Menzies listened to my story. Turning to Rupert he said, "We'd better get Burgess back here for 'bad behaviour' and for being a naughty, drunken boy. Then we can keep an eye on him."

"I met him before the war and also saw him up at Cambridge. He was locked into Donald Maclean as a good friend. Do you remember, Rupert, we saw them once at a Black Shirt meeting and gave them a lift in our cab?" I asked.

"Yes I do, and that's interesting. Because I hear that 5 have a view about him. Maybe we should let our brethren know what's happening and see how much rope to play out. With a little pressure we can see if the cat jumps," Rupert added.

Menzies agreed but wanted now to know what I had decided about the Witek proposal. "This government will never sanction an assassination plot, so this remains a Z operation of the old school, probably the final one, young Labden." His short moustache, now grey, moved up and down as he spoke. I had never favoured facial hair except for the bristling, drooping warrior moustache or the naval beard. I wondered why so many military types sported these sprouts. "It has to be clandestine and secret. The Defence of the Realm and all that. I hear you are still interested in the Sikorski affair. Is that right?"

"Yes sir," I replied.

"It would have been about motive, boy. This modern lot do not understand espionage or its purpose. The Soviets do, they know how to infiltrate, to lie deep and wait. Churchill missed the point when Canaris, the anti-Nazi head of the Abwehr, and a goodly number of anti-Nazi generals wanted to parley and still go for the Soviets. I was involved in that negotiation, but the old man remained unconvinced, relying on keeping 'good faith' with Stalin. Sikorski was not of the same opinion. Which is why he had gone to Cairo. Not only to placate your 2$^{nd}$ Corps and General Anders, but to see what might be available from the Germans he met there. Scared the proverbial out of Stalin, I can tell you! Look for the motives and you'll always find the answers. Skarbek might have some answers for you too; she was there in Cairo."

Rupert nodded. "Canaris managed to keep out of Himmler's clutches until July 1944, just one year after General Sikorski was killed. The year of Sikorski's assassination Canaris met with George Earle. Roosevelt had appointed Earle as his special representative for the Balkans. Canaris turned up dressed as a civilian at Earle's hotel in Istanbul, knocked on the door and offered a peace proposal. He proposed an honourable surrender to the Americans."

"Which partly explains why Donovan and I met with Canaris at Santander in Spain before Sikorski went to Cairo," interjected Menzies. "The plan was peace in the West. German troops out everywhere. Hitler and Company to be eliminated and the war against Communism to continue. Von Papen was also aware of the plan and backed it. We agreed in principle, but Roosevelt would have nothing to do with these 'German aristocrats' as he called them.

"We will try to keep 5 off your tail. If we are too open it will compromise both projects, mine with the moles and yours with Witek. Lay low, keep off the horizon. Now, Is there anything you need?" he asked. "Weapons, transport?"

"I do need a reliable compact radio, strong enough to reach Moscow." Witek had said that the SIS would provide one and he was right. "Deliver it via the buses parcel service, in a suitcase, this coming Friday. Mark it for collection by John Harrington at the Pool Valley depot in Brighton." Today was Monday.

"All right, we'll put the radio in a suitcase with a luggage label for a Thierry Abrupt from Paris. That will suggest it's lost luggage, that he's staying with a friend who collects it on his behalf. Remember 8 will be listening to you and will notify 5, so keep it short and obscure. It will be a late wartime Polish radio, one used by your lot which we 'acquired', so it can't be traced to us."

"Is it reliable and powerful enough?" I asked.

Menzies grinned broadly, nodding toward Rupert. "You should hear them in the Foreign Office kicking up a stink about Polish radios! Throughout the war the Poles were in radio communication with Poland all the time. Their cipher and transmitter centre was based at Woldingham in Surrey, not so far away. Believe me, Polish equipment makes all other devices look like museum pieces. We should have had your equipment at Arnhem," he sighed. "But then, it wasn't British!"

I had a lot to chew on as I took the train to Brighton and my personal bolt-hole. I felt like a kid taking that train. Opening the window and letting the strap right down to the last hole I hung out, letting the fresh air blow through my hair and mind. I smelt the smoke with its pleasing tang of sulphur. A cinder caught the side of my face. I played dare as we came to bridges and tunnels, hanging out as far as I had the courage, knowing people had their heads knocked off by such stupidity. I wanted to clear my head of confusion; what was troubling me that morning was why the war had not ended in 1943? Only Stalin had benefited. His plan to dominate Europe had been the real beneficiary, the new Soviet Empire. Was Roosevelt really so stupid or so noble? It made no sense.

At Hassocks a genteel lady entered my compartment so I had to abandon my antics and sit upright, feeling disgruntled and disturbed by her presence. At the station I made for a phone booth. When the phone rang I pushed the button. The pennies dropped and I heard the familiar sound of Kryszka's voice.

"Allo?" That unmistakeable Eastern Europe twang.

"Hello Kryszka, my old matelot, I'm ten minutes from home. Put the kettle on."

"My Gott, err, err, I happy to see you."

"No Kryszka, you can't see me yet, you *hear* me, you old son of a gun." I always enjoyed teasing him. It was great to be back. Catching the number six bus I hopped off before the Midland bank and headed up Crown Street. Kryszka was watching at the Queen Anne window. He flung the door open and we hugged. "Let me in, you old bugger, otherwise you'll get us arrested as queers," I laughed. The door closed behind us.

After a wash, and settling in and finding familiar old things as well as new things, we shared both tea and the malt. We lost no time getting to the heart of things.

"Times have changed, Tadek, people have moved on. Even the government loses power, loses spirit," Kryszka observed. "August Zaleski, the President, does not command as much respect as he should from the Generals. Time is passing. The boys are settling down, finding jobs, marrying sweethearts and having babies. The old country is fading for some, but not all.

"The anti-Polish brigade here in Britain is now turning. It has become anti-West Indian rather than anti-Polish. Those people have a disadvantage. You can spot them easily because of their skin colour. At least we can merge, being white!"

Kryszka was expecting a group of friends round to play a regular card game played for matches. He asked if I would mind. I assured him I'd enjoy the change of company.

There was a new film out called *Brighton Rock*. The town was gaining notoriety as a haunt of spivs and razor gangs, Kryszka explained. Quite a few misfits had settled round and about. The good news was that at the top of Preston Street a new Jewish delicatessen had opened, selling halva and Polish *serniki* or cheese cake. There were plans to build a new industrial estate up at Hollingbury and a big new housing estate. The Catholic Church just up the road now had mass in Polish, and they'd started a Saturday school for young Poles born in England, or young Britons of Polish descent. I recognized a familiar argument.

I asked about people we had known. One group from Halton had teamed up with a Turkish investor to form Murad Engineering, making machine tools in Aylesbury. Another group had gone off to Argentina. And then Kryszka dropped his bombshell.

"Tonight you'll meet someone else. You will meet my girlfriend. I want you to be nice to her. We are getting married." Kryszka challenged me with his eyes.

I broke into a broad grin, feeling genuine pleasure and surprise. "You're getting married? Incredible! Unbelievable! To whom?"

Somewhat bashfully, Kryszka answered, "Her name is Ruth Rosenberg. She lives in a posh house not so far from here, in Silwood Road. Her people are Hamburg Jews," he added.

"Is she pretty?" I asked.

"Very! Large-boned, German type. Neat, short blondish curly hair. Good figure, nice legs which fill her stockings, not tree legs. Good knees and nice rump," was Kryszka's reply.

I laughed. Of course he wanted to know what was so funny. "Have you been infected by Soviet realism in your artistic world?" I asked. I tried to explain why his description was so amusing but he couldn't see the joke.

Ruth was pretty and she was well covered, suiting him in both height and shape as I discovered when we met later. She was the hostess for the card party. The other guests were Wojciech Machulski, who had married an English girl and borrowed money from her father to start a small corner shop in Hove, and Marek Swarzynski, who had a young son called Zygmunt, known as Ziggie. This nickname made the father very happy. "No Polish spoken in my house," he proudly exclaimed, "My son is to be English." He was a bit nonplussed by my question why he and his English wife had not called their son Albert or William. "My wife insisted on a Polish name," he said, shrugging his shoulders.

The fourth member of the 'card school' was a young Englishman called Laurie Philps. He rented the next door basement to Marek's in Clarence Square. His wife was a German war bride he had acquired when in the forces. She was the same shape and size as Ruth, only a bit blonder. The young couple intended to open a milk bar and introduce a jukebox for teenagers. He wore his blonde hair slicked back but allowed the fringe to tumble forward in the style I had seen in America called 'rock'. He was crazy for a new song called *Rocket 88* by some group called Delta Cats, a name we all thought hysterical.

"You won't be laughing when we make our first million," said Marta, Laurie's wife.

"We shall expect free drinks for the rest of our lives if you do," Ruth added.

There was someone missing. "Where is Michałek Wojniak?" I asked as we supped tea and ate the delicious pastries Ruth had prepared.

An awkward silence fell.

"Obviously the wrong question," I observed.

"It's my fault," Marta volunteered, immediately followed by a string of protests from the others.

"No, it is not," Kryszka intervened. "Michałek and I had a disagreement. As I told you earlier, he joined the sweet company just after me. We became good friends. Now he will not come here when Marta is here, simply because she is German. I cannot accept this so I ban him from the house until he comes to his senses. My fiancee Ruth's family too are German Jews, originally from Hamburg. They came over years ago before First World but were then pilloried by the locals up in the East End as 'Krauts.' Funny how life changes!"

We talked of the 303 Squadron boys, how they had all fared. Krasnodębski, 'The King', had gone down to South Africa with his wife Wanda. The last the group had heard he was having a tough time driving a taxi because the local drivers didn't want foreigners around. I was able to tell them I'd heard they might move to Canada. Kryszka recalled the food we'd eaten at the Orchard Restaurant, and the elation and optimism of 1940 which contrasted with the later war years.

Urbanowicz had headed to the USA, to New York and Queens, where he had a poorly-paid marketing job with Eastern and American Airlines. Zumbach had started a small air charter service with some RAF pilots. I did not add that he had been named by Teresa Sawicka as an ally in the smuggling business, flying everything from currency to arms.

Witold Łokuciewski had actually gone back to Lublin in Poland, much to most people's disgust.

"Family pressure," Kryszka commented.

"Lucky to have a family left," chimed in Machulski.

"Skalski also went back," I volunteered, "even though he had commanded RAF 601 Squadron."

"Ah yes, but he was arrested . They tried him for espionage. He was sentenced to death and sits in prison today waiting for his execution."

There was a general muttering about this in the room, everyone bristling at the injustice. Eventually Machulski turned our attention to another airman, "My friend Lesniak used to be with the PAF Initial Training Unit, which was based just down the road at the Abbots Hotel in Regency Square. He is still here, now as a shop assistant."

And so we reminisced, as exiles do.

Later in bed I listened to the sound of the sea as I loved to do. *Tomorrow, I decided, I would go and look at the Old Steine fountain. Get some more air, cleanse the brain. Maybe I could look around the Lanes and find some antiques. I fancied a set of flintlock pistols. I'd be sure to find them in that shop on the corner which had a window display full of ancient weapons and militaria.* However, the thought of Kryszka kept creeping back into my mind. How would his plans fit in with Witek's? The question was one I had not dared to raise. Would Kryszka come to Russia to help me kill Stalin?

I raked my brain, teasing out memories. Captain Gripper, my mentor in the Service, had died because he had stumbled on the Red mole in SIS. I myself had been targeted by 5 because someone thought I knew more than I did. Who had tipped off the MVD in the first place? Who was close enough to Stalin to be listened to?

The sea surged and I hoped the clear air of tomorrow might supply an answer. In part it did. The next morning I sat looking at the green and yellow dolphins in the fountains devoid of water now in this English Spring. There were crocuses out, in saffron and blue. Seagulls screamed and the black-headed gulls were taking on their summer plumage. The mating game has begun, I thought. And then I thought of Kryszka. And of Ela and what should have been. It was not a good place to go.

I had needed time to plan and think and now I had it. I had realised that the Casablanca conference must hold some key I had previously missed. Never mind the 'Witek' plan for the moment. That was Stage Three. Stage One still remained the Sikorski affair. Stage Two, the moles in SIS.

Clearly there was no respectable reason why the war should have gone on. Stalin had a lot to gain by keeping the Allies in the conflict. He badly needed the second front in the West and he was totally opposed to the Sikorski plan of invasion via the Balkans. The utopians of the Comintern and the Pink socialists on both sides of the Atlantic would get the same benefits. For the former a new Eastern Empire, for the latter a Brave New World Order, controlled by Socialism from the centre, emerging from the ashes of a broken Europe.

The war was continued by FDR and Churchill quite deliberately . That must have happened at the behest of their advisors, many of whom, especially in the US, were at best Left-leaning liberals and at worst Communist NKVD sleepers.

Stalin was not present that January in Casablanca in 1943. So it was FDR and Churchill who decided only *unconditional surrender* would be accepted from Germany. They gave the public the impression that Hitler was Germany and the defeat of both was synonymous. Previously they had used the term 'Hitlerite Germany'. This subtle British twist now declared war on all the German people, exactly as Stalin intended. This gave succour to Stalin to keep fighting, perhaps. But he had no choice.

It was at Casablanca that they agreed to give Stalin every assistance in material aid. Before the conference Stalin had announced that all Eastern Poles would no longer have their Polish citizenship recognised. He was too busy to go to Casablanca, but not too busy to alienate the Poles further.

On Friday I collected the radio. Later that night I tuned it to the setting Medvedev or Witek had given me. I kept the code book by my side. 'Goose boy, Goose boy'. Nothing. I tried again. Waiting another half hour I tapped 'Goose boy' into the ether. Back a signal came. 'Plum Brandy'.

'Toast,' I replied. The correct response, 'Yellow Candle', followed.

I had my message ready. 'Harry and St. George' I tapped. Witek knew this meant I was ready, like those before Agincourt. What came back was a new frequency and a message to wait, plus an enigmatic 'Two ganders fly with cherry blossom'.

I notified Rupert. Burgess and MacLean were about to flee.

"Two of our Foreign Office diplomats are missing," intoned the voice of Stuart Hibberd on the BBC radio two weeks after they had defected. I had more news for Rupert at the end of May, 'Two ganders sitting in a flat in Moscow'. Now we knew there was an issue. Someone had tipped them off following our first radio interchange. The search would begin in earnest.

Rupert put his finger on Guy Liddell. "Look, old boy, I told Liddell we had some intelligence about a possible defection just two days before it happened. He is a well-known friend of both the bad boys and also employed some proto-Marxist called Anthony Blunt. Blunt was in the same circle, as Liddell's personal assistant for a while, and that despite objections to the contrary.

"Rum chap, I'm told. Although head of the counter-espionage section of MI5, he got all bitter and twisted when Percy Sillitoe was appointed over his head as chief of 5. Now it turns out he was told back in 1950 something along the lines of Burgess being a Comintern recruiting agent."

Remembering Witek's comments about the British spy circle I asked, "Homosexual?"

"Yes indeedee, you've put your finger on it. He was one of Burgess's lovers. Incidentally, Burgess was staying at another 'luvvies'' apartment when he fled, W.H. Auden the poet. I don't think he's a runner, just a Liddell red herring. Although 5 are chasing it down. Auden's in his lair in Italy."

"Anyone else in the picture?" I asked.

"Dick White is after a Welsh journalist called Goronwy Rees. You now the type, Manchester Guardian and all that implies, tweed etc. An MI5 man. Hard to pin down, I understand, but he had the cheek to say he thought 5 knew he was a Russian double agent, as Burgess tried to recruit him in 1937!"

"I prefer Eastern Europe sometimes, Rupert. It's cleaner. A bullet soon sorts people out."

Rupert grimaced. "So as I see it," he went on, "we seem to be in the same situation you and Gripper found yourselves in before he was murdered. We know this abomination doesn't end with Burgess and MacLean. Other bastards like Rees are being protected. To us it's clearly by Liddell, but is that for the Soviets or sex? Menzies will go shortly. Who will he turn us over to?"

"Or will he expect us to go alone?" I wondered out loud.

"An election is coming up," Rupert added. "Labour have a tiny majority. We want to go for an increase. They are still the most popular party, I'm afraid, building this Welfare State of theirs and nationalising industries. The Unions are still firmly behind them and ridden with Communist activists. So all that leaves us on the wrong side of democracy, Teddy, old man."

"But the public have no idea what this Cold War means and the mistakes Churchill made. Obviously they are going to vote for more jam, anyone would. But mark my words, one day their grandchildren will have to pay the price. The economy will get sicker. One day when the present baby-boomers will be pensioners the chickens will come home to roost make, no mistake."

"Same old Rightist, Teddy." Rupert patted me on the back.

"The other code which came through took some time to decipher, Rupert. It's 'Avoid at all costs Yuri Modin'."

Rupert looked earnest. "I should get out of the country for a few weeks if I were you. Take a holiday for your and my health's sake. This man Yuri Modin is in England at the moment, staying at the Embassy. Let's wait, see what he does now. It would appear from your Moscow message that he might have an interest in you."

I phoned Sawicka. Her phone wire would be tapped but she told me she had good friends in the East End of London, and a man known as Jack Spot would be in touch. She gave me a number to call in London which I duly did. I was handed on to a certain 'Jamie the Scot'. We arranged to meet in a Brighton pub called the Full Moon in Boyce's Street.

"Bad place," Kryszka warned me, "always fights and razors."

In acknowledgement I put on my new American shoulder holster for the Radom. It looked bulky enough to be intimidating. When asked, the barman nodded in the direction of a skinny man at a small table.

"You the bleedin Polak?" the skinny guy asked.

I thought it best to get some ground rules. "Let me assure you, you little scum, that if there are any more comments like that from that shitbag of a mouth of yours you'll end up bleeding. "

"Come on, guv'ner, I'm only a bookies' runner. I got this message fer yer, see." He held up an envelope out of my reach.

"Ten bob an' it's yours," he drawled.

"Surely Jack Spot has paid already?" I asked.

The man shifted in his seat, drawing his glass of ale to the right side of the table. "Ahm not afraid ae that wee Polish kike neiver."

"Really, something tells me different, little man." I placed my hand on the glass, squeezing his. "I'm too old for that game, Jamie. I can tell you, before the beer hit my face followed by the glass, you would be dead. Do you like pain?" I reached over and caught his nose, pulling and twisting it violently. "Now, when I let go, you say, 'Sorry sir, I meant to say Polish Jew, not kike.' You got that?" He tried to nod his head. Saliva was running from his mouth onto the table. I kept my left hand clenched on the glass as I let go. He repeated the words I had asked.

"Now, my envelope please."

He pushed it across the table. I felt rather than saw several eyes watching us.

"Be a good man and put both hands on the table, right over to me, and hold the table edge."

He did as he was told as I backed away. I did not want a knife in the back.

The letter was from Teresa. It was a dangerous communication, outlining our arms shipment plus the contacts and the drop point, as well as instructions on how I could get behind the Iron Curtain and into Poland. But it would be very difficult without more help. There is a fine line between criminality and the Secret Service. She simply suggested I contact my 'boss' to see if he could get me in. 'The Iron Curtain is just that,' she wrote. 'Goods, arms, jewellery, all can pass through with the right bribes. But people, well that's another matter.' She concluded by saying, 'If you can get in, I can get you out.' All in all, not very encouraging.

****

Far away in Moscow, Comrade General Viktor Abakumov knew something was afoot. He felt it.

Washington had reported the failed abduction attempt and the files on this Labycz person were proving as elusive as the man himself. "No one goes to this trouble unless it's for something big," he grumbled to his assistant, Mikhail Rumin. "And it started here in Russia."

Abakumov wrestled with his options. He could tell Stalin, but tell him what? That some Pole or Britisher had vanished into thin air? That would reflect badly. He could tell him his suspicions, but what concrete proof had he? Abakumov decided to do what he did best. Pass the buck. He would phone Comrade Beria and try to make it his problem.

After the phone call Beria in turn decided he needed a walk in the park. There he met with a man known as Witek.

"We may have a problem," Beria observed. "Comrade Viktor Semyonovich Abakumov needs to go."

"Only Stalin can endorse this. I will think on it," Witek replied. The two men parted. To an observer they had perhaps commented on the weather or passed a polite greeting. But both men knew another atrocity had been set in motion.

CHAPTER 19
# SHADES

Colonel Medvedev, alias Witek, turned his cigarette lighter over and over between his thumb and forefinger. The chrome had been rubbed from both sides until the brass was showing through. He frowned at this. He was very fond of this lighter, but he liked things to look smart.

Thinking of such trivia was his way of pondering matters at a deeper level. Another little trick he used was measuring space. He would listen to a person, perhaps under interrogation, and in his mind's eye he would be measuring the distance between two objects or counting the number of window frames. This could irritate the observer or conversation partner or even prisoner as he looked inattentive. Yet in reality the Medvedev brain would be working at its deepest level, listening intently for the slightest sliver of news or deviation from the expected. Or simply contemplating a solution to a problem.

Most answers came to Medvedev in a dream-like state. Sometimes he worried that he was mad, living this dream world as he did, like a second life. After many years he had come to the understanding that most Soviet citizens must live this way in order to survive. There were, of course, the masses who did not think. They were too busy finding food or avoiding punishment to worry about thinking.

Then there were the Pavlov dogs, mostly artists and writers living off the backs of the workers, whilst following the Party line. They mated or tied themselves to anyone they could find who'd give them a meal or a position that flattered their ego. Next were the *apartatczyks*, the minor bureaucracy and Party faithful, who croaked lies and propaganda like frogs, even when they knew the truth. The leaders he likened to pigs. Medvedev had always found the choice of pigs in *Animal Farm* by Orwell quite appropriate, especially as some of the leading Communist thinkers and beneficiaries were Jews. So pork was an ironic choice. He chuckled.

The subconscious picked up the word 'Jew'.

The security services were, of course, wolves. "I am not a wolf, but a Russian bear." The words had just slipped out. He wondered what the listeners with their tape machines would make of that. "Like Comrade Stalin," he added for good measure and security purposes. You had to be careful, even in his position as All Union Specialist Security Counter Revolutionary

Chief, reporting directly to Beria. Medvedev could trust no one except three people. They included Tadek Labycz. He held even Beria's life in his hand. Labycz was the Golden Child who had to be protected at all costs. The Westerners had a habit of shooting messengers and denying they'd had any knowledge of news.

There was the case of that silly young Jewish kid from whom Medvedev had confiscated the forbidden book, *Animal Farm*. The kid had insisted that Churchill was the saviour of the Jews. After re-education the boy now better understood that Churchill had known of the extermination camps but did nothing. For a while he had denied the camps' existence, and was unhappy when Polish intelligence informed the Americans, who also did nothing.

The pro-Arab British in Palestine were not helpful either.

The deep brain had now completely fastened on the word 'Jew'.

The whole American film industry was run either by Jews or Left Liberals. FDR saw himself as a cowboy, like that Donovan character in OSS. Medvedev admired the SIS, as had the Soviet system from the days of the *Cheka* and Reilly. Although brutality and terror were their hallmark the *Cheka* learned that the finesse of blackmail and 'buying' loyalty was the best of British tradition. In fact Reilly showed them the power of money and just how many had been bought by him in their own ranks. Early on, some of the Comrades had decided that the best way to defeat the British SIS was to join them. So the Comintern set in place sleepers who, by journalism or via university or the BBC, had become part of the SIS. People like Burgess. That man was a problem now however. He was also close enough to Moscow to have spotted Labycz and have fingered him years before as an enemy.

Instead of that fuddy-duddy Truman, the world needed a real American film star cowboy to run it. That would be a show indeed. Then wrongs would be righted. The British could have a woman prime minister like Annie Oakley. *What we Russians need is a cuddly bear leader, and then the world will change!* No hope of that, he sighed. Tap, tap went the lighter.

Burgess was not a fool. He had been a faithful servant, pulling many people into his web. He was not such a drunken idiot as the British made out either. As for Liddell's friendship with Burgess, either the British were being fiendishly clever or terribly stupid. As Menzies was going it was probably the latter, although Liddell could not be trusted fully by either side.

Now Burgess would start a hunt, with the aid of Abakumov. It was clear Abakumov must go. That other Britisher MacLean was played out too. Modin had wanted to bring MacLean in, but Abakumov had interfered and demanded Burgess bring MacLean to the Soviet Union. He wanted to see what Burgess knew about Labycz, to start tracking on the Russian end. *That can only mean the MGB has a more highly placed agent without the knowledge of the MVB. And that means a direct line to Stalin, avoiding Beria. This cannot be allowed to go on.* Medvedev sweated a little, imagining piano wire around his neck.

Mikhail Ryumin would be the man, Abakumov's number two. Not an intellectual, he had been chosen for his aptitude for torture and because he didn't represent a challenge to Abakumov. He was not the lead wolf but someone who needed to curry favour. *And this pack, they dance to a bear's tune,* he thought.

Medvedev had to wait a full two weeks before he could find an excuse and the appropriate meeting place. They met at the entrance to the All Union Agricultural Exhibition Grounds, under the towering statue of Worker and Kolkhoz Woman Worker with another Kolkhoz Woman. Surrounded by fraternal brothers from Africa, yearning to learn the secrets of the Soviet agricultural successes, Ryumin would not squeal. He was too ambitious for that.

Medvedev simply 'bumped into' Ryumin, who was on duty at the exhibition as a so-called grasslands expert. As the visitors were mainly from a semi-arid land there would be little chance of meaningful questions being put to him. His real purpose was to talent-spot young graduates for further training in Moscow, under a free scholarship. In other words, the old Soviet trick of free education, leading to indoctrination and the planting of sleepers. The result would be African misery for decades to come.

They arranged to meet in the Kievskiy Station, which they did two days later. Ryumin was not a fool. If Medvedev wanted to meet it was to his own advantage and certainly not Abakumov's. Medvedev began by talking with Ryumin about stateless cosmopolitans and how it had been necessary to root such people out by crushing them, for instance that Zionist organisation, the Jewish Anti-fascist Committee. It had served its purpose. Comrade Stalin felt it was becoming a place for counter-revolutionaries and Trotsky supporters to hide.

"Did you know, Comrade Ryumin, that British and Americans Jews sent the JAC thirty-one million US dollars to aid the Soviet war effort?"

Ryumin did not.

"However, these double-dealers supported the State of Israel against Soviet policy. Comrade Stalin has always been distrustful of Jews. You will know the MGB has been in the front line against these Zionists. Members of the JAC are accused of strong Jewish nationalism, of having maintained contact with Western espionage, and of having planned to detach the Crimea from the Soviet Union."

"Disgraceful conduct, Colonel Medvedev! But what has this to do with me?" asked Ryumin.

Medvedev delivered his master-stroke.

"Someone is protecting the Jews, and I believe it to be your boss, Abakumov."

He waited, allowing his words to penetrate. "I need you, Comrade Ryumin, to observe your boss for myself and Comrade Beria, in order to protect Comrade Stalin. There is a Jewish plot to poison our leaders. We in the MVD are watching over this situation closely, but we need to be aware of what Abakumov is doing with regard to those British Jew lovers and homosexuals newly arrived from Britain, especially the man Burgess. Have you seen how many of our doctors are Jewish? Or thought about how Comrades Shcherbakov, Zhdanov and Dimitrov all died so suddenly? These deaths are not coincidences, Comrade. We feel sure some Western plot in support of the Zionist doctors is afoot, with the help of even those at the top of the MGB. We must protect Comrade Stalin and the leadership of the Party."

"You want me to look into this?" asked Ryumin.

"I do," replied Medvedev, immensely pleased with the way the conversation had gone. It was just as his dream had visualised it. "Comrade Beria felt there was only one man for the job, and that was you, Ryumin. You have now become part of the *élite of the élite* of the MGB. The country's security lies in your hand. I particularly want you to look into Professor Yaakov Etinger. He treated Zhdanov."

*What a stupid little murdering bastard,* Medvedev's thought privately. *Brainless dolt. It is always flattery with second-rate men like him. Brilliant idea, though, the accusation of the doctors. Amazing how it simply fell into mind.* He had reasoned it carefully – this seemed the season to be anti-Jewish, so his remarks to Ryumin would be taken as in line with Party policy. The press had turned, by order, against all things culturally Jewish. Stalin was himself becoming increasingly paranoid about Jews. Just recently he had told Beria that every Jewish nationalist was an American spy.

*What was the dolt saying now?*

"And what if I do not cooperate?" Ryumin asked.

"Then you are an enemy of the people. Worse, you are protecting Zionist revolutionaries and helping your master Abakumov to hide spies and cosmopolitans. You will be killed. Probably in a car accident as you leave here, just as with Solomon Mikhoel's accident in Minsk - which, Comrade, you would know all about, just as you know it happened on Stalin's direct order. We all miss his great performances and enjoyed his State funeral, of course. You would probably end up in a hole."

"And if I agree?" Ryumin shifted uncomfortably.

"You replace Abakumov. You have Beria's word."

"Then I accept the assignment, Comrade." Ryumin saluted and they shook hands.

Medvedev set up another meeting and a communication link with Ryumin. When the two parted he felt pretty pleased with himself. Burgess and Abakumov could not move now without Beria knowing.

Beria listened to Medvedev's account of the meeting that evening in the garden of his house. They could not talk in the house, it being bugged. Beria listened quietly throughout and seemed satisfied.

"If we are to save Russia then we need to get this scapegoat Labycz out of harm's way for the moment. Did you hear from him if the West will accept me?"

"He tells me the Secret Services are backing our attempt. They find it difficult to believe you are not a Bolshevik still," Medvedev replied. "We are now in radio contact with Labycz."

"Put him somewhere safe till next year," ordered Beria.

"I hope Labycz told them that this Marxist Leninist system is crazy. Have him tell them that I consider Marx was a pseudo-intellectual half-wit and that Lenin was simply unable to grasp the complexity of running a State. Say too that I am not in favour of a market economy for Russia, but rather some form of mixed economy."

"I believe he conveyed your ideas, which came as a shock to them all. Unfortunately Labycz is still pursuing the Sikorski trail," Medvedev answered.

"That is a dangerous world indeed," Beria commented.

"Does he know that Stalin and I were negotiating a deal with Germany during Barbarossa? That Sikorski was well aware of it, undertaking his own negotiations? Those papers Sikorski was carrying could never be allowed to be published, either by the British or by us. We would both be sunk, Russia and Britain. Betrayal is best left undiscovered," Beria smirked.

Medvedev decided in that moment to hide Labycz directly under the eye of the enemy. He began to count the glass panels in the lamps suspended from the ornate wrought iron garden lamp stand. He counted fourteen and then went the other way round to see if he was right.

By the time he had finished counting he had a plan.

# CHAPTER 20

# GUN RUNNER

I do not believe that 'inspired' coincidence is rare; I have found that there are strange, inexplicable or unlikely coincidences in this world, as in the other worlds of the cosmos. Burgess and I being in the same place at the same time had been just such a coincidence.

Most of us assume, thanks to Copernicus of Poland and Newton of England, that the universe is a well-ordered machine. Coincidences and collisions are supposedly rare, especially if God is considered the Designer. Facts demonstrate however that collisions, catastrophes, explosions and phenomena beyond rational belief are commonplace throughout the universe.

I have come not to believe in miracles. But I do believe that we can create magic, collisions or coincidences, which to me are the same as miracles. If there is a divine wind, a divine spirit that energises and moves, it seems sensible that we as humans can catch its coat-tails and hang on. In the political world I had lived long enough to see that there was a power like the wind, a climate, a season that influenced world events. It was now winter, but with occasional flashes of palest sunshine to come.

Such a flash occurred, such a coincidence, one which moved my life onward as everyone wanted except me.

Kryszka was happy. His work was settled. I couldn't find peace with asking him to come with me to the East.

His Ruth was a good woman. As he had shown me over the last few weeks, a fine life existed here in England. Many of the Polish community were settling for it. True the émigrés might be bitter, active in émigré politics and journalism, but they had *settled*. Perhaps they were even reconciled with this being for the long haul. Very few of us were still on 'active service'. Those of us that were had roles in espionage and intelligence work, and were being run from London by the exile government. Or we were acting as agents run by the British and the Americans. The vestiges of our organisations were being used all over Europe for the ends of the Big Powers. When the war had ended we had circa three and a half thousand agents run by one hundred and seventy staff officers. I doubted that the situation was much different; only the handlers had changed. The agents would be run by SIS or CIA and for different purposes and, because they were not nationals of either Britain or the US, were expendable.

Everyone now knew that the Reds, the Bolsheviks, the Comintern – Communism, call it what you may – had always been the real enemy of free citizens and of democratic ideals, just as the Germans had identified. A war had been fought against totalitarianism. Millions had died. Yet Communism was now wider spread than anything the Nazis had ever achieved for their brand of Socialism. Millions of otherwise straight-thinking people had been misled into accepting that the 'dictatorship of the proletariat' was different to Nazism. Leftist activists screamed anti-Fascism as they had always done, without realising that their own actions were precisely the same as those they opposed. Being murdered by the Communist Secret Police was acceptable, but not by the Gestapo.

I had to wrestle with these issues, for it I did not, then I would be no better than those I hated. I was no torturer, but I had certainly killed in the line of duty. Daily I felt its pull, this siren thought of giving up the struggle. Was I going soft? Had I become so weary? Perhaps, the thought nagged, perhaps even I could make a life in Brighton too? Forget what was happening in the East? I could write articles , publish books, influence people that way. But my conscience always cried out in response. 'You would be safe whilst others are dying...'

The trouble was I had created *so many* lives. Each life was different, and I could happily live in each. It was becoming more difficult to separate them; they were leaking into each other. My mind was beset constantly, by heartbreak for my homeland one moment and traitorous thoughts of settling down to find happiness the next. No novel I had ever read showed heroes facing the dilemmas which haunted me. However hard I tried to settle to the thought of a comfortable life, duty always undermined my equanimity. What drove me on was the need to finish the job I had started. There was always this conflict between settling for what I could have and the intangible need to fight for freedom. I was not just counting the material cost but the cost to my soul. At the end of the day someone had to continue the fight. Many would do so if there was an opportunity. I realised for me this was more than opportunity. I was qualified, had even been groomed to this. It was a matter of duty above personal happiness, honour above self.

I spoke about my inner conflict with Kryszka at length. He felt differently to me. Having found contentment, he was determined to hold on to what he had.

We talked endlessly about the Polish Resettlement Corps. Set up by the British and Americans at the behest of the Soviets to solve the problem of those Polish Armed Forces refusing to be repatriated to a Communist-led country, the Corps had functioned to some extent. However, the British Foreign Office continued to view the Poles as subversive. It had even set MI5 to investigate the Polish ex-Combatants Association, known as SPK, believing it to be against HMG policies towards the new Communist puppet government in Poland. As Kryszka pointed out, MI5 were still trying to shut down the *Dwojka* groups in both countries. London and Warsaw suspected that, although officially disbanded, *Dwojka* still operated. Of course MI6 not only knew about this but had cooperated with *Dwojka*, especially the remnants of *Pralnia II*, the largest network of agents in Soviet-occupied Poland.

"Adding insult to injury," opined Kryszka, "the AK association is also under suspicion from Special Branch, as though they were Irish terrorists prior to the 1917 Rising or even German spies!"

Not only had the Poles given the West the code breaking Enigma on a plate, but I had a powerful radio produced by the Polish Intelligence Services right in my own home. The Foreign Office had never forgiven the Poles for continuing to broadcast their anti-Communist message to the old country. Particularly those messages from secret bases in Italy, which spoke out against the Labour government's policy of approving the new, illegal, Communist regime. The Foreign Office seemed determined that the ex-Polish Forces men in the West would not be allowed to become a nest of subversion against their Communist pals in Poland.

Kryszka and I reminisced like cattle chewing the cud. We had finally caught each other up on many of the stories we had experienced since the time we were in prison. Kryszka's favourite horror story was the British reaction to a request from almost three hundred Jewish Polish service men who wanted to travel to Palestine. "Parceled up, isolated and sent up to a camp in Thurso in Scotland, as far away as possible! But there's no discrimination in England," I joked.

"Have you heard about the Balts?" Kryszka asked. "You may remember Andrzej Kowerski, Krystyna Skarbek's partner in crime and long-term lover? Uses the name Andrew Kennedy, left over from his SOE days?"

"I know him," I said, "He has a damaged leg. I met him a couple of times but didn't realize he was involved with Kryszia."

"I bumped into him, literally on the sea front, one day not so long ago. We had a drink together in the Ship Inn. Fallen on hard times, like so many, but I guess he's still in the service like you, though probably with the British. They have likely given him a pension or something like Anders, to keep him stumm. He told me a fantastic but true story.

"The British, as we all know, didn't want our forces to stay but to return to Poland. However most of the DP camps were dominated by Poles, as were many in the POW camps. The Russians were all sent back to be murdered, due to Stalin's edict that no Soviet soldier should surrender, and that if he did he must be a traitor. Well, the Foreign Office has made it clear that no more Poles are to come to England from the camps. Poles are to be discriminated against, except for miners. There is an official called Hankey.

Kowerski has actual meeting minutes which record him saying, 'Let discrimination against Poles be hidden so far as possible, please. It will make for much trouble if it is revealed to the British public.'"

"That's hardly surprising, since HMG has always promised the Communists they would encourage Poles to go back to this newly contrived country," I interrupted. "What about the Balts you mentioned?"

"Well," Kryszka continued, "the Foreign Office Refugee Department has deemed, according to Kowerski's intelligence, that 'Balts should be given preference over Poles as they are of a much better type, more intelligent, honest and reliable'."

"Remind you of the Nazis? It seems the Refugee Department is infected by this idea of eugenics too. It's almost funny if it weren't true. Can you imagine, after everything we all fought for, the Foreign Office coming up with that policy?"

Kryszka was becoming more animated. His eyes were beginning to flash with anger too, and his English deteriorating, so he reverted to Polish.

"There's more. The idea is that if Britain is to have foreign immigrants then they should be of 'good stock'. They should also be white - thus excluding most of their Empire. Jews are to be excluded at all cost. Of the European DPs, the Poles are not to be encouraged to come to Britain. All true, Tadek. But there's more yet. The Foreign Office has allowed many men of the 15th, 19th and 20th Waffen SS divisions to come and live in Britain! Latvians and Estonians, too, including many war criminals, and all without question! The whole 14th Ukrainian Waffen SS Division has been allowed to settle here. It was thought best to keep the whole issue quiet as the British public 'might not understand the policy'!"

This was unbelievable. This further betrayal merely reinforced my feelings that something had to be done and I would have to be one of the ones to do it. Change or revenge? Loyalty or hatred? I needed to do something to hit out at this whole shitty carve-up that destroyed so many lives. There was nothing so devious and dirty as the British Foreign Office, except Soviet Russia.

For now there was nothing to do except wait and waiting did not suit me. I could walk and I could read, but when I know something is to happen then my mentality dictates 'sooner than later'! I decided I could never be a 'sleeper', spending long years waiting for an order. I invented a new category, a 'sitter' which amused me. Every day the arms race grew, sabres rattled and the rhetoric escalated from the Soviet Union. Apologists for Stalin occupied the press. I became more and more frustrated. Surely if Stalin was stopped now things would get rapidly better. The Russian people would have an opportunity at real freedom too, as well as the satellite countries. This idea became my fixed dream.

My next radio call from Witek brought a surprise. He suggested I 'hide out' for a while in Poland, out of everyone's way. Except of course, of the UB, the MGB or anyone else wanting to earn themselves a reward...

So it was that the wheel of chance turned for me once more. Everyone now seemed to think it was time for me to disappear. As Rupert pointed out at our last meeting before I left, "Philby has blown it too, Teddy. He's wriggled out of total exposure, but he knows that we are on to him. The CIA, knowing he was close to Burgess, wants him out. He was too close to some of theirs, like James Angleton, and they don't know what may have been passed on. He isn't any use to the Russians any more. Despite interviews we have no real proof except by association. But he is most likely to have tipped off MacLean of our suspicions surrounding the American Venona intercepts.

"What will interest you, old chap, is that Guy Liddell has just gotten the Joint Intelligence Committee to agree to a massive operation called Post Report. It is meant to screen a quarter of a million DPs of all nationalities, all foreign workers. They are not looking for war criminals but potential fifth columnists. According to your theory, Teddy, this gives Liddell the opportunity to find some people the Reds want to know about, but also to slip in replacements for the three agents you have identified so far. I believe, with the right politicians at the helm, we are being set up for a second generation of spies who will replace the old Comintern boys with a new set of Stalin's men. Infiltration. In other words, business as usual. So we should, on that basis, see some moles surfacing around the mid-sixties. These would be direct-trained MGB people, as opposed to Comintern idealists, courtesy of Comrade Liddell.

"As you've pointed out many times, Teddy, the link is with the 'luvvies'. It appears Liddell's just as likely to be a tip-off merchant as any other. You were also right that he, Hollis and White have made life a misery for Sillitoe since he became head of MI5, but it is almost too blatant. There's jealousy, yes, but something else underlies it all. There is a chap called Blunt, whom we are now keeping an eye on, another member, it appears, of the Burgess fan club. But also more than a chum of Liddell."

I interrupted him somewhat irritably. "Look, Rupert, you know better than I that all the sleepers or sympathisers, bar a few Welshmen like Goronwy Rees, are all sitting comfortably like you in the Travellers' Club. All English gentlemen together, all part of the establishment. The question is what are you going to do with these traitors? Give them a knighthood?"

"It's the British way, old man," he answered laconically. "The men upstairs think it wrong to give the plebs a bad impression of those of us born to lead. When we do get the odd bad apple we exile them to the far-flung corners of the Empire. It's like sex, old man. Just like the MGB we have our honey-traps, for boys and girls. We have our fixers, like Bob Boothby. The press is always ready for a naughty story. Hanky-panky by ex-public school boys sells papers. Homosexuality is plainly illegal, whilst underage girls simply get a wink.

"Getting a CB and a pension keeps the lid on things and so a *cordon sanitaire* is established and they become our creature once again. It's only the plebs, the little buggers, the rent boys, the prostitutes and people like you, my colonial friend, who get the knife quite literally. You are not an apostle.

"Look at Roger Hollis,[xi] destined for great things, a Somerset man from Wells. Neighbour of our family, so to speak. Married a Swayne girl, solicitor's daughter from Glastonbury. Loves the little Red Chinks as everyone knows, but Hollis was part of the establishment. All through the war he was 'reporting' on the Reds. Only 'we' got it wrong, didn't we? Stalin knew precisely how many atom bombs the West had and misinformed Churchill as to the poor position of the Red Army and the Republics' readiness for rebellion. So who helped with the information? All our now known feathered friends, and a few more. The leaks to the Soviets will not stop, I know that.

"So, Teddy, for your own safety you had better get out. From Moscow to Washington, everyone knows of this mysterious Labycz character Burgess fingered on instructions from Abakumov. It appears all hell broke loose in the cosy Soviet networks. Some coincidence, of course, but not one that has favoured you. The Soviets are out for your blood. So there are special instructions to you, my friend, from our man in Moscow. Here are your orders, and let us hope to hell he is not compromised. They come all the way to you via Queen's Messenger, and by my divine intervention out of sight of the FO! No one has opened it, old man, because we don't want to know. But we are sure from our intercepts of your radio contact that it will contain your marching orders. So as Menzies says, get out now before Liddell pounces."

Returning home, I was told by Kryszka that I had received a call from Andrzej Kowerski, better known as Major Andrew Kennedy of British Secret Service.

"Krystyna Skarbek wants a meet. She has something for you."

I knew she would come round in the end. I had sensed the night we went to dinner that she was desperate to share what she knew with someone who could put that knowledge to good use. She also knew how badly I wanted to discover the contents of the missing Sikorski briefcase. She knew what had happened in Cairo. She also knew which Polish officers were likely to oust Sikorski and which British counter-intelligence agents had been embedded in *Dwojka*. It was clearly time to tell.

I looked at Kryszka's scribbled note: Shelbourne Hotel, Kensington, Sunday 15th.

"Kowerski said to tell you 'the Ides of June' and that you were to come around the 'witching hour'. Typical amateur dramatics, if you ask me.

Krystyna has put off her meeting with Kowerski in Brussels by a day, just to meet you. It's urgent. She has taken a room there under the name Christine Granville."

London was quiet at that time of night. Enquiring at reception in the Shelbourne I was told Krystyna had gone out. So I wandered the street, waiting and watching, using the time to remember our last meeting. How vivacious and flirtatious this most famous of espionage agents was in her real life. NO wonder Churchill so admired her. I was more convinced than ever that she knew what happened in Cairo when Sikorski landed there. And I was convinced she knew how the British were manipulating disaffected Polish units. Only she could really say if Sikorski met German agents here, and she probably knew what was in that briefcase. The only other explanation for its disappearance was it being taken from the plane crash off Gibraltar by agents unknown or by Lubieński, Sikorski's aide, before the crash. It was a wonder she was still alive. These thoughts were enough to keep me occupied.

A taxi arrived and I saw her go in. Following quickly I spied her going up the stairs and called out to her. She turned to come down, smiling her delight at seeing me. I waited by the door. There were a few other men in the lobby.

Suddenly two of them were between Krystyna and me. A third man, small and dark, rushed her. I heard her shouting, "Get him off me!" The two men in front of me pushed me aside, leaving at speed. A sheath knife was sticking out of Krystyna's torso, which was pumping blood. For a second I stood motionless, dumbstruck. Her assassin simply stood there, yelling, "I killed her!"as the porter and two others rushed at him.

In the pandemonium, unobserved, I slipped out of the door and away. Just like the others who had barred my way.

Kryszka and I attended her funeral at St. Mary's, Kensal Green. The day was windy. The cross bearing her name swayed in the wind. It was Kennedy who rushed forward to stop it toppling. In the crowd there were many familiar faces. I noticed them, just as they noticed me. Especially the two men who had been in the Shelbourne that night.

Rupert maintained that Muldowney, her killer, would hang. Apparently he had been her boss on cruise ships and his crush on her had turned sour. "He'd intended to top himself with poison afterwards, even tried it in jail, but unfortunately the plods brought him back. Mentally deranged, old boy. That's the trouble with the Irish, they're an unstable lot. Some tiff over love letters. Somehow he got the wrong end of the stick from someone, went over the edge. "

I asked Rupert the leading question. "And what about the other two in the lobby?"

"Some rumour about three men, wasn't there? Not two?" he replied wryly.

I left it at that. We both knew why the security men were there. Shame the drug didn't work in the prison but then 'plods' have no imagination. Easier to fake a death or manipulate a manic depressive.

My orders from Witek were simple. The instructions read well. It was a clever plan.

I was to go on holiday near Hornsea for September the 10th, keep my radio close by, read books, go walking then get myself just north of Barmston Beach. On the four nights of the 17th to 20th, between twelve midnight and one a.m., I was to signal with a green light from the beach out to sea; two flashes, pause, one flash, pause, two flashes, pause, all at ten minute intervals. 'A red light will flash twice in answer. Wait till a small boat comes to collect you,' it read.

I recognised the dates chosen, the 'old wives' summer days', well-known periods of three calm weather days and nights on specific and regular dates. If the weather was bad I was to try again on the 30th for a further three nights. As things turned out the weather was on my side. The temperature was cool but dry, the sky cloud-covered.

I said goodbye to Kryszka. It was an emotional moment. I could tell he was badly divided in his own mind, fearful he had made the wrong decision. Choosing personal happiness over duty is not easy.

We made our parting at Skipsea near Hornsea. I had decided to rough it and camp. Kryszka took my car, now his, back down south, waving from the window till he was out of sight. I could hear the engine as it headed back up Beeford Lane, long after it had turned a bend. Feeling very alone I shouldered my pack and headed north toward Ulrome, cutting down the North Turnpike toward the coast. Crossing the main drain I headed out of the village toward a farm I had spotted. I was able to negotiate with a farmer a corner of a field for my bivouac tent, or a barn if the weather cut up rough. We agreed on a price for milk and eggs and his wife said she could get me some bread and cheese if I wanted. I paid for a small can of kerosene for my primus stove.

Being hospitable, and perhaps a little nosy, they invited me in for some brack and Yorkshire tea. I took the chance to embellish my story to match up with my eventual disappearance, saying I was bird-watching and taking the air, looking forward to walks and a good read away from the smog of the city.

The farmer was a weather-beaten sixty-something, his wife a pinafored, grey-haired dumpling in her late fifties. Their son, now living in Scarborough, was not interested in the farm, they said. He had seen action in Burma. "The forgotten war, as they call it," the farmer said. "Certainly changed our Tom."

I beat a retreat as quickly as I could. Hoisting my pack and carrying my incongruous but small suitcase I headed for my temporary shelter, praying it wouldn't rain. Over the next couple of days I walked north, up Hamilton Hill and across the fields. I found a likely landing site where the small cliffs broke. There was access to the beach for a farmer's cart and wagons, maybe to collect seaweed for the land. There was another track that ran down to the beach and a small promontory, like a little table, with the inlet to one side and a small cove on the other. Two elderly and seemingly unused dinghies lay overturned high above the tide line. They had become bleached in the sun. Thrift grew close around them on the shingle and blown sand. It was a warm and pleasant spot. I spent time watching gulls and gannets and other seabirds with my binoculars.

Most of the kit I'd had to hand, but finding a green torch had not been so easy. After Rupert's warning I no longer felt the house on Crown Street had gone as unnoticed as I had hoped. If I went sniffing around for a signalling torch there was sure to be trouble. So I had settled for a small torch and a green bottle from which Kryszka and I had cut the narrow neck with a diamond cutter. No one had specified the shade of green!

The plan was remarkably simple.

My cover was that I was now a serving officer in the MVD. I belonged to the special anti-subversive 'All Union Lightning Shock Brigade' as a special commissar, a colonel. My back-story was that I had been on special duties, finding counter-revolutionaries running guns. All my papers were genuine. When the Russian 'fishing boat' picked me up, no doubt the commissar on board would notify Moscow Central of the fact. The men would become heroes for saving me.

As the pick-up was a legitimate MVD operation there would be no trouble. The information at Central would be relayed to the 'All Union Lightning Shock Brigade', which actually existed, albeit only as one room with a phone deep in the bowels of the MVD. The phone was manned by very bored men waiting for precisely that phone call. They had been told that if anyone called the number they were to be immediately listed as counter-revolutionaries and foreign lackeys in the pay of Americans, arrested and brought to Beria's headquarters. The telephone number existed only on my documents. These papers gave me free access everywhere and demanded that everyone assist me in my enquiries. If the number was dialled it meant I was in trouble or my activities had been questioned. Simple and effective, and only possible in a nightmare state where fear dominated lives and bureaucracy was so large that such a scam could occur. *Or possibly in a Labour welfare state where similarities with the Soviet system abound*, I smiled to myself.

The first night no signal was returned. The wind had blown, the sea had been choppy. The next night a more regular swell had come. The night was moonless due to cloud, and an answering red light blinked back after my signal. Had I imagined it? Against orders I flashed again and the same double red came back.

Slinging my pack on my back I picked up my case and made my way down to the shoreline. Presently I could make out the white foam from a bow wave. Soon I could see a boat rowing almost directly to the right point, which took some skill. I took a chance and gave a green flash. Immediately I heard voices. The boat slid through the water towards me and I began to wade out, holding my case above my head. Two sailors, automatic weapons at the ready, jumped into the waves. My case was grabbed. Rough hands hauled me upward and aboard, scraping and bruising my shins in the process. The two guards were hauled aboard too, and within seconds the six rowers pulled away, turned in a small trough and headed out to sea. Nothing had been said. The only sounds were the movement of the oars in the rowlocks and grunts of effort from the men. We moved swiftly toward the growing outline of a trawler, bristling with radio masts. Scramble netting hung over the side. We were on board in minutes.

The powerful engines throbbed and the trawler began to make headway at speed into the North Sea. I stood on the deck, not quite knowing what to do next, whilst silent figures moved around me in the dark. A figure grasped my shoulder, propelling me along the deck.

"Welcome aboard, Colonel, we have some food and clothes prepared for you. And welcome home, Comrade. I am charged with getting you into the Baltic. As soon as we are out of territorial waters we can get some light, but for the moment we are making best speed out into open waters. We will have been picked up on radar and I presume the RAF will have a look at us in daylight, but I do not want a British sub shadowing us. We drifted in with the tide, so they will hopefully think we were looking for fish and moved with the sea, but you never know. No chances."

We slipped through a hatchway, closing the door behind us, and then through another doorway via a second bulkhead where an eerie green light showed a ladder descending to a lower deck. Moving quickly we passed through another door into a small cabin. There was a bunk and small table lit by low-level lighting. Laid out on the table was the field uniform of a colonel of the MGV. I had expected the uniform I had been familiar with. This was a grey-blue affair, with plenty of gold on the shoulder boards and a hat with a blue band. There was a pair of breeches and functional boots too; the clothes were worn but fitted me well. Captain Kurylenko pointed out spare sets of underclothes and shirts in the hold-all on the bunk, as well as a further uniform set, and some civilian clothes. Hanging on the back of the door was a greatcoat with MVD arm patches and colonel collar markings, as well as the inevitable brown leather briefcase. There were no side-arms, but then, I had my own. I asked for privacy to change. The captain closed the door as he left.

*Well now you have really done it*, I thought to myself. Since arriving I had said nothing, save for my last few words to the captain. I had decided my character as this officer would be reserved, formal, somewhat aloof. Changing into the unfamiliar gear I went back through my own pack. I decided to ditch all the clothes, retaining just my small arms, the ammunition and useful objects like my pre-war military pocket watch from the Polish army, my primus stove, and a marine heavy-duty pen-knife. "Complete with tool for removing stones from horses' hooves," I heard myself chant. "Well that's English done with for a while," I said out loud, instantly regretting it. The cabin was probably bugged. Too late I realized I would have to be more careful.

I had never liked the feel of ships, especially below decks. They were generally too warm for my comfort, and above decks too cold. The North Sea can be bitter, so I donned my greatcoat and made my way on deck. The ship had come to life and the navigation lights shone brightly. Aft the crews were slipping nets into the sea, using huge winding gear under blazing arc lights. The deck was slippery. Occasionally spray blew back from the bow as the trawler ploughed on, dragging the trawl, which pulled the bows down into the waves as they rolled forward. Spume stuck to my coat and the steel floor was slippery. I went to the gunwale and tossed my old life to the wind and sea. My trousers blew back, causing some amusement to a couple of crew members who tossed them further out for me. I touched my forehead in thanks.

Looking up I decided to make my way to the wheelhouse. I was half way up the stairway when I met Kurylenko coming down.

"Come, Colonel," he said, "You must be tired and hungry. There is some food prepared in the mess below. You can meet Political Commissar Egorov at the same time. He is one of yours."

My heart missed a beat. This would be my first real test.

Moments later the three of us were sitting around the table in the light pool of a single bulb. The cell-like mess reminded me of my time in MGB jails. The food was welcome, however, after my starvation rations in my bivouac. There were good potatoes, cabbage and some ham.

"Polish ham," Egorov waved his fork at the plate. "Good, eh?"

"The best!" I replied. "I am looking forward to more."

"You may be lucky," Egorov observed. "The Poles are short of a lot of things as their economy has not yet fulfilled the first agricultural sector plans due to subversive elements paid for by the Americans. Best to use the special Party *apparatchik* shops and those set aside for the MGB. Although you can always try the black market, in your position."

"You should be careful, Egorov," I replied sharply, "Otherwise I might take you seriously and imagine that you were encouraging a relaxed attitude toward black marketeers and smugglers. Especially,Comrade, as you are stationed on a ship. My job in Poland is to shoot such counter-revolutionaries and saboteurs. My aim is to break these smuggling rings. Remember this."

Crestfallen, Egorov was now at pains to ingratiate himself with me. He began to boast of his war exploits. As he talked he downed vodkas, along with Kurylenko. My protest that I drank only tea and water enhanced my strong puritanical pose. One I hoped which would not encourage too many questions in the hours I was destined to be aboard. After the third round of listening to his adventures at the battle of Kursk and how many deserters he had shot I made my excuses. The captain had already folded his arms on the table and laid his head to rest. He was snoring.

In my cabin I took off my boots but took the precaution of sleeping in my uniform with the Radom cocked and the catch slipped, to be sure that if I was surprised I would take someone with me. I slept well, comfortable and undisturbed. The next morning I was awoken by a knock and wake-up call from one of the actual fishermen on board. I emerged to a cold grey day, the drizzle making for poor visibility. I found the galley, where the cook rustled up some breakfast as I had slept through the watches that had shared earlier. It was clear the poor man was frightened of my uniform, and my taciturn attitude did nothing to allay that fear. I had the impression he and probably the other crew members would be happy when I left.

On deck I took a turn around the vessel. Denmark was on my right. The sea was leaden but with a deeper metallic tone than the North Sea, so I guessed we had entered the Kattegat or the Skagerrak - I had never bothered at school to learn which of the straits that guarded the Baltic was which. The Baltic was deep and cold.

I had already observed the steel door to the radio room and the notices saying 'Keep Out'. Opening the door I disturbed two marines, who swung round in their chairs as though they intended to jump me. Certainly one reached for a weapon. On seeing me they relaxed and went back to their screens.

"Which is this one?" I asked, pointing to a green screen with a rotating beam showing several blips.

The young signals officer spoke. "This one is tracking all air traffic within three hundred miles of our position. This is a commercial airliner from Helsinki and *this* a scheduled flight to Copenhagen. This is the one that interests us. It picked us up early this morning. From the echo we believe it to be an Avro Shackleton. It appears to be shadowing us since it came over from Lincolnshire. These two blips are Yak Ds, which we asked to go and tell them that we know they are there."

"Not the best aircraft, I would have thought, to act as interceptors," I observed.

"True, but we are short of long-range jet aircraft on this front. The best are reserved for the attack on the West," he answered. "The Yak has the range."

I noted the echo of the sonar and that the second signaller was now engrossed in his earphones. Two other metre-wide screens glowed unearthly green. Each dot represented something that the Russians wanted to know about, just as the Shackleton above us to the East was checking how quickly the Soviet response was to their presence.

*If it was a Shackleton then they must think us important. They had only introduced it this year.*

Two hours later we spotted the Polish tramp steamer which was my next destination. I watched her through my binoculars. She was marked up with the red and white trident as a Polsteam boat, the new name for the nationalised Polish Maritime Marine. We steamed parallel till the light began to fail. Dirty black smoke billowed from her centrally placed funnel. There were masts fore and aft with booms to hoist cargo, and two lifeboats aft of the central accommodation and wheel house. She was called *Kielce*.

As dusk fell the two ships came together, separated by a good few metres. There was a strong swell, and although the boats came to a virtual halt, enough speed was needed to manoeuvre. The Russian trawler shot a rocket line onto the Polish boat. Soon a Breeches buoy was rigged. I went over first, any moment expecting to be dipped in the briny as the ships rolled. But I was hauled on board safely. Next my gear was sent over and the line cast off. I waved to the trawler crew. The captain saluted.

I turned to the Polish captain, who also saluted before nervously inviting me to his quarters. I soon discovered the reason for his nervousness. Sitting in his cramped room he assured me that his ship never indulged in smuggling and 'this was all a big mistake'. "True," he stammered, "we took all these bananas on board in Stockholm, but you have to understand, they are almost starving in Poland. We never intended to steal them, Colonel. I do admit that we have been paid to import them illegally. Only the First Officer and myself were involved, even though the crew saw the contents. I believe that we have been caught up in an MGB sting operation. I am a loyal Party member, Colonel," he stuttered. "I will confess upon landing if needs be."

Apparently they had been told only that morning that I was to come on board. He wanted to know if they were in trouble. I was still only half grasping what the man had said. There seemed an overlap between Teresa Sawicka and Witek. Either way the guns were on board, apparently in banana crates.

"Let me see the cargo," I said.

We went back up on deck to the stern. On top of one of the major hold covers was a large tarpaulin-covered stack of banana boxes. They were long, stained a dirty red with rope handles either end. Ideal for carrying weapons.

"All three hundred are there, sir," the captain assured me. "The ten we were promised are below decks, all marked in red paint as we were told."

"Are you quite sure?" I demanded sternly.

"Quite sure. We know the rules," he replied.

"The rules say that smugglers will be imprisoned or shot." I stared into his eyes, holding his gaze.

"I have a family, Colonel," he whispered.

"How exactly did you intend to get this consignment through customs?"

"I was told that you Russians would pick it up. We are due to dock in the Russian section. Not all the port has been handed to the Polish authorities yet."

"And you have been paid well, in addition to the fruit?"

The captain nodded. "In dollars," he added. And then, "We sell the dollars to those who want to get out of the country."

Secretly pleased that my presence had put the fear of God into these poor bastards, I started to turn away. "I will overlook it this once since I have bigger fish to catch," I said, hands behind back like a modern Napoleon. He had almost crumpled with relief. Such was the fear and terror born of the need to survive. The man was a classic example of how the Communist system subjugated.

We steamed into port in the dark, slipping along the Odra river. The city was recovering from absolute devastation; the Allies had bombed the port to destruction and the Russians had accomplished the rest. The estimate was that sixty percent of the area was flattened.

The city was the result of the 'brilliant' Stalin, Roosevelt and Churchill plan to move Poland West.

Drawing a crude line map on the back of an envelope had resulted in this.

Before the war the port was called Stettin and had been the third port of Germany after Hamburg and Bremen. The Russians had taken the city in 1945. Of a German population of four hundred thousand, only about six thousand remained when the Poles took over. The Pomeranian Slavs had never really occupied the city since the 14th century. Now the Germans were gone, were those mysterious lost Pomeranians coming back? No, the city was full of displaced Lemkos and Ukrainians from the east. Additional Poles were being moved to the city from Polish areas annexed by the Soviet Union.

This was a stolen city full of stolen lives.

The Soviets had maintained control of the port, stripping it of everything viable as war reparations. Even though the 'New or Recovered Territories' were now Polish, the Soviets had taken possession of 'German' machinery, transport etc. The Poles had to pull themselves up by their boot-straps.

We came alongside a quay lit by floodlights. On the river side I could make out a wooded island. On the quayside three Soviet trucks had drawn up. Interior Ministry troops looked up, ready for unloading. The Polish crew lowered the gangplanks and set about negotiating with the waiting troops how to go about unloading. I could see the captain on the bridge, watching. He was rigid with anticipation. I adopted my Napoleonic pose once more, feet apart at the top of the gangplank, watching events.

The ship began to use its own booms as derrick cranes, lifting 'my' crates over the side and lowering them to the ground. They used cargo nets to hold the loads together. I watched as the officer in charge supervised the unloading quickly and efficiently. Outwardly he had not seen me but we both knew he had. He was keen to impress. As the last truck had its back covers closed and strapped, the captain turned at the bottom of the gangway and saluted before almost bounding up the gangplank. He came to a halt, saluting and clicking his heels.

"Captain Vasili Grigorevich Zabavnikov of the Soviet Border Guards reporting. Here are my papers. All loaded and ready for instructions, sir! In which vehicle would you like to travel?"

"The lead vehicle, Vasili Grigorevich," I replied. "You travel in the second."

I scrutinized his identity papers and handed them back.

"My orders are that under your orders we head the convoy to Poznan. Skirting Warszawa, we head to Lublin, dropping down to Stalowa Wola. After that we are in your hands."

"We head south still, Comrade, until Trzebuska near Nienadowka. And there we shall sit till our operation begins," I answered.

"Outside Szczecin we will be joined by another vehicle, Comrade Colonel, which will contain fuel and bivouac equipment. We shall be self-sufficient for the journey, as instructed."

"Thank you, Vasili Grigorevich. Let us move out."

He turned and I followed him down the gangway. As he called a trooper to collect my increasing gear I hoisted myself into the lead vehicle, a captured German Magirus 3-ton, still in service. The other two vehicles were ZiS trucks, also 3-tonners, the last towing a field kitchen. We passed through the city. Half resembled a building site. The other half looked like stark skeletons in our headlights. We saw no one, except for militia on the street corners. It was a dark place.

On the outskirts we picked up our small Poluturka truck, a copy of an early Ford, I remembered. The workhorse of the Red Army during the war.

I transferred with my new captain to a command vehicle which reminded me of a cross between a 1930s gangster car and an aristocratic phaeton. I knew this GAZ was four-wheel drive and comfortable. Comrade Captain Vasili Grigorevich was proud to point out that this was the chosen vehicle of Marshals Rokossovsky and Konev, and even Voroshilov. I was privileged, I realised. And our convoy was a fearsome troop.

As we drove through the dark Polish hinterland I wondered how many command vehicles had sheltered gun runners. Probably very few.

But thieves and smugglers?

Of those, many.

# CHAPTER 21

# THE REMNANTS

It took nearly three days of travel to reach our destination. Poland is a big country and the roads were in terrible condition. At some checkpoints we were stopped by what Zabavnikov termed 'over-zealous' Polish militia. Whom he made feel, in no uncertain terms, inferior to the masters of the world, the Red Army, and especially the MGB.

As we drove through the New Territories – or the Recovered Territories, depending on your viewpoint – Zabavnikov discussed the merits of the new collectivisation project in Poland and in particular the resistance of the new Polish *kulaks* in the south. In these New Territories the working peasants had no choice; they had to join a cooperative or work for a State Farm. When I spoke of the similar problems in the Ukraine experienced before the war, he shrugged these off as "negative thinking by the bourgeois and American propaganda. Here in Poland we have a tighter grip." I mused on the implication of that remark.

As we crossed into what I had known as Poland, I allowed myself the question why, having imposed these new boundaries upon the Polish people, no Western Government had recognised this Odra Nysa river line as the formal or legal boundary of Poland. If it was as if the West, having caused the territorial problem, wanted to exacerbate the issue and cause a future fault line between German and Pole. Zabavnikov was nonplussed by such political thought.

The Western politicians from Attlee to Truman had as much to answer for as Churchill and Roosevelt. Then of course there was that suave dandy Eden, whom Witek had summarised as a man open to every form of flattery, at least according to Russian intelligence. No one had the interest of the true survivors of the war, ordinary people, at heart. It was always a 'big idea' that mattered. I mulled over these things as we passed farmers in horse-drawn carts stacked with beetroot and small haystacks still drying in the early autumn sun.

We passed vast spaces of forest, home to every sort of wild life, including the remnants of the partisans.

Eventually on the third day we rolled into Trzebuska, a village spread along a beaten earth road. The weather, this glorious autumn, was dry. Our convoy left a trail of yellow dust, our speed whipping up the fallen yellow birch leaves, which danced around the convoy like butterflies. A few chickens fled us as we rolled on, any inhabitants having already taken flight at our approach.

The village looked timeless. Wooden houses neat and shuttered, some painted in yellow horizontal stripes. Others built of huge logs had their walls scorched to stop insect damage. The gaps between the logs were stuffed with neatly plaited straw. Dogs barked. Some ran to the gates, pulling and choking as their collars and chains yanked them to a standstill. Wooden roof tiles had replaced thatch in this village, but one grand house with a balcony now stacked with straw still maintained a fine thatch roof. At one spot we saw some new concrete block walls were being raised, presumably for new houses. And near the end of the village were some burnt-out barns and houses. Their charred limbs reached to the sky from blackened bodies, glassless windows like eyes without souls, unfeeling, pointless.

"AK partisans, I expect," observed Zabavnikov.

"Not Germans?" I asked mildly.

"Oh no," he responded, "I'm sure the local Party would have done something about it by now. The war has been over here for six years. The counter-revolutionary bandits of the AK *were* a problem in this area, first collaborating with the Germans and then opposing us when we came to bring freedom to the Polish working classes."

I needed this man so said nothing.

We drove through a small mixed deciduous copse into a small clearing bounded on one side by a small stream, both banks supporting a line of huge alder trees. The land sloped gently on the opposite side from open farmland, its heavy yellow soil already turned and ploughed. Ahead of us at the far end was a forest of birch trees, with some maples stretching, I could see, into conifer forest. Ahead of us was the real deep virgin forest, behind us the coppice leading back to the village. As we paused, a fox casually crossed our path, brush held straight and high. Its fur shone red in the sunlight.

"Rabid, I would guess," I commented, as it had shown no fear.

"Like us all," replied Zabavnikov.

The thought ran through my head that he was human after all. Perhaps his earlier comments had just been meant to impress me.

Immediately in front of us were two buildings. The smaller to the right was a wooden barn and in good condition, doors front and back. To the left was a modern concrete and brick extended house with tile roof and large portico. It too looked in good condition. All was silent, but we took precautions of taking our side-arms as we clambered out of the vehicles. Zabavnikov gave orders to a couple of the troopers to take up guard positions.

According to a large red tin plaque on the outside of the building by the door, this was an Agricultural Local Advisory Centre. As the white eagle had no crown and the plaque said it belonged to the People's Republic, I guessed this was one of those Communist 'ghost' institutions that existed on paper but never actually functioned, much like my own situation. I chuckled to myself. Inside, the place had been wrecked. From the graffiti scrawled on the walls it appeared to have been occupied by Germans and Russians. The bullet hole patterns suggested frivolity rather than anger, especially as the exterior was in good shape.

Desks had been wrecked and used as firewood. A few chairs were broken but serviceable still. Bullet hole-ridden filing cabinets had been slung about in another room. In the area used as living accommodation the same wreckage had transpired. Zabavnikov, beginning to reveal himself as a more civilised man than I would have expected for a Russian Communist, was as irritated as I was by this wanton destruction.

An oil portrait hung at a wild angle in what would have been the best room. The likeness showed a man in lounge suit with steel grey hair and small moustache. The background showed the place in which we were standing; coincidentally the trees were in their autumn glory as now. But the painting had been defaced and desecrated then left hanging on the wall, which was more than could be said for the wallpaper. The master bedroom had seen use as a latrine, and the fine tiled corner stoves had been shot to pieces. Tile shards lay everywhere. In the galley-style kitchen there was an inside water pump which, after a few vigorous pumps, yielded a gush of rusty brown water.

"Good for the blood," commented Zabavnikov and we both laughed.

"What are your orders, Comrade Colonel?"

"Unload the trucks into the barn. Secure it. Place the trucks in a park to the farmland side of the house. Minimise the fuel in the tanks and dig a pit to store the surplus fuel. Tonight we sleep in the open. Tell the cook to take a guard and go back into the village and buy food for tonight, and pay well.

"We need to set a watch and have a clear defensive perimeter. Tomorrow you clear this building and set it to rights as best you can."

"Yes sir," he saluted. Moments later I heard my orders being barked to our fourteen men.

My first job now was to let Witek know I was alive and well, without bringing the whole edifice down. A world of listeners was out there in the ether, waiting to trap the unwary. I thought of it as a world of intrigue, based upon crazy messages with no meaning, except to the right listener. For this side of the world, apart from one very important message, what I called the 'come' sign, it would have to be an intelligent guesswork game.

With the radio rigged and with some borrowed batteries, I sent out my call sign: 'Goose boy'. I guessed the world would wake up. From Moscow to Washington there were always listeners seeking both the message and the messenger. I wanted to tweak Witek and see how long it would take him to work out my cryptic message, saying I was okay and had arrived. 'Jack in the Green, Jack in the Green' indicated a forest rendezvous. It took only few more minutes for the response, 'A pint please', to come back from Witek. A few more twists of the frequencies to contact London and Rupert with the same call sign and message, and then an equally fast 'Who'd a Thought It' returned. This was the name of a pub in Glastonbury. Rupert and Witek were aware.

Within two days Zabavnikov had cleared and secured the area. He also gave me some information, reported to him by the cook, who had made friends with the villagers via proper payment. It seemed that the business previously run from the desecrated building had been a toy-making factory before the war. The owner had been the son of a local Polish landowner, who had lost his estates in the Second Republic's Land Reforms. His was the portrait which had been so desecrated – embellishments included a penis and the German and Russian words for Jew. Some partisans had derailed a supply train, so the local population was made to suffer. The man in the portrait had been hung by the Germans, along with a number of other local men, for the crime of being Polish. The men were neither heroes nor villains, just people.

I decided to take Zabavnikov into my confidence and warn him to expect trouble. "It's not unreasonable to want to live," I offered my new comrade. "We should be prepared to be caught in crossfire, and make our main building ready to be besieged. We are bait," I explained. "But that does not mean we have to be swallowed." So it was that we became more of an armed camp.

As we waited I pondered the chess board of Witek's mind.

The edge of the forest in the early morning is a place of magic. The sunlight streams through a world of freshness that assails the senses with the aroma of life itself. The eyes are caught by the silvered, shining, silken nets of spiders waiting for the day's catch. Birdsong echoes in the woodland edges and the yellow birch trees stir in the heat of the zephyr as the morning chill is touched by its warmth. A few leaves twist in the air, peppering the ground where leaves, once yellow, moulder to deepest brown.

I breathed in the rich air, deeply, in and out, rasping as I imagined the Samurai of Japan or the Sarmatians of Poland had done, stretching my chest. Nodding to the sentry I strode softly through the trees for my morning constitutional. The very soil yielded that indefinable sense and smell of life. The undergrowth gave way as the birch became interspersed with pine and conifer. Underfoot the ground became soft, spongy and empty, except for a russet cover of needles. Now the quietness of the solemn trees enveloped me. The sound of the forest is the sound of a hallowed temple. It is the stillness of sentient beings. On either side stood cinnamon-coloured trunks, some dark with age, some mossy, but all standing like soldiers on every side.

How easy it would be to become disoriented in such a place. I looked up over my shoulder to seek the sun sending its shafts to light the forest floor here and there. I wondered what wild life might stir there. Were the bare trunks as nature intended? Had some deer herd grazed the foliage to this near perfect symmetry of height? Or was this the job of the foresters? Had the politicians restarted the forestry service? I turned back.

A pheasant broke cover high above in the branches of the trees ahead. It sounded its sharp *trrk trrk* warning cry. The sound of its wings was like a thunderclap in the stillness; such clumsy, noisy birds. Yet something had disturbed it. A natural, primitive fear struck at the back of my neck. I stood still, every sense alert, but heard nothing. I consoled myself that it was probably a deer, but a darker thought crossed my mind. Partisans. For the first time I felt the insight of experience warning me of the fighters who fell from grace to banditry, desperate men whose ideals and loyalties had led them to this perdition.

In fact it was Zabavnikov, making sure that Comrade Colonel was 'aware of the dangers of bandits' and that 'breakfast called'.

*Or perhaps he had another motive?*

Witek was my guardian angel. However I still debated whether he was of the light or the darkness.

We had played chess incessantly. So I was sure he had a game in motion here, as well as in Moscow. It seemed to me that he must have assisted Teresa Sawicka for more than one reason. Logic dictated that when the guns were delivered to those who trusted me, if a trap was then sprung, that Witek or Medvedev, whatever he called himself, would still be in good shape with any of the authorities. He had played a clever game, in effect isolating me from the underground here in Poland and from my allies in London as a traitor. Other benefits could accrue to him as a result of my predicament, as well as the use of my money for gun-running.

So I decided that in my role as an important MVD Colonel I should pay a visit to the Polish UB, the feared Polish secret police. I told Zabavnikov to make the arrangements by contacting the HQ of the district covering our area, which I knew already to be down in Rzeszow. This particular move would not be what Witek expected.

The Poles were only too anxious to show us around. An officer named Hajduk took us in hand. To them our visit was an honour. They were out to show us just how zealous they were in seeking out counter-revolution and bandits. We were shown their new card index system, whereby every citizen was cross-matched against a file created of their actions. Artists, professors, doctors and dentists – all strata of society were represented. Cleaners and teachers, children and parents, all forced to play a role, wittingly and unwittingly. Like a web, everyone was connected to one another in a system of punishment and reward. Mrs X had been overheard to say that she listened to the BBC. She lived next door to Mr Y, whose son was seen not to cheer at the last school parade when Comrade Stalin was mentioned. Artist Z had a fully-installed set of listening devices in his apartment so that conversations could be overheard. In the local hotel used by Party officials each room was bugged. The files showed their mistresses, most of whom were informers anyway.

The methods of bribery or entrapment were varied; a car for a parish priest to 'help' him get around to visit the poor. A better apartment for an office worker to record the comings and goings of a neighbour. A university place for a son if a picture was painted of the heroic struggle of the working class. Extra rations to a factory worker's family for reporting the names of men visiting a certain lady. A web of corruption, undermining the morality of an entire nation.

Here too were the murder files. The lists of the disappeared, those men and women who had taken the amnesty and been shot. Any one of the intelligentsia who had come forward had never made it back to life. A few were imprisoned, those who had information who could, via slow torture, give their comrades away. I was especially 'impressed' by the WiN files. Carefully I noted the names of informers and those considered most dangerous. In particular I recognised the name of a doctor at the major hospital. The man was my contact for the guns. His office and his home were bugged. "An operative sits in the loft of his apartment building, sitting with the pigeons, listening every day to his family's treachery," the case officer proudly announced.

My equivalent and host, Colonel Hajduk was extremely helpful; he explained that as soon as I notified Dr Jankowski of the arrival of the weapons, that the man would be watched, monitored, picked up and interrogated for the pick-up point. When the bandits came to collect the weapons the trap would be sprung by two units of the KBW Internal Security Corps, supported by a Company of regular troops. They expected the bandits to come in a force of around thirty men, he said, mostly from the Naradowy Siły Brojne, the National Armed Forces. The UB expected to capture the officers for interrogation, but the rest would be executed on the spot. The nearby village would also be taught a lesson. Two farms in particular were trouble spots. These would be burnt out, the occupants sent off to the New Territories.

I was elated. By sheer chance I had stumbled across Witek's double deal. And now I could prepare my own chess move.

Zabavnikov and I invited Hajduk to lunch, along with his number two, a certain Major Filipov. They suggested the café in the Wanda Siemaszkowa Theater, a haunt of Party members. It was pleasant enough and quite plush, a different world from the half-starved workers' canteens and homes.

Filipov had been a Soviet partisan, caught behind German lines in Poland. He was full of the old Communist bullshit about 'bands of White Poles', proud that as early as 1943 the Soviet Partisan leadership had ordered the Polish underground be discredited, its leaders assassinated and all units 'dissolved'. And this old bastard had been part of it.

"We were ordered to call them protégés of the Gestapo," Filipov went on. "I know that counter-revolutionaries like Jankowski cooperated with the Germans around Wilno to fight us Soviet partisans," he added triumphantly.

I was surprised by Zabavnikov, who interrupted him smoothly. "If you had orders to shoot and destroy the AK, would you not think it reasonable that units sought arms and shared intelligence with German units about what was becoming a new enemy rather than their liberators? It can hardly be surprising that two enemies unite sometimes against a greater threat."

Filipov blinked, taken off guard by this remark. Zabavnikov pressed his point home.

"How, Comrade Filipov, did you come to be in the UB? I would have thought that you would have returned to your unit in the Motherland? Perhaps you were concerned that we in the MGB would look at your war record. You know that Comrade Stalin has always considered many Soviet prisoners to be deserters, and that some partisans were only forced by circumstance into soldiering after they had 'lost' their units."

The question remained unanswered, perhaps because Hajduk could foresee the two men in collision. "In the beginning we had to rely on a variety of men for the service, but today we have a predominantly Polish security force."

Joining in Zabavnikov's combative mood I followed his statement up with, "Yes, but Soviet advisors still run the system. Our Colonel Bezborodov effectively runs the Polish Ministry of Public Security. Never forget that."

I enjoyed watching him squirm. "Communist Polish partisans did a good job of betraying their own people to the Germans and the Soviets. What do you think the motivating factor was – ideology? Or love of the Soviet system? It could hardly be patriotism with a common enemy in the country."

"I fail to see your point," he responded.

"My point, and I think it is the same as that of Comrade Zabavnikov, is that we live surrounded by men who would betray their own mother. I just asked what the price was for those who desert and those who betray. We in the MVD have to be watchful of those who work for us, that's all, Comrade."

Filipov came back to the conversation. "Doctor Jankowski, the man you wanted to know about earlier, is a counter-revolutionary."

"On that we can all agree," I added. "Have some more Georgian wine. Comrade Stalin has asked us to be especially watchful of Zionist imperialists in your opinion on this matter; has the UB been purged of its Jewish elements?" I asked this smoothly, ignoring Hajduk, who was evidently Jewish.

My entire questioning was a game, to make them uncomfortable, to make them squirm, a sort of perverted personal revenge on my part. Zabavnikov I still could not fathom.

"It transpires Jankowski was also connected to that Polish woman Irena Krzyanowska or Sendler, the one who worked with that Polish organisation to save Jewish children. She placed the children with Polish families, or in convents. Some were even smuggled to priests in parish rectories and from there put with local villagers. I heard she listed their names and buried them in jars so that after the war they could trace their relatives."

"Do you have a problem with that association? For after all, she and the Polish Żegota saved thousands of Jews. You know that when arrested by the Gestapo, even after her freedom was paid for by bribes, she was dumped in the woods? She survived, even though her legs and arms had been broken. You could easily access her file, Comrade Filipov. She too is not popular with the Government here. Is she a heroine or a traitor?"

My question hung in the air like an ice-pick.

"I am interested too, Comrade Filipov, in view of the attitude you have toward the Jews now." Zabavnikov in his turn took up the game. "Comrade Hajduk, did you change your name to a Polish one? I have observed this to be a fashion here in Poland, for Jews now to use Polish names rather than family names?"

Defensively Hajduk responded, "I did so in line with other UB officers like Goldberg, now Różański, and State Prosecutor Reisler, now Sawicki. It is a tactful shift, to improve relations with the workers."

"Why was that necessary?" I enquired mildly and, apparently, innocently.

Obviously needled, Filipov took up the challenge.

"I am sure the Comrade Colonel knows well that in the Polish Eastern territories the Jewish population, unlike their brothers in the West, welcomed the Red Army as liberators. They became active in hunting down White Poles and Counter-Revolutionaries.

"Rather enthusiastically, many became involved in the murder, deportation and pillage of hundreds and thousands of Poles and Polish homes. They were the backbone of the Soviet Administration and Commissar system and did not endear themselves to the local Poles or Ukrainians. Hence the revenge Jedwabne massacre of Jews by Polish Catholic Gentiles back in '41 when the Germans invaded.

"Poles got their own back, with help from the Germans. The local Jews were rounded up, made to sing Soviet songs and break up the recently erected statue of Lenin. They were then locked in a barn with the pieces and burned alive. The Germans shot them as they tried to escape. Those were bad times. People remember on both sides."

Sipping my wine I raised my glass. Over the rim I stared Filipov out as I replied, "Bad times indeed, which seem to continue. For as I remember, Comrade, when it was necessary for the West to see the Polish Second Republic as anti-Semitic, events at Jedwabne and Kielce were widely publicised. Am I not right in thinking that the actual perpetrator, Mayor Karolak, was never found? Am I not also right in remembering that in a Polish People's Court trial some twenty or so of those supposedly responsible were judged? Most were released after it was discovered that the UB had fabricated evidence and tortured those involved until they confessed to crimes they had not committed.

"It was Heydrich's policy to stir up trouble in those territories. Reminiscent, I believe, of anti-Jewish policies now in this country – and indeed in the Motherland?"

I could see stark terror and confusion in both of our UB counterparts. They simply did not know how to handle this last remark.

For my own sanity as much as anything else, I pressed on.

"You see, Comrades, policies change and evil persists on all sides in times of war. The trials at Nuremburg gave the impression that crimes were committed only on one side. That was never true. Tell me of any Jew from that time, or any other Soviet citizen, who has been tried for crimes against Poland. Will the Jewish population apologise for their treachery toward the Second Republic? No. And why should they? As many Jews fought for the Republic. It was not the Jewish population as a whole which was pro-Soviet. That would be as absurd as the Polish nation apologising for Jedwabne – which might be a nice propaganda exercise but has no relevancy to the individuals involved. It is we, comrades, who obey orders and pull the trigger. It is we who will have to avoid the bullets of a firing-squad one day."

"If we are all done here, perhaps we should return to the office," Zabavnikov volunteered. There was a relieved consensus.

Back at the office the atmosphere became more relaxed. I explained that our job was nearly finished. We would contact Dr Jankowski and set the operation in motion. But our MGB band were mere observers, not even advisors, so they would keep out of any fire-fight. The UB man saw the sense of this.

"Leave People's Poland to do the job of clearing out any Imperialist lackeys and British spies," he agreed.

As we left the yellow ruins of what was once an elegant mansion, I was mightily pleased with myself. In fact I had an inner sense of elation which I tried not to show. Such feelings are dangerous. They lead to error.

For once I had outsmarted them all, but right now I had to capitalise on the information.

It was time to visit Dr Jankowski.

Our Phaeton, replete with red flag and staff officer flag, pulled up outside his hospital, obviously attracting attention. The reception was obsequious rather than solicitous. My request to see the doctor was accorded. Jankowski agreed to meet me in the hallway and accompany me personally to his office. I hoped this would give me enough time to warn him about the bugging and to pass on my real written directions.

Jankowski was a round-faced, chubby man with nickel glasses which suited his features. I noticed his nails were expertly manicured. We smiled at each other and for the benefit of the listeners talked of the weather and the problem I had with an imaginary ulcer.

I deliberately asked him for pen and paper so the listener would know I was giving secret instructions, to set the trap. The UB would love to have that piece of paper, I thought, so I would keep it. On it I wrote, amongst other things, 'I am sorry, doctor, but I do not see a way out for you. Will you go to the forest?'

His reply was simple: 'No, I am too tired, I shall wait for the UB to call, put up a fight and then give in and give them the facts. I know their methods. They will think I have been recruited, so I will ask to go back to my office, where I will take the capsule.'

My next question, hastily scrawled: 'What of your family?'

The reply was matter of fact: 'My wife will run tomorrow to her sister in Warsaw. My son is in the army. Who knows?'

He accompanied me back to reception after I had ascertained that he knew exactly what to say and do. This double blind rested on his shoulders and his courage.

But it was he who surprised me. "We cannot thank you enough, sir. May Poland remember you and us some day."

I felt so humbled. All the doubts which had assailed me in the West evaporated. I was not an assassin but a soldier, fighting to the death. These people needed support. They needed to be known of. They were heroes with no one to remember them. Cursed soldiers, people who were sacrificed for a Poland yet to come.

How could I have ever contemplated failing these people?

I wondered in that second how Kryszka would feel if he were here. But he was not.

"Times are changed here, sir," Dr Jankowski continued. "The people settle for whatever is on offer. Any government is better than none. The class war has been fought and the bourgeois eliminated. The intelligentsia killed or subjugated, whether Pole, Jew, Ukrainian or other. The peasants and farms are collectivised, the shoemaker, the tailor, the carpenter gone. Capitalist swine. The children are taught a new version of history. You have to queue for basic foods but you can get a job and, if you join the Party, a promotion. Slowly things get better. Keep your head down and your mouth shut and your eyes closed, that's the way now. We work till we drop, we are all so tired. Even the man who swept the floor and became the factory manager learns in time how things work, or else fools the system. Figures, norms, targets, and all the paperwork and administration to check it all. This is not the country you knew. Only the church remains a bastion. No one needs bandits today; bandits are history."

We shook hands and I watched the retreating white-coated figure walk to his destiny.

Two days later our troop decided to have a celebration. The cook had traded and bought a little suckling pig. The workers might be half-starved and everything in short supply, quotas and inspectors might be everywhere, but peasants always have a way of surviving.

We were the beneficiaries.

The Comrades, Colonel and Captain, were the good guys that night. We did not set the guards as all was quiet. The weather was fine, the fire roared, the piglet roasted, the vodka flowed, the beer was drunk. An accordion played, the old songs were sung. The troop staggered to their bed-rolls late. Some opted for the huge bonfire side. Even Zabavnikov succumbed, assisted by a little powder in his drink.

A mere fifty metres away no one saw the comings and goings of dark figures to the rear side of the barn. No one saw or heard the jingle of harness or the clop of hooves swathed in blanket to muffle the sound, or the soft click of the driver's tongue or the turning of greased wheels on axles.

The next morning brought headaches, dry mouths and preparations for leaving. The plan was that in the night or early morning the partisans would be trapped by the Security troops and regular army. Engines were started and checked over. Order of convoy was agreed. The village elder would be thanked. But it would be a night of waiting. We were ready to leave the following day.

At first light a salvo of mortar rounds 'carrumped' nearby. Polish voices echoed in the forest. Sharp cracks of rifle fire were heard at some distance. The rumble of tank tracks was heard followed by a huge explosion. The rattle of machine-gun fire broke out in staccato bursts in the forest. Some small artillery shells howled overhead, apparently fired from small field-guns in the farmland. There was more shouting. The small-arms fire became almost continuous. We could see now some khaki figures in greatcoats at the edge of the wood facing inward to the forest, firing at unseen enemies. Fireflies of return fire came and went from the dark forest. Machine-gun fire ripped through from the farmland, kicking up dirt near the edge of the wood and stripping splinters from trees. Bullets ricocheted off our building as government troops sprinted across the clearing toward the alder trees. One fell and was hauled away by his comrades. Mortars opened up once more. Zabavnikov was furious. Some of the Polish regular troops had taken shelter around our vehicles.

There were long lulls, followed by quick and short actions. From our position we could spot the firefly gun-flashes amongst the trees and hear their crackling noise. But we could see or hear little else. Some khaki regular soldiers appeared to be in the barn area. Then they appeared to be forced back to the woods. The fighting looked to move to the village.

From the farmland came the rattle of sub-machine fire and loud cries, then a silence fell and we smelt the acrid smell of gun-smoke and explosive.

Without warning five horsemen crashed from the farmland, waving and firing machine pistols, one holding a sabre aloft. They headed toward the skirmish line at the forest edge, where a line of Security troops had been formed. As the kneeling men turned and stood to face the cavalry, a mass of fire opened on them from the woods. Many fell. One of the horses stumbled and the thrown rider lay prone whilst his mount struggled.

The horsemen swerved, dismounted, and ran into the barn.

"Magnificent!" said Captain Zabavnikov. "Magnificent! I am proud to have lived long enough to see what one of the last charges of the Polish cavalry. There cannot be many more." He let out a long sigh.

As we watched men ran from the barn and vaulted onto their horses. One struggled with his reins. With one foot already in the stirrup he couldn't make the saddle. Half on, half off his horse, he vanished into the forest. Two partisans had broken cover and dragged the injured rider away. One of them shot the horse.

Everything happened in a mixture of slow motion and cinema. When the barn exploded we didn't expect it. The force blew in our temporary wooden shutters, sending shards of wood sharp as daggers into the plaster-work and walls. The sound wave of the explosion buffeted the building and our ears. Debris blown into the heavens started to rain down. Several trees were alight.

Recovering, we looked at the devastated building, which was in effect no more. Charred beams still stood, flickering with flame, but the roof had gone up. Scattered pieces of russet red banana boxes strewed the clearing floor.

"Well, that seems to be that," I muttered to Zabavnikov.

"I would have expected a real firework display from all the ammunition. You know, bullets whizzing through the air? Odd that. It was almost as if there were none there at all. But I expect the explosion will satisfy the plods."

He smiled.

Zabavnikov. Intelligent and unnervingly enigmatic.

"Next move for you, Moscow," he said.

# CHAPTER 22

# BERLING'S MAN

"But not just yet, it appears." I nodded to the tree line where a partisan had appeared with a white flag.

"Russkis! We should talk," he called.

"Shall we?" asked Zabavnikov.

"I'll see what they want," I replied. Our sergeant swung the door open, carbine at the ready, and I walked out onto the steps.

"Safe conduct?" I called.

"Agreed," came the reply.

I walked toward the partisan, who had melted into the forest. Once out of sight of the building the man turned and saluted. "Welcome, sir!"

In a clearing sat a number of khaki-clad regular troops. To one side was a row of bodies with the red flash of the Internal Security Forces. Men were working the bodies for clothing and boots. The officer in charge saw my glance.

"No quarter here, Kapitan Labycz. It is kill or be killed. All we can do is take a few devils with us. We know we have no future from our old allies. It is just that we will not give in. We hope to become a legend, to inspire a few. We have certainly been out here too long for amnesty." He grinned. "I wanted to thank you for the weapons. We are better armed now than when we were in the regular army."

In fact, though unkempt to some degree, I was surprised that many still wore the uniform of the Second Republic, or at least parts of it. Most wore *czapskas*[xii] of some sort.

"A good deal of the weapons have already gone south, toward Żywiecand Nowy Targ, into the Beskids, Pieniny and the Tatras," he said. "The government has a firmer grip in the north. I simply wanted you to see us and remember us. I want you to tell London who we are. I want you to tell New York, Washington and Chicago that we fought the fight to the end."

Moved, I said, "I will, you can be sure."

"Now, Kapitan Labycz, what would you advise we do with this gentleman?" He pointed to an officer of the Regular People's Army. "The boys we will release, but this chap, Major Eugeniusz Wieczorek, is their commander."

As the Government troops had moved into ambush position, the partisans had moved in small groups behind them. In the confined forest the regulars had been surprised. Though far superior in number they had been caught off balance and outwitted. The artillery units had been overrun and the tank disabled early on. Units had fired on each other in the confusion and in the end had withdrawn, leaving over thirty dead and seventeen prisoners, of which nine had been shot as Internal Security troops. A small victory for the twenty-odd partisans. The others had gone south with the guns, the officer explained.

"So what do we do with you?" He addressed the regular army major. "Whilst the lads here and in the UB will be happy that the arms were blown, you know differently. Are you a traitor, Major?"

Wieczorek pulled himself together and stood upright facing these men, whom he considered comrades-in-arms but misguided. "Am I a traitor? Perhaps you can tell me. In 1939 I was a lieutenant in the KOP[xiii] Sarny regiment," he said. "We had to stem the attack of the Soviet 60th Rifle Division. We held out till the 19th September. I, along with a few other survivors, headed south. We were captured on the 25th of September."

He spoke clearly, his voice unwavering. "I had a wife and a young daughter, three years old. She died in Kazakhstan when she was sent with my wife to the *gulags*. Her crime? Being Polish and the offspring of an officer. My wife survived and returned to Poland. She now lives in Wrocław but we are estranged, because she cannot accept me being in the military. Before the war we lived in Pińsk, a beautiful Polish city. Now, thanks to Comrade Stalin, it is in the country called Belarus.

"I was imprisoned with many other Polish officers at Starobelsk. We heard a new Polish Army of the East was to be formed. Names were called. People went. I was interned in a camp in Kozielsk, together with several thousand other Polish officers, professors, border guards and policemen. I was interrogated by Vasili Mikhavlovich Zarubin. Because I could speak passable Russian I was attached to a group of Polish officers being moved by train to a small station in Gniezdovo near Katyn. Some of us were sent off in buses with darkened windows. Myself and a few others, including some in the anti-Soviet Prometheus movement, were taken off in buses elsewhere.

"I now know there were about three hundred thousand Polish soldiers in the *gulags* or POW camps. Since the German invasion we had changed from enemies into allies. Comrade Beria wanted to form an anti-German Polish army. Comrade Stalin did not. Malenkov, Kaganovich, Molotov and Zhdanov all agreed with Stalin. This led to the Katyn massacre. If they were to have a Polish army it would be a workers' army and not one ruled by the legitimate London government.

"Beria himself saved some few hundred of us, me included. But I did not know this till much later. True some were communist stooges, but many were not. Those of us who ended up in the training house of Berling's army were a mixed political bunch. Of course, we had political re-education but we did not have to believe it. I was just happy to be alive.

"When you say 'training house', by that you mean the 'Villa of Delights' at Malakhovka, just outside Moscow? Beria's rehabilitation and re-education centre? " I interjected. "Where all the real turncoats or hard reds were sent?"

He ignored my inflected question and continued sidestepping the issue. "General Anders' Army left to form the Polish 2nd Corps in the Middle East. I never had the chance to join him, but I would have done, believe me. Many of us were left, unable to make the assembling stations. There was either no transport or we had the wrong papers or the information was withheld by a camp Commissar. There were many reasons why some never made it to the Army being formed.

"I did not know that Berling should have co-operated with Anders, or that during the evacuation Berling deserted and went over to the Red Army. Neither did I know that Anders' field court had sentenced him to death as a traitor. What was I supposed to do?

"I was assigned to the Polish 1st Tadeusz Kościuszko Infantry Division, later a Corps, and later still the First Polish Army. The leaders were General Zygmunt Berling, General Karol Świerczewski, an ex-Soviet commander but also a hardened Polish Communist, and Colonel Włodzimierz Sokorski, also a communist activist. Berling I believe to be an honourable man, and of the three, the only regular Polish army man.

"I accept that most of the officers were Russian but the boys were Polish mostly deportees, drawn from Siberia and Kazakhstan. True, we had political officers and true we got into bother if we sang Polish martial songs, but we were to fight Germans. I had also realised what had happened to the rest of the Polish officer corps at Katyn. I am not a complete fool.

"As we marched we grew. There were thousands Stalin had never allowed to reach Anders. Poles in gulags everywhere were now allowed to join the colours. There were refugees and POW's – they all joined. We wanted to fight our way home.

"Beria and Stalin knew we were a national army. As most had been in the gulags they were hardly loyal to the Soviet Union. So, yes, we were kept close by the NKVD and our political officers. Dissent meant death. We became five infantry divisions, a tank brigade, four artillery brigades and an airforce."

He paused and cleared his throat. I watched as he pushed a finger around his collar, struggling now with his emotions. I felt sorry for him standing there alone, smart, polished and well fed, contrasting so sharply with this ragamuffin group of partisans. Was he a sheep amongst wolves? Or perhaps a policeman amongst brigands?

"I was at Lenino where we lost almost a quarter of our men. I fought at the Vistula crossing at Puławy. I sat and cried as I watched Warsaw burn in the Uprising, whilst the Red Army sat and watched.

"*We* did not sit and watch and do nothing." He became agitated and shifted his feet, almost pacing on the spot. "We disobeyed the order not to help. We tried to cross the Vistula, but without Soviet support it was a blood-bath. We tried a second time. This time we got a foothold on the west bank for a few days. But there was no supporting help from the Soviets or the Russians. The AK was intended to die; Stalin had ordered it. We lost two thousand Polish First Army men in the attacks. We did try to cross but were cut to pieces. Berling lost his command for making the attempt.

"I heard the Western Allied radio stations broadcast that "the great Battle for Warsaw" had entered its 'most decisive stage'. I heard them praise the help 'Marshal Stalin was giving the besieged Poles'. All lies. Our Soviet radio stations, too, when it was clearly over, suddenly began to side with the 'adventurers' or, 'criminal elements' as the AK soldiers had been branded. You think I should trust the West more?

"I was with the breaking of the Pomeranian Wall and at the Battle of Berlin, and I was there from the first attack on the Seelow heights. Our Polish Army, whatever its so-called politics, was the only military unit besides the Red Army to stick its national flag over the ruins of the German capital.

"You sing of Monte Casino, but never about us at Berlin. No school child knows of us Poles, only of the British, Americans, or of the French Resistance and of course the great ally Russia. But never of us.

"And after the war…well, I am a career soldier. What was I supposed to do? I came home to a new Poland. It needed experienced army men. Yes, I knew things had gone wrong. Yes, I knew that the Polish Army was little more than a branch of the Red Army. But when my men deserted and ran to join the partisans I did not.

"I see that our schoolbooks are being rewritten, our history falsified. I see our children brainwashed as Communists. I see the food shortages and the corruption. But the country *is* being rebuilt. New flats, new industries, no crime, no unemployment, things *are* changing. The old class structure has gone. I see the theatres opening and art blossoming. It is a better world. People in Poland want to forget, to live, to rebuild."

"So why are you here today? What was your role here? What did you expect to happen? Did you intend to kill Polish soldiers? " the partisan officer challenged him.

"I am here because I am a Polish soldier under orders," he responded.

"At Nuremburg, following orders was no excuse or defence, agreed? You are here under orders from an illegal government in a territory imposed by three foreign men and subdued by a Soviet Security Force. Yes or no? Under orders from a Stalinist regime against which you fought and which still occupies our country as foreign invaders? You came here to kill us," the partisan officer cried, "To burn out farmers, whose only crime is to be anti-Soviet and be loyal to the legitimate government."

"I am a Polish soldier under orders," the prisoner replied more quietly.

His men were listening and looking on, miserably. Some wept. One rocked back and forth. One or two of them looked defiant.

The partisan turned to me. "Do you believe this is fair?"

I paused, thinking of all the warfare and blood this country had seen. I thought of my British education and how easy it would be to let that conciliatory side of me dodge the issues and compromise saying, 'it doesn't matter anymore, time has passed." I thought of the agonies people had endured, the way the country still suffered now. I heard myself say "I agree it is fair. We are all heroes. We have all fought for Poland. But the Communist regime is simply illegal."

The partisan emptied his revolver, leaving one cartridge. He waved toward the trees. "Over there," he said to Major Wieczorek and handed him the pistol.

As the man moved off I asked myself what I would do if I were him. Run? Turn, try a lucky shot and then leg it? Anything but shoot myself. But then, emotional pain is a terrible thing and should not be underestimated. How long had he suffered? What nightmares had he endured? This was no Hajduk or Filipov. Living with oneself can be so depressing. The man would know he had no real future.

I saw him lift the pistol. I would have placed it against my temple, but he placed it in his mouth. I saw the back of his head explode in a fountain of red and white. *Fitting*, I thought, *those colours.*

The partisan officer signalled to his sergeant, who had the rest of the prisoners stand. They had been roped together in one line. "Now piss off, the lot of you," the sergeant shouted, "and don't come back till you are grown up, you bunch of lily-livered fuckers! Go and sit at home and stick your manhood in your girl. But don't you show your arses round here again, pretending to be men, or else I shall stick your dick up your own backside! You want to work with the Soviets, that's your problem. But don't come back here to free Poland, here in this forest. Now git!"

Almost unbelieving of their luck but still roped together they started to shuffle out of the clearing in an ungainly conga.

"We are not bandits or barbarians, are we?" The officer's tone was pleading. I recognised in it the same yearning for understanding I had felt in myself and knew the partisan's question was in earnest.

"May I know your name," I asked.

"Best not," he replied.

"Sir, whatever your name is, you, along with your troops you are the remnants of the best Poland ever had. I would like a name to pass on in history some day."

"My name is Radian. This is Sergeant Kirszenstein."

I nodded in response, thinking how ironic that both men had good old historical names. One pure Polish, the other pure Jewish. And both men faithful to the Second Republic.

I turned and walked away without looking back.

At the building the trucks were already revving. Zabavnikov was pacing up and down, hands behind his back.

"I heard a shot?"

"Well, you can guess," I replied.

"Moscow it is then, Comrade Colonel. Let's go. To the airfield, sergeant!" he shouted over the engines' roar.

We left a trail of yellow dust in the air. It hung like a mist that – like life – is here momentarily. The fine particles slowly settled to the earth. The red fox looked unblinkingly at the clearing. It sniffed the air, separating smoke and burnt wood from dust and meat. It sniffed at the dead horse and began its meal.

Perhaps it had aspirations to be a wolf.

# CHAPTER 23

# MOSCOW

My arrival at a military base well outside the city was low key. No welcoming committee, just my ever present shadow, Zabavnikov.

We drove in through flat countryside in raw weather that had turned wet and dull. Moscow was very unlike what I had expected. The 'workers' paradise' was, in the main, a repetitive landscape of unimaginative flats interspersed with rural squalor unchanged since Catherine the Great. Once inside the garden ring, the architects had been given a free hand in modernism. The older, historic quarter was in turns either stunning or derelict. The boulevards wide but empty and the city much more open with extensive public garden areas, so different from what I had imagined.

One could not fail to be impressed by the seven sisters or skyscrapers ordered by Stalin to compete with the USA.

I had time to look around over the next few weeks. Having been given a role as a high-up *apartczyk*, I played the waiting game, sensing I was gradually being accepted and finally becoming almost unnoticed by my colleagues. Apparently I was now part of an élite group called Special Operations, *Inostranny Otdel,* which allowed me an office of my own. The one-man phone operation to secure my existence was kept in place somewhere in the bowels of the same building.

When I wasn't working I spent my time exploring and enjoying the sights. Moscow State University up on Sparrow Heights was still under construction but already nearing completion. Its façade and sweeping views were impressive. These were buildings and sites built to impress. The Ministry of Foreign Affairs was little short of a palace, with interior decorations of dimensions and wealth to match that of any *Czar*. Vast hotels were being built, all in a style I understood to be called *Russian Gothic Baroque*, but which the locals had dubbed Stalinist. To call these buildings grandiose would be an understatement.

On better acquaintance with the city, and after my first unfavourable impressions had relented, I was surprised by the many avant-garde buildings had been designed and built in the thirties. Upon reflection I had no real reason to be surprised other than my own prejudice. After all, London had its fair share of new style buildings, and in America and Canada everything was new. So why was I surprised by Russian achievement?

Once I took tea at the Zuev workers club down on Lesnaia Street. I was conscious of the use of light, the very airiness of the place. Similarly the Mostorg department store, which my companion Zabavnikov assured me was built to 'allow the curious public to see inside and feel welcome', was a triumph of minimalistic construction. Zabavnikov's cousin lived in the Narkomfim housing complex, designed to help break up the normal social family structure by having communal kitchens in a separate pavilion and minimising personal accommodation. It certainly was a brave New Order.

Of course, the jewel in the crown was the Metro. I knew it had been planned under the Czar but building hadn't gotten underway until the 1930s. But I was not prepared for its grandeur. What a sumptuous extravaganza the stations were. I thought of them as cathedrals of the Soviet religion. Monuments to the Soviet workers and tunnelers – with décor to match. What mentality drives such schemes, when people were dying and starving, I wondered? How many bones of slave labourers lay beneath those rails?

The Komsomolskaya-Koltsevaya station had opened earlier in the year. It simply took my breath away, with its soaring, ornate columns like an Egyptian temple. Huge mosaic murals decorated the walls, depicting the Russian fight for freedom. What a joke, I thought, considering the theme was Stalin's idea. The station could be best described as a large jewelled icon. Gilt panoplies of Russian history caught the eye everywhere I looked. Red granite platforms seemed to run forever. Chandeliers threw light onto the marble walls. How much cleaner and brighter than London or Paris the system was. This was the ultimate display of Soviet wealth, progress or power. But I could not avoid the question as to its human cost, not only in terms of lives but in morality.

Despite myself I was impressed by Moscow but quickly came to see how, as with so many world leaders who sit in sumptuous capital cities, just how unreal the world is.

The Cathedral of Basil the Blessed, with its ice-cream-like onion-domed towers, now a State Museum, reminded me that the progress I saw was that of a czar; czars Lenin and Stalin were as power-hungry as the rest of those whose wealth and power had exceeded their capacity for humanity. The immense sweep of Red Square, with the seat of the Government, the Kremlin, on one side and the historic merchant quarter on the other, brought home how powerful the Moscow military and workers' parades really were.

Moscow contained another lesson for me – of totalitarian power. How impoverished had ruined *Warszawa* become due to this place? And how many other places around the Soviet empire were bound in slavery due to this wealth? These were questions I asked myself sitting in the dark in my little MVD flat, aware that my every fart and sniff was recorded by some *apparatchik*.

Medvedev had met me on my arrival the first day and gone over the ropes.

"You have putting on weight since I saw you last, Tadek," was his opening remark. "You need to be fit for this job." He laughed. "You still fight me, even when we are friends. That was a good firework display you put on down there in Poland, even if it caused some paper shuffling for me. How could I otherwise explain that we are now arming the remnants of the Polish resistance!" He gave me an affectionate bear hug. I returned the gesture.

It was a genuine moment of comradeship. An acceptance that whatever the differences between us, we now had to move forward together, to finish the task we had set ourselves, for good or bad.

"Be polite but tight lipped towards your colleagues as you 'work' on the secret case assigned to you. The men with whom you will be working worship Beria," he told me. "They are the backbone of the MVD, especially of its power struggle against the MGB. They are fighting Beria's secretive war of survival against Stalin's war of selective deaths. And now you belong to them too."

I was living on the edge, whichever way you looked at it.

"Beria's men are everywhere. We have our own armoury and special units outside the MGB. Our people are mostly in leading positions, even within Stalin's personal domain. Make no mistake, Tadek. Beria is just as formidable as Stalin, for all his change of politics." He slapped me on the back. "And now you join the elite the great MVD. I will introduce you."

I was trapped now within the web of the system. Whatever my thoughts or feelings, I had a sense of living out my destiny now. To do that I had to live day by day, knowing the MGB would worm and wriggle its way to disclose or discover at any moment what this 'newcomer' was doing. Whatever Witek said about the control by the MVD if anything happened, they would look at me. But was I so very different to anyone else in the system? Every men and woman on the streets had the same problem; how to hide themselves, their souls, and stay safe.

I had been assigned a flat in a complex close to MVD headquarters on Lubyanka square. The whole MVD structure housed the hunters of the enemies of the peoples. The Special Operations unit was designed to hunt down traitors outside the USSR. My new colleagues were a select group and treated me with respect from the very beginning. As the weeks passed I played my role, appearing to them as a leading hunter, a wolf in sheep's clothing. I discovered I had access to secret police records, even from before the Revolution, right back to the Tsarist regime. Those records, I also discovered, included my mother and father's as well as their friend Ivan Patterson's, alongside such 'famous' people as Boris Savinkov and Leon Trotsky. Of Sikorski I found nothing. The filing clerk I consulted must have reported my enquiry immediately to the interceptors who then informed Medvedev.

"Be more careful, Tadek. If this had gotten back to Stalin it could have jeopardised the whole operation. With Sikorski you are prodding into Stalin's personal domain. That is forbidden." His advice was sound.

Chastened I returned to the clerk the next day to try to cover up my incaution with a more bland enquiry about certain other London Poles. There was a new corporal in his place.

"Where's the other guy?" I asked, annoyed.

"He had a run-in with a truck on the way home. He didn't make it. They're saying he was drunk and that his heart gave out," came back the laconic reply.

Moscow was a scary place.

Those around me were making the final arrangements for the purge of Jews from Moscow. Medvedev's plan to remove Abakumov by inventing the Doctor's plot had gotten out of hand - or had been further engineered by Stalin. This was Medvedev's greatest concern, since it implied Stalin had some inkling of a plot of some sort. Medvedev's agents had fed Mikhail Ryumin the story that several prominent Party men and some of the old guard in the military had been poisoned by their Jewish doctors. Abakumov, as expected, did not believe such nonsense. He had too much information on what had really happened. But Medvedev, on Beria's instructions, had urged Ryumin to go straight to Stalin and complain.

Ryumin arranged for a woman, a Dr Timashuk, to protest by letter, direct to Stalin, that a plot was being hatched in the Kremlin Hospital to eliminate the leadership. Ryumin's immediate boss was Khrushchev's protégé Ignatiev, which had been an inconvenience. Beria did not want him alerted.

Medvedev put to me in plain words that at the 19th Party Conference in October had made clear that someone was breaking up Beria's fiefdom in Georgia. Not only had there been a purge of Beria supporters in the Caucasus earlier in the year, but it was still in progress. The conference theme had been the condemnation of 'bourgeois nationalism', which could be aimed both at Georgia or the Jews, or indeed any other minority as required.

"Thinking of the Ukrainian experience, this smacked of Khrushchev of course," Medvedev explained. "Our grouping had to be cautious, but Beria, a master of snake words, was able to join in the bandwagon and highlight the negative consequences of 'Great Russian' chauvinism from Czarist days and the repression of minorities. 'Now we have a new Soviet empire,' he said, 'we need to address the needs of minority nationalities.' Beria was really crafty with this response, because he spoke about 'Russian people', not 'the *Great* Russian people', and how Leninist-Stalinist policies had already won the day against a number of evils including this 'bourgeois national-ism'. His comeback was one in the eye for Khrushchev and company, because he managed to compliment Stalin for his successes, yet trivialise the need for coming purges."

Although the MVD supposedly controlled the MGB, I saw that Stalin had recently personally removed a number of Beria men in favour of Khrushchev's men. The Ukrainian cronies of Khrushchev's murderous campaign were coming to town in the MGB, mostly military-political officers, commissars from the war. Vlasik, the long-serving, faithful Chief of the MGB Guards Directorate, had been arrested for 'passing information to Jewish plotters' just a few days previously. Beria might have power in the Ministry, but it was Stalin who held the real strings of the operatives, the MGB.

"Stalin is up to no good. Vlasik has been his bodyguard since 1931, for Christ's sake!" said Medvedev. "And we hear Beria's man Kuzmichev, Vlasik's number two, is to be arrested any day now. Beria already knows that Stalin needs an excuse the USA will bite on, to give the USSR a reason for a pre-emptive strike against Europe. Stalin is planning to win this coming Third World War. He is convinced that Harry Truman is Jewish. Stalin has been ant-Semitic from the beginning, something he shared with Hitler. He wants to use the Israelis' pro-West position to move against the Jews in the Soviet Union. Stalin's mantra for over a year now has been, 'Every Jewish nationalist is an American spy'. There is going to be a war and the West seems to have no idea of what's coming!"

The climate was being set, just as I had seen it happen in Poland.

Clearly Stalin had taken Ryumin's bait, for his own devious end. So he had attacked the Jewish doctors, convincing the nation that Jewish national-ists were planning to poison the whole Politburo. Now, a year later, a number of leading Jews were in jail, with trials set to start early next year in January. Abakumov had, as desired and designed, been arrested. Ryumin was supposed to have replaced him as a reward from Beria, but Stalin had appointed Ignatiev instead. At a stroke, Beria had removed an arch rival and enemy. As part of his game plan, he had also made sure of my immediate survival. But things had gone awry. Suspicion was breeding suspicion. Beria was not as strong as he had been.

Now it was time to meet him, this man responsible for the deaths of so many, the man to whose tune I was now dancing.

My instructions had been to go to the Sokolniki metro station and then walk along the First Avenue past the fun fair, where I would meet up with Beria and Medvedev. The bodyguards had been told to expect me. So here I was, strolling in the winter cold through Sokolniki Park, where the temper-ature had dropped to an icy twenty below.

Lavrenty Beria, my ultimate 'boss', was a surprise. I don't know what I had expected. To me the man was a monster, a sadist. Neither of those words matched the round-faced, balding family man who beamed at me through rimless spectacles. Beria was jocular, educated, well-informed, clearly powerful and very sure of himself. This was the man second only to Stalin, the man in charge of the Soviet nuclear programme, the great spymaster. But a man whose power was waning.

Yet he did not look like a loser.

"So this is our Polish ally, our executioner," he said. "Thank you for meeting me here. You must understand, my house is bugged of course. Comrade Stalin has his own security people embedded everywhere, as I do mine. His policy is 'trust no one'. He sets us against each other through flattery and fear. That murderous bastard Ryumin has been helped by Medvedev, so he will now be under immense suspicion. The old man will court Ryumin because of his injured pride at not getting the top job. I will get the blame.

"Stalin will flatter Ryumin until he is his creature alone, and then Medvedev will be done for. Stalin will want to know Medvedev's motivation. Stalin judges motives more than men. So, young man, we have no time. The purge of the Jews will begin on March the fifth, so we have to act just before then. The move against the Jews will be the prelude for war later in the year. The plan is for September.

"Stalin's plan is to march into Europe over the corpse of Poland and take it in its entirety, including Spain. Germany first, then France in a matter of hours. As for Britain, he does not care. He is betting that they will not intervene because the Reds will insist this is the will of the people of the countries. Stalin has no plans to invade Britain; the Comintern is bleeding it dry by destroying the Empire with promises of revolution and land for the African or the Indian and so on. All the old stories. But he will eventually attack the USA. I believe he thinks we can win. He wants a Communist Europe, and the Americans might just settle for that. The Democrats are always weak. They are like the British. They compromise and sell their mothers for peace at any price.

"As to you, I will introduce you to Stalin as my personal assistant, working on a project to destabilise the Polish exile community in London. We will say your secondary aim is to cause industrial problems in Detroit, then blame those problems on unrest in Europe. When Stalin quizzes you, please attack the Catholic Church. Blame them as much as you like. Stick as close to the truth as you can. If the conversation goes wrong, just stick to the truth. Stalin does not usually interfere with operatives at this level. So his wanting you to be introduced to him is probably a residue of your old enemy Abakumov. He must have fingered you or your new identity somehow.

There are spies everywhere."

He looked at me hard. "Do you trust me, Labycz?"

The wind was cold, piercing. The bare birch trees and spruce did nothing to deflect the merciless cold.

"My father said to trust everyone to act and be themselves," I replied. "The trick was, he said, to measure the person in the first place. I know neither you nor Stalin. I only know Medvedev and Zabavnikov. So, comrade, how can I trust you?"

"Good answer. Report to my office tomorrow, at ten o'clock. And remember, we shall be overheard. Just agree with me and add further drivel if you wish. Stalin will ferret about for a while. The charade will end at some point, but hopefully after March because by then we shall have removed him!" He smiled jovially and rubbed his hands together. "All this waiting must be getting you down. It is a question of timing. If Stalin discovers who you really are first your friend Medvedev will be thrown to the dogs and then you, my friend, will be shot. So you live on a knife-edge. Time is of the essence, along with opportunity."

Medvedev, or Witek, as I still thought of him, took me that night to see *Spartacus* by Khachaturian at the Bolshoi. To occupy my mind and calm any nerves, he said. But he also used the opportunity to ask me about his brown book.

"Oh, I kept the bloody thing," I told him, "It nearly cost me my life but I intend to keep it going, adding all the current details. I keep notes, just like you did."

"It's dangerous work, Tadek, keeping notes. They come back to bite you."

It was the truth. I knew this, and so had he from the beginning. Cast as a Soviet operative he had done his duty in Poland but kept a record for posterity which could have cost him his life. Now I too wanted to keep a record of Russians who were anti Soviet or who at least recognised the need for a human face to Communism. For now we were joined like brothers. But that bond had a limit; we were still on opposite sides of the curtain. In a different world we could have become friends. Now we were allies. I had learned from bitter experience that these were not one and the same thing.

"Thank you for the warning, my friend. But I still want to get to the bottom of the Sikorski affair. Until I discover the truth everything else is conjecture." I replied.

"Ask Beria," Witek suggested simply.

"Will he give me the answers I'm looking for?"

"You possibly hold his life in your hands too. He is not stupid. You are a tool, a weapon and expendable when the moment comes. We all live by his desires, die on his whim. To Beria you are merely a useful ally in the power game. Maybe you and I live, maybe we die. What he knows may be the price he pays to you for good service. But what he knows and what he says may not be the same thing. Everything here is a lie, Tadek. But you have nothing to lose by asking."

He slapped me on the back then, saying, "You won that round in Poland, you crafty sod. By the way, Hajduk got the sack and has been sent to the back end of nowhere in Białystok, to push a pen till his pension comes up. Filipov has replaced him but now calls himself Szymański! I have no news of your partisan friends, but the good doctor took a suicide pill after he was released."

It was much as I expected. I had admired the doctor but my feelings were spent. We come, we go, we do our duty.

Sikorski's assassination was raised again the following morning. Beria's big black shiny GAZ-12 limousine dripped chrome and guzzled gas. The Red élite certainly knew how to look after themselves. I was sitting in the back I stared through a sound-proof glass partition between the driver and us, a study in anticipation. I was about to meet Stalin.

It was Beria who raised the subject. "I understand you want to question me about the death of Sikorski in '43. Is that correct?"

"It is, sir," I responded.

"Comrade, please, not sir, you will get us both shot." It was not a joke.

I blurted out the blunt issue. "My real question is: Who killed Sikorski?"

"Everyone and no one, Labycz. I admired Sikorski, but he was not popular here or in certain quarters in Britain. The British, you should recall, at one point early on, even 'interned' Polish officers to keep them quiet. The British never trusted the Polish Army. Air Force, maybe, but not the Army. The truth about Sikorksi is that he was unpopular in certain factions. In fact, he was not popular even with some of the Poles."

Beria abruptly went silent. "I regret Katyn. It was a mistake. I regret a lot of things," he continued after we had stared for a few minutes at the bleak, dirty countryside, caught between winter and spring, between ice and slush. "I came from a small minority people in Abkhazia; I am a Mingrelian from Georgia. So I know about people's aspirations. You think I am a mass murderer, don't you?"

He appeared so unthreatening and the question was somewhat rhetorical.

"Yes, I suppose I do," was the answer I settled for. But I also took the opportunity to add my own concern for what I had dubbed 'the project'. "I think, Comrade, you are well known here in the USSR. But Western politicians do *not* know you, and those who do mostly know you for heading up the NKVD. As NKVD head you are seen to be responsible for various atrocities. It is not me that you should question about trust. But you should question whether or not the Western politicians trust you. I do not think they do.

"The Security Services do trust you, but in the terms I described the other day. However, you have too much knowledge of their associations and intrigues for them to favour you. How many Americans and British can you blackmail?"

It was a daring question, verging on confrontation. Beria remained calm and brooded for a while before responding.

"Labycz, you may well be right. You Poles have a knack of being a bridge between East and West, so you should know how it was here, and you know what it is like now. All of us at some time were idealists, and perhaps materialists, as I supposed all good Socialists were when I was young. I did not intend to be in the police and in espionage, it just happened. I admit in my early years to have been a thug. As you suggested I killed many. But I have matured and I have grown. I want reforms in this country and in the Party. In 1938 I was appointed to the NKVD as Yezhov's second in command or deputy. Why? Because Stalin wanted me to get rid of Nikolai Yezhov, the grand inquisitor of the Great Purge. He wanted Yezhov alone to be blamed for the excesses, not Stalin. Now I am blamed for all the atrocities in Poland and elsewhere, even in the Ukraine, whilst the Americans' so-called Uncle Joe goes unscathed and Khrushchev goes unnoticed.

"If we succeed, you should join our Foreign Ministry. You could tell the world that I reformed the NKVD from the beginning of my tenure. That I brought in order and law. I did not just purge the department; I brought the criminals to proper trial. I built loyalty by improving working conditions. I started changes in the *gulag* system, bettering conditions. I believed in what I was doing. I despised Yezhov and Yagoda before him, as well as beasts like Khrushchev. Can I alone change a terror system? I used terror, we all used terror. The society is sick. It runs on dread, suspicion and disinformation. What it stands for now I no longer know.

"I am, however, proud of my nuclear work and my son's actions and his role in it." He lapsed into silence. The car purred on and the Sikorski issue was not raised again. He seemed almost immaterial now, lost, just another part of history. Time had moved on. My mission seemed no more than curiosity now compared to the events around me. *It was true*. The past had gone. The West would never accept their complicity. I began to realise that my need to find out about Sikorski was as dwarfed by the present moment. This was revenge, yes. But it was also a private issue for me. Not revenge for my parents. They, like me, were casualties of war. No, this was revenge for the betrayal of Sikorski.

He had been a decent man, a decent politician. His life, my life and the life of millions of others had been affected by this tyrant. It was time Stalin was stopped.

Beria pointed ahead, indicating the turning for the *Kuntsevo dacha* used by Stalin. I knew the house was nicknamed 'Nearest' because the 'Great

Helmsman' had other *dachas* further out. We drove through dense forest until I saw a very high green fence up ahead. The car slowed as the gates swung open. As we entered Security Guards peered through the driver's window. Beria pulled the curtain on his side of the car.

Like me Beria had remained quiet for the rest of the journey, but now he observed, "You see how they just wave us through. I am Beria. We could have a man in the boot, they never check. The guards are too frightened, you see. You get to a point where fear paralyses the system. We are at that point.

"Are you afraid of rats?"

The question was unexpected and so out of context it seemed absurd.

"Comrade Beria, what do you mean by 'rats'?" I queried.

"Rats, man. Brown, furry rodents with long tails. Do you like rats?"

"Not particularly, Comrade. I have had little to do with rats of the animal kind." This made Beria laugh.

"I am serious, Labycz. Stalin has a phobia about rats. If you think he is paranoid about people then you should see his hatred of rats. It verges on mania. If the conversation turns to vermin simply follow my lead. You and I will be body-searched, so leave any personal weapon in the car. You can leave your official side-arm for the guards." He winked at me.

I eased myself forward and took my Radom from my belt under my jacket, placing it well under my seat. I was surprised by this mention of search for arms. Beria was a Marshal. High-ranking officers were not normally body-searched, Medvedev had previously told me. So I questioned why.

"Humiliation is the purpose of the exercise. It's done to remind me I am not above suspicion as a politician. It's his way of telling me he knows I am a danger," Beria explained.

I turned around as we drove on, looking back at the enormous fence. Alongside it ran a narrow asphalt road, illuminated by lamps and searchlights. A short distance beyond we passed through a barbed wire barrier. We were now travelling on a narrow tarmac road. Numerous paths opened up through it, either side of the car, snaking away into the trees. Gradually a two-storey building emerged from the gloom, painted green, with a glassed-in terrace. Before this was a courtyard with a typical formal entrance. To the right of the entrance was a small door, where we pulled up.

"Stalin's doorway," grunted Beria as we exited the car. "Comrade Stalin doesn't approve of the formal entrance, so we use this one.

"Before we go in I want to remind you that you have caused me a lot of trouble. Exposing Soviet spies is not a good idea if you want to remain alive. Leave things alone in London. Work with me, not against me. Learn that lesson. The old Comintern sleepers are virtually gone. Cambridge was not finished, as I suspect you know, but times change. Harry Pollitt[xiv] is a Stalin man through and through. As we speak he has targeted, under orders,

Cambridge undergraduates to massage a new breed of Left intellectual thinkers, grooming them to the idea of revolution via the ballot box in the Labour party. Labour will need our money. The Unions can provide a conduit. Who knows, England may yet have a Communist sympathiser as Prime Minister."

Nothing he ever said to me was wasted.

This was a clear warning, one that did nothing for the feeling of nervous anticipation crawling around my being. Only later I realised it spoke of a future outside Russia. So maybe there was some hope.

The house was surrounded by gardens of roses and groves of birch trees edging the conifer woods. I realised that the *dacha* had been built upon an artificial mound, surrounded by a moat with two bridges. There was a long, covered passageway connecting the house to an annexe. This held a kitchen and a dining-room for Stalin's staff, his drivers, guards, gardeners etc. Stalin apparently objected to the smell of cooking.

We entered. Inside and ahead, as well as right and left, were many doors. I noticed an elevator with a panel for four floors, so I presumed there must be a bunker below, most likely holding an underground government communications centre.

"Upstairs," pronounced Beria, "is a film theatre. Our boss watches a lot of Chaplin and Westerns, but most of all he enjoys such things as *Stalin, the Great Leader*." Beria chuckled.

We passed on to the so-called small dining-room. Here was an inexpensive sideboard of light-coloured wood displaying a set of commonly available dishes. On the same sideboard there was an open bottle of Borzhomi mineral water and a glass. In the middle of the room was a table under an orange cloth lampshade with tassels. A sofa with round bolsters and a high back stood near the window. There was also a small Soviet-style family refrigerator and a small bookcase.

"Modest, hmm?" Beria had read my thoughts. "As in any presidency, there is his real life and his public life. Come, I show you our public life, our schizophrenia." We turned left into a large, almost inappropriate dining-hall some thirty metres long. Its many windows were covered in white curtains, beneath which hung the ubiquitous yellowing, nicotine-stained roller blinds common to every Moscow institution. The room was decorated in the style of a noble's hunting-lodge. Dark wood panelling covered the lower third of the wall, topped by lighter birch dado rails.

The table was vast. I could not see if it was in one piece. It shone with waxing. Around it chairs were set out like thrones. "Like your King Arthur," Beria commented. "Our knights do not have a Round Table of equality here, however. This table focuses our minds on our position of favour. He likes to hang our portraits above our chairs as you can see."

Above each chair was a portrait of a member of the Politburo. Right next to Stalin was Lavrenty Beria. But they were all there: Georgi Malenkov, Nikolai Bulganin, Lazar Kaganovich, Anastas Mikoyan, Kliment Voroshilov, Viacheslav Molotov, and Nikita Khrushchev. There was no   portrait opposite Stalin, just dead space. Khrushchev was placed directly opposite Beria.

"Officially this is where the Politburo holds its sessions. Unofficially it's where we get drunk out of our minds and I force Khrushchev to do his party piece of dancing like a piglet. He hates me for it. But the old man loves it, so what can he do? Stalin enjoys ritual humiliation. Here is where we hold farting competitions and engage in what you would call lewd acts." He gave a quiet chuckle. "Only the old man, Koba,[XV] and I stand aside. Here in this room we stand as Georgians, whatever he may say."

Still smiling, he looked at me. "So now for our audience and your baptism of fire."

We turned right out of the room and back to a door, now guarded by two seated MGB men and a further guard standing. As the guards had clearly been posted for our benefit and the room had been empty before, I could only guess our every move had been followed.

First Beria was body searched by two guards whilst the second eyed me. Then it was my turn.

Clean, we entered the room.

# CHAPTER 24

# STALIN

Stalin, the monster of my imagination, sat behind a large desk. He was much smaller than the portrait of himself which hung behind him. I had heard he had painters shot for failing to measure his stature correctly. Even sitting down I could see he was short. His hair was thinning, the famous moustache was clearly dyed, the face pock-marked from childhood smallpox, though not as badly as some and certainly not visible on any portrait. His slightly shorter left arm rested on the table. Having been greeted by Beria his amber eyes switched to me. He gazed straight into mine. I was struck that he didn't bother to look me up and down. Instead he stared right into my eyes. I snapped to attention

"So this is your new monkey, Lavrenty? Your Polish *muzhik*? The new aide you think I should meet. Is he a piss artist or what? Someone else I shall have to cut you off from, in order to cut down your little empire? Will I have to cut off his balls to stuff down your throat?

"You, Polak," he addressed me. "I hear you lost our man in America. Three agents killed and still we lost Goretchko."

Goretchko. I almost blinked with surprise at the name. This was a dangerous game Witek was playing, fooling around with records in the Lubyanka. Now he had taken my own role and pinned it on my childhood enemy, clearly falsifying internal records. Here was something I could never tell his father back in Canada – not ever. But when you own the records you can make of them what you want.

"Well?" he barked, "I want to hear from you, not him!" Stalin said roughly, indicating Beria.

"Comrade Marshal, my job was to identify and trap the enemy of the people who uncovered our agents in America. This led me to realise that Comrade Abakumov had compromised agents in England, who were now running around loose-tongued in the States. These included one man about to expose the whole network in England, especially our political infiltration of the Labour party. I notified Comrade Beria, who made immediate arrangements for Comrades Burgess and McLean to flee and be brought to Moscow. This is easily verifiable. Our enemy" – I could not bring myself to name Goretchko – "was about to be arrested by the CIA. He was either no longer trusted or was already one of theirs, rather than an English agent. I had him marked for dead, but Abakumov's men wanted a kidnapping for his own ends. I was not informed of their attack." How near, yet how far from the truth this was. Anyone checking would see a mixture of events that would be hard to fathom or refute.

"I was recalled to Moscow. Since then I have worked on undermining the Fascist Poles in London, as well as in counter-intelligence, cutting the West's new lines of communication with the old underground, and sowing discord amongst the Detroit Polish workers. That's all, Comrade Marshal."

"Abakumov is finished," Stalin grunted.

Beria interjected smoothly, "He is fresh back from Poland, sorting out a nest of bandits and incompetent Polish policemen."

"You know, Lavrenty, that I do not like Polish Communists. I thought we had shot most of them in the purges. At least the present Muscovite crowd down there is compliant and following our line. Is he a Polish Communist?" Stalin raised a potentially dangerous question.

"Not in our sense, Koba; he is an outsider to Poland and one of ours," Beria answered.

"Do you believe in compromise with Leftist groups and a broad front alliance of Socialist groups?" The question was addressed directly to me.

"No, Comrade. Such tendencies lead to disunity and exploitation by the Jews and American spies. This was the case with Comrade Gomułka, who even advocated working with the London Poles. In my opinion this is a dangerous dilution of our strengths, built upon the foundation of the Communist Party of the Soviet Union. It is rightist nationalist deviation and should be suppressed. Comrades Bierut and Berman are on the correct path, Comrade." I replied as previously agreed with Witek, sounding exactly like an insincere parrot. In other words I was talking just as everyone else talked – in recycled politico speak.

"You have schooled him well, Lavrenty," Stalin mused. "So he is to be your mission boy for a while. Well, he becomes your problem. If he leaves as much as his briefcase behind, as you just did in here whilst you were playing tour guide, then shoot him!"

Joining in the laughter at Stalin's riposte, Beria retorted, "Ah, you know I left it in here as a test of your self-control, to see if you would peep. But of course you knew it was locked!" The two men laughed loudly at their own verbal fencing.

Without warning, Stalin shot a question at me: "What do you think of the Treaty of Andruszów?"

I could hear Beria worrying. He had no idea what the question meant. But I knew Stalin to be a great historian. He would know that to an educated Pole the treaty was a Muscovite triumph, born of many years of conflict. I had already stated my non-nationalist conviction. So I replied in kind, with a modest show of knowledge and a greater show of tact.

"I believe that what began as a rising of the Cossacks against the Poles for more money and privileges spread to the different peoples of the Ukraine. It ended in ruin, with the Ukraine divided in two. Muscovy ruled the left bank of the Dnieper river and Poland the right. The peoples there found that life under Muscovy was much harder than within the Commonwealth. That is my opinion of the treaty comrade. It worked to the advantage of what later became Russia."

There was a moment of silence. "Perhaps I should put you in charge of the Ukraine instead of Comrade Khrushchev. Poles are clever. And that was a clever answer, boy. But," he hissed at me, "never challenge me like that again. It was a test, we both know that. But now it is settled."

He looked at Beria and smiled broadly. "You have no idea of the interplay which just took place here, have you, Lavrenty? But no matter, the boy passes. But that does not mean that I either like or trust him. "

"He might have passed but your office has failed the test. Do they not clean in here these days?" Beria pointed. On the floor to the left of the sofa lay a dead rodent. A very small, very young brown rat, its pathetic little hairless tail sticking straight out like a semaphore.

"Fucking dogs' teeth!" yelled Stalin, reaching for one of the phones. "I can't bloody stand rats!"

"I'm not in charge of hygiene here, am I?" Beria replied calmly. "It's no good shouting at the maids either, so calm down. Maybe I should be in charge, and then the place would be cleaner. We should lay more poison."

Stalin retorted, "And then I *would* be fucking dead! I know what you are up to, Lavrenty, planning to sit in my chair and run the place." He broke off in mid flow, pointing toward the sofa. "How the hell did that thing get in here?"

This conversation was not banter. It had a tone of menace. Tension in the room mounted until I felt sweat on the palms of my hand.

Beria did not respond. Instead he walked over to the sofa, picked up the rat by its tail and passed it to me. "Get rid of it and check the basements, which are where this one is likely to have come from. You have a new role: Chief Rat Catcher." His anger was evident and seemed very real. I took the assignment seriously but also as a dismissal, a way of saying 'Get out of the way, now. I have things to say.'

I looked at him in disbelief.

"Are you familiar with rats?" Beria's question hung in the air whilst my brain distilled the absurdity of the situation.

"I am, Comrade, I was raised on a farm. There is rarely only one rat. I will check and make some suggestions to stop a recurrence."

"Do so. You chase rats while we work. Is that not why we brought you all the way to Moscow? Marshal Stalin does not want people on the premises he cannot trust, like Jew doctors or, it seems, Russian rat catchers. So we shall have to do the bloody work." A vein was working in Beria's temple. He glared at me, almost with hatred. A very different man to the one I had seen moments before. "Get out. Go and do what he wants," Beria yelled, banging his fist on the desk. "Get on with it."

I turned toward Stalin, blinking.

The old man was shuffling papers. He waved his hand at me. "Get on with it, boy!" Already he was speaking into the phone. "Go, go! You have the run of the place. No more rats!"

I left dangling the rat by its tail.

One of the guards slipped the Korovin 6.35mm pistol back into my side holster for me. I must have looked visibly shaken by the intensity of the outburst for he said, "That's nothing, Comrade. New people have been shot before."

The other guards laughed at me holding the dead rat gingerly by the tail. As I passed down the corridor I heard them whisper, 'Colonel Rat Catcher'. Not quite the note of authority I was going for. My new title did mean, however, that I was free to roam the building and find what I had come for. I needed to find both the underground link to the Kremlin Beria assured me lay underneath the dacha. He'd seen it once but the link hadn't been used for several years, he said. There was, he assured me, an entrance into the main office in which Stalin slept. Engineering was, after all, his forte. I had to believe it existed. All I had to do now was find it.

This tunnel was key to the action to come.

As I wandered away my thoughts were full of the man I had just met. A modern day Ivan the Terrible. Perhaps the comparison seems simplistic. Yet Stalin had studied history, he knew just how Ivan had worked, so why not make the comparison? Stalin gave his henchmen flats and *dachas*, cars and chauffeurs, in order to buy their gratitude. And every year he murdered some of them, to keep the others on their toes. It was a system that worked. After the demonstration in the office I wondered just how secure Beria was.

There was no real need to check the whole premises. The rat was obviously a Beria prop, which is why Stalin's phobia had been raised in the car. He'd clearly wanted me to have an honest reaction to it in front of Stalin. However it had been accomplished, the rat in the office was definitely a put-up job. I guessed it had been in the briefcase, which hadn't been searched, having been accidentally 'left' in the study. Sloppy security, though how many of the guards were in Beria's rather than in Stalin's control?

An elderly maid, whom I presumed to be Matryovna Petrovna, the woman who had served Stalin since his rise to power, fussed and tutted about the whole affair as she guided me about. "Mice," she said, "are not uncommon. Where else would God's creatures shelter in the winter? But not rats!" I surmised she was not a good Communist. She believed in God.

Taking leave of her and the two upper levels, including the cinema, I took the lift to the lowest floor, hoping the guards would not notice I missed the middle level. I was in a hurry. The doors opened to reveal a very bored guard just rising from his seat and slinging his submachine-gun to his shoulder. From his breath he had drunk more than tea to keep him warm down here. It was chilly, to say the least, with no evident heating. Just a cold concrete square with one steel door and three bolt-style locks.

"Keys, Comrade," I snapped.

The man was no ordinary guard. I had noticed that all these *chekists*, as they were called, took turns at all the different locations and duties, whatever their rank. This one I recognized to be a deputy commissar for the *dacha*.

"I have no keys, Comrade Colonel. No one is supposed to come down here."

The stubby barrel of his crude but highly effective PPSH 41 began to swing toward me, his finger on the trigger. Equally deliberately I moved my hand to my holster, and with my hand on the butt slipped the catch. It was a short weapon, semi-automatic, one favoured by the old NKVD and Russian officers. Never a standard military weapon, it had been gifted to me by Witek. "I know from New York you like to carry two calibres," he had said. "The MVD can match the CIA." He was making reference to the Ruger I had left with Kryszka in Brighton. But also telling me indirectly just how much he knew about me.

The pistol was no match for this guard's weapon, but my rank and its implication were enough for him to pause.

"Down here in this basement, Comrade, I guess you were forgotten. You should have been told that I am to be given free run of the building to find the source of rats that have invaded our great leader's office."

"There are no rats down here, Comrade. Three of us work shifts here. There are no rats. Where would they come from? You could not even slip a paper underneath these doors," he replied sourly.

"True, Comrade. It is not from this room that rats may come, but from the space beyond the door which has access to Marshal Stalin's office. So I suggest you phone upstairs and get the keys fast or else you and I are going to fall out. You will have plenty of time to consider the implications of our argument when you are somewhere east of the Caucuses."

He moved to the wall telephone and rang upstairs, now pointedly aiming the gun in the direction of my stomach. As he spoke into the phone his eyes wavered. I slipped my pistol from its holster, resting it in the crook of my arm, aimed directly at him.

"Yes, yes," I heard him say. He turned to me and observed my pistol. A silly grin appeared on his face. "I am sorry, Comrade. I cannot be too careful, you understand. No one ever comes down here. Always they stop on the floor above, the telecommunications and signals unit. No one ever comes down here." Turning back to me he said, "He is bringing the keys now, Comrade."

The tension eased and I replaced my pistol. The lift whirred and head guard Colonel Khrustalev entered. Barely glancing at me he unlocked the three rooms and waved me in. There was a pull chord switch. It worked. Light flooded the room. I swung the door closed behind me and shot the bolts. The air was stale and smelt of dust. It was a mirror image of the room behind me, except for two more doors, one to my left and a larger door just ahead. I went first to the larger door and swung back the wheel lock as though it were a safe. The heavy steel door opened, revealing pitch black. The secret tunnel. The light from the chamber in which I stood soon faded to a black nothingness. Inside the door and to one side was a series of grey painted electrical fittings and fuses.

I pulled the master light switch; the clunk echoed away down the brick chamber. Fresh cold air swept along the tunnel. Heavy duty wire-encased lights disappeared into the distance like Christmas tree lights. There was a single narrow gauge rail track gleaming in the light and a low platform. I was standing at the end of it. Otherwise there was nothing except for a small metal table and a metal cupboard. Inside the cupboard were some overalls and maintenance equipment, shovels, crow bars, an oilcan, hammers and the like.

Movement. A rat scuttled away and I laughed, the sound booming and disappearing into the void. I walked into the tunnel, hopping from one sleeper to another. They seemed spaced specifically to be awkward and break my stride.

It was evident the tunnel had been here for some time. An occasional tungsten bulb had blown. At one point water had seeped through the red-brick lining. The ground had puddled a few centimetres deep. Miniature stalactites of lime from the mortar of the brick pointing. The occasional rat's eye gleamed red ahead of me in the tunnel. Eventually I came to the main steel door, the door to the outside world, which evidently slid to one side. There was plenty of access room for rats, which had clearly tunnelled under the main slide guide-rail. Within the door was a low, recessed, steel pedestrian access. I swung the locking bar open and pushed the door wide. It opened to a view of the main perimeter fence about fifty metres away. I closed the door but carefully left the locking bar in the open position and hurried back along the track. Reaching the low platform I shut down the electrics and closed the main door with a thud.

I looked around the chamber, which was bare except for the other door. This one was secured by a locking bar and padlock. I set to with the skeleton keys supplied by Witek, which had been concealed in my boot. Their rubbing had caused a blister on my ankle. Soon the door opened to a flight of stairs leading upward. It was clean, with no spider webs, yet the unsealed concrete had shed dust. I was aware I was leaving footprints as I went up. Treading quietly at the top I entered a narrow concrete corridor. At the end was a doorway and a large plain wooden door. There was a simple recessed latch which appeared to move to one side to open, nothing elaborate. I guessed it was matched on the other side. The grease was aged, cracked and black. I wondered what would happen if I tried it. I could hear nothing on the other side of the door. But then, I was here on official business. Inch by inch I teased the latch back, praying that whatever lay the other side was not observable or making noise I could not discern. Everything was silent. Large, heavy, piano-style hinges lay to my right, running top to bottom of the door. This indicated that the door was heavy, although evidently, from the latch, not that thick. I pushed but nothing gave. I set my shoulder to the door and the hinges groaned. I stopped.

I remembered the oil-can in the cupboard. Quietly I made my way down to the platform, losing precious time. I let the oil run down the hinges, its smell tainting the otherwise clean air. Setting it carefully to one side in case I kicked it, because there was little room in the confined corridor, I leant against the door. Heat from another room seeped to my nose as it gave a millimetre. I could hear muffled voices but couldn't make out any words. Another millimetre and I realised I was listening to Beria and Stalin. Success. But how far dare I go? I listened intently, easing my way forward, opening up a gap that showed me the sideboard I had seen earlier. I felt myself sweating. Stalin should be directly in front of me - but where? Had he changed position? I tried to pull the door back but it would not budge. I realised too late that I had miscalculated; there was no handle this side, just a latch. My God, what if I couldn't get it closed! I tugged hard, but nothing.

Just as I contemplated bursting into the room and damn the consequences, I heard Beria say, "Excuse me, Comrade, but I must go scratch my bloody back, it's driving me mad. Must be those fucking rats and their fleas."

"You think so, Lavrenty? I shall be sure to have the place fumigated."

I heard the scrape of chairs and then footsteps on the rug and the more energetic sound of heels on wood block. Then I felt pressure on the door as it closed. "Ah, that's better ..." I heard as the door shut home. I imagined Beria rubbing his back on some cupboard attached to the door.

My heart thudded for long moments. I hurried back the way I had come, switching the lights as I went, barring and padlocking the passage door. I got back to the main room, slid the three bolts home and found my guard sitting on the chair.

"Don't you get bored down here, Comrade?" I asked jovially.

"No," was his desultory reply. "I had plenty of practice in the Butyrka prison, until Comrade Beria's reforms."

"I share your experience," I added. He blinked at that. "What is your name, Comrade?"

"Piotr Lozgachev, Comrade. Here, let me brush you off if I may. You are covered in white dust on your shoulder and side. Did you find any rodents, Comrade?"

"I did. Rats follow wires and pipes. They are probably entering through the small rail tunnel. They must have holes that take them upwards into the house, although I saw no signs of rats, except the dead one in the office."

Whilst still dusting me down Lozgachev explained that the rail link was mostly over ground and travelled underground only at the Kremlin end and just inside the perimeter fence. The tunnel entrance was closed by steel doors which could only be opened from the inside. "Rats could easily tunnel in there I guess, Comrade." He called Khrustalev for the keys. Whilst waiting he told me that the tunnel link was designed primarily to get Stalin out of the Kremlin unobserved. "There is a GAZ 12 rail car limousine that runs along it," he revealed, "with a bevy of security guards in the one behind. But Stalin only used it once or twice."

Khrustalev arrived and Lozgachev shut up like a clam. "Whatever both of you think, you need to lay rat poison down here and in the room next door and in the tunnel. Just do it," I ordered and proceeded back to the ground floor.

"Ah, so my rat-catcher and spy is back. Have you cased the joint, as the Americans say?" Stalin asked in his disarming but devious way. I'd heard it said of him before. You always had the feeling he knew what you were up to. It was a strategy that had served him well. Stress people, and eventually they make a mistake, take the joke or barb and give themselves away. I was wise to this game.

"Comrade Marshal Stalin, I have ordered poisoned bait to be laid at the rail tunnel exits. It is clear that they are coming along this route. We must also lay bait in the communication area, as rats like to eat the coating on electric cables."

The response was immediate. "Did I say you could enter the forbidden section, boy?"

"No, you did not," Beria interjected, "but I clearly heard you tell Comrade Labycz to search everywhere. Let us get on with business now. Labycz, the Marshal wants to know more about these other rats, the London Poles. Tell him your opinion, starting with Anders. After that he would value your opinion on politics in Britain. We believe the king is not likely to survive the year – who will succeed him? We succeeded in helping with the Unions to bring in a pro-Soviet Government. So why, the Marshal wants to know, when so much nationalisation has occurred, did the British back the Conservatives again? How can we best influence the Labour Party to our interests?"

"These are big questions," I began…

We did not leave until the early hours of the morning. I was way over the top with drink and kippered by smoke. Just about in control of my senses, we were driven back to Moscow.

"Thanks for noticing the door," I ventured.

"Lucky escape," murmured Beria. "Standing bookcase. We shall have to work out how to close it. Altogether a successful day," he offered.

I retrieved my Radom and slipped it back into my belt.

"Would you like a woman?" The question, even from Beria, was a surprise. "We could pick one off the street, willing or unwilling. Or I could order you one from Lubyanka office?"

Taken by surprise I responded shortly, "No thanks, I can find my own if needed." This was the first and only time I encountered the so-called Beria predilection for sex.

"Today is the 26th of February. We shall make our move on the 28th, the day of Holy Basil the Confessor. I trained to be a priest, you know. My mother dedicated me to God when I was a baby. Sikorski was in everybody's way in the end." The lightning change in his conversation yet again took me by surprise. I had decided to leave the question but now he was opening it up again. Perhaps it was because he thought I would not come out of this alive.

Or perhaps it was simply time for me to know.

"Sikorski held several cards. He was loved by few and courted by many – the Germans, ourselves, and the British – but he always put Poland first. He had upset Anders by conceding territory in the east, but he had not conceded Wilno or Lwów or the oil fields. Anders could accept this, so could we, and it kept the British happy, but Stalin personally wanted Sikorski dead. Sikorski was a Polish officer who had avoided Katyń. A Polish officer who had played a large part in defeating the Bolsheviks just twenty years previously. It was Stalin's desire to kill all Polish officers. A class thing, one we Bolsheviks had practiced since the Revolution. Stalin knows me well. He *wanted* me to advise him to kill the Polish officer corps and so I did. However I made sure that Stalin signed the death warrants.

"Stalin had decided that Poland's borders were now immaterial; he was going to take Poland anyway. So a few kilometres made little difference. He was scared that Sikorski would conclude a peace with the German Army. Quite possible, you realize, as the German Army wanted shot of Hitler and the worst of the Nazi crimes were still yet to come. Sikorski wanted the Polish Army, which was after all a sovereign army, to barrel up through

Yugoslavia. He had the forces to do it. That would really have put Stalin in difficulty in the West. Sikorski, in his own negotiations with the German Army, had evidence that Stalin too was suing for peace and would go back to the '39 pact with Hitler. The German Army had given evidence to Sikorski of the Stalin negotiations with the Nazis against the Allies. They wanted nothing to do with Stalin. The Soviet plan was then to neuter the Poles by killing the head. There was no one else to replace him but Sosnkowski, and the British would not accept him at any cost. In Poland itself Stalin got General Rowecki out of the way, along with Colonel Oziewicz of the NSZ, all in the same year.

"Who killed Sikorski? Well, we can say the thinking was with the British, but not the order. The intention was Soviet. And the implements were the Security services of both nations, but serving only one master, Stalin. We are experts in poison, as you shall see. The main players were dead before they hit the water. Survivors were taken off by the Philby team. Small, fast boats waiting for the belly-flop. You recall people were seen on the wing? Prchal had a short neck jab like the one you have experienced, a momentary blackout and memory loss. The drugged pilot was dressed in his Mae West, supposedly the person to blame, but that was fucked up. Maisky had delivered the poisons and drugs which had previously ended up in Cairo, but not the assassins. They were already on board the Liberator, part of the regular party and crew. Forget Gralewski. He may be a mystery man, but Sikorski was meant to die on his way *to* Cairo, not on his way back. This is mostly forgotten. Hence you can discount the Poles themselves from doing the job.

"So who pulled the trigger, so to speak? I do not know which Britisher or Pole, or even Soviet citizen did the job. It was a joint effort, of which Stalin was supremely proud, and of which the British government, bar one or two, were blithely unaware. It was a security job. Maisky was a great pal of Churchill before the war, did you know that? Pre-war Churchill was very keen that Poland should derive its security with an alliance with Soviet Russia not Britain. He opposed the treaty to support Poland in time of war. I doubt you knew this. Poland was never his favourite country!

"That is all I can tell you. There, that is my part of the bargain sealed. Do not trust records, Labycz. We are all masters at changing them."

I had learned nothing new but at last I had real confirmation that Sikorski's death was no accident. I kept quiet.

"It was Cairo which sealed his fate and made for a joint operational decision with the British Secret Service and the NKVD. You needed to ask your little whore friend Skarbek if you wanted more. She knew what was in the missing Sikorski briefcase, but she is conveniently no more. Though not by our hand." This was his last remark before dropping me off.

Krystyna had hinted during our meetings that she knew the truth. Perhaps she was the only one who ever did.

I was dropped outside my apartment building and made my way up the stairs. Sitting in the gloom on the floor outside was a female MGB NCO. She stood up and leant against the door as I climbed the last few echoing steps. I had seen her before, in the Lubyanka, on the same floor as me. I had assumed her to be some sort of guard. She often sat on duty in the corridor outside one of the cipher offices, wearing a side arm, which was unusual. I had judged her of no particular importance, but at this moment, in these circumstances, she could be dangerous.

"Comrade?" I questioned.

"You want me. I have seen it in your eyes, Comrade, when we have seen each other in the canteen," she said. Her directness was just yet another surprise in this day of surprises.

"Did Beria send you?" I asked arrogantly.

In answer she grasped my lapels and pulled me close, pushing her hips hard against me then swaying them from side to side. "I choose my own man. You intrigue me," she replied. "Is there lead in this pistol?" She meant more than the gun she had slipped from my belt, the barrel of which she was now holding to her lips, her tongue touching the steel.

She was right of course. I had picked her out from the crowd. She was not voluptuous in any particular way, but long-legged with shapely thighs, her breasts full and heavy. Her beautiful face was narrow but with wide-set delphinium blue eyes. Raven hair. Lips small but well shaped. She had that intrinsic look of sexuality, that look of eroticism, that indefinable look that played across the mouth. The one that said, "Desire me, taste me, fuck me so we can swim in our lust and our emotions'.

My mind was torn between fear that she was an MGB plant, disgust that Beria had sent her against my wishes and that she had obeyed, and my simple desire, my need for release which had risen instantly. Perhaps Beria was right. 'What the hell!'

She was not Russian but from the Caucuses. Her skin smelled of some sweet oil that gave it a sensuous sliding touch. She oiled my body as we entwined, sliding, moving limb to limb, feeling the crevices and spaces left untouched by common behaviour. A thin wisp of silky black hair led me to the Mount of Venus and beyond, to the warm depths of her moist abyss. Lips dripped with nectar. Saliva tasted of honey. My phallus was anointed, caressed and explored by lips and tongue. Pert nipples held to mouth. Sweat joined oil, softness turning to grinding intensity. Oil was poured between the cleft of my buttocks and a finger explored me, strangely arousing me further. I returned the compliment, delving deeply and inducing a soft rhythm that subtly demanded more. We danced like snakes. We came together. There were short rasps of breath, a holding for a moment, then expression, wetness and a slow recovery.

About an hour later she dressed. I watched her.

"I must go now, Comrade. Duty calls."

I pondered love. This city was run by automatons, unfeeling robots, Pavlov's dogs. This was a country with so many ordinary people, who must live and love, eat and sleep, live out their existences. Every mother must love her child, surely. Yet so many bright children were taken at birth to be farmed for the good of the people. Did some son love that old *babushka* who swept the streets?

Her scent lingered with me. Next day Witek exploded my dreams, telling me she worked in the diplomatic section as a professional seductress. "She's very good," he said. "She has several Americans here in Moscow on the blackmail list. She works part time at the Lubyanka and gets paid for 'extra duties'. She's MGB not MVD of course. Keeps an eye open for everything she can sell I guess. Ultimately I don't know whom she supports. But Beria sent her, so we can assume the best."

I objected to Beria undermining me, but as Witek said, I had only to refuse and I had not.

Moscow was a strange world of depravity, of moral or political stricture. It was a place of fear, a place to do as one was told. Not easy simply to live by the rules as they changed so often. You could enjoy the moment if you tried, and if not, it was best to pretend. Go to the fair, enjoy the expositions of Soviet engineering, agriculture, power, smell the flowers. But do not think or speak freely.

Pavel had passed to Witek the poison to be used. We went over the plan.

"Sudoplatov is one of Comrade Beria's special multi role chief fixers," Witek said. "It was he who chased off the Ukrainian partisans we were involved with, and a host of other special tasks. He's been in and out of favour with Stalin. Eventually he was given the job of heading up the MVD poison laboratory by Beria, to bring it to some order and sanity after the removal of Marianovsky. The man was a brilliant biochemist, but he went too far with human experimentation. Too many *gulag* prisoners died. The experiments were supposed to have been stopped but I doubt it. And we moralise about Nazi crimes."

Witek had known about the 'dead rat trick' too, but like Beria hadn't told me so all my reactions would be genuine. He laughed at my description of events.

I did not laugh at the ugly syringes provided to me.

"First you use the paralytic, and then you have to administer two separate poisons. Above all, it is vital that his death look natural. To achieve that the poison must be slow acting, and it must be expelled in his urine, leaving no trace. So, Comrade, it will take time. We have to *buy* you time. You cannot be seen. Everything must appear normal, natural.

"It will not be an easy experience, Tadek." He had not called me that for a while. "Remember, you do it for your fatherland. This cannot be a personal vengeance, dismiss from your thoughts your parents, friends, any thought of revenge. You are under orders, even if only from yourself as a freelance. People can moralise all they like, but this deed needs to be done. It is easier to be in a fire-fight, we both know that. This requires a cold, calculated courage of a strange sort. You know Sikorski and others were killed in the same way. What you are about to do is not new or extraordinary, here or elsewhere. Do you think the CIA is any different? I accept that your British education and your Polish honour fight against this, but a gun has the same result. And the British just use proxies to salve their conscience."

"Yet you are not handling it yourself?" I asked the question knowing the answer to be one I had heard so often before. I recited the answer before he could speak. "Because I am the fall guy should things go wrong; the goat of Azazel, the sacrificial lamb, a foreign agent, an imperialist lackey."

Witek paused, placing an arm on my shoulder. "I have taught you well. Of course, you have lost your romantic illusions on the way. This is a dirty business, wiping the backsides of politicians, supposedly for the greater good. But I work with my few friends and you are one. We are enemies at one level but friends at another. I will get you out of this if it is the last thing I do."

I did not respond to his show of emotion except by gripping his arm firmly. "Don't worry," I mumbled, "I have a host of reasons for being here and doing this. It will be done." But I needed to ask a question that had been nagging at me, "What if the drugs don't work, like with Rasputin?"

"Make a better job of it than Yusupov. This job requires finesse. You will be using this new C-2 drug, tried and tested, tasteless and odourless but too quick. We have to make it look real, drag it out. So you will have to drip feed him the poison slowly, so that he dies little by little, till in the end he has a stroke or heart attack. It matters little which, so long as he pees first and dies naturally. On a full dose he would be dead in fifteen minutes, becoming calm and peaceful and with no post-mortem trace unless you were looking for it, just slight shrinkage of the body. Remind you of a certain Polish prime minister?"

The implication was not lost on me.

The time came. Stalin was working in the Kremlin, so mid-morning I made the trip with Beria to Kuntsevo, only this time in the boot of the car. My heart raced as we stopped at the security check-point but as before it was not searched. Why should it be? As we neared the house we slowed and stopped on the bend. The boot was opened, and I recognised the driver as

Zabavnikov. He said nothing but winked. Scrambling out, I dived into one of the birch glades. It was one thirty in the afternoon and a clear day. The frost was still heavy. I followed one of the guard tracks toward the rail link. We had specifically asked the guards to check the rat bait at the tunnel entrance, so I knew they had a regular half-hour beat. I walked carefully and quietly in their footsteps. In the distance I heard Beria's car purr away and then stop. Stillness and quiet were everything. Now was the moment. My every nerve was tuned to this stillness, this quiet which was inside me and yet around me in the air, in the trees and in my breathing. I was ready.

At the tunnel entrance the ground had been trampled by the guards. A cigarette butt lay on the frozen ground. I took a still warm rat from the greaseproof paper bag in my pocket. About two metres from the doorway I wiped the ground with it, using the paper bag to hold the rat, being careful not to touch the dead animal with my bare hands. It had been injected with some dog-appealing smell, Witek had told me. I tossed the rat some distance, knowing that the guards would be pulled away by the dogs, otherwise they would have picked up my stranger's smell en route. This way hopefully the rat smell would attract them, or at least distract them from my scent which would linger around the door. Striking a match, I set fire to the greaseproof paper and watched the black and glowing flakes rise into the cold air before drifting to the woods and ground. There was the smell of burnt paper, but I hoped it would pass as the cold settled onto any debris. I pocketed the dead match.

The service door swung opened without a hitch. I closed it behind me. Dropping the locking bar with a clang that echoed on and on down the dark tunnel I headed off down the line into the pitch black. I had brought a stick to guide me and held it firmly against the rail so that I kept a straight path. We had decided that lighting was too risky as it might shine through any gap or rat hole. I had had no real way of checking. Better safe than sorry. The stick told me the awkward sleeper spacing. By the time I arrived at the platform my legs were aching. The luminous dial on my watch, bright in the intense dark, told me it was an hour and a half since I had left Beria. I felt safe enough now to use a small pen flashlight. I left my stick unobtrusively by the maintenance cupboard. As quietly as possible I entered the first chamber, securing the door behind me. I decided to sit and wait here for evening. I dozed on and off, getting colder and stiffer.

My dreams were wild and I fought real sleep. I jerked awake, my mouth open, hearing a snore which was mine. Stretching my limbs I walked quietly on tip-toe around the room. Beria had told me that he, Khrushchev, Bulganin and Malenkov would probably watch a movie at the Kremlin that night and then Beria would drop Stalin off some time after twelve. At midnight I started up the stairs to my own, and perhaps everyone else's fate. It was now Sunday, the traditional day of rest. I pushed the secret study door open a few millimetres. A single lamp was lit. Everything else was in blessed shadow. The warmth from the Dutch stove seeped into my passage way. On my side of the door I screwed a large 'eye' into the wood, very slowly so that no tell tale wood particles dropped to the floor, and then slipped some rope through it. Now I could close the door from my side.

Leaning stiffly against the wall I waited. And waited. At some point I heard shouting and laughter vaguely drifting through the room. I stiffened and readied myself as a door was opened, but it was only someone stoking and feeding the stove. From the shuffling gait I guessed it would be the elderly maid. She must have left the door to the small dining-room ajar as I could now clearly hear voices. I could make out Stalin's and Beria's amongst others.

The voices stopped. I heard doors close and someone enter the room. There was heavy breathing, a belch, breaking wind. I heard him ease himself onto the couch. Boots fell to the floor. A big sigh, a strange chuckle, some coughing, and then silence. Shortly afterwards there came the sound of rhythmic breathing. I swung the door wide.

As the cars swept away bearing the Politburo members to their Moscow homes, I knew the guard commander Khrustalev would have told the bodyguard, "It's a night off, boys. The old man has ordered you to get to your bunks." I hoped they would make the most of it and not come back until twelve noon sharp, as Beria had instructed. The guards would be grateful for the extra sleep, a full eight hours for once. Stalin normally kept them so sleepless they were next to useless.

From my pocket I took out felt overshoes and slipped them over my boots, with some difficulty. We wanted no footprints in this room. I took out a small chloroform bottle and tipped some onto a pad. I approached the couch.

There he lay, the Great Man, short, shrunken, elderly. The foulest murderer in history, the evolutionist, the Communist. Mouth slack, saliva dried at the corner.

I became calm and cold as I placed the pad over his face. There was no real struggle, some jerking of limbs, but he was already asleep and within seconds he went limp. I put the pad into the stove and opened the windows, triple framed, to remove the smell of the chloroform. The levels had been low so as to avoid too much smell, but I hated the stench and was sensitive to it.

Picking up his hand I chose the worst nicotine stained finger. Taking the first hypodermic I slowly pumped the paralytic into his system, just as he had ordered it to happen to so many of his victims. It would be slow and there were better sites, but it would work. Plus there would be no obvious bruising amongst the staining. I squeezed the finger to stop the little bead of blood from escaping.

'Now, you bastard,' I thought, 'let's see how you are in fifteen minutes.'

Closed the window and opened the stove to get some warmth back into the place. It was 4.45 in the morning.

Half an hour seemed a lifetime. I watched the man. He blinked, slowly. His amber eyes met mine.

"Death comes to us all, Comrade. I don't know whether you can hear me, but this is how it will happen. In a moment you will take some warfarin. I trust you had plenty of garlic tonight to help elevate the effects, Comrade, and though I hear you have cut down on drinking, tonight was special, wasn't it? Now you know it was more than fruit juice. Lavrenty got you to drink more, didn't he? So at some point you will bleed and vomit blood, but do not worry, you will not die. Then I will have to get you to pee, to rid the traces of the anti-coagulant. If we can induce a proper stroke so much the better, as then I will finish you with a cushion. If not, Comrade, it will be C-2. Remember General Kutepov? Yes, you do. I see it in your eyes."

His eyes had flashed at the name of the kidnapped Kutepov, the last great White leader who had been taken from Paris by Soviet agents.

"Or General Evgeny Miller, another White you never forgave. You harboured so much resentment, Comrade. You never forgave the Poles, did you, for defeating you in the south when you were the political commissar? They made you look a fool. Is that what it was all about? Your legacy, your reputation? You never forget or forgave, do you? Well, I am the same. You killed my parents. Did you know that?"

Taking a small packet and a teaspoon from my pocket I took a flat spoon of the stuff and carefully opened his mouth. He resisted mentally with all his being. I could see it, but he was like a doll. I remembered it well, the helplessness of your whole being, all your bodily functions being taken over by someone else as they manipulate you with drugs. I shuddered as I remembered my time in the clutches of this man's MGB.

"There's a good boy. Now take another one. Drinkies now, you son of a bitch," I crooned. I took the water from a side table and dropped it in, making sure his mouth and false teeth were undamaged. He gasped and gurgled but it went down. "A single dose won't kill you. It takes a few hours, even days to be effective, depending on constitution and food. This dose will just help it look as though you died naturally. Now get some sleep and let nature do its work," I told him. I switched off the light, sat in an easy chair and nodded off myself. Now it was a waiting game.

Light came through the window blinds. I felt dry and hungry. Stalin was awake. His eyes bored into me. I held my fingers to my lips. "Shhh!" I whispered. He had wet himself in the night, I could see. I tip-toed over and forced more water on him, nearly a litre. "Drown, you bastard!" I muttered under my breath then tip-toed to the door and listened. Nothing stirred. My watch told me it was nine o'clock in the morning on the first of March. Outside there was movement, but inside, so far, there was nothing.

"Time for more medicine," I said, as I gave him another dose of the paralytic.

Around noon I heard the guards moving about. Listening at the door I heard them debating what to do. It was unusual for Stalin to be asleep so long. Mentally I kept saying to them, 'Wait, children, just wait.' I saw the handle being tried but knew the door was locked. My mind raced; had Stalin had enough already to do the job? I thought of smothering him now and making a dash for the exit route. I picked up a cushion to finish him but then mercifully I heard their steps moving away down the corridor.

It was quiet again. I breathed slowly conscious that my heart was pounding. I swallowed hard and sat down again, replacing the cushion.

The light came and went. I dozed, and finally I heard the sound of Stalin relieving himself fully. I looked at my watch in the gloom. Its luminous hands showed me it was now the evening, around half past six. I switched the light on to check and decided to leave it on. I guessed the guards would be really worried now as to what to do. But Khrustalev would have been ordered to hang on until the last moment.

I went over to Stalin. "It's time, Comrade." I took another nicotined finger. "You will die slowly now. The doses are accurate and your mind is going. If you are lucky you will shortly have a genuine stroke. If not, you will fade. I would lie quiet if I were you. Someone might come in. You might have the strength to say something, but that effort might finish you. So think about it. I know you still can for the moment."

Pulling him off the couch I let him lay on the carpet in his own urine. Carefully I placed him the near the table in such a position that I could see him through the gap I would leave behind the almost closed hidden door. Then I hit his pocket watch, hard enough to jump the balance wheel so that it stopped and placed it on the floor along with a few papers.

Fumbling in his pocket I found the keys to the two safes. Opening the safes, which were identical, I found what I had been told to collect: a number of dossiers and leather-bound journals. There was some cash, a pistol, and, surprisingly, what appeared to be family photos. I took the files, bundling them into the haversack I carried. I guessed the staff must have seen the light go on and so would not dare enter for a while more, at least not without knocking. I reckoned I still had a few hours.

I sat and leafed through the files and notes. Everything was there. The Kirov dossier about his death, how Stalin had used this to rise to power and start the Great Terror. The entire Politburo, past and present, had their sins filed and documented. He was certainly about ready to get rid of Beria. The Khrushchev files revealed a catalogue of terror as great as Stalin's. There were secret notes on meetings with Allied leaders in the war. War strategy documents, showing the planned invasion of Western Europe. The new

Purge, meticulously planned and aimed directly at Zhukov, together with the replacement of the present military regime with one more favourable to Stalin. It was clear Stalin had already fabricated information to Zhukov that Beria was after his blood. Uncle Joe liked to be seen to be clean.

Another hour slipped by. I made as many mental notes as I could from the files on Polish leaders both here and abroad. Certainly the British had removed Sosnkowski on direct request from Moscow. Roosevelt had done a deal to give away a Poland he cared nothing about, except for the Polish vote, for which he had cynically lied. There were pictures for blackmail, bank statements of politicians and union leaders in the West. The folders were dynamite. No wonder Beria had ordered me to take them.

Eventually I padded to the bookcase door. I pulled it to, leaving sufficient gap to observe the door. In the gloom of the shaded light I guessed no one would notice immediately a bookcase slightly askew. Details would come to mind later.

At ten o'clock exactly the door was opened gingerly and slowly. The guard Lozgachev entered. Through the crack I saw him peering down at Stalin. He went out and closed the door then re-entered with Khrustalev. I heard Stalin attempt a noise.

"Call Beria, Comrade, let him sort it out," I heard Khrustalev say." They left the room and I closed the door then hurried back along the passage. Replacing the oil-can I had forgotten I grabbed the stick and began the stumbling journey back to the gate. Swinging the bar back I stumbled into a gentler, natural darkness. I breathed in fresh cold air, standing there for a moment. It was finished.

All I had to do now was survive.

Emerging from the blackness I saw a shadow. It came nearer, its belly close to the ground, the eyes catching the brightness of the arc lights on the fence. Low it came, slow, placing one paw in front of the other. I froze. It froze. The German shepherd raised itself, contemplating a spring. It waited for my arm to rise, so it could spring at my throat. Its ears pricked up as it watched me intently, a snarl escaping through its teeth.

I watched it, willing myself not to emanate fear. I *was* frightened. I hate dogs. Did I dare risk a shot? How fast could it move? How fast could I get to my gun? The questions pounded my brain and I was conscious of a background disturbance at the house. The news was spreading that something was up. I heard voices near the fence. A searchlight suddenly went out near where the gateway should be. I heard a shrill whistle and the dog turned and loped away. The tension eased from my legs. I had been rigid as any tree, rooted to the spot. True to the plan, the guards were being called to the house, so there would be no more dogs for the moment. I ran like hell in order to arrive before Beria. I saw his headlights coming to the bend. The car slowed.

The moment of truth. *Was I to get a bullet?*

No, the door swung open. Moving fast I got to the running board and swung myself in.

Beria first question was, "Did you get the safe contents?"

I passed him the haversack. He chose some files, including two bound albums which he pushed into his briefcase, forcing it to bulge.

"And the old man?" His second question.

"He can't talk and will not survive. He should die very soon, or might even be dead now, of natural causes. He is beyond recovery. If he is not dead then lean on his face with a cushion."

"I am not a murderer," Beria retorted.

Russia was indeed a charnel house for the insane. But then the Soviet Communist mind was beyond normal intelligence.

We entered the building as usual. Khrustalev spoke to Beria in low tones. Zabavnikov had entered too, which was unusual for a driver. "Let me brush you down, Comrade. You are covered in dust." He began flapping at my uniform as Lozgachev looked on.

"Wait here," Beria commanded. We did as we were told. Beria entered the office and closed the door. He was in there a long time. There was a smell of burning. Eventually he emerged. I noted his briefcase had returned to its normal size. He spoke to Khrustalev and Lozgachev. "We are leaving. I was never here, you understand. Call Ignatiev at the MGB, and failing him, Malenkov."

We slipped out and the car raced down the track and out on to Moscow where we pulled up outside my apartment. "Your job is done, so now off with you. We shall not meet again. Go in peace. Whatever your suspicions you have nothing to fear from me. The concierge is well and truly drunk so will not remember you, and you have been signed in and out. What? Don't tell me you expected to be shot or something." He laughed. Those were Beria's last words to me. I never saw him again.

# CHAPTER 25

# AFTERMATH

That same Monday morning Witek phoned to say he would collect me from the apartment. I was told to collect my grip with anything I needed and dress as a civilian. Part of me felt numbed and highly mistrustful. I felt like a fish in a net, wondering if I could wriggle my way out of the death to come.

I trusted no one here. I had signed my own death warrant. Without speaking we headed in his car toward the Lubyanka but suddenly stopped near Kitay station. Leaving my things in the car we went for a walk around the green. Was it here I was to have an 'accident'? Was it here I'd meet my fate, perhaps a gulag or back to the mental hospital? Witek seemed in good spirits. He saw my mood and clapped me on the back, sighing, "Surely you do not expect a bullet from me? Have you learned nothing about me? I keep my word, Tadek.

"A job well done, my friend. Colonel Khrustalev called Ignatiev at the MGB but, as was expected, it was too hot a potato for him. The coward told them to phone Beria, again just as we expected. They phoned Malenkov, who could not raise Beria because he was with you. He told them to keep trying Beria. Get the picture - Beria was *to be seen* not to be involved. Beria phoned the *dacha* when he was free and then, collecting Malenkov, went back to the *dacha,* which was now fully roused, not just a handful of guards.

"The guards had put Stalin back on the couch. Even though he had evidently wet himself Beria and Malenkov together concluded he was just asleep after being so dead drunk. Eventually the household staff and some of the guards began making a fuss, demanding that the house doctor be called. The leaders demanded he be put in a more seemly bed and cleaned up before medical attention, which the staff did. Beria and Malenkov had already called a heart specialist, a Doctor Myasnikov. He said he would bring other specialists. So they waited. Someone had told Khrushchev and he turned up at around 7.30. Don't tell me his little pet Ignatiev hadn't phoned him the previous night. I understand Molotov is on his way over now. I bet Bulganin is already there. Did you know you should not move someone with a possible cerebral haemorrhage? Unfortunate that Stalin has been so mauled about, don't you think?

"So now the Politburo will sit, waiting for him to die, deciding who will replace Stalin. The doctors will sweat, knowing he will die and they will have to give the reason. Like Rasputin, he was tough. It was planned perfectly though, one must hand it to Beria."

Witek lit a cigarette, flicking his ever-present lighter to life. Inhaling deeply, he let out a stream of smoke before speaking. He looked at me long and hard.

I stood like a condemned man awaiting his fate.

"Now as for you, I am afraid your life here is at an end. You are, even as I speak, disappearing from our records. The few who knew you are being bought off, and those who refuse will come to a sticky end. Not only do you not exist, but you never did. Records in this country are everything. So I'm afraid only Teddy Labden exists now, and he is booked on a train to Paris in about three hours. Get out, Tadek. Take a breath in Paris before you decide what to do. Go to ground, disappear. Keep away from the British and American embassies. One thing for sure, whoever wins the power game here, the immediate threat of war is over. We have achieved that much at least.

We shall meet again, my friend. Think of me favourably. I am as much a patriot as you. Just on a different side."

A wave of relief swept through me and I blinked back tears. Witek placed a hand on my arm. It was a moment of intense emotion.

It appeared I would be let go. He and Beria were to keep their side of the bargain. Perhaps this was to be a new Russia after all.

Unsure what to say and wanting to cover my loss of control I said, "I am retiring, disappearing. I intend to move to Somerset in England. I decided that whilst I sat there with Stalin those long hours. There is a small town called Glastonbury, the ancient Avalon. King Arthur, Merlin and all that. I visited there once. I've decided I prefer mystery to reality, Witek. The land is not unlike some parts of Poland, rural wetland with lazy rivers and big skies. I am not ready for the Great Plains and the Rockies. Everything is too big across the pond. I am a natural European, with an eastern perspective. Look for me there if ever you come west."

He gave me my papers and passport. "Genuine Canadian," he added, "we all have our contacts. Discharge papers from the Polish Air Force and matching ones from the RAF, so you are no longer technically a deserter. You may also remember these." He handed me my original Polish documents, lost to the Soviet Security forces such a long time ago when Witek had 'betrayed' me. "Mementos," he said. "And this is my personal present for you, a French passport and a Swiss, all kosher, not forged. Just a few more lives taken and recycled. Stolen Lives, eh? Supporting documents, certificates, discharge papers, family records. Keep them safe, they may help keep you alive someday."

It reminded me of Rupert and the passports offered to me in Germany on our escape from Poland. The Security Services invent and reinvent people on a whim and eliminate them as they wish. The law is no boundary.

The journey home was long and uneventful, except for the borders. I had to change trains from the Russian wide gauge to standard gauge. All through the Iron Curtain countries, even with my papers in order, I felt I was watched, an interloper, an alien. Fear lived in me, just as it stalked everyone else. At the border in Germany I saw a family being taken off, literally kicking and screaming. I wondered what their 'crime' had been. Probably wanting a better life. As the train pulled into the West, I wondered if there'd be a 'welcoming committee'. But Witek kept his word. It was to be Paris in the Spring!

The death - there was only one death for me to think about - was announced officially on the 5<sup>th</sup> of March. I was in Paris by then. The phrase 'the death of one man is a tragedy, the death of a million is a statistic' seemed particularly poignant at that time. The official reason, I read, was 'cerebral haemorrhage. I smiled. For the British the illness of Queen Mary was more important. Having lost a king and gained the new Queen Elizabeth, there were more important things like a coronation to consider, not what was happening far away in some vague, snowy country.

From Paris I began organising my affairs with my old lawyer friends in London. I made arrangements to sell all my British property and made over the house in Brighton to Kryszka, my old friend. I did make one trip to England to meet Rupert, taking the Golden Arrow boat train. We decided to meet at the Horse Pond Inn in Castle Carey, out of the way and far from London. The town was a beautiful mellow yellow in the May sunshine, the soft sandstone houses timeless and welcoming. The air tasted good and the sun danced on the water of the pond.

Rupert was as suave as ever. "We all owe you a lot, old boy. We do wish, however, you would drop this Sikorski affair. It is such an embarrassment to HMG. My advice is to look no further. No one is interested in recent history and wounds now need to be healed. Leave it to the scholars fifty years hence. Heard you, or more accurately one of your Canadian companies, is looking at a property over at Shapwick, a small stately pile. Don't worry, your name wasn't mentioned. I just recognised the solicitors' name. Your secret is safe with me."

He saw my look so added, "It really is, Teddy. I don't want to see you go down. And don't look so surprised, old friend. It isn't 5, the brethren, it's even worse; the Somerset unofficial league of property price speculators! Don't forget my family home is just down the road the other side of Langport. Little property news gets past mater and pater, even if they are in the dodder years. Not much land, I believe, but a nice dovecote. Could make a nice hotel, blue lias, grey stone and all that country retreat stuff. Pater told me that Prince Rupert hanged some rebels in the hallway. Or was it the other way round?"

Surprised by his intelligence on my house purchase, I realised his curiosity had gotten worse since he had been at the Foreign Office. "It was Prince Rupert's lot that did the hanging. I've agreed a price and signed the contract. What can I tell you? I fell in love with the fireplace. God knows what I'm going to do with the space. I would like to turn it into a hotel. Eventually people with money will want holidays. Or I could make it a home for wounded or damaged soldiers. I don't really know. Property is cheap now, so those of us with money should grab what we can. "

"You sound like pater," Rupert grinned. "We got Comrade Beria's list of rogues, by the way," he went on. "As you know, we don't eat our true English traitors any more or send them down the Thames to the Tower. We just mothball them, isolate them. If a Dago or something like turns up, we might still hang one as a lesson. So tell your Polish friends to keep quiet in their little world in London." The warning was well meant but it grated on me.

"By the way, I thought you ought to know our American friends are not at all happy with your pal Beria. Their choice of successor is Khrushchev. We don't have a choice any more. Not after the cock-up of not marching on Moscow in '45. They still blame us for the wrong intelligence."

I felt I had to say something about the sordid cover-ups. "I blame Cambridge and the old school tie, whether Winchester or even Sandhurst."

"Blessed be Catholic Oxford then," he answered.

"It's the arms race, you see. Good for business. Beria has already reformed the MVD and MGB into the KGB to tame the goons. Your friend Lavrenty wants peace and Marshall Aid. He wants to take Russia from a super poor country with nuclear arms to a modern state. There is talk of arms reduction. He wants the Soviet federation to break up into a trading bloc and Poland back on the map, with concessions on the Eastern border. He wants a friendly, neutral Poland with a sphere of influence from Kiev to Riga. Not a good idea, we think. To cap it he wants a reunified Germany and is going about it. Can you imagine the consequences?

"How can we keep the prols happy if we didn't have an enemy? What happens to the American arms and technology industries when the tax payer is no longer driven by fear? No, the safest route is to keep the arms race going. It will cripple the Soviets and keep them caged. Not my idea, old boy, but I thought you ought to know. I have it on good authority from Chuck that a coup will happen with American blessing. Your pal Beria is going to take the rap for Stalin's excesses. The Democrats don't want red faces over their hero Roosevelt.

"Zhukov and Khrushchev, that's the axis, the military and a new murderer for us to play with. June, old boy, June."

Rupert shook my hand warmly. He wanted to catch the train to London.

His last remark was less than reassuring. "Be careful, Teddy, and keep a gun handy in your new manor house".

I waved goodbye as the City of Truro locomotive pulled away from the platform.

There was just one thing left for me to do; trace Crabbe, the SIS diver who first went down to Sikorski's crashed Liberator. The search initially drew blanks and I was in no position to draw attention to myself. I would have to wait.

I contacted Kryszka and caught the Brighton Belle Pullman to the town, eating dinner on the way. I had much to tell him and Ruth, and spent half the night relating my story. Kryszka and Ruth were embarrassingly grateful for the house. I explained it was all part of shedding my past and getting 5 off my back. I managed to convince Kryszka that his phone was tapped, so we agreed in future to use different public call-boxes. Ruth found it all hard to believe. She was very British. She couldn't fathom that parts of the Intelligence community could be at war with each other or that 5 would be happy to see my end.

Next day I heard more about how all the boys, Kryszka's group of friends, were faring. On the whole they were settling down. Generally Poles were found to be good workers. From agriculture to mining they were slowly getting past British xenophobia. "Blacks are coming in from the West Indies. The New Poles they call them, dirty dogs taking 'our' jobs! We are white, you see, so now we're back on the British side again," Kryszka said sarcastically. "The boys and girls in the camps were getting married and being slowly assimilated," he said. "Babies are being born. I learned there was one resettlement camp near my new home. I decided to take a look at it, over near Westonzoyland.

Kryszka was still involved with exile matters, but clearly the Exile government was becoming an anachronism. He'd tried to set up a gliding club too, to keep the air force boys active. What I wanted to know was what was being done for the Polish children born here and growing up without the Polish language. I felt anger that the Church was the centre of organisation, not the government.

"Why the Church, Kryszka? Haven't they done enough damage? Everyone has a right to religion, but being Polish is not the same as being Roman Catholic. Just check your history!" I was raising my voice.

"Calm down, Tadek," he answered, "Where else will we get premises and money if not from the Church?"

"Don't tell me you don't pay something! There is always a price to pay, Kryszka even if it's not in cash," I countered. He remained silent.

Next day we agreed I should leave at night over the roof-tops into Dean Street. I gathered up my other weapons and ammunition, some favourite clothes, and that was it.

We had a plan. Kryszka regretted that he had failed to come with me on the last mission. He had put family first. We felt it time Teddy Labden disappeared. I had a couple of spare identities, thanks to Witek and his papers. And I had my true identity in Canada and the papers to prove it. But here we were in England, on paper two Poles, according to our air force papers. Two aliens, who were now stateless.

We decided to simply swap identities. Confuse the enemy. That was how I became Jerzy or rather Jurek Oliszewski, Kryszka's true name. Whilst on paper he became Tadeusz Labycz, sometimes known as Ted. It sounded a crazy idea but it was strangely realistic in those strange times which were so open and messy. Officialdom was still somewhat confused with regard to Poles. People were popping up all over the place, displaced Germans, Czechs, Ukrainian prisoners of war, Jews changing names, Germans playing the innocent. The British loved to be confused by foreign names and to give more civilised names to their foreigners. Labycz was not an uncommon name, anymore than Tadek. We looked nothing alike, so if Labycz was pursued or identified the obvious physical difference would stop 5 in its tracks. A few photograph changes by an expert called Michał in London would soon sort that out. After all, Michał had been forging documents for us and SOE for years. In fact I believe he was now working on bank notes. Kryszka took his alien resident's card and my passport and other documents and said he would pass them on by post to my lawyer.

We agreed that from now on we would swap names for official papers and for life in general. To anyone else but our intimate friends, the name Kryszka would now be used by me. It was after all a pseudonym. But now I too would use it.

Going through his papers, Kryszka found a letter which had arrived at my lawyers. The Red Cross, active in tracing refugees, had somehow found a connection to him and through him to me and so on to the lawyers. It was addressed to us both. It had been sent on to us by the son of the old man who had helped us escape from Poland, the night Elk had sacrificed his seat on the plane for his sister. He'd wanted us to know what happened to a hero, he said. Kryszka pointed at the section he wanted me to read. It told the story of what happened that night, after we left.

*"Elk had pushed through the undergrowth at the edge of the trees. He must have known he was leaving a trail like an elephant. The stalks were pushed inward. It would not have taken a boy scout to reason that someone was headed back into town. If I know Elk he was thinking of me and the closeness of my cottage. So he moved sideways pushing away from my farm, so that the security police trackers would not suspect me.*

*His sister was gone and with her his home. I suppose he realised it* would not be long before the UB worked that out. So his only choice was to go back to the Forest Lads. Back to the bivouac, back to the fight with no end. Back to a damp, half-sunken wooden hut.

He'd told me that he hated the loss of his civilised life. That he hated Germans and he hated Russians. He hated Jews in Polish UB uniforms. He hated Communists.

At some stage he had sat down with his back to an old tree. *It's said you can gain energy from a tree, son,"* the old man had written. *"I can see that young man pushing his back hard up against it trying to feel something, something magic, but it was just wood. From the earth around him I could tell he'd touched the ground, running it through his fingers. He had exposed the velvet moss-covered roots, digging his fingers into the sod, identifying by touch the twigs and leaves and pine needles and humus. Perhaps he held some dirt to his nose, breathing in the sweet smell of the earth. The world would have been quiet. No sound of pursuit. The aircraft had gone.*

At some stage Elk took out his Tokarev pistol. He'd been proud of it. Won from a skirmish with NKVD troopers a couple of years earlier. He told me he'd picked up the pistol from a dead NKVD soldier near the village of Kuryłówka. I'd watched him a couple of times trying to remove the red star from the butt, rubbing the metal, scraping and pushing at it. Of course the embossed metal did not yield – how could it – flesh against metal?

We'd spoken about his experiences. About the good times, like when some deserters from the Communist People's Army had learned of the presence of his NZW unit in the village and come over to our side. They were about two hundred strong then.

He'd said the Reds came at them on the seventh of May. His leader was Major Franciszek Przysiężniak. They were outnumbered and out-gunned, but the Reds got the bloodiest nose and a shock into the bargain. They counted nearly sixty dead NKVD men after they ran. Their unit cleared out straight away to avoid reprisals to the village. But the reports had come in anyway. Two hundred plus houses burned out, nearly a thousand people left homeless and driven away. Six civilians shot as sympathizers.

*I can see him sitting there, son, gun in hand. Only the trees breathing an answer. See him sitting there in the silence. A silence that was cool, refreshing and very dark. Did the Lady beckon? Did he hear her whisper, "Come, let me enfold you in my spirit"?*

A tempting idea for a young man with no future.

*I heard the shot echo through the night air. Just the one shot. Fondling the back of the dog's neck, I felt sad. Thank God I know the woods like my own backyard. I had marked the spot in my mind from the sound of it and I wasn't far wrong. I grabbed a spade and it wasn't too long before I found him. He'd shot himself through the mouth. The pistol lay to one side. I picked*

*it up and rummaged through the pockets of his jacket and found a few more*
*rounds. I kept them, son. Just in case.*

*I knew I couldn't dig too close to the tree, the roots would be too thick.*
*Through the morning I toiled, sheltered from the warm sun by the trees. A*
*breeze got up and the leaves and needles rustled in the wind. The leaf edges*
*were turning brown and winter would soon come. The ground did not*
*permit a neat grave. Elk was a big man, his body heavy. I dragged and*
*pushed him into the hole. He assumed almost a foetal position. I filled up the*
*earth on top of him, jumping on the loose turned soil to tamp it down.*

*The dog watched me make the sign of the cross in the Orthodox fashion.*
*Then we both walked back home. Over the winter I felt drawn to the spot*
*again and again. The sadness of it, the senseless loss of this young life. I*
*carved into the tree a face. I don't know whose face it was, but it appeared*
*to be a woman's face, about a metre long, half hidden in a cloak. I just felt*
*there should be a memorial to this young forest soldier.*

*It was a kindly face, an ancient face. And I carved my real initials into*
*it, NH for Nykyfor Hudak. So in a way it became a memorial for me too."*

"Christ, that's so bloody sad, so very sad," I said. "It really was the end
already, even by then. The fight was hopeless I suppose, futile…Though we
kept our honour if nothing else."

"One day I'm going to write my memoirs of what happened," Kryszka
swore. "You could help me with that notebook of yours. That notebook,
Teddy, is what the brethren and everyone is after, the *real* record of what
happened."

Life began again. Somerset assimilated me. I watched events in Poland
unfold and assisted where I could.

Many years later I attended the real Kryszka's funeral in Devon. My old
friend lived to a ripe old age. There were only a few mourners, an older
Englishman with a young woman, some staff from the old folk's home and
a couple of elderly ladies. Two men in city suits. They paid no attention to
the other spry older chap who stood to one side, watching curiously at a distance. Neither would they have known why he smiled at the gravestone a
week later to read: 'A Polish Airman, known to the world as 'Kryszka'. Here
lies Bartomiej Oliszewski. A *Dwojka* joke.' Beneath it was the date and a
carving of an eagle with swept-down wings, neck curving down to its right,
holding a wreath.

Only Kryszka and I and a very few others knew that *Dwojka* meant
Section Two of the Polish Secret Service to which we both truly belonged.
Fighting from within the offensive intelligence department our whole lives
had been nothing but a double entendre. I enjoyed my friend's last joke. As
for the eagle, many would know this to be the badge of the famous Polish
Air Force. At least for a while, until time stole all our lives.

It made me think once more of the many events which stole my life. Made me think of all the people I had known, the lives they might have had. All gone.

Gone like precious gold, stolen by thieves in the night.

As for Teddy Labden, he simply vanished.

# EPILOGUE

*In the year 2007, in the month of May, called Maj in Polish, two young men stand in front of a tree in Poland. From the way they speak and are dressed, they are clearly American. The two men had met at Illinois State University, ISU. The ISU's motto was 'Gladly we learn and teach'. Both hoped to do just that, teach. ISU students are known as Redbirds, due to their sports colours of red and white, the national colours of Poland. The irony of which is lost on these two at this moment. The State emblem, the Cardinal bird, is also a good Catholic and red. Both men are history students. One is studying the Philosophy of History and the other The History of East Asia.*

*"This is the place Ed, for sure, just as your granddad described. So somewhere under my feet my great-uncle lies dead and buried?"*

*Both peer at the old tree, with the carving of a woman's face staring back at them.*

*"So the old stories were right then." Marek speaks. "The carving looks like something from Walt Disney's old Snow White film, the wicked witch and all that stuff."*

*The third person standing nearby is a local government official.*

*The 'boys' are over from the USA on a trip of discovery. A 'trace the ancestors trip', which many members of American Polonia have undertaken since Communism fell in 1989. With money collected and donated from local Polonians in Marek's home town, the local Gmina or District Council here in Poland has agreed that a small memorial or plaque should be put on this spot to commemorate all the Forest soldiers who fought against the Communists in this part of the forest.*

*The official, a man in his late fifties, clearly has reservations, but the money is there and the approval has been given. It will be done. He has not made it known to these two brash Americans that he was a Party member and an informant against his neighbours. Times were good then. Today work is hard. As he stands there he remembers one of his relatives, gunned down by bandits right in his own home in front of his children. Why, he asks himself, is there no memorial to that hero of the People's Republic?*

*Half listening to the two young Americans he idly thinks of the films he has seen at the cinema where the bandits held up trains and robbed the peasants and shot good Party members. Fiction, of course, portraying the events of those times, the fight against fascist counter-revolutionaries. And now that bloody Institute of National Remembrance was poking its nose into good Party members' pasts. The Institute was supposed to examine records of Communist, Nazi and other crimes committed against Polish citizens in the period from September 1st, 1939 to December 31st, 1989. As well as political repressions carried out by officials of the former Polish investigative and justice organisations of that time.*

*The official gobbed and spat on the ground – his comment.*

*Ed and Marek are anxious to leave and get back to Rzeszow. Each had their photograph taken, individually, together and then balancing the camera on a rucksack, shaking hands with the really nice guy who took them to the spot. Family duties done, they have discovered Polish girls and a pizza place in the local Galeria. Two American girls wait for them up in town being chatted up by two young Polish men. One wears a pink tee-shirt with the slogan 'Polish princess'. She wears it because she is in love with Ed and he is sort of Polish. He wears a matching tee-shirt, displaying 'Proud to be Polish'. The locals wonder that anyone should wear such slogans, after all Poland is a poor country and the young want to work abroad. Times move on.*

*The trees whisper, "Did he die for this? For pizza? Will those girls ever think of him?"*

*"No," the Lady sighs into the wind. "He died in vain, as mankind does."*

# END NOTES

[i]Wolność i Niezawizłość. Officially the AK Armja Krajowa had been disbanded on the 19th January 1945 on instructions by the Polish president in London. This was in accordance with the Allies agreements and wishes. The supreme commander of the Home Army Gen.Okulicki and sixteen other underground leaders were invited to meet with the Soviet Authorities. They were kidnapped, taken to Moscow tried and imprisoned. Okulicki was eventually murdered. The Polish Underground was effectively relieved of its leadership. No Western ally protested at this obscene act of betrayal. WiN was created to help AK soldiers make the transition from life as partisans to that of civilians. However as arrests of AK members continued it began to function as an anti-communist semi-military organisation in its own right. The last AK active soldier commander Józef Franczak was killed only in 1963.

[ii]House or hearth spirit

[iii]The Polish underground leaders, the bedrock of the Polish Secret State, whilst on a visit to Moscow with Allied guarantees of safe conduct were kidnapped by the NKVD on Stalin's instructions. All were accused of collaboration with Nazi Germany. The trial took place between 18 and 21 June 1945, in the presence of foreign journalists and political observers.

[iv]Historians now acknowledge British responsibility for the introduction of the Curzon line, not Stalin.

[v]All the named partisan leaders, having remained loyal to Poland, were savagely tortured and beaten over years. They were all tried as traitors and shot in the head in 1951. Their bodies have never been found. Two of them already held the Virtuti Militari (a Polish medal similar to the British VC). All had fought against the Germans. However it can be put, they were murdered by their own people, Poles, Communists.

[vi]KPA stands for Korean People's Army.

[vii]The operational name for the German invasion of the Soviet Union.

[viii]Venona was not always the code name for this project, as for security reasons it was often changed. It is used here as the one most widely used.

[ix]The Soviet military intelligence service.

[x]Admiral Sinclair's nickname.

[xi]Despite known Communist sympathies, Sir Roger served as head of MI5 from 1956 to 1965. Margaret Thatcher's famous statement to the House of Commons neither damning nor clearing Hollis is in contrast to the many, including Christine Keeler, who assert his guilt as a Soviet plant or agent.

[xii]The traditional four-cornered hat of the Polish military.

[xiii]KOP is the abbreviation for the élite Border Protection Corps formed to hold against a Soviet attack.

[xiv]General Secretary of the Communist Party of Great Britain.

[xv]Stalin's Party nickname.

# HISTORICAL NOTES

The factual background to this novel makes the point that Poland receives little recognition for its valiant fight against the German and Soviet invasions of Europe. As an ally of Britain and the USA there is still no real recognition of the illegal invasion of Poland and other free states of Europe by the Red Soviet Empire. Only the Nazis are seen as invaders, yet the truth is, the Red Soviet Armies invaded just as Nazi Germany did. We must remember that Germany and the Soviet Union were in formal alliance until they fell out and the Soviets switched sides!

The British in particular have a penchant for forgetting their first ally, Poland. Consider how blithely it is stated that the Red Army liberated Berlin. The role of the Polish Army is entirely forgotten. Similarly at Narvik, Tobruk etc. The British forget that the Poles were therein force too.

And, of course, Poland is bad at publicity!

There are three main historical events which provide the basis for this novel.

The first to be considered is the little-known armed struggle on behalf of the remnants of the Polish Underground against the Soviet takeover of Poland following the end of the WW2. This struggle took place against a backdrop of forced mass movements of population, on the lines of ethnic cleansing, in order to create the borders decided upon by the Big Three. In the same territories Ukrainian Nationalists also fought the Soviet domination of their areas.

The last known or reported partisan death, that of Józef Franczak, occurred as late as 1963 when he was killed in a fire-fight with 35 ZOMO Polish paramilitary police near Lublin. His head was removed and only his body was returned to the family. Andrzej Kiszka, a survivor of the Garbaty unit, was finally caught in a forest bunker in 1961. He was sentenced to life imprisonment as a reactionary bandit. Interested readers may like to follow the circumstances of these people, known as cursed soldiers, by visiting the website www.doomedsoldiers.com.

The second main political event in *Stolen Lives* concerns the death of the Polish Prime Minister, General Sikorski. His death continues to court controversy. Whilst the official verdict remains that it was a tragic accident, the sheer convenience of his death to the big three Allies causes alarm. The facts and 'coincidences' surrounding his death stretch credulity to breaking point.

In November 2008 the Polish government exhumed Sikorski's body. Tests did not reveal any trace of poison or shot wounds. Experts concluded that Sikorski died of multiple organ failure and shrinkage of the kind typically sustained in a plane crash or in a fall from a great height. The Institute of National Remembrance, Commission of the Prosecution of Crimes against the Polish Nation, which is notably responsible for the investigation of Communist and Nazi crimes in Poland during the Second World War and post-war era, is still considering whether or not sabotage caused the plane to crash.

The missing bodies, which include that of General's daughter, Zofia Leśniowska, raise unanswered questions. The bodies are supposed to have been carried away by sea currents. However in the bay in question, on the eastern side of the rock, the currents are minimal. More importantly, Gibraltar was surrounded by a metal grid installed against Italian miniature submarines operating from Spain. Any body would have been trapped by that grid.

Reliable reports of the sighting of Zofia Leśniowska in a *gulag* after the event cannot be dismissed.

As in all good conspiracy stories, mysteries surround some of the characters in Stolen Lives. Krystyna Skarbek referred to in the text had a close confidante in Countess Teresa Łubieńska, who like Skarbek was mysteriously stabbed to death in 1957. Major Ludwik Łubieński was the adjutant general and liaison officer in Gibraltar and a witness of the plane crash which killed Sikorski. Commander 'Buster' Crabbe, the diver sent to retrieve the bodies of the Sikorski Liberator, was of course found in the waters around Chichester, headless and handless (readers will recall the method from the text) following the visit of Soviet leaders to Portsmouth harbour in 1956.

The third fact that underpins the story of *Stolen Lives* is the character of Lavrenty Beria. After his death he achieved greater notoriety than whilst alive. His reputation as a murderous sex maniac survives. Khrushchev ensured Beria's reputation was destroyed. The facts remain that all the Soviet leadership were guilty of heinous crimes; Beria was in charge of the Secret Police apparatus for a time. Set against this are his reforms.

Beria set a series of changes in progress which reversed many Stalinist policies. In the 112 days of his regimen, counting from the death of Stalin until his arrest on June 26 1953, Beria had begun a process towards the reunification of Germany as a neutral state, a Nationalities policy that was essentially a de-Russification of the Baltic States and a move towards a non-Communist Poland. He also investigated rehabilitation and compensation for those unjustly convicted by special judicial bodies (*troikas*) and the NKVD's Special Commissions as well as amnesty for over a million of those imprisoned for crimes against the state.

Beria wanted closer economic relationships with the West and the building of different economic structure with less military expenditure. This may be the reason why the coup organised by Khrushchev had the backing of Zhukov and the Moscow military district, which effectively disarmed or neutered the MVD troops.

Apart from his commonly alleged crimes, Beria was accused by Khrushchev of being in the pay of British Intelligence.

Although Beria was supposedly given a trial and executed in December 1953 the author believes that Beria was shot and killed on the day of his arrest and never came to trial.

He simply knew too much.

Beria's son Sergio asserted that his father and Stalin had agreed the need to get the Communist Party out of direct management of Soviet society: "My father's relations with the Party organs were complicated... For example, he told Khrushchev and Malenkov directly that the Party apparatus corrupts people. It was all appropriate for earlier times, when the Soviet state had just been formed. 'But,' my father asked them, 'who needs these controllers today?'This would certainly have signed his death warrant."

Three controversial areas for any history lover to research more fully!

If you enjoyed reading *The Engineer* and *Stolen Lives* then the concluding book in the trilogy of the *Chronicles of Love and Honour* called *White and Red* is real must. A preview is on the following pages.

CHAPTER 1
# EBB AND FLOW

Sławomir Labycz, Sławek for short, stared gloomily but thoughtfully down at his boots. Where the black polish had worn away they had assumed a dull grey sheen. The leather was hardened by continual soaking, the boots caked in clinging ochre mud. As he lifted his feet the ground squelched, making a soft sucking sound as though reluctant to release him from its grip. If he stayed still he sank fraction by fraction into the earth. When he moved to new footing coloured water welled into the footprint, leaving yellow scum around his imprint. His right boot toe had opened from being drowned in the river bed of what was purported to be a trench. The leather of the sole had parted company with the upper. He kicked it against the dugout wall to shake the mud from it.

Some of the mud slid slowly from the boot. He watched its descent, calculating when it would drop away. There was not much else to do. The mud slid down, making a plopping sound as it hit the sodden trench floor. There was no splash as the ooze greeted its child. The boot grinned at Sławek through gaping lips. Its rusted tacks looked like teeth, like the maw of some strange hungry fish. Sławek's foot was wet. He walked as though with a limp to stop the gap widening and the sole coming off entirely. The bindings around his feet were sodden and chafed his toes.

The trench was too shallow. The pioneers and engineers had done their best, but the advance had been too rapid. They had dug the trench just waist high then piled the earth as a rampart in front. The weather this July was appalling. Every day it had rained from leaden skies. The rampart was slippery, just clinging, filthy mud. There was no true field of fire, although the wood had been cut down for some fifty metres to the front. Instead of reinforcing the walls or providing duckboards for the floor, timber had been used for fires and cooking. So if you wanted to fire at the enemy or if the enemy advanced all you could do was hurl yourself at the rampart, take a few pot-shots and then, due to the recoil, slide down the mud and start again.

'At least we have weapons,' Sławek mused 'and we've had some rations'. The Kerensky offensive had begun with a massive artillery bombardment of the Austro Hungarian lines. Shells had whistled overhead as never before. The boys, elated, had run forward but found only empty trenches, the network wrecked by the artillery, the troops gone. And so they had gone further forward, on into this mess.

*So here we are, stuck in the mud with over extended lines*, he thought. "And why are we stuck in the mud?" he asked out loud.

The answer came from the lad next door, grinning through a face grimed the mud. "Because the Petrograd news media and our deserters told them we were coming."

Sławek grinned and called back down the trench, "And because the whole show up there in Petrograd is run by shite workers who are safe and comfy in protected industry jobs and have never seen a battlefield. All they do is strike for more money, whilst we die out here." He winked at the lad, knowing that his comments would be making some of their more Lefty comrades squirm. "They sing songs and print leaflets and send agitators down here. Nothing but a bunch of self serving, sloganeering shites. That's what they are," Sławek added. "And they can't even cobble boots right," he humphed as an afterthought.

No one answered.

The lad next to him in the line was less than eighteen. Sławek wasn't sure himself of his true age. It hadn't seemed to matter when he was just a peasant from Wołyn. Most of the Imperial Russian Army was made up of conscripted peasants like him, drawn to the colours from the land. The revolution affected us in a different way from the workers in the cities, he realised that now. They believed in the holiness of mother Russia, if they came from Russia. But many were from the minorities forced into serfdom under the Imperial system. Czechs and Poles were particularly troublesome and often Social Revolutionaries, troublesome and quarrelsome Mensheviks. He himself was a Pole and a Social Revolutionary and a supporter of the provisional Government of Alexander Kerensky, well at least to some degree.

Kerensky had asked the soldiers to take up their weapons and free the ancient soil from the Austrian and German invaders, so that the people's revolution could nurture itself. The soldiers had done so, but the lad standing by Sławek wanted to go home.

Politics was like the mud, Sławek thought, a stinking morass. The Revolution itself was a mess. The Bolsheviks were adamant about ending the war immediately. They were being paid by the Germans. Their leader, Lenin, was a traitor to the dead soldiers, that much was clear. The Social Revolutionaries' representatives were now making pro-German speeches and were in direct communication with the German government.

Kerensky was an honourable man though.

It was difficult to know what to think.

The two of them, standing there in the mud, were just a minute speck in the Russian Eighth Army, in the south of what should properly be called

Poland. Eight infantry divisions and four cavalry divisions had attacked the Austro-Hungarian Third Army on the 7th of July. The enemy commander had thrown in his best German reserves to stem the tide but the Russians had chewed them up and spat them out. They had taken over ten thousand prisoners.

But then the rain came and then the mud. Everything stopped at the Stryi river. It raged and burst its banks. Tranquil streams turned to torrents, trenches turned to streams, redoubts to ponds and the good earth to mud.

Then came the counter attack. The Germans carried the Russians' first defence lines at the point where the Eighths hard won salient hinged with the Russian Seventh Army. They had pushed forward. The Eighth had to withdraw and stop a route. Dagestani, Circassian, and Kabardian Regiments came to stem the flood. Briefly the Germans and Austrians were held at bay but a general retreat had already begun to their flank. Thirty-two kilometres south of Brody, the German divisions were momentarily held up but the rot came when the soldiers' committee of the 607th Mlynovskii Regiment voted to retreat. That caused a domino effect of unit pullbacks all along the line. A gap of forty kilometres opened. Into it poured the Central Powers' soldiers.

"We of the 607th Mlynovskii Regiment began the end." Sławek spoke out loud again, to no one but the mud wall. "Our soldiers' committee decided we should retreat and so we did. So here we are now, hounded by the Germans. We opened the gap and in they came." He sighed and turned his face to the sky for a moment, feeling the rain on his face. He let the water trickle into his mouth and thought of food. With his left hand he rubbed some slimy mud from the three faded red cloth stripes on his arm marking him *starshina*. First Sergeant. Not that anyone took much note these days.

Ahead in the gloom of the late afternoon a stirring was felt – or was it heard? – coming from the woods. There was a moment of suspense, a silent portent of arrival. It was like a wind stirring before the rustling of leaves. It was the sound of voices and movement, mingled with the snapping of twigs and the brushing of undergrowth, the breath of menace, the wave of aggression, of animal fear. They were coming again. The two soldiers, the lad and the sergeant, together with many of the lads, threw themselves up and onto the mud ramparts.

Sławek pushed his Mosin-Nagant rifle over the rampart and sited forward, sliding the bolt back, making ready for action. He loved this weapon. He oiled and polished it as though his life depended upon it, which indeed it did. He had smoothed and polished the wood stock till it shone, as good as any table top in a magnate's house. Small calibre, high velocity and five shots, how he wished the army had been this well equipped in the past two years when the Tsar's inept staff had sent unarmed troops to conflict.

A young officer staggered rather along the back of the trench line, shouting something like, "Steady men, make your shots count. Fire only when you have a target." About the same time German voices were heard calling and hallooing from the woods opposite. It was a moment of fear.

The officer was a *praporshchik*, an ensign. Sławek reckoned him to be about twenty, fresh-faced and eager. He'd heard him talking at one of the committee meetings – workers solidarity and equality and even votes for women. He thought he came from an aristocratic family somewhere up north, in Latvia. He was waving a pistol vaguely at the sky. He was young and gallant and looked, Sławek thought, like an angel of war, inspiring his troops to honour and fatherland even in the dreary weather. He was fighting for Honour and the Revolution.

The shot rang out just a few steps away. The boy swayed and tottered as he looked down at his chest. A brilliant red stain was spreading quickly as his life blood washed from him. He looked up once, catching Sławeks's eye. He looked surprised. His arm fell limp, the pistol falling to the mud as his body pitched forward, crashing into the muddy floor of the trench.

"Peace and bread," the shooter in the trench cried, the old Bolshevik cry. Two riflemen were now crawling from the trench, away from the enemy, one of them the shooter. As he stood he was taken in the back by a bullet from the trenches. Others began to leave the dugout. Those who stayed shot at those who left, who in turn shot back.

On Sławek's other side a man began to climb out. Sławek pulled at his boots. The man turned and tried to stab downward at Sławek with his fixed bayonet. The lad stabbed the man in the thigh with his bayonet. Another trooper pushed by. Sławek found himself standing on the dead young officer. As men pushed by the Ensign was trampled. His dead body turned the colour of mud.

"It's time to go home," Sławek said.

The lad laughed. "And where is that, Pan Sławek? Tell me where are we to go?"

Sławek grinned at the boy. "Are you trying to get me shot?" The boy had used the term *Pan*. The word, meaning nobleman, was anathema to the Left, especially the Bolsheviks.

"For me it is Odessa. And for you?"

"Oh, I shall tag along with you for a while. I have to keep you safe."

Sławek roughed the lad's hair in a show of camaraderie.

"As long as it is 'Comrade' from now on then. Is that a deal?

"It is Comrade Pan Starshina Labycz. Odessa is a long way from Volhynia, but you will get me back there one day, of that I am sure."

Sławek was not so sure as they made their way through fields and woods. At first they hid themselves from others but as they moved on troopers sloped up to them asking, "Where are you headed comrades?"

Always the answer was the same, Odessa. Some joined, others went their way. Soldiers recognised the stripes, recognised Sławek's age and experience. They thought he must be a survivor. Troops came in groups of two and three, rarely as individuals. They did not think of themselves as deserters. Before long they had become a well armed band of almost seventy men.

They passed others marching north, some going east, others headed their way. At one stage an organised detachment from a traditional regiment still moving to the front confronted them as deserters. Their officer said he would shoot. Sławek said they would shoot first. Sławek's band had a machine gun. It was hastily set up, trained on the opposing column. They parlayed.

The confrontation took place at a small rail station, no more than a shed with a water tower and wood pile next to it. The countryside was flat, devoid of immediate habitation. Smoke rose from some village behind a stand of birch trees just starting to show the first buttercup yellow of their autumn leaves. A field of sunflowers, running to seed in the early September sunshine, stretched toward the trees. Sławek had ordered his men to line the field edge. The train was slightly elevated on its built-up track. On the other side of the track the steppe stretched to the horizon. Clouds scudded the blue sky like painters' brushstrokes. Birds wheeled, chasing flies high into the sky.

The regular troops had been surprised. They'd come off their flatbeds to bask in the sun and to set up a listening post on the telegraph wire that ran far away to somewhere. The little khaki clad group had attached a wire to a machine on the ground. The operator and officers were intent on their machine, tapping out in Morse their orders and directions. The troopers had been lolling about on the bank smoking, talking enjoying the sun. No guards had been posted.

Sławek and a small detachment approached openly, but arms at the ready. Some soldiers jumped to their weapons as the group approached. Others just laid or stood where they were and watched to see how events would unfold.

"Deserters," the officer shouted, "Stand to and take aim." Some of the regulars obeyed. Others still just watched.

The small group, clustered at the portable telegraph machine, consisted of an older man with the insignia of a full *Podpolkovnik* or Lieutenant Colonel, supported on his right by a Kapitan, a Yunker or Cadet officer and two NCOs. Arms were levelled both ways.

"Give yourself up and drop your weapons," the *Podpolkovnik* demanded, cocking his pistol and aiming it directly at Sławek.

Whilst they were talking the rest of the 'Labycz' band, following Sławek's strategy, had crept up to the track and occupied the rail line whilst everyone's attention had been distracted.

"Look to your right, Comrade *Podpolkovnik,* and you will see you are in no position to bargain."

The sun glinted on bayonet and barrels ranged behind the rails.

The train engine shone blackly in the sunshine. The driver was very proud of it. Not the biggest of engines but it did the job. He had been polishing the brass whilst his fireman was taking on water and then he'd gone round to the front of the engine, to make sure the two red flags were still in situ on the front of the train. It was best to show you were pro-revolution, though frankly he cared nothing for politics and had liked the Tsar. He used to keep a picture of the Tsar in the cab but that had gone with the revolution. As he turned around the front of the engine he faced a scruffy bearded soldier who aimed a pistol at his chest whilst holding his finger to his lips indicating to him to be silent.

The engine driver shot his hands in the air and walked quietly to join his fireman, sitting morosely to one side, hands on head. The engine driver had but one thought: 'Please God do not let these bandits kill us. I want to go home.'

The three cattle trucks at the end of the train had travelled with their doors slung wide open to let the fresh air blow through. The train with its heavy load had paced slowly over the plain. It was not an unpleasant ride. They had stopped near villages where the villagers had sold them basic foods, milk and water.

The occupants were mostly women and children and few men folk. The latter were mostly elderly. The able bodied had gone to the front long ago. They were trying to get away from the front when the regulars had commandeered the train yesterday. It was a mess. The officer had said they could stay on the trucks with no engine and wait for the engine to come back. He was a kind man, had said an alternative was to stay attached to the train and go back to the town they had fled from. He was sure it would be back in Russian hands again. They had voted to stay with the engine. After all this was now a democratic Socialist country.

They had seen the ambush coming. There had been a stir but they had learned where armed men were concerned to keep quiet. There had already been trouble with the younger women and some soldiers. The officers were not in command as they should be. There were some male students amongst the civilians; they had kept well back and out of sight. Valuables had been hidden in the straw and jewellery pressed into cracks in the floor and side panels, just in case. The newcomers amongst the sunflowers looked no worse or better than the regulars. These soldiers could be worse or better. Events would tell.

So they had sat, some in the shade of the trucks, others dangling their legs over the side blinking into the sun enjoying the moment of calm before the storm. They sat like Russian peasants, although many were not, letting the world unfold their fate.

The older officer lowered his weapon, as did Sławek.

"We are not deserters. We are Revolutionary Guards," said Sławek. Not that he knew himself what that might mean but it sounded better than deserter. It meant somehow that they were an organised band and he their elected leader.

"This is now the territory of the *Rumcherod* the Central Executive Committee of the Soviets of the Romanian Front, Black Sea Fleet, and Odessa Military District." He had picked up this gem from one of the soldiers, a Menshevik and anti Bolshevik who had joined the growing band a few days ago. "In the name of the *Rumcherod* Soviet we are commandeering this train, Comrade. We are going to Odessa."

The older officer turned and quietly spoke with the other leaders. All the time he pulled on his moustache. He turned back to Sławek and his group, holding out some paper taken from their telegraph machine. "Kerensky has arrested Kornilov and let the Bolsheviks out of prison to support him. It looked as though Kornilov was for a coup to overthrow the Provisional Government, at least according to what the Petrograd Soviet says."

Sławek absorbed this piece of information. He chewed it over in his mind for a moment, realising that the opposing group was virtually doing the same. He turned to his group and they talked amongst themselves. None believed that Kornilov would do such a thing. Most of the men were anti-Bolshevik and the Petrograd extremists.

"We are still going to Odessa," Sławek said, "It changes nothing." But in truth they all knew that it did.

The opposing officer group called for a soldiers' committee meeting and Sławek's group agreed to hold it jointly. The discussion was heated. Several factions emerged. In the end it was decided both groups would join as one band. The leader was voted as Sławek Labycz, the Pole. He would lead the band to Odessa. After that each would decide his own destiny. His second in command would be the regular officer, provided that his shoulder boards would be taken off. He agreed and later confided to Sławek it was better having them torn off than having them nailed into his shoulders as had happened so many times to his brother officers.

The two of them talked. The older man said toSławek, "You know this is the start of a Civil War. It will be fought against the Reds, the diehard Bolsheviks."

"So what are we then?" Sławek said. "We must be White. You know, purity of thought and all that – all those splendid old Tsarist white and gold uniforms. The Bolshevik's have stolen Red – which just leaves White." He paused for a moment "Although for me, truthfully, in the long run, white it will be. White together with red, the national colours of Poland".

"This is going to be a long, bitter confused struggle," the older officer said.

Returning to his own lines, the young lad teased Sławek. "So you have gone up in the Revolutionary world, Comrade Pan Labycz? You are now well on the way to being a local Tsar. Give the Revolution a while and we will be back at the beginning with the same people. Different horse, same colour."

Underlying the humour was the greed and jealousy of the underclass.

The next day the train left for Odessa, sporting one white and one red flag.

# NOTES ON POLISH NAMES

Polish belongs to the Slavic language group. Eastern Slavs use the Cyrillic alphabet whereas Western Slavs use the Latin. The Polish language, like those of the Czechs and Slovaks, employs a number of letters and sounds foreign to most Western languages.

The Polish language contains many subtle sibilants but there is little difference to an untrained ear between an rz and a ż! It seems that Westerners find Slav names difficult to pronounce, even when given a list of equivalent sounds.

Unlike *The Engineer,* the text of the last two volumes of the trilogy *Chronicles of Love and Honour* use mostly Polish spelling for names. Sometimes an English name appears alongside to provide some context. The partisan *Łoś,* for example, is also nicknamed *Elk,* and *Warsaw* is written as the Polish *Warszawa.* I chose deliberately to mix the usage so the reader will find no strict continuity, part of a hidden learning curve of authenticity.

Don't let pronunciation of names spoil your enjoyment of Stolen Lives. Just go at them like a hurdle and see what you come up with. Make your own nearest equivalent. If you want to be more accurate, assistance is given below.

Below is a list of Polish letters and their sounds:-

The Polish Alphabet contains 32 letters. Specific to Polish are the letters: ą, ć, ę, ł, ń, ó, ś, ź, ż. Ą, Ć, Ę, Ł, Ń, Ó, Ś, Ź, Ż.

## Approximate Pronunciation of Polish letters which differ from English:-

A – sounds like "a" in the word "Apple"

C – sounds like "ts" in the word "Tsar"

E – sounds like "e" in the name "Elsa"

G – sounds like "g" in the word "fog"

H – sounds like "h" in the word "hello"

I – sounds like "ea" in the word "beam"

J – long "i" sounds like "y" in word "bye"

K – sounds like "c" in the word "colour"

O – sounds like "o" in the word "top"

U – sounds like "oo" in the word "pool"
W – sounds like "v" in the word "love"
Y – sounds like "y" in the word "pity"   Ą – nasal A, sounds like French
"bon bon" or "ow" in the word "own"
Ć – sounds like Chinese "chi"
Ę – sounds like "en" in the word "engine"
Ł – sounds like "w" in the word "wedding"
Ń – sounds like the word "knee"
Ó – sounds like the double o in "pool"
Ś – sounds like "sh" in the word "ship"
Ź – sounds like "ge" in the word "genie"
Ż – sounds like "g" in the word "mirage"


Double letter sounds in Polish are: CH CZ DŹ DŻ DZ RZ SZ; they all pronounced like one letter, with the exception of DŹ DŻ DZ, which are read in usual way.

CH – sounds like a Polish "h" with a rough edge
CZ – sounds like "ch" in the word "chocolate"
RZ – sounds like Polish "ż"
SZ – sounds like "sh" in the word "gosh"